THE WAR ETERNAL

THE LESSONS NEVER LEARNED

ROB J. HAYES

FOR ALL THOSE WHO HAVE FELT LIKE GIVING UP
YET FIND THE STRENGTH TO GO ON

PROLOGUE

I'VE HEARD PEOPLE TALK ABOUT HELL AS though it is some place that awaits them when they die. A land of eternal torture for those who have committed the worst of atrocities. They're wrong. Life is hell. Living is hell. And there is no greater torment than the ones we fashion for ourselves. I have done a great many things in my life; more bad than good, I think. The memories of them play out in my mind again and again. I am ashamed of so much of what I have done. The guilt of my actions remains even after all other consequences have faded. People may speak of hell as though it is some other place, but I say I am living it every day of my life.

The Pit was finally behind me, or more accurately below me. I struggle to say exactly how long I spent down there. My mind tells me it was just over six months, but my body tells me it was over a decade. All part of the unnatural ageing, I suppose. Ten years stolen from me by the magic of Chronomancy. Ten years paid to save Hardt and Tamura. Ten years lost to kill the man I considered my brother. I suppose it was a small price to pay all things considered, and I paid it willingly. I would freely pay it again and again and again. To save my friends there is no price I wouldn't pay. That doesn't mean I'm not bloody well bitter about the cost.

It is a strange thing, but I have noticed the older I get and the fewer years that remain to me, the more I dwell on the choices of my past. I consider my mistakes and belittle my accomplishments. I find myself reliving the hardships, as though they are old friends long lost and fondly remembered. I brush over the joyous times as though they mean nothing to me, the things I have achieved minor in the face of the mistakes I have made. My life has always been fraught with hardship, but rarely has it only been that way. Down in the Pit, I will admit I struggled to find any happiness. But then prison is not meant to be a nice place.

The war was lost, the Orran bloodline was gone and their lands engulfed by the Terrelan empire. It is somewhat odd to think I went into the Pit bound hand and foot, beaten and bloody and stripped of my magic; my Sources taken from me. Down there in the dark they tortured my body and mind. The overseer, the man in charge, did everything in his power to make me swear allegiance to the Terrelans. Not once did he manage to break me, though I have already admitted he came fucking close. I think he made one vital mistake: he tried to use Josef against me. The overseer enlisted the aid of my oldest friend to help turn me. That, more than anything else, galvanised my will to defy. Defy him, defy Deko, defy Josef. I fucking-well defied them all!

I went into the Pit as an Orran, daring to hope my emperor and the resistance was still alive. I came out of the Pit as a Terrelan; not because I was broken or my allegiance wavered, but because we were all Terrelans. Six months of peace after the greatest war mankind has ever known had given the Terrelan empire more than enough time to secure the last of the Orran lands. I doubt they did it peacefully though. I met the Terrelan emperor eventually. He made Deko seem like a puppy.

I stared back into the cave that led underground. We were finally free, after so much blood and sweat and sacrifice, and yet some part of me yearned to go back. Some fucking weak and pitiful part of me had decided the dark was my home, that I deserved to be there. As Tamura played in the snow like a child seeing it for the first time, and Hardt stared at the back of Yorin; marching away from us... No, not us. And not marching. Yorin ran away from me. Away from me! From the fear I put in him after he killed Josef. I stared into the darkness of the cave, little more than a crack in the cliff face really. I imagined I could hear scratching, scrabbling. I imagined I could hear the screams of the Damned chasing after us. Still, that weak little part of me wanted to go back. Fuck it! Maybe it wasn't really a part of me at all. Perhaps it was Ssserakis, the ancient horror I had agreed to carry until I could send it home. Ssserakis hated the light, that was why I found it deep underground where the darkness was complete.

For so long I had equated the sky with freedom. Long before my incarceration I looked up at the sky and it was full of promise and wonder. Down in the Pit I used to dream of it, blue or grey, clear or shrouded in cloud, it didn't matter. I used to dream of the sky and promise myself that one day I would see it again. One day I would look up and see stars shining down upon us, the twin moons locked in their crushing embrace as they passed overhead. Now I was free. Now I could see the sky again I found it scared me, made me uneasy. The light made my skin itch. My little victory had been stolen from me and I resented it. I resented the horror that possessed me and the fear it inspired within me. But resentment wasn't enough. I was stuck with it.

We had all sacrificed so much to the Pit. Tamura had long since lost his sanity, though in truth he had perhaps never had it, but I doubt it helped that he had been trapped underground for longer than I had been alive. Hardt had lost his brother, Isen. I would say I regret my actions with Isen, I certainly didn't enjoy it, but that would be a lie. It has just taken me many years to see the truth; of what it cost me and what I gained. I had also lost Josef, though I lost him long before Yorin slit his throat. I think I lost him before we were even sent to the Pit. I lost Josef up on the tower of fort Vernan. I lost him the same day the Orran empire fell. It is a loss I have never quite managed to come to terms with.

But I should move on. The Pit was finally behind me. The sky and the freedom I associated with it were in front of me. There were brighter times to come, and darker. Not just for me but for all of us. I will pick up where I left off: staring into the darkness of the cave, my bare feet cold in the snow, and a clear sapphire sky above.

CHAPTER ONE

A TERRAN PHILOSOPHER ONCE TOLD ME THAT when you stare into the darkness it stares back. I've always thought it was yourself you should find staring back at you. I found Ssserakis. The ancient horror wore many faces, always of those whose deaths weighed upon my conscience. I stared back into the cave on that cliff face and I saw the ghost of Isen standing there.

My friend. Hardt's only brother. My first love, though I'm not sure I should really call it that. My first lust maybe, my first encounter with sexual desire. My first time with a man inside of me. Isen was a mess, his leg cut open and oozing, his rags torn and bloody, his eyes were pale and misty. For just a moment I hoped it was him. I hoped he had somehow survived. I hoped Hardt would turn and see his little brother and all the pain his death was causing would be forgotten in an instant, but I knew better. I knew I was looking at nothing but a ghost conjured by Ssserakis in an attempt to scare me. But I wouldn't let it. I was not afraid of death. I would not let it affect me. I am the weapon. The mantra drilled into me by the tutors at the academy, designed to absolve me of guilt, of conscience, of doubt.

I was still staring at the face of my lover when a creature erupted from the darkness. It was not much larger than a child, but then, neither was I. The creature hit me and we went down in the snow. Sharpened nails tore at my skin as I fought to keep the thing from my face. The wail it let loose set my ears crackling. Hardt tells me I screamed bloody murder and his recollection is often better than my own. If I did, I'm sure it was more battle shout than cry of terror. I think, these days, the little beast wouldn't have shocked me at all. These days I expect monsters to come flying out of dark corners. Such is the way of raising mischievous children.

Hardt was there in a moment, dragging the wailing thing off me and throwing it to the ground. I have no doubt he could have crushed its skull in his giant hands, but Hardt wanted nothing more to do with violence or death. Too much blood on a person's hands can do that. Blood never washes off. It sinks into the skin and stains a person's soul. I didn't know it then, but Hardt was stained the deepest of crimsons. I was relatively clean of it at that point, though I soon managed to change that.

I saw then the creature was one of the Damned we had met down in the ruined city of the Djinn. It was small and stooped at the shoulders with grey skin and wispy hair on its head and arms. It wore no clothes and I could see yellow puss oozing from a number of wounds that looked to be caused by tooth or nail. The poor man, and it had obviously once been a man, writhed on the snowy ground. It clawed at its face and shrieked loud enough to raise the dead. And believe me, it takes quite a din to bring anything back from the grave.

We stood there for a while watching the thing roll about and wail. I think none of us knew what to do. Hardt had already killed so many of the poor creatures and I could see the guilt written in the dirt-smeared lines of his face. I've always thought it foolish to feel guilt over killing the Damned; they're little more than beasts and I wouldn't feel guilty over killing a lion before it killed me. Tamura obviously felt no guilt either, by the look on his face he was probably thinking about jumping down beside the creature and joining in with the thrashing about. The crazy old man likely thought it looked a lot of fun.

"What's wrong with it?" Hardt asked, his voice a deep rumble like drums in the distance. "I didn't hit that hard."

"Absence followed by excess. It is easy to drown when you don't know how to swim," Tamura said with a grin before turning away from the writhing creature.

I could see Hardt's jaw clenching. He finds Tamura vexing, always has. Some people don't like riddles, and Hardt was one of them. Unfortunately, that's just the way Tamura speaks. I decided to put myself between them lest the misunderstanding grow. It's probably worth repeating that Hardt had just lost his younger brother. The big man was putting on a brave face, but there was grief festering below the surface and I know first-hand how grief can cloud judgement.

"It has spent its entire life underground," I said. I should have left it at that, but I foolishly thought I could ease my friend's pain. "Even before that, imps come from the Other World and there is no sun there. It's a place of darkness. And wonder."

"It's not an imp." Hardt caught me in the lie designed to spare his feelings. Lies are useful things, especially when designed to save others, but lies can sour a friendship within moments, almost as quickly as betrayal. Luckily Hardt has always been wise enough to see the reason behind my lies. I wonder which of us is more at fault there. Me for telling so many falsehoods, or Hardt for excusing them.

"It's never seen the light before," I said, forging on before either of us could dwell on my mistake. "It probably burns. We should go. Before it gets dark." It's strange to think back on it, but my voice sounded different even to my own ears. I still had the slight croak given to me by Horralain the first time he tried to strangle me to death, but there was something else now. I sounded… older. One more thing I could *thank* Chronomancy for; due to the magic of time, I no longer recognised my own voice. Change is like that. When it happens over time it's insidious, subtle alterations here and there, you don't even notice it. But when there's a catalyst for sudden change, it feels so wrong and alien. We resist sudden change, perhaps because we fear it.

I turned towards the forest in the distance and started walking. I expected them both to follow without question. I had gotten used to being in charge, to the others responding to my leadership, and my decisions being final. Tamura fell in line, dancing his way through deep snow just as a child might, stopping to marvel at the sight of his own footsteps in the powdery white. Hardt remained, staring at the creature now quieted to a low mewling.

At first, I thought Hardt might kill the thing, reach

down and end its suffering. It was a miserable looking creature even in the dark, but out in the light it was truly pitiful. Small limbs, wasted by malnutrition, and cracked grey skin. A stench of rot and decay rising off it that even we could smell, and I assure you none of us smelled pleasant. It had been so long since I last bathed, I couldn't even remember the true colour of my own skin. The Damned might have been terran once, but too many generations underground, inbreeding and infighting, feeding off imps and each other... There is nothing terran about the Damned anymore. Perhaps there never truly was. They are a plague upon the dark places in this world.

Hardt reached down and picked the little creature up as though it weighed nothing. It screamed and thrashed, yet Hardt gave it no time to strike, he threw it towards the cave mouth and into the waiting darkness. Then he turned and walked past me. I hurried to catch up, eager to be away from the cave. Somewhere inside, deep within my mind or heart, Ssserakis mourned the loss of the dark. I felt it as a strange pull, like a rope stretching between myself and the cave, trying to drag me back as it pulled taught. Resisting that pull was hard. But I would not go back. I could not go back.

I stole one final glance back towards the cave. For so long it had been my focus, my way to escape the torture of the Pit. It had been my path to freedom and my glimmer of hope. Now, as I looked back, it seemed a portal to my past. A dark place that held some of the worst mistakes of my life. I once again saw Isen's ghost staring back at me.

For a long time, none of us spoke. Unless you count Tamura's humming and occasional muttering. We were, all three of us, exhausted. It's probably not surprising. We lived in a constant state of fear and tension down in the Pit, never knowing when we might wake to find that day our last. Never knowing when Prig or Deko would decide they had had enough of us. If anything, things only got worse in the Djinn city. Surrounded by the dark, the unknown, trapped down there with the imps and the Damned and chased by Josef and the overseer's cronies. Now the tension was gone and I felt weariness flood me in its wake. I believe I could have slept for days. But we had no time for that. We had to get ahead of those chasing us. We had to get away before the overseer sent more of his minions to find us.

We aimed for the forest as the sun made its slow daily routine across the sky, warming our backs. Maybe it was the weariness or maybe I misjudged the distance, but it was almost night by the time we reached the first of the trees. That was when my strength finally gave out. I collapsed into the snow, ankle deep in powdery cold, and felt myself slump. The last thing I remember seeing was Hardt rushing towards me, then everything tilted sideways and went black.

CHAPTER TWO

I DREAMT OF THE OTHER WORLD, THE PLACE where monsters and horrors reside. It was not the first time I had been there; as an Impomancer I was long since used to contact with that world. It is a place of muted shadows drawn in grey, as though permanently lit only by moonlight. Though there is no moon, no sun, no stars. I'm not even certain that place has a sky. I suppose it must. I've never seen any clouds, just a lighter shade of grey above the landscape.

The Other World is a vast expanse; even after a lifetime of study I have barely begun to investigate its wonders. But for all its vastness it is surprisingly empty. There are nightmares there, plenty of those, but they haunt the cities and places where the mindless monsters congregate. For as different as the Other World is, and as different as its inhabitants are, they are also strangely like us. They gather in great communities, both the mindless beasts,

and the horrors like Ssserakis, insidiously intelligent. I knew
none of this at the time, the tutors at the Orran Academy
of Magic were fools who taught lies and half-truths, but
their teachings were all I knew. It was Ssserakis who truly
furthered my education, though I feel I may have seen
everything through the horror's tinted vision.

I stood on a rocky plateau, far too sculpted to be
natural, with sharp edges leading to a severe drop. There
were no loose rocks, no dust, no signs of erosion at all. A city
spread out before me glowing green with lethargic pulses of
light. Strange to think about it, but it reminds me of blood
pulsing through veins; as though the city were somehow
alive, and the green light was its essence. The city was built
in ordered blocks, symmetrical in every way. It started off
small with low buildings before growing to mighty towers
and one impossible spire that reached into the grey expanse
above. It was larger than any city I had yet to see, though
my experience was somewhat lacking, and it buzzed with
activity. Even from far away I could see the roads were
crowded, though I recognised few of the creatures I saw.
Some were huge hulking monstrosities, others were smaller
beasts dodging around their larger cousins. There was peace
there. It seemed so strange, perhaps because we Sourcerers
always used the denizens of the Other World for war.

It was a dream, I knew that. I had visited the Other
World many times through Impomancy and knew a
Sourcerer has no body in that world. They exist only as a
disembodied spirit, invisible to all but the most powerful of
horrors. But not that time. I stood on that plateau. I could
see my arms and legs, my body, all just skin and bone. I
was still wearing the rags from the Pit, torn and shredded
and identifying me as an inmate. A criminal. I could feel

the stone beneath my bare feet, and the breeze stirring my matted hair. I would be lying if I said it was not somewhat surreal. I had never heard of any Sourcerer actually visiting the Other World as anything other than a spirit, but there I was. The air burned in my lungs and I felt heavier somehow, as though gravity was stronger there.

I wasn't alone.

Isen stood next to me. It wasn't the Isen I remembered though. The rugged man, handsome despite the grime and scars, was gone. What stood beside me now was a ghost. The same ghost who watched me leave the ruined Djinn city. He looked just how I had left him. His left leg was torn open, muscle and blood bulging to escape the wound. His right arm was bent backwards, bone poking through skin. His face was mashed and broken, crumpled on the right side from where Josef had crushed him against the ceiling and then the floor. I have no doubt I would have vomited from the sight, but it was a dream. Neither of us were really there. The mess of a terran that stood beside me wasn't even Isen. It was Ssserakis, wearing the bloodied corpse of the man I had, just a few days ago, fucked.

"Is this my dream or yours?" My voice sounded wrong in that world, as though a terran voice had no place there. I half expected every creature and horror to suddenly find and evict me.

Is there a difference? Isen's mouth moved to speak the words, but the voice was not his. It was the same voice I had heard down in the Pit the first time I met Ssserakis. It is hard to describe, and I have tried many times in my life. I think the closest I have ever come is that it sounds like a bag full of snakes. Angry snakes.

"This is your home." I knew it was true even as I

said it. That should have tipped me off that Ssserakis and I were more closely linked than I believed. I knew it was the horror's home, because it also felt like my home. Despite how alien it appeared, I was comfortable there.

That is my home, Ssserakis hissed and pointed with Isen's good arm towards the very top of the great spire in the centre of the city. *Before I was taken. Now...* Isen's body walked in front of me, obscuring my view and then stopping on my right.

The city had changed. Where before it pulsed with a strange green light, it now stood dead and dark. Nothing but grey stone, still artfully sculpted and symmetrical, but no longer beautiful. The activity in the streets was gone. The creatures that moved about the city were gone. It stood there empty and lifeless. I couldn't say why exactly, but I mourned its loss.

I tore my eyes away from the dead city to find Isen gone. I stood alone on the plateau and realised what little light there was had started to fade. I think, more accurately, the darkness was rising around me. The world dimmed until I was engulfed in a void. I heard only the rapid, fearful beat of my own heart. Icy claws closed around it and the pain in my chest became stifling. It hurt to breathe. I was frozen by a cold that sank so deep into my bones I was beyond shivering.

"Wake up!" I shouted into the darkness. I tried to reach up and slap my own face, but I had no arms, no head. I was nothing. Just a disembodied voice floating in nothing. I screamed.

I woke screaming, clutching at my chest. Hardt tells me he's never seen me look as terrified as I did in that

moment. As though every horror and nightmare, every
fearful thing that has ever existed in this world, had all
visited me at once. And I suppose Hardt would know best.
He has seen me at my best and worst. He saw me down
in the Red Cells, beneath the Terrelan capital; he saw what
tortures the emperor visited upon me. He stood by me as I
made the hardest choice, the impossible choice; he witnessed
the fear of that decision. He was even there the day I died.

"It's alright, Eska," Hardt said, his voice deep and
soothing. He held my cheek in one of his giant hands and
stared into my eyes; an anchor to bring me back to the real
world. It's surprising what eye contact can do that words
cannot. "Just a dream. You're out of it now."

He held that eye contact until my breathing calmed
and the panic left me. Then he nodded and helped me up
to sitting, my back against the rough bark of a chessop
tree. I knew the type well; I had spent my first six years in
a forest after all. Chessop trees have short needles instead
of leaves and can resist just about any type of weather.
They grow far apart from each other and produce a strange
earthy smell when burned. I smelled it then and it brought
back memories of a carefree time before the Orrans turned
me into a weapon. Before the Terrelans turned me into a
prisoner. That, too, helped calm me. The thought of a home
I would never know again. The memory of our little house
and the bed I shared with my brother, my father snoring at
night, and waking to the smell of porridge as my mother
cooked breakfast.

Hardt nodded and sat down, finding his own tree
to rest against. I still didn't trust myself to speak, so I sat in
silence. The memories of that city in the Other World, the
fear Ssserakis had put in me, were still close to the surface.

The horror's voice echoed somewhere within me.

Home. I want to go home.

We were surrounded by trees on all sides, a small copse of them forming a little clearing, somehow free of snow. There was a fire going in the centre, just a few feet away. The heat warmed my feet but it only went skin deep. I could feel the cold inside. Tamura was sitting by the little fire, his hands slick with blood as he tore the skin off a little animal that looked as though it might once have been a rabbit. To this day I still don't know how they caught the creature, nor how they managed to find wood dry enough to burn. One of Tamura's many talents hidden behind layer upon layer of crazy old man.

"Here," Hardt pushed a sack towards me. "Eat."

I started to protest, but as soon as I thought about it, I realised I was ravenous. It was a hunger that went deeper than a need to eat. Again, I looked down at my arms to find them stick thin, bones visible under skin that looked like dirty paper. I dug into the sack and pulled out a handful of shrooms. They were a gift from the imps down in the Djinn city and they were starting to run thin. They also tasted like chewing on an old boot. I am happy to admit that was the very last time I ate shrooms. Even to this day, the thought of them makes me feel queasy.

"You've looked like that since after the fight with Josef," Hardt said as I shoved shrooms into my mouth and went about unenthusiastically chewing. He placed our one clay cup on the ground in front of me and I saw it was brimming with water. There is something to be said for a land coated in a blanket of snow, it is easy to find water. It was icy and refreshing,

"Chronomancy," I said it around a mouthful of

chewing and I doubt it sounded right, but Hardt seemed
to understand and Tamura had a look on his face that said
he already knew better than I did. "Speeds up the body but
comes at such a heavy price. A double cost, it both ages the
Sourcerer and burns the body's resources."

"That's why you suddenly look so much older?"

I nodded. I still hadn't had chance to look at myself.
Mirrors weren't just lying around. But we had water. I
picked up the little clay cup and held it below my face,
looking down into water as the sloshing quieted. I did look
older. It wasn't just the gaunt complexion and papery skin. I
had new lines on my face. The jagged scar of flesh on my left
cheek looked weathered. I had lost so many years in so short
a time. Age is odd like that. The more years you have, the
less you have left.

There was nothing I could do about it. I lifted the cup
to my lips and drank deep. I was quite thirsty and it wasn't
long before we were melting another cup of snow over the
little fire.

"Where are we?" I asked after I'd had my fill of
shrooms. It wasn't so much that I was feeling full, but
I don't think I could have stomached any more of the
things. Besides, Tamura had spitted the rabbit and was
busy cooking it and I could feel my mouth watering at the
thought of real meat. I wasn't the only one. In all the time
we were down in the Pit we ate stale bread, cold gruel, and
shrooms. I had been down there for just over six months.
Tamura had been down there for longer than I had been
alive. I doubted he even remembered the taste of meat and
not just because of his addled mind.

"The Forest of Ten," Tamura said. "Ten fires in the
night. Ten knights to rescue ten damsels. Ten times thrown

back from the forest edge. Ten times they tried. Ten cries went up when morning broke and ten damsels were never seen again.

"Ten tears were shed by Lokar and Lursa. Ten rocks made holes in the ground. Ten weapons found where once were none. Ten brothers went to war. Ten thousand died upon the fields and ten times that number grieved.

"Ten weapons lost and forged anew. Ten Sources to lend power. Ten artefacts of great renown hidden from greedy eyes. Ten kingdoms built and then ten more. Ten wars fought, ten empires burned. And now, just two remain."

"One," I said, my voice bitter with the admission. "One empire remains. Terrelan."

Tamura looked up from the spit. "Then ten weapons have become one. Or maybe lost again." He giggled then and let go of the spit, spreading his arms wide. "The Forest of Ten."

I glanced over to find Hardt staring into the flames. "You butchered the song, old man. The bards sing it with ten verses."

Tamura shrugged. "The truth is like power. Many claim to have it, but few really know what it even means."

"What?" Hardt asked.

"Your bards are fools," Tamura said and then broke into a wild giggle.

Hardt sighed. "It's just a forest. A place we can hide for a while. It'll keep us covered while we go wherever we're going." He looked at me then as though I should have the answer. I had led us all from the Pit and through the ruined Djinn city, but here I was lost. I knew nothing about the area. I had never seen a map with the Forest of Ten on it. I was also too weary to care.

"For now, we just keep moving," I said. "Josef said the overseer would send others if he didn't return. And Yorin was heading west when he left. If he keeps going, he'll head right back to the Pit and they will probably torture our story from him. We'll just keep going." It was the closest I had to a plan.

"And then what? We just run? Keep running?" It was clear Hardt wanted to know my intentions there and then, and he wouldn't take no for an answer. I think maybe he wanted to know what his brother had died for. I sometimes wonder if I had given another answer, whether he might have left me and stormed off on his own like Yorin. Maybe he wanted to with the answer I did give.

"And then one day we return and pay back Prig and Deko and the overseer and everyone else who made our lives hell down there." Cold rage made my words sharp. I glanced up at Hardt, pinning him with a bright blue stare. "And the emperor as well. But first I need power. I need Sources, ones that won't kill me."

I was naive back then, foolish even. I thought just having a few Sources inside my stomach would make all the difference. I never even stopped to consider how little difference it made when the Orran empire fell. No, back then I had no idea what true power was. And I had no idea what strength really meant. Some lessons take longer to learn than others. Some knowledge comes with a terrible price.

Hardt fell silent then. He looked old suddenly. Sat against a chessop tree, his shirt long since lost to the clutching claws of the Damned, his body covered in little red scratches. I wondered when he had stopped shaving. The fuzz on his face was starting to curl and mat together. I think

I saw him crying silent tears, fat drops of water catching the firelight as they ran down the lines of his face. I wanted to comfort him. But I didn't know how. We had both so recently lost a brother and I knew there were no words that could help. I wasn't even sure I was the right one to offer any. It was my brother who had killed his, after all. Instead I turned away from his grief, and shoved down my own. It was easier to not feel it, than confront the tempest of emotions.

"We have these," Tamura said and I looked across the fire to see him playing with two small crystals, each no larger than a marble, and each coated in blood. Sources. A Chronomancy Source from deep within the Djinn city. And a Kinemancy Source, given to Josef by the overseer. It was Josef's blood on the two Sources.

I'd be lying if I said I didn't crave them. It wasn't so long ago the Chronomancy Source almost killed me, and it wasn't so long ago that Josef almost killed me with the Kinemancy Source. If I swallowed either of them then I knew they'd complete the job. Sources were never meant to be ingested by people, even those attuned to the magic are hurt and eventually killed by it. The only way to stop that is to retch up the Source before too much damage is done. But my body has never liked to give up the power once it is inside. Only Spiceweed has ever allowed me to regurgitate a Source and I used what little we had to stop Josef. Still, even knowing they would kill me, I wanted them. I knew, no matter how many shrooms I ate, my hunger would never be sated until I had a Source sitting inside my stomach. It's an addiction, you see, one all Sourcerers share. To feel that core of power inside, leaking magic into your body, there is no feeling quite like it. It's not quite pleasure, and it is often painful. It is like raising your face to the sun after a long night of cold. Filling your belly after a year of starvation. Not pleasure, nor pain, but comfort. A feeling of rightness.

I think I may have been staring. The lust for power has always been strong in me and never more so than back then, when my vengeance was so strong in my mind. When I thought I had no power of my own and wanted it, needed it to burn away all those who had wronged me. Tamura lifted the Sources up to his face and poked his tongue out at me. Despite everything I had been through, or maybe because of it, I laughed. Then Tamura opened his mouth and popped one of the Sources inside.

"NO!" I screamed; leaning forwards and knocking the little cup over. I think Hardt was confused, maybe he thought I had fallen asleep again; another bad dream plaguing me. But it was far worse than that. Only Sourcerers could wield the magic of Sources, anyone else would be consumed by the power in a matter of minutes and the death would be far from pleasant. Tamura had just fucking killed himself!

The crazy old man chuckled, his jaw working around his mouth. Then he spat the Source back into his hand. "This one's for you." He flicked the Source over the fire. I'm a little ashamed to say I scrambled for it. I'm more ashamed to admit I had to fight the urge to swallow it. Instead, I clutched it to my chest as though fearing someone might try to take it from me again.

"This is…"

"Kinemancy," Tamura said with a sage nod of his head. "The power to move things." A basic description if ever I heard one. Basic and very lacking.

"What just happened?" Hardt asked.

"I think Tamura just identified a Source by taste." It's

fair to say I was a little surprised. Back at the academy we were told there was no way to identify a Source until the Sourcerer swallowed it, until they could access the power. We were instructed to memorise the Sources we were given; their size, shape, flat surfaces, edges, imperfections. Everything, including the most minute details. That way we would know which of our Sources we were swallowing even while blind.

"Tastes like a river; always moving, cutting its own path." Tamura smiled and went back to turning the spit as though he hadn't said something entirely crazy.

I wondered if I could trust him, trust his judgement, his memory. His sense of taste. I will admit I thought about popping the Source in my mouth, to see how it tasted myself. I had never even thought about it before, I had always swallowed the Sources down as quickly as possible. The very idea that they might have a taste was alien to me. Right then I knew I couldn't trust myself not to swallow it, and placed the Source instead in the little leather snuff pouch tied to the rope around my waist.

"It's not enough," I said. I was attuned to six different types of magic and if I had a Source for each of them it still wouldn't have been enough. "I need to know how to fight as well. I need you to teach me."

"Who?" Hardt asked.

"Both of you."

Tamura giggled.

"You're not built for what I do," Hardt said with a sad shake of his head.

"Then I'll get stronger." I have always had determination in spades. Determination, and a relentless drive to get what I want. There have been many times in my life when I have relied, instead of using a convincing argument, on wearing down the other person. Hardt has never taken much wearing down. At least not where I'm concerned. "I need to know how to protect myself." I didn't point out that it was more about learning to hurt others. Sometimes you need to tailor an argument to the person.

Hardt nodded slowly. "Remember, you demanded." He shared a look with Tamura who just giggled. It was decided, but there was no way my training would start that night; we were all far too tired.

There are three ways to deal with grief, and make no mistake, I was grieving just as surely as Hardt was. I might have cut Josef loose down in the Pit, pushed him away and left him there, but I loved him. I fucking loved him. He was my best friend and my brother in every way that mattered. My safety and my comfort. Without him I felt less somehow, as though the better part of myself had been cut away along with his throat. But pushing someone away is not the same as watching them die. I saw the life fade from his eyes. I saw the blood spilling out. Even if I had hated him, truly hated him, not just trying to convince myself of it, I would still grieve for the loss.

The first way to deal with grief is to confront it, to meet it head on and accept it as a part of yourself. It is, by far, the hardest thing to do, but also the only way to truly move past it. I wish I could give some sage insight into the process, but I have never been good at confronting my grief. Hardt, on the other hand is a bloody master. His grief for Isen showed for a while, both in the tears he shed and the smiles he shared. He told us stories of a younger brother who followed him everywhere, copying him as he chopped wood or collected water from the well. I think that was the way he coped and the way he moved past his loss, by remembering the good times. I couldn't help but notice that all the stories he told were from their childhood, and not one of them contained even a mention of their father.

The second way is to wallow in it. At first it might seem a lot like a confrontation. Both forms certainly contain a lot of spilt tears and even more spilt booze. But the key difference is those who confront their grief move on; eventually they make it out the other side and put the pain, sorrow, and tears behind them. Those who wallow don't even try to move on. Maybe it's the pity that they heap upon themselves, and that which they take from others. Maybe the attention is addictive, or maybe they just don't have the strength needed to pull themselves out of their misery. I don't know. I've never been able to stand people who wallow in grief for very long; their pain and tears soon become annoying. Or even worse, they clamp down and refuse to feel anything. At that point they are little more than golems made of flesh. I cannot abide wallowers.

The third way of dealing with grief, and I count myself as one of the great followers of this belief, is to run from it. Rather than allow myself to feel the pain and heartache, I throw myself into activity. I use the desire to escape my grief to drive me. Some of the most successful periods of my life have come about because I needed to run from my feelings. In the Forest of Ten, I was doing just that. I made both Hardt and Tamura teach me, to distract both my mind and body, because it was easier to wear myself to exhaustion than it was to deal with the fact that Josef was dead and a part of me had died with him.

CHAPTER THREE

JOSEF

I didn't die.

I write those three little words to affirm it in my own mind because it still seems impossible to me. I sit here, weak and weary, with wounds that should have killed me. But I am alive.

I didn't die.

I. Didn't. Die.

But I wish I had.

She betrayed me. I don't know how else to say it. Eska betrayed me. I had a way out, for both of us, a way out, and a way to be free. But she didn't care. All she wanted was to keep fighting. All she wanted was vengeance for something that no longer matters to anyone save herself. Stupid bitch!

I wish I could say sorry. I killed Isen. I don't even know why. I think I was jealous. Or maybe I just wanted to hurt her. To hurt him. To hurt them. I killed him. Hardt must hate me. Eska must hate me.

I know this isn't what the overseer wants. He gave me paper and ink to write down what I saw. To tell him what happened down there. I can't speak. My voice is gone and I don't know if it will ever come back. The knife cut too deep, severed something that should never be cut. It hurts to breathe and swallow. They spoon feed me gruel and it feels like eating knives.

But what happened? There were creatures down there, I think. Monsters I had never seen before. Creatures from the Other World. I don't know anything about that place, except that Eska knows. She tried to hide it. She did a good job of hiding it. But I ~~know~~ knew her better than anyone. Eska is drawn to that world in some way I can't begin to understand. I remember finding her staring off into space so many times, and I know it looked like she was daydreaming, but she wasn't. She wasn't here. She was there. She was in the Other World, searching it for... I don't know what she was searching for. After everything I shared with her, everything I gave her, it still wasn't enough. Eska was always withdrawn. Even from me.

I want to hate her.

~~I do hate her.~~

We followed the lights to find her, through a city that was old and buried. Gemstones in the walls, I think, that held the light of torches and reflected it back. Then, when there were no more lights, we followed the carnage. Whatever creatures she found down there were not friendly. There were dozens of them. Hundreds, maybe, and so many of them were dead. When we finally caught up to Eska. She had a Chronomancy Source. By the moons, where did she get a Chronomancy Source? I should have let her die. But I didn't. And then someone else was there. I felt so helpless as the knife cut.

I didn't die.

I should have died, but I felt something. I felt the warm touch of Biomancy stemming the blood and healing my wound. I don't know how. I haven't so much as tasted a Biomancy Source since the fall of Orran. Yet I could feel it working within me. I guess such lengthy exposure to the magic has made it seep into my flesh. I've never heard of anything like it but...

I didn't die.

I saw those monsters, the ones from the city. After Eska left me, I could barely move. I saw them come and drag away the bodies. They're still alive down there. Monsters so close to the Pit. I have to tell the overseer. He must know.

Horralain found me. I guess Deko had sent him and some others. Horralain went on, following after Eska, but he told the others to drag me back to the Pit.

And here I am. No one has been to see me in days, except for the guard who feeds me the porridge. The overseer left me these papers, my only way of communicating. My only voice. I don't think the guard can read. I grunted at her and she just shook her head. I have to be useful to the overseer. I must give him what he wants. Maybe if I do, he'll send me to find Eska again.

I know you'll never read this, Eska, but you've taken my voice from me so I have no other way to tell my story.

I'm sorry.

I didn't die.

CHAPTER
FOUR

I STOPPED KEEPING TRACK OF THE TIME WE spent in the Forest of Ten, but Tamura counted the days and remembered, despite his addled memory. I once asked him exactly how many days he had spent down in the Pit and he replied instantly with *seven thousand one hundred and eleven*. Half a lifetime spent underground; no wonder he can remember so little. For two months we moved through the forest, making a new camp every day, Tamura hunting and scavenging to feed us. I ate a lot during those months, though thankfully not a single shroom, and the flesh burned away by Chronomancy quickly returned to me. The years I had lost, however, did not.

Each morning I would wake, force down some cold meat or berries from the night before, and set about training with Hardt. It was tough going at the start and I would like to say it got easier, but that would be a damned lie. With the big Terrelan as a teacher no matter how much I improved, I was always a lifetime away from his equal. At first much of the training was designed to make me stronger. Hardt claimed there was no sense in teaching me how to punch unless I could make my target feel it. I remember bristling at that, but I was skin and bone since leaving the Pit, and even before that I had never been strong of arm. I've always been something of a slight woman and I relied on magic, wit, and guile. Regardless, a well thrown punch can hurt, no matter how small the thrower.

I was exhausted every day by the time we broke camp and started walking. I say walking, for me it was very much trudging. Hardt stayed beside me. He was always there in case I ever needed him though he never offered me help I didn't ask for. I carried everything we owned every day that we were in that forest to improve my strength and stamina. Admittedly, we didn't own much and what we did was worth nothing, at least except for the Sources, but I carried it all the same. Tamura ranged ahead and around. He couldn't tell us how he knew about forests and tracking and hunting, but the skills were there even if the memories were not. Every day he found some fruit or berries or some small animal to cook. There is much to be said about the bounties of a forest; three people can live off it indefinitely if they know how.

My evenings were given over to Tamura and they were even more frustrating than the mornings. By campfire light he would instruct me in the basics of whatever martial art he practised. The basics included, for the most part, learning to fucking breathe. I was fairly certain I had the art of breathing figured out, having been doing it all my life, and, in fact, having been tutored on it previously by tutor Bell at the academy. Tamura was not impressed with the academy teachings. I cannot blame the old man. I have learned much since leaving the academy and a lot of what I have learned shows their teachings for lies, half-truths, or the ignorant babbling of fools. Still, at the time I was sure of myself. I spent almost as much time complaining, as I did learning the new method of breathing.

For the first week all I did was sit and breathe. It was bloody frustrating. I had set my mind on learning the old man's mysterious arts, and instead I was sitting still and doing nothing. I may have unnaturally aged a decade, but I still had the foolishness and impatience of youth about me. It didn't help that the forced meditation gave me a lot of time to think, and that was something I was actively trying to avoid. More than once, my breathing turned to sobs as grief snuck up on me. It does that, lies in wait for a quiet moment, and before you know what's happening you are feeling utter loss. Remorse for the things taken from you, taken from the world. The second week Tamura had me maintaining my breathing while holding various positions, none of which seemed likely to help me disarm a foe or break any limbs. What can I say other than, it was a slow process.

The snow soon melted away and the forest went from powdery white to damp green and brown. It was beautiful, and there were many times during my breathing exercises I found myself drifting off and remembering Keshin, the forest village where I was born. The snow barely touched us there, despite how cold it could get in the winter. It is odd but no matter how many places I have called home, and no matter how long I have called them such, it is still the forests that make me feel most at ease. I sometimes wonder if I would have led a happier life had I called off my quest for vengeance and settled down amidst the trees. Perhaps taken up basket weaving like my mother before me. But I could no more give up my quest than Tamura could give up his crazy. It was set in me, branded onto my soul. Back then I had nothing else to drive me, only my need to see my enemies as broken as I felt. As broken as they had left me. Grief and self-pity often go hand in hand. That's one more reason I run from my grief; pity does not suit me.

At night Ssserakis flooded my mind with nightmares. Sometimes they were visions of creatures from the Other World, sometimes they were memories of the things I had done and seen. Sometimes they were visions of a home in flames, and friends in pain. I lost track of the number of times I watched Keshin burn. Each night I would wake in a sweat, despite the cold, and each night I would see a ghost in the darkness, just beyond the reach of the firelight. More often than not, it was Isen, but sometimes it was others, those from the Pit whose names I couldn't even remember. Ssserakis only ever visited me with the faces of the dead. I thought the horror was just trying to scare me; it fed off fear, and down in the Pit it had grown fat, but in the Forest of Ten there was nothing to be afraid of. I imagined it was starving, and only by inspiring fear in its host could it survive. There was much more to it though. More I didn't yet know.

Once, Ssserakis took me to a mountaintop. In Ovaeris, the air grows thin as you ascend, but in the Other World there's no difference, regardless of altitude. We stood on that mountain, Ssserakis appearing to me as formless shade, and watched a migration of monsters. I thought myself knowledgeable of the denizens of that world, I had read the Encyclopaedia Otheria cover to cover on more than one occasion, and even added some of my own notes, but there were things I saw there I could not name. Giant creatures with front legs larger than the rear, they glowed red from within as though some fire burned inside of them and only their purpling flesh stopped it from spilling out and setting the world ablaze. They carried smaller beasts on their backs, creatures of half a dozen limbs all ending in sharpened blades of carapace. There was a symbiosis there, the larger creatures plodding along, forever moving forward, while the smaller ones leapt down to hunt prey where they found it, carrying food back to the larger ones after they had torn it to shreds.

But it was not the ground Ssserakis wanted me to see. The horror told me to look, instead, to the featureless sky and there I saw something wondrous: a serpent so long I couldn't guess at its true size, winding its way through the sky. Its body shimmered between green and blue hues even in the grey light of the Other World, and thousands of spines stretched out across its body. It had no wings to carry it and I couldn't fathom how it flew, but it moved in such a way I found myself mesmerised by the undulations. Ssserakis told me its name was Hyrenaak, the Landless, and not once in the eternity it had been alive had it touched the ground. I watched it dive towards the migration and snatch one of the giants from its path, crushing it between jaws that made it look tiny. Molten flame gushed out over the serpent's teeth, dropping fire toward the ground as it wove its way higher into the sky. The six-legged creatures that had been riding on the giant fled its carcass before the serpent swallowed it down, they scurried onto Hyrenaak's body, spreading out over the length and falling still. That was when I noticed that what I had taken for spines, were actually thousands of those little blade-legged monsters, all crowding on the back of something that dwarfed them.

Hyrenaak flew past us and I saw it had dozens of eyes on each side of its head, each of them a twisting mass of madness. Yet it watched us. I'm not sure how I knew it, but it watched us as it passed and there was recognition. One king to another. *King* is the wrong word, but I have since discovered that the Other World is ruled, just as ours is, by individuals. Monsters like Hyrenaak, horrors like Ssserakis, and others too. I have also discovered that they war endlessly amongst themselves but are united in their hatred of both the Rand and the Djinn. A worthy cause to unite for.

As the weeks wore on, Hardt started to change my training. He would still watch over me while I performed the exercises to strengthen my body, but afterwards he would teach me to move. He insisted much of the art of pugilism was based on staying light on your feet, stepping quickly and keeping your opponent in front of you. We would adopt a stance with our hands held up in front of us, and he would dodge left and right, moving around me. My job was to keep up with him. You might not think it so difficult, considering he is the size of small tree, but Hardt has always been swift. More than once I ended up with crossed legs, pitching onto the needly floor of the forest. Trust me when I tell you, an arse full of needles hurts.

Tamura laughed at us from time to time. It made Hardt angry. Tamura's teachings seemed completely at odds with Hardt's. Where Hardt taught strength, Tamura taught leverage. Where Hardt taught movement, Tamura taught stillness. My mind was a whirl with the conflicting teachings. It's fair to say that I was foolish trying to learn two different styles of combat at once. I have ever been a poor student and I excelled at neither, though Hardt insisted

I was making fair progress all things considered. Tamura just laughed and said *even mountains were once rocks.*

As the cold seeped away, replaced by new warmth from the sun, I felt stronger than I had ever been. I had put on weight and much of it was muscle, and the old Pit rags we all still wore were barely large enough to cover me. Tamura had fashioned us all cloaks made of sewn animal hides, but it was clear I would need new clothing and soon. I washed regularly, having found a few streams and pools within the forest, and Hardt actually told me I looked quite pretty underneath all the grime and filth. I'm not too proud to admit I took solace at the compliment. I have never been a vain woman, but after ageing a decade in a matter of minutes and having my face quite horribly scarred it was nice to know I had retained at least some of my looks. My hair was a mess, growing at odd lengths. It was a reminder of Josef, that he had cut my hair so short to try to mask my gender down in the Pit.

Times were hard. The weather was cold, and our provisions were scarce. Yet I found myself smiling and laughing a lot during our time in that forest. Maybe it was the relief of being able to see the sky after so long underground. Maybe it was because of Hardt's good nature and Tamura's wit. Maybe it was because we didn't know what was coming. I count our time there as a happy one, and I think it may be the longest I have ever gone without making a mistake. Unfortunately, our time in the Forest of Ten couldn't last. As we drew close to its eastern border we were found.

CHAPTER FIVE

JOSEF

I'm more of an outcast than I've ever been. The overseer isn't pleased with me. I failed to bring back Eska. I lost my Source. I almost died. He called me useless and threw me back to the Pit. The way he looked at me, like I was nothing. It was horrible. It was even worse when he turned his back, waved for the soldiers to drag me away.

I'm mostly healed, I think. I still can't speak. When I try nothing comes out but a painful croak. I think perhaps the overseer is right. I am useless. Not even Deko or the foremen want me. I've been assigned to no team. Lessa hasn't come to put me back to work. I think I'm glad about that. No more beatings for failing to meet the digging quota on time. No more being rudely awakened by a kick to the ribs. No more mattering to anyone. They all just ignore me. The other scabs are in on it too. Those that are left.

I wonder if Eska had any idea what she was doing when she started that riot over the food. Did she know how many lives would be lost? Did she care? Somehow, I doubt it. She always was a heartless bitch. That's not fair of me. But I'm not going to scribble it out. Not this time.

The Pit almost feels empty. There's so much space. I can go a full day without seeing anyone, without them seeing me. Except when it's time to eat. Deko and his thugs still hoard the food. Even though there's fewer people down here, we still go hungry. We still wear rags while they have fresh clothes and boots. Scabs still dig. Scabs still fight in the arena over nothing at all. For all the anger Eska caused, for all the pain and death she brought down upon this place, nothing has changed. Except she's gone. And I'm still here.

I dreamt about them catching her last night. I saw her thrown into a dark pit where hungry wolves were waiting to tear her apart. I watched it happen, stood by and did nothing as my only friend was savaged by teeth and claws. I watched her die and... I won't write it. I won't write what I felt. I won't admit to it. What does that mean? I think maybe I deserve to be here. And I think she deserves to be here as well. After all the things we've done, we both deserve the punishment.

They caught Yorin. The overseer questioned him, had him beaten. Now he's down here with us again. I see him staring at me sometimes, over his bruised lips and blackened eyes. The look in his eyes scares me. There's so much anger there, I know he'll kill me if he ever catches me alone. I don't know why. I did nothing to him. Maybe he and Isen were friends. Maybe Eska cut him loose because of me. Maybe Yorin was the one who cut my throat. I must keep my distance. I have to hide from him. I can't let him finish the job.

I have to hide my paper and my charcoal from the other scabs. I can't allow anyone else to find them. But that's easy now. There's so few of us left I can sneak away to sit alone in the darkness. Like a shadow at night, invisible. I sleep on my own, eat on my own. No one notices me and I hate it. No one but Yorin notices me. I've been forgotten. Not even the overseer pays me attention anymore. I'm useless. And I'm mute, and the wound on my neck never stops hurting.

    I love you, Eska.

    ~~*I hate you, Eska.*~~

    I write them both to see which is true. I'm not sure I can tell anymore.

CHAPTER
SIX

THERE IS A SOUND OF A BOW BEING DRAWN. Some are like the creaking timbers of a ship on the water, bold and unmistakable; others are more like a whisper, the promise of swift death. This one was more like the latter and it came from behind. I froze, one foot barely touching the ground.

"Don't move," said a gruff voice from somewhere in front of us. I knew then that we were surrounded.

It was mid-morning with a high sun, beams of light streaming through the canopy. My breath steamed as it passed my lips, and the hairs on the back of my neck tingled.

"Stay close," Hardt hissed. He was frozen to the spot, head twitching about as he searched for the source of the voice.

Tamura was further ahead but he stopped as well. He was staring at the exact spot where a tall man stepped out from behind a tree, just a short distance ahead of us. Huntsmen have a way of stepping in the forest that masks their movement; it is a trick I have never managed to learn. This one was silent as calm waters, despite having a fair belly beneath his jerkin. He held no bow, but I counted three knives and a small axe hanging from his belt. They all looked like they could be thrown, and I doubted he would miss. Some people have that air of competence about them. It's all in the way they stand, somehow both at ease and ready to spring into action. Back then I certainly had no such air about me; I was rigid as rock and shivering from the cold.

"Fair warning, we have you dead to rights," this voice was from behind. I glanced over my shoulder to see a much smaller man, both in height and girth, with a drawn bow trained on Hardt. "No threatening moves, please." In all my years and everything I have witnessed I don't think I have ever seen a more unruly, unkempt beard than that on the man with the bow. I wondered how so much hair couldn't affect his aim.

A third man stepped out from behind the first. That last man looked older than the others, with grey shocks of hair on the side of his head and a grimace with every step he took. He was huge, maybe a little smaller than Hardt, but big all the same. Go wondering in the woods, and you're likely to meet huntsmen and woodsmen, and neither live easy lives. They are what the forest makes of them. I suppose the same could be said of all people; we are what our environment forges us into. Well, I was forged by my recent experiences in the Pit, and one thing it certainly made me, was ruthless.

Hardt held up his hands. Maybe he was trying to look peaceful, show the men he carried no weapons. The problem

with being as big as Hardt is that you look even bigger with
your arms held high, and big men often appear threatening
even when they're harmless compared to the small woman
they are standing beside.

"We mean no harm, friends," Hardt said. He looked
at me, clearly expecting me to follow his example. I didn't.

"I don't remember us being friends," said the man
with the grey hair. His accent made all the words a lazy
drawl. I took him for a woodsman, he had the kind of brawn
that is used to swinging something heavy at something hard.
I had seen many just like it down in the Pit, what with all the
digging we did. "And it's not every day we find strangers in
the woods. Especially not an odd group like yourselves."

"Nothing so odd about my family," Hardt continued,
his hands still up. "Unless you count my father, Tamura.
He's got a touch of the old age. Mind isn't what it used to
be."

Tamura let out a giggle. "The mind is what we make
of it. Too sharp and it cuts, too dull and it rusts. Bends too
far and it can break. Shattered, like a mirror. Have you ever
tried to put a mirror back together?"

"Enough, old man. Quiet now." I think it was the
first lie I ever heard Hardt tell. I remember it seemed wrong
somehow, as though he should always tell the truth. I
wonder if that was because I have always seen him as the
only true and just person I have ever known. I decided to go
along with his ruse; after all, he was far more worldly than I.

"Family, huh?" drawled the grey-haired man. I felt
eyes turn my way. My skin bristled.

They won't believe it. They're going to kill you all. It had
been so long since Ssserakis had spoken to me directly I
almost believed the thought my own. But I recognised the

horror now and it wouldn't manage that trick a second time. Still, the words did feel like they had the stench of truth about them.

"What are you running from?" asked the man with the grey hair.

"We're not running from anything," Hardt said. "Just looking for a place to settle down. New town and new roots, is what my father used to say. He moved us around a lot. Before he lost his mind, that is. Now I guess it's me moving us around." Hardt kept to his ruse with a tired smile and a jovial chuckle. I could see the play he was making, from my time gambling with dice and cards down in the Pit. When caught in a bluff there are two options available; you can either fold or double down. Often times it's better to back out, count your losses and be happy you weren't taken for the whole lot. However, if the woodsmen caught us in the lie, I couldn't see any way it would end well for us.

I inched my hand towards my belt, feeling for my snuff pouch. I have to admit there are benefits to standing next to a person as large as Hardt; he tends to draw all the attention away from the real danger.

"What is it? Debt? Crime?" The older man continued. "The three of you don't look like you own much. You must be running from something."

"Prison rags," said the fat huntsman, his drawl a match to his friend's. "They're wearing what those down in the Pit do. It's been a while since I ranged that far, but I once saw a bunch of prisoners being sent underground. They were all wearing the like, though not quite as ragged."

Well, there goes the lie. Either they kill you now, or send you back. The problem with having a voice in the back of your mind is it's very hard to shut it up. The other problem is that it sometimes speaks the truth when you'd rather hear a lie.

"Alright, it's true," Hardt said, taking a step forward.

"NOT another step!" shouted the older woodsman. "If he takes one more step, Deryl, you put an arrow in his back."

My left hand found the snuff pouch tied to my belt and I started working my fingers inside. I could see the older man and the fat one talking quietly, sparing us glances, but trusting in Deryl to watch us from behind with his bow. No doubt they were deciding what to do with us. We were escaped prisoners from a prison where only the worst criminals are sent, they were probably thinking it was easier to kill us than capture us. Or maybe there were already posters up in the local villages, my likeness scrawled on paper, the word *WANTED* underneath. I had no doubt the overseer was hunting me still. How little I knew; there were far worse things than him hunting me.

Hardt still had his hands up, frozen to the spot and awaiting whatever judgement was thrown our way. But Tamura… Tamura was no longer watching the men; he was staring at me. I met his eyes and he nodded just once. There is a ruthlessness to Tamura. He may seem to be little more than a kind, crazy old man, but he is more capable than most people I have ever met, and he is fiercely protective of his own life. The lives of others mean little to him when his own lies in the balance. I think we are all that way to some degree. I know I am.

My fingers brushed against the Kinemancy Source hidden in the snuff pouch and I snatched it into my hand, slowly raising it to my lips. I popped the little crystal into my mouth. Nobody seemed to notice. The two men in front

of us were still arguing, and the one behind was focused on
Hardt. I tensed my throat and swallowed, feeling the Source
start to slide down and almost catch. I gagged a little then
but managed to swallow it.

The feeling that comes with a having a Source in my
stomach is intoxicating. It's more than just power, though
I will admit to enjoying the sense of power it gives. There
is a feeling of being connected to something that I cherish.
For Impomancy it is a connection the Other World and all
the horrors and wonders found there. For Pyromancy it is a
connection to fire and ice and all the things in between. For
Kinemancy it is more like a connection to myself, to my own
mind. The tutors called it psychokinesis, the ability to create
waves of force as an extension of oneself.

I saw Tamura grinning at me, knowing what I had
done. I think Hardt was still unaware, I believe he still hoped
to settle the situation without violence. I look back now and
think he had the right of it. Those men were not soldiers,
nor bandits trying to rob us. They were just woodsmen,
hunters who stumbled across three strangers wandering in
their woods. I think I could have handled it better. But I have
always been one to lash out first and use diplomacy only as
a last resort. That probably says a lot about my brief stint as
a queen.

Looking over my shoulder I saw Deryl, the man with
the bow, still watching Hardt beside me. His eyes flicked to
me for just a moment. I grinned at him. I sometimes wonder
if, in that moment, he knew what was coming. Luckily for
Hardt, I was quicker.

All it took was a flick of my fingers and an invisible
wave of force hit the man's bow, knocking it sideways
just as he loosed the arrow. I suppose it was lucky he was

standing just a dozen feet away; I have never had the range that some Kinemancers do. He shouted out a warning as his arrow disappeared into the trees. I turned back to the others and pushed out with both hands, putting as much force as I could into the blast. The other two men were quite some distance away and much of the force had dissipated by the time it reached them. Much, but not all. The wave that hit them sent the fat man careening into a tree and the older one rolling in the needles scattered about the forest floor.

"Eska, what are you doing?" Hardt's objection was only on his lips; he made no move to stop me.

I am the weapon.

I spun around on sure feet, just as Hardt had taught me to only a week earlier, dragging my right hand through the air and sweeping a wave of force with it. The blast hit Deryl like a moving mountain, crushing him against a nearby tree even as he fumbled for a second arrow. There was no mistaking the sound of cracking bones, nor the splatter of blood. Any force strong enough to splinter a tree is strong enough to kill a man.

Even with my head swimming with power I took a moment to consider what I had done. Deryl's body was half embedded in the tree, a broken and bloody mess. The sight reminded me of Isen, of what Josef had done to him. I think it may have been the same for Hardt, maybe that was why his voice cracked.

"Eska?"

If any of them get away, they'll turn you in.

"You think I don't fucking know that?" I hissed the words under my breath, but Hardt still heard them.

When I turned back to the others, I could see the fat huntsman lying on the ground, shaking his head and struggling to get his arms beneath him. The older man, the one with the grey in his hair, was up and running already, dashing between trees as he tried to get away. I launched after him, flinging my arms backwards and letting loose a wave of force to give me some momentum.

Tamura was already moving towards the fat huntsman and I trusted the old man enough to leave the job to him. I went after the grey-haired one, the largest of the three men. For just a moment, I questioned why I was chasing him, asked myself if he was still a threat to us with his two friends dead. But Ssserakis' whispers had lodged in my mind, convinced me that the man would warn any others he found. Before long the Terrelan army would know where I was, and they would not rest until I was either recaptured or dead. I set my mind to the grim purpose and crashed headlong through the forest, chasing, even though I could barely see my quarry.

It had been a long time since I had last sprinted through a forest. When I was a child I didn't care about branches slapping at me or needles poking into the soles of feet. But as I chased that woodsman through trees that passed as little but green-brown blurs, I found a lot had changed. I resented the constant need to shield my face from low hanging branches, and more than one toe stubbed on roots almost convinced me to give up the chase.

Eventually I lost sight of him and slowed to a stop, doubling over as I fought to fill my lungs. Sprinting is very different to running and I was no longer used to either. Somewhere in the distance, behind me, I heard Hardt shouting my name. A beacon to guide me back to my friends. I straightened up and took one last look around the forest, trying to spot any sign of the old man. There was nothing; no sight nor sound, and I have never been very good at tracking. With a weary curse I turned towards the sound of Hardt's voice.

He's here. Close. My thought or Ssserakis', I'm still not sure to this day. But it was Ssserakis' strange power that convinced me it was true. I could feel the woodsman's fear.

I moved slowly, careful to make each footfall as silent as possible. I concentrated on the feeling of fear. It is hard to describe; not a scent on the breeze, nor a sound. Not even something I could see. But something I knew was there. An impression left upon the world by strong emotion. Ssserakis drank the fear in and I felt new energy in my tired limbs, a strange sense of tension as though my body needed to move. Keeping still was difficult.

Either I was still too new to the power, or Ssserakis was still too new to sharing my body. Maybe it was a little of both. I could feel the old man's fear, but I couldn't place it. I couldn't find it. I couldn't find him. That is why I startled when he stepped out from behind a tree just in front of me, an axe already swinging towards my neck.

There is no doubt in my mind that I would have died there if not for Hardt's training. My body was already moving, while my mind was still cursing my poor luck. I ducked underneath the swing and swept a hand, releasing a wave of force that took the man's legs out from under him. Then I stood and brought both hands down on his chest, complete with another kinetic blast. He died instantly; his chest caved in from the force.

So fragile. So easy to break.

"Shut up!" I snapped, my voice high with fear and shock. I stood there, staring at the body of the grey-haired woodsman for a long time. I'm not sure if it was the impact of my magic or the collision with the ground that killed him, but he died with his eyes open, staring up at nothing. And there was no doubt about it, his death was on my hands. There wasn't much blood, just a trickle from the corner of his mouth. I thought there would be more, but not every death is a bloody one.

"I am the…" I couldn't finish the mantra as bile rose up in my throat.

I was retching my breakfast onto the forest floor when Hardt and Tamura found me. I had killed before, I knew that, and I had seen people killed in horrible ways. But this was the first time I had killed someone with my own two hands, and the first time I was truly confronted with the body. He was no soldier fighting in a war, trying to kill my emperor. He was no criminal living out punishment for crimes worse than my own. He was just a man, trying to make living in his forest, trying to survive. And I killed him. Took him away from his world, his forest, his family. I murdered him. I never even knew the man's name. I've known so very few of their names over the years, I only knew that he was a grey-haired woodsman, and that he would still be alive if not for me. One more skull paving the road behind me.

My Kinemancy Source lay on the forest floor, coated in bile and half-digested strips of pheasant meat. The instrument of my slaughter. I snatched it up and frantically wiped it clean, as though that would somehow mask the crime I had just committed. I think, to this day, that remains the only time my body has ever given up a Source without the aid of Spiceweed.

"You didn't have to kill them." Hardt's first words after catching up to me. It was not very consoling.

It was you or them.

I felt the need to defend my actions. "They would have killed us or turned us in. Even if they had let us go, they would probably have told the authorities. The overseer is still hunting us, Hardt. We can't afford to let him catch us." Who was I trying to convince?

Hardt was silent for a moment. He was probably considering my words. Though, knowing him as I do, I think he was looking for an excuse to agree with me. Hardt has made a habit of excusing even my most heinous actions.

"Three lives for three. An even trade," Tamura said with a grin as he knelt down by the woodsman and started looting the body. I noticed he was already wearing a new coat and our sack of belongings looked significantly fuller than it had that morning.

"You don't just trade lives," Hardt argued. "This isn't a game."

"Belmoroes Treatise on War disagrees." Tamura started wrestling with the woodsman's boots. "Any fight is a trade. The combat is merely the act of haggling for how many lives are lost. Here." He held out the first boot to Hardt who just stared on in disgust.

I have since read Belmoroes Treatise on War. I have a copy in my library, though I must admit it is in fairly poor condition and I have dog-eared quite a few pages. Tamura quoted it many times in the years that followed and eventually I decided it might be worth leafing through the sections. Belmoroes had some strange insights into the art of war, and also some truly disturbing ones. I remember one quote that was of particular relevance to Hardt that day: *Never pass up a good pair of boots.*

"Do you see that?" I asked, pointing east. A gap in

the trees showed us the edge of the forest and beyond it I saw green fields, a couple of fairly expansive hills, and a barn. Beyond that barn lay the first I had seen of civilisation since the fall of Orran. A village. For just a moment, I felt my spirits soar. Then I realised it was probably the home of the three men I had just murdered.

Ssserakis woke me that night with nightmares of being chased by an unknown terror. I ran through forests and fields, cities and battlefields, snow-covered mountains and mines sunk deep below them. I never caught sight of the thing that chased me, but I knew it was there, dogging my every step just beyond my vision. And I knew what would happen if it caught me. I think I hated those dreams most of all. More than the memories of the things I had done, more than visions of monsters not of this world. The terror of being chased by an ambiguous foe, knowing that it would never stop and I could never lose it. Knowing that if I stopped running, even for a moment, it would catch me. Those dreams scared me most of all.

I woke shaking, either from the fear or the cold. The fire was low, but still crackling away. Tamura watched me with curious eyes as he chewed on something. He wasn't the only one watching me. The old woodsman was there too. He stood just out of the firelight, before it gave way to the darkness completely. His eyes stared straight ahead, unfocused but watching me. I got no more sleep that night.

CHAPTER
SEVEN

WE LEFT THE BODIES WHERE THEY LAY IN THE Forest of Ten. We had neither time nor shovels to bury them and Hardt claimed we couldn't risk a pyre. I, for one, was glad. I didn't want to revisit the sight of my handiwork. Tamura did a good job of looting the corpses and both he and Hardt claimed a new pair of boots each, mostly fitting, and both trousers and coats. I, on the other hand, claimed only an ill-fitting shirt, far too big for me. None of the three men was carrying much else save for weapons and a few copper coins.

There was some debate the next morning as to what we should do. Standing at the edge of the forest, staring out towards the village, I found myself aching for a chance to visit it. To see people again, those not trying to kill me. I hoped they had an inn. I was still naive in so many ways. I had never visited a tavern, but I had read about them in the bards' tales at the academy. Those stories always had adventurers visiting small villages, weary and dirty from weeks on the road or exploring dungeons. There was also music and merriment in the taverns and plenty of beer. I had yet to try my hand at getting drunk, and now that I was free from the Pit, the need to give it a go seemed pressing. I imagined we would saunter in and strike up a conversation with the musician, telling them a tall tale about our trip through the Djinn city; something heroic that the bard would turn into song. I also imagined a hot bath and a hearty meal, a real bed to sleep in. It's funny how I took those things for granted during my years at the academy, yet after six months in squalor they seemed the greatest luxury I could conjure.

Hardt argued that the men we had killed were most likely from the village and we were wearing their clothes. The last thing we wanted was to be recognised. I argued that when a man as big as Hardt walks into a place, people rarely look at his clothes. Tamura argued that *Even a storm blows in gusts.* I must admit I still don't understand that riddle and judging by Hardt's growl, neither did he. Eventually our need for provisions won out. The forest might be able to provide for three people indefinitely, but it looked as though we would soon be walking over hills and through fields and there would be far fewer chances to catch any prey. We needed food and skins to hold water. And I needed a pair of boots. As soon as the others had a pair, my feet started to ache with every step.

The moons hung low in the sky, visible even through the light of the day. Lursa, appeared the larger of the two, a pale red disc that almost seemed to be eating the blue of Lokar. Soon the two moons would appear as one,

Lokar hidden behind Lursa, and then the tides would be highest. Then Lokar would start his assent, spinning so Lursa disappeared behind his bulk. The celestial dance of our moons as they twirled about and ground themselves together. It was always most dangerous when Lursa was in power over her consort, the chance of moon showers are so much greater. The tutors at the academy once explained exactly why, but I have never had much of a head for their astronomy. Strangely, in the lands that were once Orran, we used to think of a person as lucky if they were struck by a moon shower. The rocks that fall from our moons are valuable, rich in an ore that can be found nowhere else, the only metal that can accept a bond with a Source. If a falling rock from a moon shower strikes a person, then it is considered their property. Unfortunately, that person rarely survives, but their family will suddenly find themselves in possession of a rock they can sell for a great deal of money. I admit, it is an odd form of luck. Still, people gather around areas they believe will receive the showers, hoping they get *lucky*. Hoping that one final act of random chance will see their family fed for the rest of their lives. I imagine most people would rather keep their family member around than lose them and find themselves rich. I know I, for one, would never give up any of my friends no matter the number of coins offered.

There were animals in the fields between us and the village. Monstrous abbans, larger than any I had seen before, chewed away at clumps of grass, ignoring us as docile beasts are like to do. I counted ten of them, each with a shaggy coat of hair and six legs, making them all female. I wondered where the bull might be and squinted to try and make out a four-legged abban amongst the others, but it was likely kept away from the females until time came to mate. I must admit, I have a taste for abban steak, cooked only slightly more than bloody and dripping with gravy. It has been a favourite meal of mine since I first arrived at the academy. As we passed those beasts, my mouth began to water as I remembered the taste. It had been a long time since I'd had abban steak and I dreamed of the inn serving it to us, of the meat melting in my mouth... Hardt brought me out of my reverie with a sharp finger to my ribs.

"You were drooling," he said with a smile.

"Was not." I wiped at my mouth just in case. I honestly can't remember if he was right or not, but I like to think not. Memory is such a fallible thing.

A shepherd watched us pass, leaning on a heavy staff and squinting against the sun. Hardt called out a friendly greeting but she ignored it and kept watching. I noticed a small horn hanging from her belt, no doubt to call a warning to the village should any of us think of causing trouble. We continued and the abbans hooted at us as we passed, each one raising their head in turn and blasting out a single note. We saw more farmers as we neared the barn, three men loading up a cart while a trei bird, as big as a horse and just as flightless, clawed at the ground and *squawked* at us, small jerky motions of the head keeping us in sight. Eventually one of the farmers pulled the bird away and started fixing a harness to its chest. It was the first time I had seen a trei bird put to a use other than racing or war. They make for excellent mounts; swift, vicious, and deadly.

I felt eyes on my back after we left that barn behind. That familiar sensation crawling between the shoulder blades.

They know what you did. Murderer. They'll turn you in.

I tried my best to ignore it, but Ssserakis was insistent and eventually I turned, yet there was no one watching.

No one you can see.

The village of Low Haven was quite large as far as villages went. At the time it sported a single tavern and a single shop, the rest was given over to homes, workshops, a blacksmith, and a sawmill. Most of the villagers traded what they needed amongst themselves and we later heard, on good authority, that strangers were rare, other than the logging caravan that passed through three times a year, and the odd trader. We earned quite a few suspicious glances walking into the village mid-morning.

"We'll see if we can find a store." Hardt stooped and lowered his voice to a whisper.

"And a tavern," I added.

"What do we need a tavern for?"

"Somewhere to sleep, somewhere to eat. Somewhere to drink?" I grinned up at him and Hardt frowned back and shook his head. "I have never been to a tavern, Hardt. I want to go."

"They're not like you think."

I fixed him with a cold blue stare then. "How would you know what I think?" I could have been a bit less of a bitch, but I've always played to my strengths. "We're going to a tavern." I made my decision and Hardt was never one to deny my orders.

He was right about that tavern; it was not how I imagined it. There was no bard, no music, no merriment of any kind. The place was empty so early in the day, save for toothless old men sitting around a table playing at some game with a board and stones coloured black and white. Hardt used what little money we had left to buy us a meal, vegetables and small chunks of meat in a watery broth, and a drink. It was the first time I had ever tasted ale and I must admit I found it bitter, sharp, unpleasant, and oddly moreish. I ordered another once I was done, and another after that.

That was the first time I ever tried beer, but far from the last. One thing I have learned over my years is that taverns in cities tend to water their ale down, to allow the drunkards to drink all day without passing out, and to keep the flow of coin steadily moving one way. Taverns in villages, however, are not so devious. If ever you want a good strong beer it is best to find a village to visit. I can recommend Low Haven, if it's still there.

I'm afraid I remember very little about the rest of that day, only flashes of things said and boasts made. I would tell you of them, but I find them far too embarrassing to recount. I can't explain how thankful I am that Hardt has never told me the full extent of my foolishness that night. Tamura, I hope, has already forgotten.

I woke to an earthquake. The world was dark and shaking so violently I thought a Geomancer had decided to bury the whole damned village. Then I opened my eyes and found there was light streaming in from a nearby window and the world wasn't shaking, rather, Hardt was shaking me.

Kill him. Ssserakis said sullenly. It appeared I wasn't the only one suffering from my hangover.

"Up, Eska. Now." His voice was strained, urgent. There was fear in his eyes and I could taste it. That was about all I managed to make out before the headache and nausea hit. I feel it's a certain kind of malfeasance that I barely remember the first time I got drunk, but I remember the morning after so fucking well, even thinking about it now, so many years later, makes me feel ill.

Hardt kept shaking me. It wasn't helping the situation. It dawned on me then that I was on a bed, surrounded by four walls with light streaming in through a window. Hardt had hired us a room for the night. My first time sleeping on a bed in almost a year and I couldn't even remember it. I think I silently swore to myself then and there never to drink again. One of many promises I have broken in my lifetime. I shoved at him feebly, trying to free myself.

"We're leaving," Hardt said. "Now, and quietly."

It was a great effort rolling out of the bed and even greater one standing up without falling over. My new boots were lying in the corner of the room and I wondered if I had pulled them off or had it been Hardt. I also wondered if I had crawled into the room and bed, or if he had carried me there. I have never asked and Hardt has never told. I think I prefer to keep it that way.

Hardt dragged me down the stairs of the tavern and we found Tamura waiting in the common room, our meagre belongings already packed. My stomach growled at the thought of stopping for breakfast, but Hardt gave us no time to eat. We were out of the tavern within moments and already on our way north. The sun had only just risen and still hung low. I looked up and saw the twin moons fading away against a light blue sky, Lokar almost entirely devoured by Lursa. There is an old shepherd's tale about seeing Lokar and Lursa in the morning. I can't remember the rhyme that goes with it, but the gist is that if they appear in the morning then their embrace will be violent. It is a warning about moon showers.

The light hurt my eyes and my aching head made every step a misery, but I soldiered on. Eventually Hardt pulled us off the road, once he was certain no one was following us. We moved east in an attempt to lose ourselves in the hills, or maybe just lose anyone who might decide to try tracking us.

It was then that Hardt decided to tell me what had happened. The men I had killed had indeed been from Low Haven and their disappearance did not go unnoticed. A search party had been sent out early in the morning, just before Hardt roused me from my hangover. By midday the bodies would surely be discovered and after that it wouldn't take much of a leap to connect us to the deaths.

It wasn't until early afternoon that I realised I hadn't dreamt the night before. It was the first time in months Ssserakis hadn't plagued me with nightmares. In honesty, I think I preferred the nightmares to the hangover.

CHAPTER EIGHT

JOSEF

I saw Death today. I see death every day. Things are different ever since the riot and Eska's escape. Deko is ruthless, merciless. Much more than he was before. Scabs are killed every day down here, some for almost no reason at all. Deko makes it public, a spectacle designed to keep us all in line. Nobody wants to be next. I saw Maeter die just last week. He was about as close to a friend as I can claim these days. Deko doesn't have enough of his captains or foremen left for every job, so us scabs are given some of the more laborious ones. Maeter was given the task of spooning out the gruel at feeding time. One ladle per scab. One ladle per scab. One ladle per scab. Last week he missed a bowl, just a little. I think the woman was pushed as she raised her bowl, I saw her stumble, and a little slop of gruel fell to the floor like a sodden cloth. The scab complained and Maeter gave her a second ladle. But Deko was watching. Beady little eyes shining in the gloom. I hate him. I hate all of them. I hate Deko and his foremen. I hate the scabs. ~~I hate the overseer.~~

> *Deko pulled Maeter away from the gruel and shut down the Trough. More than half the scabs went hungry that day and the bastard said we could all blame Maeter for the growling of our stomachs. That could have been punishment enough, Maeter would have caught a beating or two for his mistake, and the scabs would have dished it out. It should have been punishment enough. But of course it wasn't. Deko is a fucking tyrant! He forced gruel down Maeter's throat, made him eat while the rest of us watched. He made Maeter eat until he couldn't anymore, until he was reeling from the pain in his stomach and gagging with the effort of keeping it down. Then Deko took him up on one of the lifts, all the way up to the third level. And pushed him off. It's a long way down, but Maeter didn't even scream. And then he hit the floor and many of the scabs who had eaten that day lost what little they'd had. I've never seen a body burst like that. Deko knew what he was doing. He knew it would happen. I hate him!*

> *Deko put me in charge of the gruel after that. I don't know why. I don't know if it's some sort of punishment for something. Maybe he still thinks the overseer is protecting me and this is his way of getting back at me. Maybe he just wants me to screw up so he has a reason to kill me like he did Maeter. I won't. I won't give him a reason. I won't give any of them a reason.*

> *At least everyone sees me again.*

> *I think I preferred being invisible.*

> *But that isn't what I wanted to write down. I keep this diary in the hope it will someday lead to my freedom. I know the overseer reads everything I write. Why else would soldiers come, once a week, down here in the darkness to take my pages and give me more, fresh ones? I know you read this, overseer. Please, let*

me out. I can still be useful. I'm still a Sourcerer and I'm loyal to
Terrelan. I don't care about Eska or her stupid need for revenge. I
just want out of the Pit. I just want to be free of Deko. I just want
to be free of the damning stares and whispered insults. Please let
me out.

Death. She walked into the Pit like it belonged to her. She
was a vision, tall and straight, dark hair cascading like a waterfall
of onyx. Maybe it's just from spending so long down here in the
darkness and filth, but I've never seen anything so mesmerising.
She wore red leather on a black uniform with golden plate on top,
etched with enchantments. The way the lantern light caught it
made it shine so bright I thought I might go blind. I wasn't the
only one. Even Deko shielded his eyes. Even Deko stayed out of her
way. She rode the lift down to the floor of the main cavern and two
others came with her, wearing the same red and gold. One of them
was wrinkled with age yet carried his years well. He wore a shield
strapped to his back, wrapped in cloth, and an axe in hand. The
other was a giant of a man, taller even than Hardt had been.

I still wonder if he blames me for Isen's death. He should. I
am to blame. I killed him out of...

The other man was a giant and had a hammer slung across
his back. I remember the look in that one's eyes as he swept the
crowd as if he didn't see people just the stench that comes off us.
Who can blame him? We're little more than vermin to those above
us.

But Death, she was different. She looked at us, each of us.
She met our eyes and held them. She walked through us, close
enough to touch, and didn't flinch. She wasn't scared. A single
standing figure of beauty down with the filth. Down with the
very worst Terrelan has to offer. Murderers and thieves and war
criminals, and worse yet. We're monsters. Everyone down in
the Pit is a monster. If we weren't when we came in, the Pit soon

turned us into one. She didn't care. Death walked among us as
though we didn't even pose a threat. And I'm not sure we did.

She carried a sword I have seen just once before. It used
to hang on a wall at the Orran Academy of Magic, in a locked
room with no lock, hidden away from us all. I had to pull Eska
away from the sword when we snuck in that one time. The way
the metal shifted and moved held her mesmerised. There was a
plaque underneath it. I think it read "Neverthere". Maybe that
was the name of the sword. I don't know. It was definitely the same
sword, though. I remember the way the metal seemed to bubble
with a sickening yellow shine. A hideous blade. I can feel my skin
crawling just thinking about it.

Death stopped in front of the Hill and Deko's cronies
parted, like the skin of an orange peeled away. I miss oranges.
I miss fruit. I can still just about remember how they taste, so
sweet it's almost sickening. My mind keeps wandering. Ever since
I didn't die, I find it hard to keep everything straight. Hard to
concentrate. Deko wouldn't meet her eyes. Death stared through
him and he looked away. He knew where the power lay, and he
knew it wasn't in his hands. I bet the slug kisser hated that, to
have everyone in his little kingdom see who held the true power. To
have everyone reminded that the Pit is just that, a pit where all the
refuse is thrown. Deko is nothing but a shit king ruling over shit.

When Death turned away, I expected Deko to make a move,
to leap at her and stab with one of his little shivs. He carries a
few, we've all seen it. He didn't. Deko sat there as quiet and meek
as the rest of us. All the population of the Pit gathered around. I
don't know how everyone knew something was happening, but for
the first time since I've been down here, I couldn't hear digging. It
echoes throughout the tunnels, a permanent ringing that hammers
against my senses. I hear it everywhere, all the time. Even alone
in the dark, as far away from everyone as I can get. Even with my

hands pressed so hard against my ears until I feel like I'm crushing my own skull. Even then, I can still hear the digging.

But not when Death stood there watching us. For the first time in months, I didn't hear the digging. I almost threw myself at her feet for that. For that one brief moment of respite.

She asked for Yorin in a voice that rang like tempered steel. There was strength there, strength, and power, and grace all in the sound of her voice. How did she do that?

When Yorin came he matched her in height and stood as straight as Death herself. His bruises, given to him by the overseer's soldiers, had mostly faded; a lifetime of pit fighting will do that to a person, bruise hard and heal quick. He had the brawn, but they looked a true pair, Death and Yorin; both strong and proud and beautiful.

They fought then, only briefly. I don't know when they decided to fight, nor who made the first move. They didn't speak to each other. One moment they stood facing off, both pillars of strength and beauty, and then they came together in a furious rush of fists and feet and elbows. Death didn't draw her sword. I thought that foolish. I'd seen Yorin fight down in the arena once or twice. He was fast and brutal and no one, not one of his opponents had ever stood a chance. He killed them all; fast, efficient, and with no more regard than stepping on a bug. But not Death. They clashed only twice before she had him face down on the ground with both arms twisted behind his back and a knee pressed into his spine, holding him down. She didn't even seem tested by his strength or skill.

Death's huge companion stepped in and took hold of Yorin, keeping his hands twisted behind him and hauling the bastard to his feet. He struggled, but there's no fighting the sort of strength that giant possesses. The more Yorin struggled the tighter his arms twisted until everyone heard the pop of his shoulder screaming from its socket. He stopped struggling then, slouching against the pain of it, and the big man wrapped an arm around Yorin's neck, holding his head in a vice.

Then, Death asked her question.

She had just the one. Where has "Eskara Helsene gone?" I think I knew it before she asked it. I think Yorin did too, that's why he fought. Of course, he didn't know, and he told her as much, said he'd tell her if he did know. He called Eska a monstrous bitch and I think there was fear in his voice. He should have been more scared of Death. She gave him a second chance, asked her question again. Yorin struggled once more, but it was no use. The strongest of us scabs, the best of us, the champion of the Pit, beaten for everyone to see. With one arm hanging useless by his side and the other twisted so tight I could see the muscles straining. He gave in. Yorin gave in. He told Death all he knew, that Eska was last seen headed towards the Forest of Ten, but he had no idea where she was going. It was clear for all to see that Yorin was broken, no fight left in him, no chance to struggle free and no hope save giving Death what she wanted. I don't think she was satisfied with his answer.

She pulled a knife. I was too busy watching Yorin to see where from. Death asked him one more time where Eska had gone, and Yorin just repeated his answer. The Forest of Ten. I've heard of it, a giant forest stretching for leagues in every direction. It makes sense she'd flee there, Eska always did like the trees. She used to tell me stories of climbing them before the Orrans took her.

I don't know if Death didn't believe Yorin, or if she just wanted to make a point. I suppose it doesn't really matter anymore. Yorin screamed as she dug out his eyes. Who wouldn't? I can't imagine the pain. I don't want to imagine it. She didn't stop with the one eye, even after she'd pulled it out of his head and crushed it underfoot. Some of the others turned away, walked away. Even Deko turned his shiny gaze elsewhere. Not me though. I couldn't.

*I couldn't stop watching as the most beautiful woman I have ever
seen stabbed into Yorin's face and cut his eyes from their sockets.*

*I wanted to feel. I'm not sure what I wanted to feel. Yorin
slashed open my throat and tried to kill me. I hated him for that.
A part of me blamed him more than Eska for her escape. Maybe if
Death had just killed him, I could have hated him all the way to
the end. But now, I just feel sorry for him. Pity. Even a Biomancer
can't undo the damage done.*

*They left Yorin mewling on the floor, clutching at his
maimed face, crying a crimson flood. No one moved to help him.
No one dared to move at all. We all just stood and watched as
Death wiped her knife on a cloth and turned towards me.*

*I've never felt fear like that. Not during the fall of Orran.
Not during all my time in the Pit. Not even lying there with my
throat cut, watching Eska walk away and leave me to die. This was
something else. I was frozen. Rigid and unable to move as Death
advanced upon me. She knew who I was. She knew what I was, and
how I was connected to Eska. She knew it all and she held my life
in her hands. I don't remember dropping to my knees, but I found
myself staring up at her. Death has brown eyes, the colour of coffee.
They were so deep I thought I was drowning.*

*I would have told Death everything I knew without even
being asked. How Eska always loved trees. How she dreamed of
the sky and called it freedom. How she longed to sail the sky on the
flying city of Ro'shan. And how she wanted to visit revenge on the
Terrelan emperor, and everyone else who had a hand in the fall of
Orran. But the words couldn't make it past my throat. As much
as I wanted to, I couldn't make so much as a sound. I suppose I
should retain some pride, I managed not to cry, though the terror
Death put in me made my blood run cold in my veins. I could still
see Yorin curled on the floor, not moving, and I wondered if I was
next. I knew then that I never want to go through life without my*

eyes. The fear was not of the pain, or the possibility of death. I was terrified of never being able to see a sunrise ever again, or snow falling, or a fire crackling away in a hearth. I was scared of never seeing children laugh and play, never seeing a beautiful woman lost in a dance. I feared never seeing colour ever again, and living my whole life locked in total darkness.

I would have done anything Death asked of me right then. Anything at all just to not end up like Yorin.

She passed me by. Never saying a word to me. Barely even acknowledging I was there other than to stop and wait while I struggled to speak. I knew then that I was nothing to her, not even worth maiming.

I was still on my knees when Terrelan soldiers appeared to drag Yorin away. He hung loose in their arms and made no sound, but I could tell he was still alive. I could feel the spark still inside him. I don't think anyone has seen him since.

Please, Overseer, I know you'll read this. Please let me out. I'll do whatever you ask. Anything. I just don't want to be locked in the darkness anymore. I just want to see the light again. Please let me out.

CHAPTER NINE

THREE MONTHS OUT OF THE PIT FOUND US closing in on the city of Yun. I could smell the sea; we were so close. We saw no sign of pursuit from either the villagers of Low Haven or the overseer's people, but I knew both were still on our tail. I could feel them chasing me, trying to drag me back to the Pit. Fear snapping at my heels. We needed to find a way to escape their reach before they caught up to us. I woke from nightmares more than once, certain that I was being chased, certain that enemies lurked just beyond the range of my vision. I wasn't entirely wrong about that. Ssserakis lurked there, wearing the faces of the people I had killed.

My training continued and both Hardt and Tamura said I was making progress. Well, Hardt said that. Tamura said *It takes a long time to walk the length of the world*. I took it to mean I still had a long way to go.

By then I was starting to show. The others noticed it, I think, but neither of them said anything, at least not yet. I tried to ignore it, as though it might go away if I pretended hard enough. I wasn't ready. I couldn't be. All the signs were there, and I knew enough of them from my studies at the academy. I was pregnant.

It was a thing I had been trying desperately to ignore. I was terrified. Isen was gone, and though Hardt and Tamura were with me, they were also not. I was pregnant and it was something I would have to go through alone. I could feel the life growing inside of me. Part of me wanted it gone. It was unwelcome, a burden I had to shoulder alone, and one that was already starting to impact my life in ways I was not comfortable with. Another part of me, a part I didn't understand, wanted to protect it with a fierceness unmatched even by my hatred for my enemies. I was so damned confused by it all.

I decided to carry on as though nothing had changed, at least until I couldn't anymore. But something had changed. Back at the academy all the girls were required to sit through a lecture on pregnancy for Sourcerers. They didn't tell us what to expect, or ways to prevent a man's seed taking root, nor what to do to get rid of it, not that I intended to. For whatever else that child was, and what it might mean, it was mine. A part of me, though I had so little to offer it. No, the tutors at the academy only told us things never to do while pregnant.

The first was never to use a Source while pregnant. The permanent effects were undocumented, but we were told that the rule was there for a reason. I had already used both Chronomancy and Kinemancy. I wondered how both might affect the child. It is a strange thought that different

Sources may affect an unborn baby in a variety of ways. What could Pyromancy do to a foetus? Would they suffer burns even inside the womb? Or would they be born with fire running through their veins, a veritable inferno in human form? How would Necromancy affect a pregnancy? Would the child die inside and yet still come to term, an undead monster caught between life and death? So many questions, and not a single answer for one of them. I suppose it is hard to find women willing to risk both themselves and their child in order to test the results. I certainly wasn't willing to risk it any further than I already had.

The second precaution was to avoid close contact with creatures from the Other World. Again, the reasons were not very forthcoming at the academy, and it was another rule I had already broken, though not willingly. I was hiding it from everyone else, but I had an ancient horror living inside of me, possessing me. I'm fairly certain contact doesn't get any closer.

We joined the road as we approached the city of Yun. Traffic increased, both that on foot and carts pulled by either horses or trei birds. The city lies in a bay, sprawling out from the sea in every direction. Just beyond its limits, to either side, are the Cliffs of Dry Ice, though in truth they are formed of chalk, not ice. They look very impressive all the same. The road slopes down quite sharply as it begins to lead to Yun and the sight there was one that brought back fond memories.

In Picarr, on the days we were allowed out of the academy grounds, I used to love dragging Josef to Braggart's Tower. There was an old tale about Aeromancers, convinced that they could use their magic to fly, leaping off the top of the tower only to realise the limitations of their power.

I was never certain how true that tale was, but I did know
the tower was tall and open to the public. From the top
of it I could see out across most of Picarr. I used to love
watching the day pass by, watching the people of the city
go about their business. Maybe it was the humbling feeling
of watching so many people moving on with their lives
without even the knowledge that I existed. Or maybe it was
the heady feeling of seeing so many people down below and
knowing I had something none of them did: the ability to
wield magic. I was special and they were not. I don't know.
It can be hard to think back over such things and remember
with any real clarity. Time has a habit of eroding memories
down to their base emotion. Faces fade, details blur, and
eventually all that is left is an impression of how it made
you feel. I know I loved going there, loved looking down on
the city. And there, on the approach to Yun, I found a similar
feeling. A city laid out in front of me, both giant and tiny all
at once, and beyond it, the fathomless blue of the ocean.

I think I must have stopped in the middle of the
road. Maybe it was the pleasant memories the scene stirred,
or perhaps the humbling sight before me. I know I was
grinning. Then someone bumped into me and the feeling
vanished. I heard a mumbled apology and rubbed at my
arm. I was still hurting from the light punches Hardt dished
out when I fumbled in our training sessions. He dished them
out quite regularly, though he had started pulling his blows
since realising my condition.

"Come on, Eska," Hardt said. He was still so worried
that someone might recognise the clothes we wore, or maybe
that someone from the Pit would be there waiting for us.
He frequently told us not to draw attention to ourselves. I
grumbled but set off into a jog to catch up. I knew with some

certainty, though I couldn't say how, that the danger was behind us, chasing us, rather than waiting before us.

There is a weight to something you carry with you, and at all times crave. A temptation and burden rolled into one. It's a reassuring thing to know that you can crack at any time and give in. That was how I felt with the Kinemancy Source I carried in my little snuff pouch. Barely a moment went by when I didn't think about popping it in my mouth and swallowing, or the sense of power that came with it resting inside my stomach, the sense of completeness it gave. The craving of hunger that only it can end. It was a weight that I had gotten used to, a weight that I checked regularly without even realising it. And that was how I noticed that the weight was gone. My hand brushed my hip where the snuff pouch usually hung, and I knew right away something was wrong. A panic rose up in me, and for just a moment I didn't understand why.

You're defenceless without it.

"Eska?" Hardt's voice somewhere behind me. I barely heard him, I was already turned around, walking back through the crowd, searching for the person who had bumped into me.

The problem with a busy port town, especially in the early morning, is that the roads to it are often packed with people making their way to sell or buy. Added to that was my distraction upon seeing the city. I didn't get a good a look at the person. I don't think I knew what they looked like at all. I was just wading back through the crowd, grabbing people and hoping I would see my snuff pouch in their hand.

There are times when blind panic pays off, though it is usually more by way of luck than anything else. I got

lucky that day. I pulled on the arm of a small figure, dressed
in the grey robes of a scholar or priest. If I had been thinking
clearly, I would have realised that the people of Terrelan
don't worship anything greater than their emperor, and
even their most juvenile scholars are older than the girl
who stared at me from the depths of that hood. Her eyes
met mine for an instant, so fast I barely had time to see the
dirt on her face or the sunken look about her eyes. Then
she shrugged out of the robe and was off, sprinting away
through the crowd. I hesitated, shocked for a moment,
holding the robes. Then I threw them aside and leapt after
her, letting loose a wordless cry that might have been more a
growl. I heard shouting behind me; Hardt or Tamura, most
likely, trying to figure out what was happening. I ignored
them both.

Run her down and take back what is ours!

"What do you think I'm doing?" I growled as I ran.

The girl was running through the crowd of people,
bumping into some and dodging around others. She was
moving at quite a pace, but there is only so fast you can
run when surrounded by a moving crowd of flesh and ill
attitude. I moved to the side of the road where the people
were thinnest and sprinted until I was alongside the girl.
Then I made a mistake. I shouted at her to stop, thinking she
would realise she had been caught and give up. You would
think half a year in the Pit would have burned the naivety
away, and you would be wrong. The girl glanced just once
towards me, then turned and ran away again, putting the
entire road and the people on it between us. I spared no
time bemoaning my stupidity and charged into the crowd,
threading my way through to reach the other side.

The little bitch had a head start on me, but if I have

learned one thing over the years it is never to discount the kindness of strangers. I shouted again as I passed through the thickest of the crowd and the thief turned for just a moment. I saw a wild grin on her face, the smirk of the victorious. Then a nearby cart owner leapt at her, tackling her to the ground.

By the time I reached her, she had kicked the man's face bloody and was scrambling away, just about getting to her feet. I kicked one leg out from under her and stopped to catch my breath. She was small, almost of a height with me, though maybe with some growing to do given her age. Red hair, the colour of dying embers, sat tied back behind her head, a few rebellious strands escaping the tight braid. She was skinny and dirty and reminded me of myself not too long ago. I wondered if I had looked so unkempt down in the bowels of the Pit. Actually, I know I had looked far worse. Despite her situation she grinned at me, dark eyes twinkling. That grin remained even once Tamura and Hardt arrived at my back.

"Must be important," the girl said, her accent a hurried drawl, irritating to my ears. She glanced behind her, probably looking for somewhere to run to. We stood between her and the city, there was nowhere she could hide. "I'll tell you what, lady, I'll fight you for it."

Mistakes are usually only apparent after the fact. I knew this one was a mistake even before I made it. I had no need to agree to her terms, the pouch and the Source within were already mine. She was a thief and we had caught her. Despite knowing this, I still accepted her challenge. I was eager to put Hardt and Tamura's training to use against an opponent who was taking it seriously. I whispered the academy's mantra to myself, *I am the weapon,* as a way to erase any doubts. I would win with ease. What a fool I was. I thought myself further along than I was. I thought myself stronger and smarter than the thief in front of me. Hardt argued against the decision. I didn't listen. Tamura sank down into a cross-legged position and told me to *show him what I had learned*. I think I disappointed him.

It is important, I have to come to realise, when learning two distinct forms of combat at once to pick one and stick to it when involved in a fight. I went into the challenge thinking to fuse both styles together and bring the thief down hard and fast. I think I landed one punch before the girl hand me on my back with one arm locked against my chest and the other failing to ward off the blows she threw at my face. I lost the fight convincingly and I might have lost some teeth too, had Hardt not waded in and picked the girl off me. She struggled against him of course, but there is very little struggling you can do against a man of Hardt's strength. Eventually she found her arms twisted behind her back and realised there was little she could do but grumble.

One more fight lost. Have you ever actually won one? Ssserakis' thought echoed inside my head and I tried my best to ignore it.

"I won the fight. Let me go!" Now I got a good look at her I realised just how young she was. No more than thirteen or fourteen and already as tall as I, and I was certain my growing years were behind me thanks to the Chronomancy Source. I may not be considered short, but I will certainly never be considered tall. "Look, lady, I won. You agreed. The pouch is mine."

It's fair to say I did not accept my defeat gracefully. I struggled back to my feet, staggered towards the girl, and punched her in the cheek. I wonder if it hurt her as much as it did my hand. The pain made me consider whether martial combat was really something I even wanted to learn.

You'll always be weak. You'll always fail.

"Argh. Shark-hugging bitch!" the thief spat in her drawl.

Hardt let out a sigh but he kept a good hold on the cursing thief. "Eska…"

"Easy to hit a girl when you have a twice fucked slab of arse holding me back." The girl was wincing, and I could already see a red mark on her face where I'd hit her. A slight cut and blood starting to leak out. I shook my hand to try and rid myself of the pain. It didn't help.

"When the storm rages, people watch," Tamura said, though he made no move to stand. He wasn't wrong. Quite a few people were watching now, and I saw a couple of them were wearing Terrelan military uniforms.

"Where the fuck is it?" I hissed, already patting at the girl. "Where is my pouch?"

She smiled at me. "Hidden."

Tear her apart until you find it. It's ours!

"This is too much attention, Eska." Hardt was worried, and with good reason. If the soldiers looked too closely, they might start asking questions.

"She took my fucking Source, Hardt. She's not going anywhere until I get it back. Tell me where it is and we won't hand you over to the guard, thief."

"Hand me over to the guard, and you'll never get it back, bitch." I will admit I very nearly hit her again and damn the pain it might cause me.

I let out a frustrated sigh. "Hardt, break her arms."

The girl let out a squeak, fear rolling off her, but it didn't last long. "I'm not breaking anyone's arms, Eska."

"How about a deal?" the thief asked, a note of panic creeping into her voice. "You escort me into the city, one of your little gang, hidden from the guard. Once we're inside the limits, you get the pouch back."

"Or we just strip search you here," I said.

"I don't have it on me. Passed it off as soon as you caught me. Either you help me get into the city, or you'll never see that pouch again."

I had heard thieves worked in groups, but I never thought I'd run afoul of them. Back in the academy I had nothing to steal, my only riches were carried around in my stomach. Down in the Pit everyone was a thief or worse. My first real taste of civilisation, life outside the academy or a prison, and I had already been robbed and then beaten by the robber; like a mugging but in reverse.

"Back to the road. Keep a good hold of her, Hardt." I had already formed a strong dislike for the girl. I wonder how much of my life might have turned out differently if I had just given her to the guard. Maybe I would be dead. Maybe my daughter Sirileth wouldn't be a monster.

CHAPTER TEN

THE SECOND TIME WE APPROACHED YUN WAS far less pleasant. My memories were no longer happy but tainted with anger. Instead of remembering my time atop Braggart's Tower I found myself ruefully remembering the fight I had just lost. After three months of training with both Hardt and Tamura, I still couldn't beat up a half-starved gutter rat. I wanted to be strong, powerful enough to defeat all my enemies. Instead, I seemed destined to lose every fight whether I picked them or not.

We descended into Yun. It is strange to descend into a city. It feels like being swallowed up by the ground and I had so recently escaped the earth. The guards, men in military uniform, spared us but a glance. I was glad of that; I half expected them to stop us and discover where we had come from. Houses soon cropped up either side of us and with them came merchants lining the sides of the streets,

attempting to hawk their wares to passers-by. The thief
warned us not to bother wasting our coins, that we could
find whatever we wanted further into the city, and for far
cheaper. Little did she realise we had just two coins between
us and one of them was clipped.

The crowd thinned a little at the outskirts, but as
buildings rose up before us, obscuring the view of the sea,
it soon swarmed back in so that I found myself jostled with
almost every step. She led us deep into the city, all the way
to the docks. Dozens of ships lay at anchor in the bay and
I saw four crowding the berths. I had never seen anything
larger than a fishing skiff before and found myself awed by
their beauty. It is hard to imagine that such fragile constructs
of wood could survive out in the waters of a hostile ocean. I
found Hardt smiling at the vessels, probably remembering
fond times. Then the smile turned to hurt, and I guessed the
thought of Isen was still painful to him. It was painful to me
too. I didn't miss Isen, my opinion of him had soured too
much and too fast, but now I had consequences to live with.
I glanced down at the small bump of my belly.

*You can't raise a child. You can't even get your Source
back.* Ssserakis whispered in my mind. I'd like to say I
ignored the horror, but I was never very good at ignoring it,
especially when its fearmongering rang with uncomfortable
truth. At least it moved me to action.

"You're in the city now, thief. Where is my fucking
Source?" I was brusque, but I wanted my magic back. Even
if I couldn't use it. I needed the reassurance that I had the
option. Like a soldier misses their sword, a scholar misses
their pen, a fisher misses rod or net. *Like a scared little girl
misses her friend.* I missed the Source at my side and found
my hand groping for something that wasn't there over and

over.

She smiled at me and nodded to a building behind us. It appeared to be a dockside tavern named *William's Rest*. We crowded through the door and I got my second taste of a tavern, though this one was far more like the stories I had read. There was music and dancing and drinking and sailors sharing tall tales of the sea. We sat down at a dirty table in the dingy light and I sulked while the bar maid brought us a drink each. We parted with one of our last copper coins at the tavern and at least I can say it was the clipped one. I barely spared the beer a glance.

"So where is it?" I leaned forward as I spoke so I didn't have to shout over the music. The girl leaned away from me, smiling again as she lifted the mug to her lips.

So smug. She doesn't even realise how insignificant she is. I smiled at Ssserakis' words. *Neither do you.*

"It'll be here soon. Patience. Is it really a Source? Are you a witch?" The thief sounded excited by the prospect.

She was baiting me. I knew it. She knew it. Hardt and Tamura knew it. I'm certain we all knew I would rise to it as well. "I am a Sourcerer, not some witch from a backwater village."

"Is there a difference?" she drawled.

I think I might I have leapt across the table and got my myself beaten up a second time had Hardt not decided to play the role of diplomat. I look back now and I think I forced him into the role. I have never been very good at making friends, much better at keeping enemies, and once Josef was gone there was no one to make up for my lack. Luckily for us all, Hardt was there to smooth over the rough edges I was left with.

"What's your name?" The big man asked.

"Imiko," said the thief.

Tamura let out a gasp just as his beer reached his lips, sending a frothy spray across the table. "Like the second pillar." I had no idea what he was talking about, but it seemed to wipe the smile from the girl's face.

"Yes. Like the second pillar." Imiko took to looking into her own drink. "I guess my mother or father had a sense of humour. Hard to ask them now."

I glanced at Hardt and he just shrugged back at me. I felt a little emboldened by that. For once I wasn't the only ignorant one of the group. *The only excuses for ignorance are apathy or stupidity. It doesn't matter if you're not alone.*

"Shut up!" I hissed into my mug of beer. "What's the second pillar?"

Tamura laughed. "The second of eight that keep the world from being swallowed." He grinned, as though that were enough of an answer. Imiko was silent on the matter.

"Care to explain any of that madness, old man?" Hardt asked.

Tamura giggled, took another swallow of beer, and let out a happy sigh. He's always had a way of telling stories, a ritual before starting them, as though his addled mind needs to arrange the words into a fathomable pattern.

"Long before Terrelan, the people of old Isha believed the world exists in the maw of a great monster." Tamura grinned at us all. "Called Ufta. This monster is constantly trying to devour us all. The stars we see in the night sky are Ufta's teeth, sharp and piercing, but never moving, held at bay. The darkness that surrounds the stars is Ufta's endless hunger, ever trying to swallow us all. But the world does not wish to be swallowed, and so the pillars were willed into being by the collective consciousness of us all. Eight pillars of light, each one representing one aspect of the terran soul, hold open Ufta's mouth, preventing the monster from swallowing us. Bren, our will. Imiko, our greed. Kairn, our wisdom. Toro, our compassion. Poena, our ferocity. Non, our imagination. Zeke, our anger. Yorella, our body. Only through the combined strength of all eight pillars is Ufta's ravenous hunger kept at bay." He finished by pointing at Imiko. "Greed."

I'll be the first to admit that some of the stories our ancestors came up with were quite absurd. I've always wondered what they thought of the daylight if the night was supposed to represent Ufta's hunger. Perhaps sunlight is supposed to represent our desire not to be eaten. More importantly, I've always wondered how Tamura knows all the old stories, though he can't remember his own past.

Hardt let out a sigh and turned his attention to the thief. "Why did we have to sneak you into the city?" He tipped back his mug and swallowed and I found myself the only one at the table not drinking.

"The locals have branded me a thief," Imiko drawled. "Which is probably because I steal from them. I don't really fancy having my fingers broken so I'd rather they didn't catch me. There's not many better places to hide than in the shadow of someone your size." I'd be lying if I said Imiko and I didn't agree on a great many things. I still didn't like her. "So, who are you on the run from?"

There is a certain silence that can descend upon a conversation. I have seen it many times and I have seen the aftermath. Sometimes that silence leads to good humour and friendships that can last a lifetime, sometimes it can lead to violence and enemies who will chase you to the end of the world. Most often it settles somewhere between the two. I might have opted for violence if not for Hardt.

"So, you're probably about to deny being on the run,"
Imiko said with a grin. "But this silence and glancing at each
other thing you're doing now has convinced me." Imiko met
each of our eyes in turn. "You're on the run, I'm in hiding. It
seems to me like…"

"Where is my Source, Imiko?"

The thief fell silent, staring at me across the table. I
might have imagined it, but I could swear the light in the
tavern dimmed a little.

*Kill her and take it. Negotiation shows nothing but
weakness.*

With a sigh Imiko reached down into her trousers and
a moment later pulled out my little pouch before dumping
it on the table between us. I'd like to say I showed some
restraint, but it would be a lie and I think we all know that.
I reached across and snatched it back, pulling open the little
string to find it empty inside. Panic clutched bony fingers
around my heart, and I tried to remember the last time I
had seen the Source. I touched the pouch often, but I hadn't
looked at it in weeks, choosing not to in an attempt to spare
myself the temptation. When I looked up, I saw Imiko
rolling the little Source across her fingers, staring at the way
it caught the light. It wasn't a large Source, about the size of
peach stone, and it had one hard edge, rough to the touch. I
knew the thing better than I knew my own body; I had spent
hours and hours rubbing it between my fingers, learning
every curve and contour. I wanted it back. I needed to hold it
again.

"This thing is really magic?" Imiko asked.

Each Source has its own light, a glow that comes from
within. But that light only shines when the Source is inside a

Sourcerer and fades quickly once it is regurgitated. However, sometimes it is possible to hold a Source in such a way that any light passing through it gains a tint, a small hint at the power contained within. Kinemancy Sources shine purple and as Imiko rolled it over her fingers I caught glimpses of that light. It took a lot of self-control to stop myself from lurching across the table and snatching it from her hand.

It is yours. If only you had the strength to take it back.

"Yes," I said it through gritted teeth.

"Huh. Tell me again how you're not running from someone." Imiko placed the Source on the table and rolled it across to me. I grabbed it, pushing it back into the pouch before I could make the mistake of swallowing it. I kept my hand on the pouch, gripping it tightly.

Both Hardt and Tamura looked at me. Hardt has always followed me, ever since our time in the Pit. I have often wondered why, what I did to earn the trust and loyalty of such a man. I have no answer. I'm as much a monster as the creatures that inhabit the Other World, perhaps even worse, for most of them are mindless and don't understand what they do. But Hardt is a good man. He would be a good man if not for the things I've made him do over the years. Tamura, too, followed my lead and accepted my decisions, but for him I know why. He saw power in me, the potential to be part of something great or terrible. I think I ended up being both. And I don't think it mattered to him either way.

"You want to know who we're running from? Everyone," I said it with as much menace as I could. "We escaped the Pit…"

"No one escapes the Pit." Imiko looked sceptical; I will admit it pleased me.

"We did. And the military know it. They don't want

us staying free. Especially not me."

"Because you're a witch?" She flashed that same self-satisfied grin.

"That's why we're in Yun," Hardt said. "We can't stay in Terrelan. We need to run." I decided not to mention that one day I intended to return and reduce the Terrelan empire to ash. I didn't think it wise, considering all three of the others around the table were Terrelans.

Hardt turned his eyes on me. "I know you don't know how to sail, Eska, but I think I can get us on a boat. I have some experience. Maybe we can pay our way to Polasia."

"I have a better idea," Imiko said and then paused to take a lengthy sip of her beer. "Come with me. I'll show you." With that the girl was off, moving towards a doorway at the back of the tavern. None of us followed. When Imiko reached the door she turned back, rolled her eyes and waved at us.

It's a trap. She's leading you to your enemies.

"Do you think we can trust her?" I asked Hardt.

The big Terrelan shook his head. "No. But then, I remember telling Isen we couldn't trust you once. It seems I was wrong on that account. Maybe I'm wrong again."

I looked at Tamura and the old man grinned wide as though happy to be included. "It is hard to catch fish unless you are allowed near the water."

"Just once, old man, I'd like you to say what you mean," Hardt replied with a grunt of frustration.

"He means trust is earned, and it's hard to earn it without a chance. I think." I looked to Tamura and he nodded. There have been many occasions where Tamura's madness lies beyond my ability to grasp. I wonder how much wisdom I have missed out on because I did not understand. Then again, maybe it is the understanding of that wisdom that drove Tamura crazy in the first place. Stare at a light too bright and it will blind.

I stood from the table and crossed the room to Imiko before I could decide it was a bad idea. Hardt and Tamura followed, and I was thankful for that. Walking into the unknown is always easier with friends at your back. Imiko sent a quick nod towards the tavern owner, then disappeared through the doorway and up the stairs beyond. I followed slowly, straining my ears at each step, in case of ambush.

"Oh, come on." Imiko's voice drifted down from a turn in the stairwell. "We'll be all day unless you hurry up. We're only going to the roof."

No ambush came, and eventually I stepped out into sunlight, raising a hand to shield my eyes against the glare. It was still winter and bitterly cold, but that didn't stop it from being bright. The roof of the tavern was flat and there were two wooden chairs set up around a small table. From that vantage point I could see out towards the docks and the water beyond it. It was a beautiful sight. I have always liked a good vista. Imiko was waiting nearby, a look on her face that said much about her impatience. She looked so young in the bright light, truly just a girl.

"You're looking the wrong way," Imiko said and pointed north along the coastline.

Tamura giggled and Hardt let out a grunt. I found myself speechless.

"You want to run. Get away from Terrelan? That is your best bet, not some rickety old pile of logs trying to survive the ocean. And I can get you up there." Imiko nodded, her grin showing just how pleased she was with herself. I might have bristled at it, but I was too awestruck. In the distance, little more than a speck on the horizon, I saw a mountain turned upside down, flying in the sky. It had been many years since I had last seen Ro'shan.

The boats no longer mattered to me. I knew just how I was going to escape Terrelan. In a flying city.

CHAPTER ELEVEN

IT WAS THE THIRD TIME IN MY LIFE THAT I HAD seen Ro'shan gracing the sky with its monumental presence. The first was when I was five years old and the city passed over Keshin. It rarely moved so far west, most often passing only over the eastern coast of Isha as it floated in orbit of its sister city, Do'shan. I felt my breath drawn out of me and all words with it. Even now, to this day, I still marvel at its graceful journey through the sky.

The second time I saw Ro'shan, I was still at the academy. Picarr was in an uproar about it. Apparently, the flying city had passed overhead only once before in living memory. There was a festival, a celebration that lasted three days. Even the academy got involved. Our usual lessons were suspended and the tutors had us students making paper lanterns. It has always been customary in all areas of Isha to float messages up to the city when it passes by. Each lantern is a small balloon of paper with a cup at the bottom for a candle and a string with which to tie a written message. Some of the balloons are plain, functional and nothing else, whereas some are decorated. I chose to paint patterns of flame on the lanterns I made. Everyone has a chance to send up a message, whether they are too old to see, too poor to afford, or too young to care. I must have made at least twenty lanterns, and written messages on many more for those who were unable, and yet I only used one myself. Strange to think that we were at war at the time and yet the city celebrated.

When the great anchor fell, I remember the excitement, and not just my own. A sense of anticipation passed through the city like a fire gone wild. I stood with Josef on top of Braggard's Tower, part of a crowd nearly twenty strong, and we watched the anchor fall. The ground shook as it hit. A couple of the crowd fell, one almost toppled over the edge of the tower. It is hard to imagine how such an anchor, or the chain attached to it, was forged. It is metal, probably steel, and it made the grand hall of Picarr look small despite its three storeys. Each link in the chain, and there are hundreds of them, is longer than three grown men standing on each other's shoulders.

We stood there on top of the tower, fighting for a space near the front as I was far too small to see over anyone's shoulders. Ro'shan kept drifting onward, even once the anchor was embedded in the earth. Before long the chain pulled taught and we saw the anchor drag only a little before the great city came to a halt. After all was said and done and the flying city had moved on, I went to see the scar that anchor had left in the ground. A wound in the earth tens of feet deep and almost a hundred feet long. It takes a lot to bring Ro'shan to a stop and there are lands all over the world that bear the proof of it.

After the crowd dispersed to their celebrations, I stayed up on the tower with Josef. I think he wanted to leave, but he wouldn't abandon me there. I could have stayed to watch that city for all three days. I remember the flyers, little boats with windmill blades atop and behind them, float down from Ro'shan to land outside Picarr's limits. Merchants with carts, escorted by soldiers, went to meet the visitors from Ro'shan. I did not bother to go and see the visitors myself because I believed them to be terran and paid them little mind, but now I know better; there are few terrans up on Ro'shan. The visitors from that city were more likely pahht and I missed my first chance to see one of the other peoples of the world. These days I know them all well; the pahht, the tahren, the garn, and even the mur. I also know the Rand and the Djinn, though I doubt anyone can claim to know them well. They are as Gods to us mortals, or so they would have us believe.

Eventually Josef dragged me away. We walked back to the academy and were quickly put to work creating lanterns. That night the sky was crowded with little flames all rising to the city above. I doubt many of the lanterns reached Ro'shan, but that isn't the point. It was still a beautiful sight to behold, the darkness lit up by thousands of lanterns drifting on the breeze. I even remember the note I attached to the lantern I sent up. It was a simple thing, but the words meant so much to me at the time. *One day I hope to walk the streets of Ro'shan.*

I thought Imiko had a way to get us on one of the flyers. The little ships ferried goods and people to and from Ro'shan and were almost as much a wonder to me as the city

itself, but they are not there for tourists or stowaways; only
registered merchants or officials were allowed passage on
the flyers and we were most certainly neither. We would be
turned away or, worse, turned in to the authorities. Luckily
for us Imiko had another option. I use the word *luckily*
somewhat hesitantly.

It was not the first time Ro'shan had stopped outside
of Yun. According to Imiko, it passed over head twice a year,
most years, and usually dropped its anchor for a few days.
The citizens of Yun would celebrate, a festival much like
I had seen in Picarr so many years before. The merchants
would trade with their counterparts from Ro'shan; I have
often found it amusing that the Terrelans are so prejudiced
against the other people of Ovaeris yet are so willing to trade
with the pahht from Ro'shan when they appear. I guess it's
true that enough money can buy anything, even friendship.

Imiko claimed she had been to Ro'shan no less than
six times, sneaking around to see the sights and stealing
whatever she could. She said the flyers were heavily
guarded, but the great anchor and chain were not. I think
that was when Hardt decided to put his foot down. He had
seen Ro'shan before and he had seen the chain. I can't blame
him. At the time I thought it sounded a challenge, and one I
was eager to try my hand at after failing so completely in my
first fight. Unfortunately for Hardt, no matter how big his
feet might be, I wasn't about to be deterred. And the more
he resisted, the more determined I became. The ships in the
port no longer interested me. I had already decided I would
make my escape via Ro'shan or not at all.

Our last coin was spent on food and they were
meagre rations at that, barely lasting us the two days until
our climb. Imiko disappeared, despite Hardt's watchful

gaze, and I suspected the worst. I didn't trust her, and with
good reason. You have to remember the little bitch had
stolen from me and beaten me at our first meeting. I was
quite damning of my opinion of her when speaking to Hardt
and Tamura, but I didn't let my bile get in the way of a
potential trip to Ro'shan. Eventually Imiko reappeared with
enough rope to make her the second richest person in the
Pit, after Deko.

It is hard to truly describe the size of the flying city.
I have likened it to a mountain turned upside down, its
pinnacle pointed towards the earth hundreds of feet below. It
has contours and peaks and troughs just like any mountain,
but at its top is a flat base and upon that base sits a city
larger than any terran hands have ever built. I have been
to the Terrelan capital of Juntorrow and I was there when
the Orran capital of Lanfall fell. So, when I say Ro'shan is
larger than any city terrans have ever built, I know it to
be true. Three small islands orbit Ro'shan, though what
connects them to the main land mass I do not know. Despite
my research, I have no idea how the city stays up in the
sky and defies gravity like it does. It's Sourcery, I suppose,
but certainly none I'm familiar with. Both the Rand and the
Djinn are true masters of the arcane and they do not share
their secrets with anyone. That is not strictly true. The Djinn
shared some of its secrets with the Iron Legion, and I came
to know more about the Rand than is safe. But I'm getting
ahead of myself again.

That first night we joined in the celebrations. Imiko
found us all paper lanterns and we sent them into the sky
with thousands of others. I don't know what the others
wrote on their messages, it's rude to ask. I wrote only one
word: *Tomorrow*.

The next morning, we set out hungry and ill-prepared for the ordeal to come. Hardt still wasn't pleased. He championed giving up the plan and returning to Yun right up until the last moment. I think he might have continued past then, but we were all sick of his complaints, his reasoning falling on deaf ears. My mind was set. Imiko claimed she had done it before, and Tamura only giggled at every argument against the plan. The more Hardt argued against it, the more it became my will. Set in stone. No. More permanent that stone. Set in blood.

We avoided the traffic to the flyers Ro'shan sent down. I wanted to get a look at the visitors, but we didn't want the attention. Couldn't afford the risk. Instead we set out straight for the anchor. Or at least we tried. I should have been watching for an attack, paying closer attention to those lining up to enter the city. Instead I was so fixed on my destination, my eyes so filled with the vision of the flying city, that I was caught completely by surprise. At least I wasn't the only one. No one expected Horralain to come charging out of the crowd.

I would have been dead before I realised what was happening, but the giant had to push his way through a group of merchants leading a trei bird and cart. I glanced over just in time to stumble and then the giant fucker hit me. I have experienced a great number of punches in my life, both given and received. Some are little more than a slap, more shocking than painful. Some are violent and brutal and unrestrained; if ever you get to raise an unruly boy you might experience one yourself. Children don't hold back; they live in the moment and are ruled by emotions and sometimes those emotions drive them to violence. I suppose that says a lot about my failing as a parent, both to my own children and those I chose to raise. But some punches, often those delivered by men or women of great strength and skill, feel like being trampled by a herd of abban. Hardt punches like that, and so did Horralain. I suppose I should feel lucky that his fist hit my chest rather than my face. I certainly didn't feel lucky at the time.

The world turned into a bright blur of pain. I think I must have rolled on the ground, struggling to gasp in some air and I inhaled dust. Coughing while winded is not pleasant, but I didn't have time to do much else. Horralain was on me in moments. I caught a glimpse of his snarling face set against the brilliant blue of the sky, and then a great hand wrapped around my throat. It was the second time Horralain had choked me like that.

My vision dimmed and my world became dominated by pain and the desperate struggle to breathe even while my larynx was being crushed.

So weak. Ssserakis' words barely made it past the pain and panic and terror. I clawed at Horralain's fingers to no avail. I opened my mouth to breathe but couldn't even force a sound past his grip. My vision went dark as my eyes rolled back of their own accord.

Hardt was there in a moment, his promises of pacifism forgotten. I find it strange that down in the Pit he was willing to let Isen fight and die at the hands of Yorin, but when my life was threatened, violence came to him so easily.

I often wondered back then just how Hardt saw me. As a sister who needed protecting? A wilful daughter who was almost more trouble than she was worth? A young woman whose friendship made him happy? Maybe none of those things. Maybe he just saw the life I was carrying inside of me as the last connection to a younger brother he failed to protect. Some things are better left unsaid. Some mysteries are better left unsolved. All I can say for certain is that I am glad Hardt was there to protect me that day, and all the others after.

By the time I came to and managed to suck enough air down to allow my mind to catch up, I was down in the dust with Tamura knelt over me. The old man had a hand placed against my chest and was staring into my eyes, breathing deeply. In and out. In and out. I found my own breathing mimicking his and soon I had it under control. I still don't know how he performed that little trick. Hardt was clutching an arm to his ribs, and bleeding from a cut on his head. The blood trickled down towards his left eye and he had it squeezed tight. Horralain was down on the ground with five men wearing guard uniforms kneeling on his back, twisting his arms. He growled and struggled, but there's really only so much you can do with the weight of five men pressing down on you. We locked eyes as the guards bound his hands and pulled him upright. I don't think I've ever seen such rage in a simple gaze. I couldn't fathom why he hated me so, nor why he'd chosen to pursue me even after escaping the Pit himself. The truth, I think, is that Horralain was a simple man. Deko had given him an order to bring me back or kill me, no matter the cost, and Horralain would pursue that task until the end of the world if need be. I don't think it ever even occurred to him that he was free of the Pit and free of Deko. That he could now do and be anything he chose. I've heard it said some people never escape captivity, even once they're free. I think that was Horralain. His life was the Pit. It was all he knew. No matter where he went, he would always be a prisoner there. Such people deserve pity, but I have none of it to give, so I gave him rage instead.

"Fuck you!" I screamed at him, one hand clutching my neck and the other brushing against the Source at my belt.

Another fight lost. You truly are weak. But I could make you strong.

"You know him?" asked one of the guards desperately trying to hold Horralain down.

I shook my head slowly and met Horralain's furious stare with a deadly cold one of my own. "No. He just attacked me. I hope he rots in gaol."

The struggle, brief though it was, cost Hardt dearly. Horralain had broken a rib and had given Hardt a cut that quickly caused his left eye to swell to the point that he couldn't open it. Shortly after Horralain had been dragged away, Imiko reappeared. I had not even noticed her sneak away, but that was one of her many skills. Whenever a fight started the little thief vanished. For someone usually so loud and vibrant, it was quite a skill to disappear like that. She handed Hardt a long strip of bandage and some ointment that smelled like ground Everberries. Never ask a thief where they found a thing; at best you'll receive no answer at all, at worst you'll find your pockets emptied for being so rude.

We were soon underway once more, though in a much worse condition. Hardt's injuries slowed him down and I found talking quite the struggle with a bruised neck. At least Tamura was jovial. The crazy old man looked up at Ro'shan filling the sky. "Once around and back again. Then once more and once again. Two cities, you see. Two. Not five. The path used to be less predictable." I had no idea what he meant, and not the will to puzzle it out. Ro'shan was there, in front of me. And after so many years I was finally going to fulfil my younger self's promise. I was going to walk the streets of the flying city.

CHAPTER TWELVE

RO'SHAN FILLED THE SKY. THE FLYING mountain loomed above us, blocking out everything and casting us in a shadow so great it almost felt like night. I could feel the excitement, the nervous anticipation, a thrill running through me like lightning or the gentle touch of a new lover. I will admit that it soon gave way to exhaustion, terror, and a biting cold that I think even Ssserakis felt. But right then, in that moment, I was full of nervous energy. I was ready to climb.

We used the rope to tie ourselves together. Imiko went first, claiming she knew which links were hardest and could pave the way for the rest of us. I was second and then Tamura and finally Hardt. Imiko made a harness of the rope and tied it around our shoulders and waist, each of us was separated by a length of rope as long as two Hardts. Finally, there was nothing else to do but start the climb.

So long and such a drop. So easy to slip and fall. You're all going to die.

I very nearly backed out then. Standing next to the anchor, dwarfed by it, and that was just the start of the climb. Cold metal sunk deep into the earth. Above it, links in a chain that didn't rattle but groaned in the wind. I looked up at the climb ahead of us and I couldn't see how it was possible. Hundreds of links extending into the distance. It was a climb that made our efforts in the Pit look easy. I have always enjoyed a good climb, spending much of my earliest years scaling trees just to get a glimpse of the sky. There is something thrilling about being high up and having a lethal drop below. A certain satisfaction with the burning ache of muscles used to pull yourself higher. A wild excitement when you encounter a broken branch, and that brief elation when the body thinks it is falling before the mind convinces it otherwise. Even so, the climb that chain presented me with was daunting, to say the least.

The rope attached to me pulled taught and I realised Imiko had already started the climb. She glanced back at me, red faced and sweating already. "Are you coming or not?"

I won't say that first part of the climb was the hardest, that would be a lie, but it certainly wasn't easy. I failed twice at the start before Hardt moved forwards to give me a boost, lifting me up as though I weighed nothing. Before long, I was scrambling up the side of the anchor, using the dents and pits for holds. Imiko guided me at some points and I hated her for it even as I thanked her for the advice. I have no idea how long it was before all four of us were standing atop the anchor, staring up at the chain stretching away before us. I'm still not certain whether the first or last link looked the most daunting.

"Last chance to back out," Imiko drawled, smiling because she already knew I wouldn't. It wasn't that she had gotten to know me well over the past day, but more that even those who barely know me know I hate to back down from a challenge. Especially when there is someone else so willing to undertake it.

"Just climb," I said. I stared out towards the length of chain and wondered if the others were feeling as apprehensive as I.

More so. Can't you feel the fear rolling off them. Can't you taste it. I could. I hated to admit it, but I could taste it. It had a sour flavour that should have been repulsive, but instead I wanted more of it. I wanted to feel my friends' terror, and that sickened me.

"Hands and knees all the way," Imiko said. "Follow me as best you can and shout if you get in trouble." With that the girl dropped onto all fours and starting scrambling across the first link in the chain.

I gave Imiko a head start, making certain there was enough rope between us so I would not be crowding her. Maybe I was hesitating, but I felt a hand squeeze my shoulder just once and then Tamura's voice in my ear, "When the destination seems so far away, instead pay attention to each step. Step. Step. Step."

"Will it make the journey seem shorter? Easier?"

Tamura laughed. "No. But at least you'll be moving." He gave me a gentle push and then I had my first foot on the chain.

I dropped onto my hands and knees. The first thing I noticed was how slick the chain felt beneath my hands and when I looked at it, I saw a coating of grease. "Wonderful," I groaned before starting my climbing crawl up the first link.

I have done a great many harrowing things in my lifetime. I've crossed the Seras Desert with nothing on my feet but callouses, hoping every step wouldn't be my last and that the scorpions and snakes that infest the dunes wouldn't take the opportunity to strike. I have stood face to face with creatures older than the entire terran race and I have screamed my defiance at them. I have given birth. Twice. But few events really compare to that climb.

I tried to do as Tamura suggested, keeping my eyes on the chain and each inch I crawled along it, but I soon found my vision swimming. As large as the links were, they couldn't entirely obscure the sight of the ground far below. It wasn't too bad at first. I saw greenery, bushes and fields, below me. The problem was the further up the chain we moved the smaller and blurrier the ground became. Closing my eyes only made things worse and I found myself clutching at the metal below me hard enough to crack nails. The horizontal links were terrifying enough, yet they were child's play compared to the vertical links. Each one required a leap, complete with clutching for dear life, and a scramble to get on top of it. The balancing act that followed the crawl across it had me clenching my teeth together so hard both my jaw and head soon began to ache.

You might think it would have been a perfect time for Ssserakis to remind me of the predicament I found myself in, but the ancient horror was silent. Despite that silence I could feel how content it was as it drank in our fear. It wasn't just me feeding it, either. Like a cloud surrounding us, I could feel all of our fear. Even Tamura was scared during the climb, though I doubt he'd ever admit it. I'm not even certain he can remember it. I sometimes envy Tamura's ability to forget things.

Before long I was shaking from the exertion, and a little after that I was shivering from the cold as well. In case you have never shook and shivered at the same time I can tell you this, it is not pleasant; especially when crawling along a loop of metal with a fatal drop beneath you. I felt as though we had been crawling for hours and I looked up. Ro'shan seemed no closer than when we had set off. I wasn't foolish enough to risk a look back. I didn't want to know how far we had gone because I had a sinking feeling it would only make the rest of the trip seem that much more unbearable.

Imiko set a slow pace and looked back regularly. I occasionally saw her staring towards us, and her grin was long gone. It might be true she had indeed made the climb before, but never had she done it tied to three fools who had no idea what they were doing. I admire her courage in that regard. I heard grunts from behind, but no words. Tamura and Hardt laboured on in silence just as I did.

The wind picked up. Whether it was a change in weather or because of our ascent, I'm not sure. I first noticed it when an errant gust caught hold of my coat and threatened to pull me off the chain. I collapsed flat against the metal, hugging it despite the coating of grease it left on my face and clothes. I think I heard someone calling my name, but it was hard to be certain over the crashing of waves in my ears. For those few moments all that existed to me was the slick cold of the chain and the icy bite of the wind as it whipped through me, trying to find purchase enough to drag me to my death wherever it could. Eventually I pushed back onto shaking hands and continued my crawl.

At some point Imiko called for a halt. We rested

there, part way up the great chain, each of us a link apart.
We wedged ourselves into the crannies where links met,
and waited. That was the first time I got a good look at
how far we had gone. The chain stretched away behind us,
far but not far enough. It was hard to gauge, but I guessed
we had gone no more than a third of the way. There was
a figure standing next to the great anchor, little more than
a dark blur, but I knew the shape of the man well enough.
Horralain was free once more and had found us. Luckily for
us, he couldn't get to us. Even that monster thought twice
about attempting the climb up to Ro'shan.

Looking the other way, past Imiko, I could see
nothing but the mountain looming so high above us, and so
far away. It awed me that we had gone so far and still had so
far to go, and yet the great lump of rock filled the sky. I don't
think I truly appreciated the length of the chain until that
moment. I tried my best not to look down, but it's like asking
someone not to look at a wound. They will always pull the
bandage away, desperate to get a look despite not wanting
to see it. I can say this for a certainty. Don't. Look. Down.
My vision swam and I pulled back, pushing myself further
into the chain and closing my eyes against the vertigo. It
didn't help. I might not have been able to see it, but I knew
the drop was there, waiting for me. Almost calling to me. A
part of myself, that incessant seed of self-hatred and doubt
that the bitch-whore, Lesray Alderson, planted in me so long
ago, told me to let go and throw myself off into the drop. It
is an unfortunate truth of my life that suicide has never been
far from my thoughts, and it most often tugs at me when
there is a height to launch myself from. The call of the void. I
fought it. I have been fighting it my whole life. I am so tired.

As we began our climb again, I could see the last few

rays of light disappearing over the western horizon. Lokar and Lursa, ever grinding their way into each other, were high and bright and gave us new light to work with. It was Lokar's time for dominance, his blue a muted brilliance in the sky, and I consoled myself that at least we were unlikely to find ourselves in a sudden moonshower. The going got slower from then on. And the chain only got colder. More than once I pulled my hand away and left a patch of skin frozen to the metal. The pain of it was intense but it served to sharpen my senses and chase away the insidious fingers of sleep that were worming their way into my mind.

I almost slipped and fell the first time I put my hand on a patch of ice. The freezing burn of it startled me and I pulled my hand away, a thrill of terror coursing through me. I felt myself toppling sideways and slammed my hand back down, clutching at the greasy metal. By then I couldn't stop the shivering.

As the night wore on I glanced up more and more often. Ro'shan was a dark stain against the night sky, blocking out the stars behind it. It was so large now I couldn't see how we weren't almost there. The chains moved more as well, groaning and grating as they shifted against each other. The closer we got to Ro'shan the more pronounced the movements. There were times when all four of us were clutching onto a link for all we were worth while the wind buffeted us.

We stopped again, when Lokar and Lursa were high above. I sat there, shivering, with my greasy coat pulled close around me. I looked back down the chain and wished we could all huddle up on one link together to share warmth. With Sserakis inside of me I was never warm, but up there, on the frozen chains… I have used Pyromancy

to freeze people solid before. I sometimes wonder if that
was how they felt as the ice took them. I wonder if they
experienced the shivering and the lethargy that comes with
it. I almost didn't notice when Imiko shouted at us to start
moving again. The wind was howling and my mind was
lost in the chill. I think if we had waited there much longer I
wouldn't have moved again. What an end that would made
for the great and terrible Eskara Helsene; frozen solid half
way up the chain to Ro'shan. I wonder if my body would
have shattered when it hit the ground, or maybe I would
have become frozen to the great chain, stuck to it for all
eternity. A monument to my own stupidity.

They say misery loves company, but up there, even
attached to the others by rope, I felt alone. It was as though
the whole world had ceased to exist. All there was, was the
chain, the cold, and me. I crawled along and my mind took
me to places I didn't want it to. At first, I thought it was
Ssserakis trying to scare me, trick me into dropping. But the
things and people I saw up on that chain had nothing to do
with the horror. I saw Josef's face floating out in the void. I
saw him alive and happy, smiling at me the way he used to.
I almost started to reach out to him. I'm certain I would have
pitched over the side. But the memory of my friend's death
came flooding back, and bitter determination to survive
came with it.

Suddenly I was surrounded by dozens of tiny flames.
Paper lanterns rising around us, bumping into the chain.
Some faltered and went out, falling back down to earth
while others kept on floating up, blown by the wind. I let out
a giggle. Perhaps you have never heard someone shivering,
cold to their core, giggle. Far from a happy sound, it is quite
eerie, like a ghost mocking the living.

I heard the shout from behind over the sound of the wind. It was a grunt followed by a cry of terror. Some instinct quashed my desire to look back, to see what was happening. Instead, I flattened myself against the link and wrapped my arms and legs around it, hugging it as tight to my body as I could. Then the rope went taught and Hardt and Tamura tried to rip me from the chain, dragging me down to death with them.

CHAPTER THIRTEEN

THE WORLD WENT DARK WITH CRIES OF
terror. Pain kept me anchored. The pain of two grown men
trying to rip me from the chain, their weight dragging
down on my arms and chest. The pain of my own nails
cracking against the metal, ripping from their beds. My arms
wrapped around steel so cold it seeped inside, weakening
my grip. I clutched onto the link with every bit of strength I
had. It wasn't nearly enough. We were going to fall, going to
die. I knew it. They knew it. We were all going to die.

Would you give up so easily?

I was scared. We were all scared, filled with a terror
born from the absolute certainty we were all going to die.
The strength Ssserakis gave me allowed me to hold on, but
even that wasn't enough. I could feel myself slipping.

"Don't let go!" Imiko's voice, screamed over the howl
of the wind. A hundred scathing replies flitted through my

mind, but I could barely breathe, let alone tell the girl how stupid a command that was. I was well aware there was a fatal drop below me and letting go was the last thing I intended. I would have let the strain tear my arms from my sockets before I let go.

"What do we do?" Hardt's voice, full of fear. I have seen Hardt with a knife to his neck, already bloody from the fight, and there was no fear in him. Together we have faced down monsters made from nightmares, and not once did he falter. He has spent months on the torturer's block, and never broken. But hanging there, I could hear his terror. I could feel it. It pulsed in waves, the stench of it thick. It should have revolted me, but I felt heat stirring inside from it. I enjoyed the fear. I welcomed it. The fear made me feel strong and whole.

It is mine! I allow you to taste it.

"Cut yourself loose." Imiko's voice held her own note of panic.

"What?" I honestly didn't realise Hardt's voice could reach so high an octave.

"Cut yourself loose or she falls with you." It was not lost to me, even then, that Imiko did not include herself in the statement. She had cut the rope binding us the moment she heard Hardt cry out. I suppose I shouldn't really blame her, having only known us a couple of days. She did not have the bond forged from months in the Pit, from the hardships we had suffered, from the losses we had endured.

"Don't you dare, Tamura!" Hardt again, grunting with effort.

I clutched the chain and squeezed my eyes tight. The initial shock had driven the air out of me and even now I was breathing only in short gasps, body rigid against the strain and the pain. I think I might have been crying, tears forced to run down greasy cheeks, freezing before they even left my skin. I was, after all, dangling upside down, my arms and legs wrapped around cold metal, my face pressed against it. The seeping cold of that link numbed me. The strain was too much. I felt my grip slipping, my strength failing. That ever-present call of the void sounded stronger then. Lesray Alderson's most insidious work daring me to finally end the pain and suffering and misery. The promise that it would be so easy. But it wasn't just me I would be condemning. It wasn't just Hardt and Tamura. It was the life I harboured inside. The life Isen and I had created. I couldn't allow my child to die before it had even had a chance to live.

There is a point, I have come to realise, where death becomes so certain that the fear of it vanishes. Holding onto that chain, my arms and legs wrapped tight around it, my face coated in the grease of it, the weight of my friends dragging me down… I stopped fearing. We were going to die. I knew there was no stopping it. And the fear just went away. In its wake I saw Isen staring at me from the darkness. The fear Isen had felt down in the Djinn city had been real, driving him almost to madness. I saw that now. I think that was why Ssserakis chose to wear his face, crushed and bloody as it was, I could see the anger there. The ancient horror was angry because the fear was gone. I felt new strength in my arms, enough to clutch just a little tighter. But strength alone wouldn't save us, and strength was all Ssserakis could give me. The determination, the stubborn refusal to give in, was all mine.

"Cut yourself loose or you all die," Imiko screamed. She was close, the sound of her voice made my ears crackle.

"All men are ladders for their sons," Tamura said and

I could hear the strain in his voice.

"What?" Hardt screamed back at the old man.

"CLIMB!"

I heard grunting, growling, and the occasional curse that could only come from Hardt. The strain on my chest and arms became a tug as well as the constant pull. I couldn't breathe. My vision was nothing but darkness, my eyes squeezed tight, but even that started to fade. I felt hands on me, clutching at me. Cupping my face with a gentle touch. Then it was too much. My arms simply fell away and I felt myself drop.

There is a place people go sometimes where there are no dreams and there is no thought. It is a void, a place without. I was there. I felt nothing. I thought nothing. I dreamed nothing. I remembered nothing.

When I woke my mind was slow to catch up. I saw rock above, hewn and shaped. For a dreaded instant I thought I was back in the Pit. *You never left*. Ssserakis, whispering in my mind, lies and truth all at once. I sometimes wonder if the ancient horror was still aware even when I was not. When I disappeared and went to that nowhere, did Ssserakis take my place? I wondered if that was how the horror had taken over my body and almost killed Josef. The mocking laughter I heard in my mind at that thought did little to answer one way or another.

It took some time for me to realise that the chain was gone. I was no longer dangling above a fatal drop. There was no wind, no grease-coated metal beneath me. Though I was lying on something quite sharp and uncomfortable poking into my back. I tried to move, but my arms felt leaden, dead weights that barely twitched no matter the effort I put into them. I think I might have groaned or maybe grunted. Imiko's face appeared above me, staring down into my eyes.

"The witch is awake," the girl said. She laughed, but I caught something in her eyes, something that hadn't been there before. I wasn't sure what it was at the time, but these days I know it. It was respect. The type that is earned through action and given only grudgingly. We did not like each other, but I had just done the impossible and that was enough to earn some small respect.

Tamura appeared next, his dark face lined with worry. I managed to cough at him, though any words I attempted made it no further than that. When Hardt's face appeared, I felt a weight lift off my chest and found I could breathe again, though it hurt to do so. I realised then; I had been bracing myself for bad news. A part of my mind retreating and hardening for a blow that never came. He said something, but I didn't hear the words. I was too busy revelling in the relief, like a torrent of cheering sounding only in my head. They were alive. Hardt and Tamura were alive. We had all somehow survived. No more losses. No one else left behind.

For now. I would have told the horror to shut up and let me have my moment of victory, but as I have said, words were beyond me.

Big hands moved underneath me and Hardt helped me sit up. If you have ever needed help sitting up then you understand the state I was in. My arms and legs tingled and I could barely feel past that. When I did finally manage to move them, little more than closing my fingers into a fist, the pain was intense and travelled all the way up my arms. I don't think I have ever felt quite that helpless, not even chained to a table with a knife in my chest.

We were in a cavern, massive and dark and clearly not natural. The walls and ceiling were too flat, and I could just about make out steps carved from the rock itself. I heard wind nearby, that same whistling howl that had given me hope down in the Pit. It was cold. I shivered and that sent a whole new list of pains through my body. Pain is a constant companion throughout life. It is something we can get used to if it is frequent enough, but rarely something we enjoy. I have noticed the older a person gets, the more they complain about the pain, as though tolerance for it erodes with age. Maybe it's because pain comes more readily with years, or maybe it's because pain serves such a good use, to remind us all that we are, over time, falling apart. Hurtling, moment by moment, towards an inevitable death.

A water skin was lifted to my lips and I sipped as greedily as Hardt would allow. When he pulled it away I think I may have glared at him. He drew away from me, a cautious glance sent towards Tamura.

Imiko was up on her feet and looking skittish. "See, she's fine. We really should go before one of the golems comes to check on the chain."

"What happened?" It took some time before my memory of the chain returned to me. I tried to think back, and everything was blank. One moment we were crawling towards Ro'shan, and the next, I woke up wracked with pain and on solid ground.

"You saved us." Hardt's voice was full of respect. I felt oddly embarrassed by it. "I don't know how you held on as long as you did, but you did. Long enough for me and Tamura to climb up the rope. After that, we hauled you back up and carried you the rest of the way."

I knew exactly how I held on, where the strength

came from. I considered telling them about Ssserakis. It's quite difficult telling the people you care about that you are possessed by an ancient horror that uses you to scare them so it can feed off their fear. Honestly, even to this day, I have no idea how I would approach that conversation. Through all our time together, our travels and trials, it may be the one secret I have never told anyone. Partly because I was ashamed, partly because I've always been scared of how they might react, of losing them.

Having finally convinced my limbs to start moving again I gave myself a quick inspection. It was hard to be certain, but I could feel bruises all over my arms and chest where the rope had dug into my flesh. Even with Ssserakis lending me strength, there is a limit to what a body can endure. There comes a point where muscles simply can't go on. I had reached that point and it took me weeks to recover fully.

"We really don't want to be here when a golem comes. They are not forgiving of stowaways. I've heard stories of people being thrown out and we've just proven that none of us can fly." Imiko sounded worried and I could well understand. Golemancy is a powerful school of magic. Golems don't quibble over orders, nor hesitate. No morals or conscience. From the outside it might appear as though the magic is limited in its purpose, but it can be used for far more than just creating semi-sentient constructs. The Iron Legion was a master in that particular school, but then he was a master in all the Sourcery schools he practised.

"She's right," I said. I didn't doubt Hardt would stay and protect me for as long as it took, but I also didn't like his chances against a rock golem. "Help me up."

Tamura hauled me to my feet and kept hold of me

while my legs remembered how to function. I'd be lying if I said it didn't hurt, but I limped towards the stairs. I'd also be lying if I said Tamura didn't help me with every step. We had to duck underneath the chain and I glanced first right to see it disappearing out into the night sky, and then left to see the great mechanism that wound the chain back inside the mountain when it was time to leave.

The steps led up and up and I was sweating and exhausted by the time we reached the top. They opened out into a building that sat near the edge of the mountain. The sky was already starting to brighten, the first rays of the sun yet to appear, and in that light, I could see a dozen golems in the building. Six were huge monstrosities with four legs and as many arms. They stood half again as tall as Hardt and looked as though they were formed of the same metal as the chain below us. The other six were small, maybe half my height, and looked as though they were made of rock. They almost looked terran, though without any defining features. All twelve of the golems stood dormant in that building, watching us, but not moving.

Have you ever seen what a golem can do to flesh? Ssserakis' whispering conjured disturbing images.

"Can't you just let me be?" I whispered, my voice breaking on my exhaustion.

I'm hungry. Ssserakis sounded as tired as I did.

Hardt was staring at me strangely. I can't really blame him; I had just been whispering to myself. "What do we do?" His voice a whisper, as if that was all it would take to wake the slumbering constructs.

"We should leave before any of them wake up," Imiko said. "I've been here before. They'll ignore us when they're like this, but if they start moving, we're dead. So, let's get out of here."

Hardt looked at me and I nodded. Neither Orran nor Terrelan ever had much use for golems and in my youth, I often wondered why. I have since learned that it is a rare school of magic, one that both empires coveted. I have also learned that Polasia has an abundance of Golemancers, and along with the Demonships, they are a military force to be reckoned with.

We crept from the building, careful not to disturb any of the sleeping golems, and hopeful that there were no more-sentient sentries nearby. As we passed through the doorway and into the open air, surrounded by trees on all sides, the first rays of sunlight broke over the horizon. It dawned on me then that I was finally on Ro'shan, the floating home of the Rand.

CHAPTER FOURTEEN

BEFORE WE MADE OUR WAY INLAND TO THE city, I crept closer to the edge of the mountain where the ground became rocky and uneven and the horizon was nothing but sky. Tamura kept hold of me, my right arm slung over his shoulder. We stood there for a few minutes watching the sun peak over the ocean so far below. It is hard to gauge just how high Ro'shan floats until you are up there, looking down on the world. That lofty position is one of many reasons both the Rand and Djinn consider themselves above the other people of Ovaeris. From a literal standpoint, they are.

I realised then how calm it was. Climbing the chain, we had been buffeted by gusting winds that threated to drag us off into the drop. But standing up there, looking down, there was nothing but a calm breeze. It seemed so odd. The temperature, too, was mild, yet it was the tail of winter down on the ground. Even with the sun blazing and a clear sky above, it would be chilly down in Yun. Yet up on Ro'shan I felt warm for the first time in a long while. It might almost have been pleasant if not for the stirring of the horror inside at the sight of the sun.

Even inside you, it burns. You should go back to the underground.

"I think I'll stand in the sun a bit longer," I said with a grin. I received nothing but sullen silence to that.

Hardt joined us staring out over the edge of the mountain. He was smiling, a genuine smile that was infectious. It seemed a long time since I had seen true good humour on his face.

"Yes, it's a wonderful view," Imiko said impatiently. "But we really should go. We need to find somewhere in the city we can hide."

"Hide?" I turned from the view and felt my spirits drop a little. I saw a figure standing just beyond the treeline ahead. At first, I took it for Isen or one of the others I had murdered, conjured up by Ssserakis. Then the figure turned away and vanished into the trees. "We've been seen."

"Well, that's going to make things more interesting." Imiko shot me a disingenuous smile. "Feel free to stay here, but I'm gonna find somewhere to hide before we get ejected the quick way down."

We made our way to the treeline and followed along behind Imiko. The thief seemed to know her way through, but progress was slow. More than once, we stopped, waiting when Imiko thought she heard others moving through the forest. It might seem surprising that there is a forest on the top side of Ro'shan; many people believe there is just a city up there, but that is far from the truth. I have explored the forest of Ro'shan, and I have swum in the lake. I have also walked every street the city has to offer and visited every tavern. I have seen it from above and below, and for a long time I called the city my home. Yet I am no longer welcome there, for Ro'shan is the domain of the Rand and she does not like me very much. I assure you the feeling is mutual. I'm no longer on good terms with any of our gods.

It was mid-morning when we left the forest. We might have made better time, but we stayed away from beaten paths. When we stepped out of the final line of trees and I saw the city in front of me, I will admit I forgot myself somewhat. We were stowaways and should have hidden away instead of announcing our presence, but I ignored Imiko's frantic attempts to pull me back and wandered straight towards the spectacle.

The buildings in Ro'shan are all white, almost polished to a shine. From a distance they look like marble, but it is only when you get closer that you realise they are, in fact, formed from bone. The city stretches out wide in a circle around the central palace, a series of giant arches all looping over, under, and through each other. At first it looked like chaos, a haphazard series of architectural madness. But I have studied the pattern of those arches, and though I cannot grasp it, I am certain a pattern exists. I know now that nothing in Ro'shan is haphazard, it is all by the design of the Rand.

I have since learned there is a monster sleeping in the centre of Ro'shan. A giant none save the Rand has ever seen. Its bones grow out from its skin, out through the rock above, and they grow into the shapes of buildings. I often wonder if I could have found a way down to it, maybe I might have talked to the giant, but a creature that size probably wouldn't even see me. After all, I have never taken the time to talk to an ant, and, if I did, I doubt it would have anything interesting to say.

Our arrival did not go unnoticed. Dozens of tahren swarmed over the nearby buildings, each one wielding a cloth and polishing the bones. They are ever the caretakers of the world, the tahren, as eager to preserve as we terrans are to destroy. They have a library, I have seen it, larger than any other in the world. Some people say every book ever written can be found in that library. I would argue with that claim and I would win. I have been to the tahren library, and I have stolen a few choice tomes from their endless bookshelves.

One of the tahren stopped and cocked its head towards us, listening. It was the first time I had seen one, the first time I had seen any of Ovaeris' people other than a terran. I don't think I made a very good first impression, but then my mind was reeling somewhat from the shock of such a sight. They have no eyes, yet they see more clearly than any of us that do. The tahren are small, even the largest of them are just half my height. They have small heads and large ears, and they are covered head to claw in a shaggy fur. I've seen terrans mistake tahren for animals, believing them to be unintelligent and docile. I've also seen terrans lose digits before for trying to pat a tahren on the head like they might a dog. As a rule, tahren are fiercely intelligent, prideful, and quick to anger. But then, as a rule, terrans are self-important, resourceful, and warlike. I like to think I break at least one of those rules, but thinking about it now, maybe I'm not so different as I like to believe.

"Huh." My first response to seeing a tahren was not particularly articulate. It was about all I could manage.

The others fared better, I think. Imiko had been to Ro'shan before and knew what to expect. Hardt had sailed across the seas and pirated many of the other races; I think he was more worried someone might recognise him for his crimes. Tamura... Well, it was hard to gauge Tamura's reaction. Maybe he had seen it all before. Maybe he didn't care. He kept muttering that it was *Just like back home*, not that I could see how that was true. There is nowhere in the world quite like Ro'shan. Not anymore. There hasn't been for almost six centuries.

I continued stumbling into the city and more and more of the nearby folk stopped to watch us. Well, the pahht stopped to watch. The tahren stopped and their heads certainly followed us, but they listen rather than watch, I suppose. Honestly, I have never asked any of them about their lack of eyes, I think it would seem rude, even by terran standards, and they already consider us uncouth.

Most of the nearby pahht were children. They appeared to be chasing each other around a tree while an adult watched, though they all stopped to stare at our passage as though the sight of a terran loose in the city was as rare as an abban with wings. The pahht are cat-like in appearance, though I have learned from experience not to call them such. It is considered quite an insult no matter how accurate most terrans might believe it to be. They have the face of a cat and the fur of a cat, but they stand as tall as I do and on two legs. I think I may have been staring at them a little too intensely; the adult quickly gathered up the children and ushered them away.

None of those watching us made any attempt to approach, but the dead silence that surrounded us was more than a little damning.

"What's happening?" I asked. "Surely they've seen terrans before?"

Imiko shrugged. "Maybe not. One thing you'll soon learn about Ro'shan is there really aren't that many terrans, and those there are, are usually restricted to the docks where they trade and then leave."

"Why?"

"Because of Terrelan." Hardt's voice was a sad rumble. "Because of people like me and Isen, and what we were ordered to do."

Down in the ruined city Hardt had admitted he and Isen were once pirates, ordered by the Terrelan empire to board vessels sailed by the other races, steal whatever they could, and leave none alive to tell the tale. The problem, I have found, is that no matter how few witnesses you leave alive, the tale always gets told. This is especially true of atrocities, and Hardt has committed almost as many of those as I have. I wonder if they weigh as heavily on his conscience as they do on mine? I would wager so, Hardt drags his guilt with him and wears it like a noose around his own neck.

"We should probably go." Imiko sounded a little worried. I thought her foolish at the time and scoffed at her. "Back into the forest, maybe. I think it's fairly obvious we're stowaways."

"What are the buildings made of?" I ignored Imiko and when I approached the nearest building one of the tahren sitting on it hopped down onto the ground and stood before it, staring up me without eyes.

"Back," the little tahren barked, its voice high and accented in a way I had never heard before.

I might have bristled at the order, but my curiosity

won out. I shrugged free from Tamura's support and took
another step forward. "What are the buildings made of?" I
asked the tahren.

Another tahren dropped down beside the first and I
looked up to see three more posturing on a nearby rooftop.
They didn't look dangerous until they opened their mouths,
revealing two rows of sharp teeth. I will admit I took a step
back, caution finally overcoming curiosity.

"It was just a question." There are moments in
life when perception gives way to reality. I saw the city
of Ro'shan as a wonder, a marvel, something new that I
had never even imagined might exist. I saw the tahren as
harmless creatures dutifully looking after the city. But to
them Ro'shan was not some spectacle, it was their home,
and I was a stranger, and a terran. To them, I was dangerous.
I think that realisation took some of the shine off Ro'shan for
me.

"Eska, I think Imiko is right. We should go." Hardt
ever the voice of reason. Unfortunately, I am not particularly
good at backing down.

"I'll go when they answer my question." I fixed the
tahren with a hard stare. I've always had quite a piercing
gaze, a savage intensity combined with eyes the colour of
blue ice. However, no matter how intense the stare, it is
somewhat wasted on a creature who cannot see.

Hardt laid a big hand on my shoulder. He didn't
mean to hurt me, but I winced at the pain. He gently steered
me away from the confrontation and I hadn't the strength to
resist. I noticed then that we had drawn quite a crowd. No
doubt the nearby citizens of Ro'shan thought me just another
Terrelan. I had, after all, been on the verge of starting a fight
with a tahren I had only just met over so little an issue. As I

have said, I did not make the best first impression. As a rule, I don't. We'll call it one of my many failings.

Hardt was clutching at his ribs as he pulled me away, and I think we supported each other as we made our way down that street, further into the heart of Ro'shan. His fight with Horralain had taken more out of him than he wanted to admit, and our ordeal on the great chain was far from easy. The truth was, we were all of us weary beyond words and filthy from our climb. I don't think the fact that we were terrans drew nearly so much attention as the fact that we looked like vagrants, and the dishevelled raise an innate fear in people. Children were pulled from our path and merchants kept a wary eye on their goods. I think I would have been angry at that, but I couldn't quite find the energy for anger. It was taking everything I had left just to keep one foot plodding in front of the other.

The city passed by in a blur, but I remember bits of our first morning there. Tahren diligently cleaning the buildings, others going about the daily toil of city life with pahht and even a few terrans. For all its majesty and wonder, Ro'shan is a city like any other. It has butchers and bakers, blacksmiths and wood carvers, city guards and thieves to keep them occupied. We saw children at play and others learning the crafts of their parents. We saw people laughing with others, wiling the day away over laborious tasks, or taking time out from the sun to have a cool drink in the shade of a tavern. A city like any other, though perhaps a bit more cosmopolitan than most. I even caught my first glimpse of a garn while we trudged further into the city with no goal in mind. A great hulking thing slithering across the ground like a snake. Dangerous things, are garn, but also so incredibly polite. Unless, of course, you're another garn; in which case they are as likely to cut you in half as wave good morning. I suppose the world should be grateful the garn are constantly at war with each other, or we'd be overrun by them within a few months. They breed prolifically and have a habit of regenerating from wounds instead of dying.

I can't tell you when Imiko disappeared, only that one moment we were all together, and the next I glanced around to find her missing. The little thief has always been like that. She vanishes without a trace and leaves no indication as to why.

The size of the palace became more apparent as we moved towards it. The arches rose up from different sections of the city and all crossed each other near the centre. I glanced up to where they met and found myself awestruck at how such a large structure could be held suspended above the city.

I suppose we were going towards the palace, not because any of us had some grand plan about meeting the Rand, but because we had nowhere to go and were all far too exhausted to think about it. We just aimed towards the centre of the city and kept walking. Even Tamura's attitude, normally so jocund, was muted. The crazy old man even quit his mumbling and giggling for a while.

Then I met Silva for the very first time. A chance meeting that shaped so much of my life. A woman stopped us with a raised hand, a small book in her other. She was beautiful. I do not mean handsome or pretty, but beautiful in that way some people are. That way that demands attention. Appreciation. That type of beautiful that comes from both within and without. Her eyes were light green and she had a way of looking at you, as though she were looking inside of you to your core. Her golden hair, even tied up behind her head, made her pale skin seem almost aglow. She was taller than I, though not so tall as Tamura, and had an easiness about her; a grace that showed through with every movement and every stillness. Perhaps it was the weariness, but I found myself struck dumb at the sight of her.

"You don't look like locals." Her voice always sounded like bells to me, softly chiming in the distance. Hardt disagrees with me there, but then he was always suspicious of her.

I heard my name shouted from somewhere behind us. It is always strange to hear your own name used as an accusation, almost like it is too long to list all your crimes, but your name works as a brutal summation. I turned to see another woman striding towards me. She was tall and broad and wearing red leather over a black uniform with golden plates etched with enchantments. Her dark hair, such a contrast to Silva's, cascaded down around her shoulders and where Silva was soft, this woman was sharp. Her eyes were fixed on me and me alone, her stride, long and purposeful. I should have seen it coming, but my exhaustion had blinded me to the subtleties of body language. I didn't realise what was happening until the woman's sword tore a scream from me.

CHAPTER FIFTEEN

HARDT SAW THE DANGER BEFORE I DID, BUT not soon enough. He started forward just as the woman in red and gold reached us. She barely even spared the giant a glance but drew her sword, pommel first, into his stomach. As Hardt staggered back and fell, clutching at his broken ribs, the blade cleared the scabbard and the woman turned it on me and thrust.

I remembered the sight of that blade from another time. The yellow-tinted metal with a shifting pattern as if it were boiling steam. Then the blade bit into my flesh. Only my lack of grace saved me. I tried to turn and run only to trip over my own feet and the momentum carried me further and faster than I could have moved otherwise. I fell, and the strike that had been meant for my heart instead sank into the meat of my left shoulder. I screamed. I'm not too proud to admit that. I had been beaten and bruised, lashed and broken down in the Pit, but never had I felt steel thrust inside, parting flesh and sinking deep. It was a new experience, and not one I enjoyed. Some things fade, the effect of time working its irresistible erosion on memory, but that one moment, that memory, that feeling of pain and helplessness and confusion, is as clear to me now as it was then. If I close my eyes, I can still feel the sword in my shoulder, invading my body. I have tried to forget, but it has stayed with me all these years. And every time my shoulder aches, and it often does, I remember that day and that wound, and the woman who dealt it to me.

As quickly as it had pierced my skin, it slid free. I fell away from the sword and left the tip slick and dripping with my blood. I landed next to Hardt and what a pair we made; both moaning in pain and trying to crawl away from our attacker. The woman took a step forward, her bubbling blade lowered towards me. There was no emotion in her dark eyes, no pleasure in her actions nor pride in her victory. She intended to finish the job and see me dead, and I didn't even know why. I didn't know who she was or why she was going to kill me. I find that somewhat discourteous. People should know the name of their slayer, the reasons for their murder. No one should be sent to the grave with the questions of why and who on their lips. We should know, so in the possibility of there being a next life, we know who to hunt down and visit our vengeance upon. I wonder how many times I've played the nameless assassin. How many people I have sent on ahead of me with those questions racing through their minds as their very last thoughts.

"Asylum!" Tamura shouted. One word standing between life and death. It's surprising how many times a single word can save a life.

It made the woman pause, just long enough for Silva to stride past me and position herself between us. I didn't know her name at the time. I knew nothing about her, not who or even what she was. She looked terran, at least. And she stood there facing off against the woman trying to kill me. Putting her own body in harm's way and standing as though completely at ease.

I noticed then my attacker wasn't alone, there were two men with her, similarly dressed in gold plate on red leather and a black uniform. Terrelan uniforms. One was grey as an autumn storm, wrinkled with age but still strong, still full of energy and life despite the years he wore. The other was a giant, as big as Hardt or Horralain, with a cruel set to his mouth. I have noticed you can often tell the ones who truly like to inflict pain; like Prig down in the Pit, they have a way of looking at people as though they are food. There is a lust in their eyes, an insatiable hunger they cannot hide. That giant was one of those, and he looked at me as though I were his next meal.

Exhaustion made my mind weary and much of the day had passed by in a blur. The pain from having my shoulder sliced open gave my mind a razor-sharp focus, but it didn't last long. Soon, the blood loss made my mind wander and my agony let me focus on little else. But I remember the sight of the stand-off. Silva standing in the light, alone and so bright she almost seemed to shine. My attacker, with sword still dripping my blood onto the stone streets, stood in the shadow and darkness seemed to pool around her. It's strange, but I could feel Ssserakis leaning towards her. I think, perhaps, the horror sensed something in that woman, a kindred spirit, maybe. The potential to cause fear in others, even greater than the potential it saw in me.

"We're Terrelan Royal Guard," said my attacker, her voice as sharp as the blade. "This matter doesn't concern you." Oh, I cannot quite describe how much I wanted that sword. It wasn't just because I had seen it before, and not just because it captivated me even then, though both were true. I wanted that sword because I wanted to take it from her and run the bitch through with it. It had already tasted my blood at her hands, it was only fair it taste her blood at my hands, too.

My vision was dimming, blurring. I knew the feeling all too well. Exhaustion, pain, and blood loss were causing me to lose consciousness. I tried to blink away the fuzziness and found the two women swaying. The whole street was swaying as though dancing to a mournful tune lost to my ears.

"You have spilt blood on the streets of Ro'shan," said Silva, her voice sounded like soft music lulling me to sleep. My eyes closed; my limbs went weak. "That makes your matter the concern of the Rand. And any concern of my mother's, is my concern as well."

I lost consciousness for the second time that day.

CHAPTER SIXTEEN

PAIN IS A RELATIVE CONCEPT. WE ALL FEEL IT;
terrans, pahht, garn, fish, abbans, snakes, even the Rand
and Djinn feel pain; trust me, I've been the cause of a lot of
it. But there are hundreds of different forms of pain, and
each individual experiences it differently. It is a concept,
an idea with as many different expressions as there are
stars in the sky. The Terrelan emperor believed himself to
be a connoisseur of pain and claimed terrans held eleven
different screams depending on the stimulus imposed
upon them. I have met tahren up in the high mountains of
Erekfend who are able to suppress pain by entering a trance,
not unlike the deepest of meditations. I tried to learn the
technique, but I do not possess the necessary focus. Besides,
those tahren appear to be joyless as well as painless. I
wonder if that is the point somehow, the need to experience
one in order to appreciate the other? All I can really say is of

all the expressions of pain I have experienced, being stabbed by a sword rates high on my list of the worst.

When I came to, my head was pounding, my mouth tasted like sun-baked slug, and I could hear voices, not raised but urgent. People were arguing and I'm certain I heard my own name in the mix. I opened my eyes to metal bars set horizontally into the bone of the building around us. Hardt knelt over me, wincing from his own pain but seeing to mine first. He was wrapping something around my left shoulder, causing it to flare with an agony that set my nails digging gouges from my palms.

Hardt smiled down at me, a weary smile of relief. "I was worried we'd lose you this time," he said.

Tamura crowded in beside Hardt, staring down at me. "When riding a horse, it is unwise to cross ice." His eyes flicked down to my belly and I caught his meaning.

Dead inside.

I reached down and cupped the bump of my belly, fear making me shake. I felt nothing under my touch, no movement, no sense of life. Nothing. Had I really gone through so much to lose the child on the cusp of safety? Had I so little to offer it, that I could not even give it life? I felt the call of the void so strongly, pity and grief stealing my breath, pushing me over the edge.

She lives. Ssserakis said. I felt something from the horror. Disgust. It had meant to pull fear from me, not pity, not grief.

"What?" I had no control over my emotions, a ship lost in storm, pulled this way and that, completely at the harsh mercy of the ocean.

"It doesn't look good," Hardt said and I realised he was talking about my shoulder. "That woman, Silva. She's in charge or something. Gave me some bandages, but nothing to clean the wound or close it. I can stop the bleeding maybe, but I can't tend the wound properly." He grit his teeth and tied the bandage about my shoulder a little more tightly than he intended. I gasped and he apologised.

A slow death. Bleeding out your life trapped in a cell. You might as well be back in the Pit. At least down there, there was darkness. I ignored the horror's words. Mostly because it was easier than facing the truth, but also because I was trying to concentrate on the argument happening beyond our little cell.

Tamura leaned against the bars and stared ahead, watching the argument taking place, a look of fierce concentration on his face. We were in a cell, a gaol, with a guardroom beyond our bars. In that guardroom, Silva argued with my attacker, while the other two Terrelans stood nearby, guarded by a pahht soldier.

"She's some sort of Terrelan elite guard," Hardt said. "Called herself Prena Neralis."

Tamura glanced back at me. "First blade of the Emperor." He giggled

Hardt grunted. "The other one called herself Silva. Claimed to be the daughter of the Rand." I wasn't even sure how such a thing was possible.

All the stories we are told as children say the Rand and Djinn are gods; all knowing, all powerful, and above the concerns of us mortal people. The stories are not strictly true, but they do hold kernels of truth, as most good stories do. Some say that between them, the Rand and Djinn created the world and everything in it, us included. Some say they just improved upon what was here already. The truth, I think, is that both the Rand and Djinn were far too busy trying to destroy each other to create much of anything. I've read extensively on the subject and I've even spoken to our so-called gods. What I do know is there used to be many more of them, hundreds or thousands even, and the more of them there were, the more powerful they were. But they argued and fought over the world and when gods fight, it's us mortals who suffer. There is a crater on the western side of Isha, in the lands that were once Orran, so wide it takes three days to walk from one side to the other. Nothing grows there except rock. It seems odd to say it that rock can grow, but I have long since learned that the truth often breaks the rules of what we consider possible. That crater is a blasted land full of jagged rocks, ancient ruins, and ghosts. And it is there because the Rand and Djinn went to war with each other. Nor is it the only such proof of their power. In Polasia, deep within the desert, there is an oasis where the waters run red and the trees grow purple. Above that oasis the sky is cracked open, and through the jagged scar above a great eye stares down on the world. And yet, in all the stories I had heard of the Rand, nothing had ever been said of them having children. Yet there Silva stood, radiant as the dawn and living proof of an impossibility.

I struggled to sit, gratefully accepting Hardt's help, and then relied on him further to stand. I was leaning heavily on my friend, but a man of Hardt's size rarely quibbles over the additional weight of someone as sleight as I. Together we stumbled towards the bars and looked upon the argument that would determine our fate. The guardroom beyond our cell was austere, just a table and a few chairs. At the doorway, silhouetted by light pouring in from outside, stood the two men from before, dressed in their black and red and gold. I touched my hand to the snuff pouch only to find it missing, and the jolt of fear *that* sent through me made Ssserakis surge to life, feeding on it. It might have been my imagination, but I am certain the room darkened for a moment. Maybe the sun just dipped behind a cloud. There was one other in the room, a single pahht leaning against the far wall, arms crossed and slitted eyes locked on the two men and their weapons. I have never been good at judging pahht facial expressions, perhaps there is simply too much fur for me to catch the subtleties, but it certainly seemed to be sneering at the men.

Tamura glanced at me and tapped at the bars. "Trapped once more. But look, stars." He pointed towards the single window, but all I could see through it was the washed-out blue of the sky. There were no stars to be seen during the day. Perhaps there was some deeper meaning to his words, but I think not. He just likes stars.

My attacker, Prena Neralis, looked past Silva and her dark eyes met mine. There were hard lines to her face, not from age, but from experience. I had never heard of a Terrelan elite guard before, but I knew the enchantments on her plate would protect her from most Sourceries, and the sword she carried was no mere blade. It was one of the ten weapons that fell from our twin moons the day they became locked in their destructive embrace. She turned her gaze back on Silva and the argument continued.

"She is a war criminal and a fugitive on Terrelan sovereignty," Prena said, her voice hard and spoken in the clipped accent of central Terrelan. I've always hated the way people from Juntorrow speak.

"We are not on Terrelan soil," said Silva. Her voice was strong, ringing with authority, yet she spoke softly.

"We are above it," Prena said sharply. "Your anchor

rests in Terrelan soil and as long as it does, as long as you and your city float above our lands, you will cede to our demands over matters of state security. Eskara Helsene is a fugitive wanted for crimes against the Terrelan empire."

Silva smiled apologetically. "Crimes committed during a war. I will wager both sides committed atrocities, and there are doubtless Sourcerers on your own side of the conflict who have done far worse and are still free."

Prena shook her head, her mane of dark hair rippling. "Crimes are for the losing side, Aspect. The winning side calls them heroic deeds."

It is a strange thing listening to people argue over your fate and knowing that you have no say in it whatsoever. Silva, a daughter of the Rand, had no reason to fight for my freedom other than obligation due to Tamura's request of asylum. She knew nothing of me, of the crimes I had committed in the name of the Orran bloodline. She knew nothing of the crimes I had committed since my incarceration and escape. She knew nothing of the ancient horror that rested inside of me, possessed me. Yet she fought for me all the same.

"I'm not here to quarrel over the semantics." All I could see of Silva was the back of her head, her golden hair pinned up with a long shard of bone, and her sleek yellow dress hugging her body, dusty from the morning's work. "I'm here to save a woman's life. You have provided no proof of any crimes other than your word."

"Is that not enough? I speak with the authority of the emperor himself." I felt my heart thump at those words. And there it was. I had come to the attention of the emperor himself. Not just the overseer, or some general or court official. The emperor himself had sent Prena Neralis, his elite guard, to hunt me down. What a heady feeling that was, I had come to the attention of my enemy.

And still you hide behind others.

My elation evaporated like mist before the sun. The horror was right. My enemy had sent his strongest to bring him my head, and here I was, trapped and protected by a woman I didn't even know. And I wasn't alone. I had dragged my friends into my fight. *My* fight. Not theirs. They wanted no part of it. They certainly didn't deserve the consequences of *my* actions.

I sagged against the bars of my cell as I summoned the will to tie my own noose. "My crimes are mine alone," I said. "These two had nothing to do with them. They did not fight in the war. There's no blood on their hands." I wonder if a greater lie has ever been told.

"Eska..." Hardt started to say something but I wouldn't hear it. I couldn't hear it. It would not have taken much to sway me from my course. But I didn't want his fate sealed along with my own.

Silva turned around in her chair and pinned me with a stare as green as the first blooms of spring. "You admit to your crimes?" she asked sadly.

"I am the weapon," I whispered the mantra aloud, using it to draw courage. I nodded once. "Hardt and Tamura have nothing to do with it."

"Tamura?" the pahht said, finally shifting her gaze from the two soldiers.

"Hello." Tamura waved at the pahht, completely at ease despite the weight of so many eyes. "Chased by fog so thick it covers yesterday."

"Still as mad as ever, I see." The pahht shook her head and turned dangerous eyes back on the two Terrelan guards.

Even injured and with my life hanging on a thread, I felt my curiosity piqued. I knew almost nothing about Tamura, and that was partly because he seemed to know so little about himself. If the pahht knew him, had met him before, perhaps she could shed some light on the mystery of his past.

There was a sad look in Silva's emerald eyes. I think she would have fought for me, argued for me. I think, if I had just kept my mouth shut, she would have managed to save me, but I am a fool, and I have never been able to keep my mouth shut. I have spent a lifetime fighting every battle regardless of who it might hurt along the way. I have made choices that have condemned friends to death, or worse. But there, in that cell, with not just my own life, but Hardt and Tamura's also, I felt the need to take responsibility and accept my fate. I believe Silva had something to do with my decision. I think I did not want to seem childish to her eyes. I did not understand why, but her opinion of me mattered. I wanted her to see me taking responsibility. And perhaps even more than that, I wanted to take control back. I was sick of being locked away. Even if it meant marching toward my own death, I would make the decision on my own terms.

"Do you accept the terms, Prena Neralis?" Silva asked, turning away from me.

Prena nodded. "Their crimes are each their own. But I would warn you, Aspect Silva, all three are criminals. They started a riot in their prison, and murdered a number of guards before making their escape. But I am only here for the Sourcerer, Eskara Helsene. The others will find their own justice in time."

Silva looked over at the pahht. "Any objections, Coby?"

The pahht snorted, her whiskers twitching. "I'd have

let them kill each other on the streets. The tahren would have
mopped up the blood, and we wouldn't have to sit through
this tedium." She spoke the terran tongue surprisingly well,
all things considered, though her accent was oddly lilting to
my ears.

Silva shook her head. "We are responsible for keeping
the peace on the streets."

The pahht let out a growl and pushed away from
the wall, striding towards the doorway. "So. Dull." The
two Terrelan men stood fast, blocking the door. They both
towered over the shorter pahht, but when she pushed
between them, both men stumbled as though Hardt had ran
at them full sprint. Coby has always been far stronger than
she appears, no matter which skin she is wearing at the time.

Silva waited until the two men had recovered before
offering them a smile and then turning it on Prena. "I must
apologise for my sister."

Hardt laid a hand on my shoulder, gently turning
me around. It hurt. He knew it hurt. He did it on purpose,
nothing like pain to get your attention. "Not like this, Eska."

I shook my head at him. "It's already done." My
voice quavered. I will admit, the implications were starting
to dawn on me. I suddenly realised I had just sacrificed my
life for theirs. Prena had meant to kill me earlier, there was
no doubt about that. Only tripping over my own feet had
saved me. She was not under orders to bring me back. As
the last Orran Sourcerer left alive, she was under orders to
finish it once and for all. To see me dead and put an end
to any rebellion before it started. So much for Terrelan law
forbidding capital punishment. Had I really just sacrificed
my own life?

Don't forget the little life inside. It dawned on me at the same time Ssserakis' mocking voice sounded in my head. My child! If I died, so did my child.

"Are you ready?" Silva was at the bars, small key in hand, sadness and understanding in her eyes.

Hardt has never been one to let me go. Not when I push him away, nor when I try to sneak away. He has always followed me into the danger and done everything within his power to drag me back out of it, even against my will. "She's pregnant," he growled in a panicked voice. I hated him for saying that. And loved him also.

It was the first time anyone had mentioned it. Until that moment, locked in a cell and awaiting my execution, we had all just pretended it wasn't there. I wanted to hit Hardt for saying it. Strange, that I wanted to hurt him for speaking up. It wasn't for finally broaching the subject, but for taking so damned long to work up the courage and waiting until I was facing the sword to say anything.

Silva glanced down at my body, and then back up, a smile lighting her face. Silva's smile has always had an effect on me. Strangely enough, it's the same effect as Ssserakis. That smile puts a fear in me like no other and dims the light around me until she is all I can see. When she turned back to Prena, I found I could breathe again. I turned to Hardt and stared at him for a moment, an apology frozen on my lips. I'm not even sure why I felt the need to apologise to him. Maybe because I hadn't had the courage to talk to him about it. Because it wasn't just my child. It was Isen's too.

"Asylum is granted," Silva said, spreading her hands as though the matter were no longer up to her.

And now you hide behind your unborn child. Still too weak to face your enemies.

The big guard at the doorway bristled, his greedy

eyes flashing hatred. The older of the two just shook his head and laughed. But it was Prena whose reaction interested me. She took a deep breath and stood, both hands gripping the edge of the table hard.

"You made an enemy this day, Aspect." Her eyes were dark as onyx and just as hard, but she made no move to object further.

Silva was a diplomat first and foremost, but she never shied away from wielding her mother's power like a hammer when she wanted something. "I imagine Terrelan will fare worse from that proclamation than Ro'shan. But making enemies was not my intent. Criminal or not, she is with child, and I cannot in good conscience allow that child to suffer for her parent's crime. I grant asylum until the child is born. After that, you may return and make your case again."

"We both know she will have fled by then. You leave me no choice but to chase your city around the world, waiting for my moment."

Again, Silva spread her hands. She left the cell door locked and crossed to the doorway, ushering the other two Terrelans out into the street beyond. The woman with the sword lingered, eyes locked on me once more. She approached the bars, and I realised, for the first time, just how much taller she was than I. Prena Neralis, First Blade of the Terrelan Empire, Captain of the Ten, wielder of the sword Neverthere. I name her in full to impress upon you that I was not chased by just anybody. The Terrelan emperor had committed his finest warrior to hunting me down, and it seemed she would not stop until that task was complete.

As she came closer, I saw her tense, the training Hardt had given me taught me the signs of a strike before it comes. Unfortunately, I was far too weary to get out of the way. Prena drew Neverthere into a wide arc and the blade passed through the bars as though they weren't there. That is the magic of the sword, the ability pass through metal and strike at the flesh beneath. Tamura saved me, pulling me backwards just out of range of the attack. I crumbled to the floor of the cell, cringing at the pain in my shoulder as a grim reminder of what I had so narrowly avoided.

Tamura waved his hand in the air. "Snow on a warm day. Fleeting." He smiled as he met Prena's eyes. "Your moment has passed."

Then Silva was there, an eyebrow raised at the bared steel. "This way please." There was an edge in her voice, something hard and sharp underneath her pleasant tone. "My sister, Coby, will see you safely back down to the ground. It's quite a height and I'd hate for a foreign dignitary such as yourself to accidentally fall."

Prena gave me one last look and nodded. "Until next time, Eskara Helsene."

I should note Silva did not unlock the cell door before she left. She might well have saved us from death at the hands of the Terrelans, but we were still stowaways and criminals. She was gone for some time, seeing Prena and her lieutenants back to Ro'shan's docks, and I was still arguing with Hardt when she finally returned.

I had questions. So many questions. First and foremost, was *where was Imiko* and *what had happened to my bloody Kinemancy Source*. I had a suspicion both questions had just one answer, but they weren't questions for Silva. As soon as she walked back through the door to our little gaol, the first question burst out as though I couldn't hold my tongue. It might have seemed rude to her, childish and impulsive, but the truth was, I wanted to stop arguing with Hardt, and Silva provided just the excuse I needed.

"Why?" I asked. Questions are an odd thing when we allow them to stew inside for a while. We ask them in our heads over and over and dream of the answers. We ask them so many times that when finally, we get to ask the target of that question, we sometimes forget they haven't been present for the previous hundreds times the question has been asked.

Tamura giggled. He was sitting on the floor with his back against the wall. I thought him sleeping until that moment. "Ask the sun why it shines, the river why it flows, the bee why it makes honey. No one can fight their nature." He opened his eyes and set them on Silva. "I wonder what aspect that is?"

"At least some of that made sense." Hardt was sulking. He wasn't pleased I had tried to sacrifice my life for his. I thought him quite selfish at the time, but that was my own churlishness. I was the selfish one. I've always been the selfish one.

"Why save me?" I asked. "Why save us? Why do anything?"

To control you. You belong to her now.

Silva frowned, just a slight wrinkle of her brows, and I felt so guilty. I couldn't explain that guilt at the time and I'm not sure I want to explain it now. "You believe it would have been easier to do nothing? Four lives held in the balance and all I had to do to save them was spend a few hours of my life arguing for their worth. I have a great many hours of my life to spare, so in truth, I feel it cost me nothing. I saved you because it was the right thing to do, and because I don't

think I could have lived with the guilt if I had stood by and
done nothing. Is that so alien a concept?"

It was. I didn't want to admit it, but it was. I had been
brought up in the Orran Academy of Magic, and trained
to be a weapon. Sourcerers intended for the army were not
meant to think of the lives we were taking, we were meant
to kill with impunity. It was one of the things Josef always
had trouble with, separating his conscience from the lives he
had taken. Time down in the Pit did nothing to teach me the
value of life. Down there, it was cheap. There were always
more scabs to take the place of those who had died. But
there in that cell, confronted by Silva's earnest declaration, I
realised myself for what I was: a monster who cared little for
the lives of others. I couldn't help but consider if I was truly
any different from those I fought against.

You are. You're worse. I winced at the horror's
accusation but bit my tongue to stop from arguing.

I think my conflict showed both in my silence, and the
way I sank back into the cell, collapsing against the far wall.
Hardt, came to my side quickly, our argument forgotten. I
wondered if this was how he felt all the time, the weight of
the dead a damning noose around his neck, dragging him
down with its weight. I saw the huntsman from the Forest
of Ten, standing in the darkened corner of the gaol, his
ribs buckled in and blood leaking from his lips. Ssserakis
compounding the guilt I felt. I wanted to disappear. To stop
feeling. To stop being.

"I need to clean and close her wound." There is little
more reassuring and comforting to me than the sound of
Hardt's voice. Even when I want to claw his eyes out.

I glanced down at my shoulder to the hasty
bandaging stained a deep crimson. Can guilt cause a person

to bleed? Can it open wounds and fester? Or does it only take root inside, corrupting our minds and hearts? I was lightheaded from exhaustion and blood loss, and my mind wandered to strange places.

Silva opened the door and between her and Tamura they carried me to the table and laid me upon it. I was reeling and dizzy, and I think I may have pawed at Silva's yellow dress, guiltily trying to wipe away the grime I left on it. I made the staining worse, but she didn't complain. Before long I had a belly full of alcohol to numb the pain, and Hardt was stitching the wound closed. I was quite drunk by the time he finished and was satisfied enough to sit me on one of the chairs. I threw up on his boots, and spent some time crying. It shames me that they all saw me in that state. I kept apologising to everyone. Odd that apologies come so easy to me when drunk but must be ripped from me while sober. We slept in the gaol that first night in Ro'shan. They put me back in the cell, in the single little cot, and that's the last thing I remember.

CHAPTER SEVENTEEN

WHEN I AWOKE THE NEXT DAY, I WAS FEELING much better. Well, apart from the incessant headache and the dull throbbing in my shoulder that seemed to run bone deep. I smelled fresh baked bread and bacon, and that quickly brought me around despite the grogginess. Tamura had slept on the floor beside me and Hardt at the table, a chair pushed back against the wall. Silva appeared with the sunrise and she brought enough food with her to feed twice our number. We demolished it all in moments.

Silva introduced herself formally, both as a city official, and as daughter of the Rand. I once asked her what it was like being the daughter of a god, she asked me what it was like being the daughter of basket weaver. I didn't bother to introduce myself; she already knew who I was and had a long list of my crimes. After we had eaten and Hardt had checked on my latest wound, Silva set about telling us the rules of Ro'shan. We were safe there, at least until my child was born, but asylum did not mean a free ride on the flying city. We needed somewhere to live, and we needed to eat, and those were things that cost money. Ro'shan traded for most of the things the city needed so money was the true lifeblood up there. If we wanted to stay, we needed to earn our place. I had just one idea of how we could do that there and then.

"How much is a Source worth?" I asked. My hand brushed against my belt, searching for the snuff pouch that was missing. It had not escaped my notice that Imiko had yet to reappear.

She's long gone, and all your power went with her. My horror was part right at least. Imiko had taken my Source again, and I was furious. I wanted to tear the city apart looking for her, and when I caught her I would teach her to fear me!

"A great deal," Silva leaned back in her chair. She had a small book in her hand, opened to a fresh page. That book was never far from her person and contained a list of all the favours she had collected, the names of all those who owed her, and how much. Silva liked to collect favours, almost as much as she liked to call them in. "My mother will offer a fair price, dependant on the nature and size. You might be able to get more from one of the less reputable dealers within the city, but then you also might be robbed and find yourself with nothing. Despite fervent attempts, Coby has found it quite impossible to stamp out crime in Ro'shan."

"Tamura, show her your Source." The crazy old man startled and for a moment I thought he might refuse. Instead he let out a sigh and raised both hands in front of him, holding them out and turning them over, showing us they were empty. Then he raised one hand to his mouth and patted his stomach with the other. He coughed and then widened his eyes in mock surprise, opening his hand to show a small crystal, round and no larger than a marble. I couldn't figure out how he managed the trick. I had seen sleight of hand before, but Tamura wore no sleeves.

"A Chronomancy Source. Those are quite rare." Silva said with an appreciative nod.

"Identification from sight alone." Tamura paced towards Silva and dropped the Source on the table in front of her. Then he bent at the waist and stared at her hard. "I see you." He grinned and straightened before walking back into the cell and collapsing on the cot.

"Don't mind him," Hardt grumbled. "He's crazier than a bucket of spiders."

They set about haggling, Hardt and Silva, and I turned my attention elsewhere. I went to the doorway and looked out upon Ro'shan. We were close to the palace and I could see the great arches intersecting high above. It was dizzying looking up at it and humbling too. I realised how small we must look to those so high above, and how small we would appear to those on the ground so far below. It's all a matter of perspective, really. Eventually a price was agreed upon and I'm told it was quite a sum. The truth is, I've never had much of a head for figures and money has always seemed a means to an end and nothing more. I had no need of it at the Orran academy, and down in the Pit we traded and gambled for everything we needed. I had honestly never even really thought about money and how much we might need it before my time in Ro'shan.

Silva led us from the gaol when all was agreed upon, and Hardt proudly admitted part of the price of the Source

had been a house within the city. We were now residents of
Ro'shan, as well as refugees fleeing Terrelan for our lives. I
paced down the street behind them, wincing at the pain of
every step and already wishing I could spend another day
in bed. I hurt everywhere. Much of the grandeur of Ro'shan
had rubbed off already, but then being stabbed in the streets
will do that to you.

One moment the four of us were walking down a
street, surrounded by people we didn't know, the next Imiko
was beside me as though she hadn't vanished earlier, leaving
us to our fate. I was angry. I had given it some thought,
and I couldn't blame her for abandoning us. Stealing my
Source for a second time is another matter entirely. It would
have been wiser to put aside my fury and spend some time
pondering what brought her back to us. At first glance, it
seemed that she needed to get away from Yun, that her
exploits were too well known. The truth was far worse.
Imiko was running and we were her protection as much as
her escape.

There were some charged insults exchanged in that
street. I think we drew a few stares from those nearby. Two
terrans fighting in the middle of the road was apparently
quite the spectacle to the citizens of Ro'shan. Eventually
Hardt convinced us to stop, putting himself between us and
ushering us on. I found it so easy to forget back in those days
how young Imiko was. Or maybe it was just that I still saw
myself as close to her age, but Chronomancy had robbed
those years from me.

Silva said nothing of the little thief's appearance, and
we continued on. The house she took us to wasn't large,
but it was big enough for our purposes, and Hardt assured
me it was what we could afford. Silva left us there with

promises she would return the next day. I was glad of that, I still had questions I needed answered. No sooner was the door locked and the beds made, before I collapsed into mine and slept. It was not the dreamless sleep I desired. Perhaps because I found myself feeling safe for the first time in so long, surrounded by sturdy walls and sturdier friends, granted asylum in a city I had dreamed of visiting all my life. Ssserakis dragged my unconscious mind to the Other World and showed me a forest where the trees stalked those who entered, crawling across the ground like great wooden spiders. It was a place of nightmare, existing in a world of nightmares. Those trees did not appear in any Encyclopaedia Otheria before I added them; they don't respond to the ethereal presence of Sourcerers, so most just considered them normal trees. I fixed that. Thanks to Ssserakis, I discovered over thirty new types of monster and horror residing in the Other World. I call those trees Creakers on account of the sound they make as they move. I would advise against summoning one though, they are quite painful to bring across and it takes many days and many ales to get the taste of rotten wood out of the mouth.

Silva came calling the next day as the sun was just peeking over the horizon. I was going through my morning stretches with Hardt, as much of them as I could with my injuries. I think it was a token gesture on both our parts, keeping up the tradition though neither of us were in any fit state. She brought with her a credit note that turned us from the poorest of people into poorly dressed rich folk. I had questions for Silva, so many questions, yet she answered none of them and left me burning to know more. Who was she, exactly? Was she a true daughter of the Rand or just some orphan taken in? How is it she was clearly terran yet

called a pahht her sister? Why did Prena Neralis call her by
the title Aspect? What did I have to do to secure myself an
audience with the Rand? I will admit I was quite excited
when I asked that last one; it's not every day you get to meet
a god.

I have admitted I have never been very good with
money, then or now. Spending it has always seemed so easy
and saving it so pointless. It's not exactly a good trait for
a queen which might explain the destitution of my reign.
Hardt claimed responsibility for our funds and I certainly
didn't try to stop him. Our other choices were a crazed old
man who could barely remember his own name, or a young
girl who had already stolen from me twice. Some decisions
truly do make themselves.

We barely had time to count our good fortune
when the whole city started to shake. I rushed outside to
find no one looking in the least bit concerned. At least I
don't think anyone was. My trouble understanding pahht
facial expressions is one thing, but tahren are even more
inscrutable; eyes are often the most expressive part of a
person and they have none.

It took some coaxing from the locals to discover that
the shaking was normal when the anchor was winding back
up. It went on for some time, maybe half the day, and only
my little group seemed to care. I trekked to the western edge
of Ro'shan, where the land stops and there is nothing but
a long drop. I got as close as I dared to that edge, though
the shaking seemed more pronounced there so I played it
somewhat safer than I am known for. Hardt and Tamura
followed me and we watched Terrelan disappear over the
horizon. Ro'shan does not move particularly quickly and we
were there most of the day, until the land was just a line in

the distance and all we could see below was water.

It is strange to say it, but it felt like running away, like I was fleeing from my enemies, from those I had sworn to kill. And from those I had sworn to avenge. I think I hated myself a little. I thought myself a coward, running and hiding under the skirts of the Rand where the Terrelans couldn't get to me. My desire for vengeance only grew along with my anger at my own cowardice.

"I'm coming back," I spat the words. I wasn't talking to Hardt or Tamura or even Ssserakis. I wasn't even talking to Terrelan as it vanished beyond the horizon. I said it to myself. There is a power in spoken words; saying something aloud makes it more real somehow, releasing a thought to the world and claiming it as your own. By saying those words aloud, I made them a promise, an oath I would keep no matter the cost. I was coming back!

Hardt placed a big hand on my shoulder, the uninjured one this time, and nodded. "One day."

Tamura let out a content sigh as he laid on the ground and stared up at the sky. "All of life is a circle. Round and round and round and round and…"

Neither of them understood. It wasn't their fault; I left half of the promise unsaid. Ssserakis heard it though; the ancient horror was in my soul and in my head, it knew my thoughts as well as I did, maybe even better.

The fear we will cause will be a fitting meal, and our power will grow. I smiled at the thought. *But don't forget your promise. You* will *send me home.*

I didn't just intend to return to Terrelan. I intended to destroy it. To burn the empire to the ground and see the emperor suffer just as I had. I didn't care what it cost me or any others. It was a matter of vengeance, of justice, of a

burning need to do unto others as was done to me. I would
see Terrelan in ashes and blood, regardless of how many
lives it would cost. For my loyalty to the Orran Empire
for all it had given me. For justice for the hurts committed
against me and my friends. For the loss of the one person
who had ever understood me. I was the weapon, and even
without a wielder I would cut out the heart of the Terrelan
Empire.

I think I realised then that I had been running ever
since the fall of Orran. Even locked down in the Pit I was
running away; from myself, from Josef, from what the
Terrelans wanted to make me into. I was running away
again, but one day I would stop running and when I did, my
enemies would finally learn to fear me.

CHAPTER EIGHTEEN

JOSEF

I realise the true punishment Deko dealt me when he put me in charge of spooning out the gruel. The shiny eyed mud fucker is more devious than I ever gave him credit for. I think the overseer gave him orders to keep me alive. And I think that's why he hates me. He hates me being down there, one of the scabs, but protected.

The scabs are never happy with their portions, and they don't blame Deko. That would be far too dangerous. They blame whoever is dishing out the gruel. That's where the punishment comes in. The hatred from the other scabs. Dishing out the gruel turns you into a pariah, and I still have the bruises to prove it.

But it's over now. Deko and the scabs and the gruel and the overseer. It's all behind me. I'm out. I'm free!

I HATE the overseer! I HATE the overseer! I HATE the overseer! I HATE the overseer! I HATE the overseer!

It feels so good to write that, to admit it and not scribble it out for fear he might see. I may have no voice, but I still have words and I use them to admit that I hate the overseer. I hate Deko. I hate the Pit. I hate everyone in it. And I hate Eska. I won't scratch it out. I won't deny it. I won't pretend she didn't betray me.

Death returned to the Pit. She came back for me. No one else. No one else down there was important enough. Because no one else knows Eska. Even my escape is all due to her.

It was feeding time down there. Hundreds of scabs with their bowls raised, hungry eyes hating me for the portions that I had no choice but to dish out. From up there they all look so worthless. Scabs is a good name for them. It suits them. Something to be peeled off and discarded. Something disgusting hiding a festering wound. But today, Death came. She rode down the lift alone, the other soldiers nowhere to be seen. I spotted her though, striding towards the Trough as though she weren't surrounded by thieves and murderers and worse. They moved out of her way like ice retreats from a flame. It was so satisfying to see Deko watching from the Hill, just watching and nothing else. He's scared of her. Scared of real power. He should be.

She looked at me and said my name. My full name. Josef Yenhelm. It had been so long since I heard it, I almost didn't respond. I had almost forgotten what my name sounds like. All I could do was nod. I wish I had my voice still. I wish I could speak. She took me with her when she left, ordered me to follow. I did. I left the Trough and the scabs and the Hill and Deko all behind me. We rode the lift all the way up and the soldiers didn't stop us. They stepped aside, nodded to Death as she walked past and said not a word. I wonder who she is to inspire such fear and respect among others.

I shied away from the exit. I slowed and dragged my feet to a stop. It wasn't the thought of freedom after so long that stopped me. It was the light. The Pit opens out into exactly that, a tunnel of stone that leads to a pit dug into the earth, wooden stairs sticking out of the sides, and a giant crane above. Those last few steps of the tunnel were so bright, I found myself squinting against the light, barely able to see anything. It scared me. Death noticed I had stopped. She turned to me and beckoned. She stood in the light, sun glinting off her golden plate. I stood in the dark, shrouded in the shadow of the Pit, and she beckoned me towards her. I felt a pull I couldn't resist. My feet moved of their own accord. And then she took my hand. I expected Death to have a hand as cold as ice, clammy, maybe. But it wasn't. Her hand was warm, her skin tough with callous, and her grip strong. She didn't pull me out of the Pit but led me out. And I went willingly.

I write this entry from a tavern. I'm clean, bathed, shaved, and dressed in new clothes. It's not the military uniform the overseer made me wear when he sent me after Eska, but it's a lot better than the rags of a Pit scab. Sturdy riding leathers with a symbol on the breast. Death's symbol. Lursa and Lokar crashing into each other, and ten weapons falling from the sky. I don't know if this makes me her servant or prisoner. I don't think I care. I have never been so grateful for anyone before.

I know Death is not her name, but I know whose death she seeks, and I mean to help her. I will do anything to remain free.

CHAPTER NINETEEN

WE SPENT MONEY WITH WILD ABANDON. We bought ourselves new clothes, no longer dressing in threadbare rags or garments stolen from the corpses of people I had killed. Honestly, it had been so long since I had been clean and dressed in fresh clothing, I think I had forgotten what I looked like under it all. I stared at myself in a mirror and barely recognized the woman staring back at me. I was older than I remembered, my skin weathered. The scar Prig gave me stood out on my left cheek, proud and ugly. I hate that scar and yet I wear it with pride. It is a constant reminder of how helpless I felt and that I escaped the Pit. I have been told I could cover it up with powder and certain oils, and I would be lying if I said I haven't considered it. But the truth is, I never will. Scars are proof of a life lived, of hardships that changed us yet didn't kill us. I wear mine with pride and I have many of them.

I suffered through having my hair cut so it was less wild and unruly. The barber, a pahht man who wielded his scissors with more skill than I ever have a sword, cut it short and told me it would need to grow back in. He also left me with strict orders to wash it more regularly than never. I bought a dress and I was quite happy about that. I have always liked wearing dresses though I have rarely found opportunity to do so in my life. They have always given me a sense of freedom, and I will admit to some vanity; I can look quite pretty in a dress. I bought two dresses up on Ro'shan. The first was made of blue silk the same colour as my eyes. It was beautiful, but it didn't fit me. It has never fitted me. I think I bought it for a woman I would never be. The second dress I purchased was more drab, designed for everyday use and for constant adjustments to a woman of increasing size. And I felt like I was increasing in size every single day.

I was soon far beyond the point of being able to hide my pregnancy and I quickly found it changed the way people dealt with me. Some would treat me like a fragile flower whilst others would keep their distance as though I were a wild animal, likely to bite. I didn't mind it from the people I didn't know, the citizens of Ro'shan, but my friends also started treating me differently.

Hardt refused to keep training me, and right when I felt I was starting to make progress. I was furious with him for that. I watched him chew over a question for nearly two months before he finally worked up the courage to ask me if it was Isen who put the child in my belly. He already knew the answer, but he wanted to hear me say it. I think it made Hardt happy, knowing that Isen had left something of himself behind, other than bad memories. After that, he tried to do everything for me, as though I were some kind of invalid. More than once, I considered swallowing my Kinemancy Source just so I could push the man away, but I wouldn't risk what the magic might do to my child. Of course, I still had Ssserakis inside, coiled around my mind and soul, and that put enough fear in me to keep the horror well fed. I could only hope it was not inflicting that same fear on my child. It is a mother's job to protect and nurture the children they carry, and I could not even do that.

Tamura started to act even stranger around me, though he was not nearly as infuriating as Hardt. I have discovered that pregnancy affects women in different ways, and for me it makes me sleepy during odd hours of the day. I am not usually one for napping, but while carrying my first child I honestly found it hard to stay awake at times. A few times I woke to find Tamura whispering a story to my swollen belly. I will admit, the first time it happened I was confused and angry, and it took some time for me to calm down. Despite my anger, Tamura just laughed and walked away, promising my unborn child he would finish the story later. Once I calmed down, I realised there was no real harm in it. Tamura is a crazy old man who can barely remember yesterday, but sometimes it seems he knows every story ever told and he tells them well; without having to resort to his usual puzzles and codes. The next two times I caught him whispering his stories to my belly, I let him, feigning sleep so I could listen in as well.

The months wore on and Ro'shan continued its migration across the world. I saw so much in that time, but always from afar. None of us dared leave the flying city for fear Prena was still chasing us. I started to think of it as my home, perhaps even more of a home than any other I've ever had. I continued my training with Tamura as much as I was able, but I soon discovered that pregnancy does not well lend itself to balance and I have never seen a martial art that does not require balance. I also found it quite difficult to practice patience when I needed to piss every few minutes. You may notice that I do not look upon pregnancy kindly. There is a reason for that.

Our money supplies began to dwindle at which point Hardt had to admit he, too, was not very good with money. We had spent a lot on clothes and exotic foods, and we were quite free with our spending. Before long we had but two choices; either we sold my Kinemancy Source, or we found work. So, we found work. Hardt did what men of Hardt's size often do; he lifted things, carried things, occasionally chopped things. I think the only thing Hardt truly refused to do back then was hurt things. He also refused to dig and that was not something any of us could blame him for. Tamura found work in the taverns; he might not be able to sing, but his storytelling brought in many a coin and he returned each day on the sour side of sober. Imiko… Well, Imiko never told me what she did, but thieves will ever be thieves and there is plenty of crime to be about even up on Ro'shan. I have never met a city that didn't support a healthy population of rogues.

That just left myself and I soon came to terms with the fact that I simply didn't have much in the way of marketable skills. I was a Sourcerer, and until the child was out of me, I couldn't use my magic. Even if I could, I'm not sure how much use I would have been. Kinemancy can be used to move things, much the same as Hardt's muscle, but it requires precision and that is simply something I didn't have. I'd be more likely to dash a crate and its contents

into a hundred pieces than get it to where it needed to be.
I suppose I should count myself lucky there was a basket
weaver on the same street as our house. It turns out some
skills get rusty, but you never quite forget them. I found it
somewhat ironic that in the latter stages of my pregnancy I
found myself weaving baskets just like my mother. It gave
me a small taste of what my life could have been if I were
not a Sourcerer. If the Orran recruiters hadn't come for me. It
was not entirely unpleasant, but it also wasn't me. Every day
stuck there, weaving baskets, was one day I wasn't moving
towards my goals. I had too much drive and anger to sit and
do nothing with my life.

Silva visited more and more often. At first it was
under the pretence of checking on us; we were, after all,
some of the only terran citizens of Ro'shan and that put us
as something of an oddity. We were also the only refugees on
the run from Terrelan for war crimes. She said she needed to
make certain we were fitting in and that we weren't causing
any trouble. She never seemed to care too much about how
Tamura, Hardt, or Imiko were *fitting in*. We became friends,
and I will admit I had never had a friend like her before.

Many times, I would walk down the streets of
Ro'shan beside Silva. I could talk to her, I found, about
almost anything. In some ways I think she filled the hole in
my life left by Josef, but there was always tension between
us. I knew from the very start Silva was lying to me. She
refused to answer my questions about her mother. I think
it was my curiosity that drew me to her early on. I wanted
to know what she was, how a child of a Rand could be so
terran. But Silva always changed the subject and I quickly
found we were talking about other things without even
realising it. She made me talk about myself, the things I

had seen and done. More than once I ended up crying in
front of Silva and she always knew what to say to comfort
me. I blamed those tears on the pregnancy, it can affect a
woman's emotions. But that was lie. They were tears of
sorrow and they needed to be shed. I see that now. Without
even realising it, she coaxed me into dealing with my grief,
and though the betrayals Josef and I visited upon each other
still stung, I soon discovered I could remember my friend
without either running away or bursting into tears. And that
led me to realise just how much I missed him. But he was
gone. Dead. And my last words to him were spoken in anger.

It was hard to fathom how everyone in Ro'shan
seemed to know Silva. We couldn't walk down a street, nor
sit in a tavern without people greeting her and with real
kindness, often asking her for advice. I think in many ways
we were complete opposites. Everyone knew her and loved
her; no one knew me and those that did feared me, or at least
they feared what I might do. Maybe that was what drew
us together and made us friends. I have heard it said that
neither light nor darkness can exist without the other.

I never told Silva about Ssserakis. Just like with Hardt
and Tamura, I feared what she might think of me if she knew
what I harboured inside. She knew, though. Silva knew
from the very start. Saw it in me even back in that cell. That
was her power, her gift. She saw it in me and she didn't shy
away.

Ssserakis grew more sullen with each passing day, at
the same time as growing more outspoken. It's strange to
think a disembodied presence in my mind could feel sullen,
but it did. I think it was the lack of progress that made
the horror so. I had promised to send it back to the Other
World and there I was, putting down roots in Ro'shan and

spending my days weaving baskets and complaining about the child growing inside of me.

Each night I dreamed of things chasing me. Sometimes it was Terrelans, sometimes creatures from the Other World. Once I was even being chased by myself; an angrier version of me wanting to catch and displace me. I woke screaming so many times Hardt stopped checking on me. I think I made life in our little house quite unpleasant for the others.

Routine is the death of progress and I had fallen into quite the routine. I hated myself for it. I suppose I have my daughter to both blame for that routine, and thank for finally shifting me out of it. Believe me, there is nothing quite like giving birth to shake up the status quo.

CHAPTER TWENTY

WHAT IS THERE TO SAY ABOUT GIVING BIRTH that hasn't already been said? It is loud, messy, and fucking painful. I would not recommend it. By all accounts, the garn have a much easier time of it, though I hear anyone within line of sight is likely to end up covered in some sort of secretion. At least I can say this: I gave birth to my first daughter with no complications… Unless you count Hardt fainting at the sight.

It took a while, though I expected that. My midwife, Coechee, a pahht woman with fur the colour of almonds striped with fire, coaxed me through the worst of it with promises of it being almost over. I have since discovered that it is standard practice to lie to women giving birth. It was exhausting, far more so than my second time. I wonder if that was because my second daughter, Sirileth, was in such a hurry to come out, to inflict her presence upon the world. It is with no hesitation that I call my second daughter a monster and half the world stands with me in that judgement. And yet I love her. With everything I have, and despite all that she has done, I love her. But we're not at that part of my tale yet.

I was utterly exhausted by that labour. It was that type of exhaustion that can push a person out of themselves and into nothingness, but I held on. Lying there, covered in sweat and barely remembering to draw breath. I could see the midwife and Tamura crowded around a small table. My daughter didn't scream. She didn't make a single sound. Despite the exhaustion, I felt a cold fear crawl inside, wrapping itself around my heart.

It's dead. Ssserakis' thoughts mirrored my own. *Nothing comes from you but death.*

"Shut up!" The words issued from me as a squeak. I couldn't face the possibility the horror's whispers were true, that I had so little to give my child. Nothing to give, not even life. A lump formed in my throat so tight I couldn't speak, couldn't breathe. I think I might have started crying, but it was hard to tell, my face was already slick with sweat and tears. I reached out a weary hand towards them, crowded around the little table, around my child, my daughter. At the time I didn't even know why I cared. I had never really considered the child as anything other than a nuisance, slowing me down and feeding off me, reminding me of the mistake I made with Isen. It was a parasite I was glad to be rid of. Or so I told myself. Hardening myself against the possibility that she would be something less than terran, changed by my use of Sources and my connection to the Other World. But none of that mattered anymore. Now she was here all I wanted to do was hold her. I wanted to see her face, this life I had created, protected, carried, and brought into the world.

When the midwife looked back at me, I felt my heart stop. I find it impossible to read pahht facial expressions, I didn't know what that look meant. Then Tamura turned a wild grin my way. It was as though my body had been frozen in time and suddenly it all started again. The pain and exhaustion, the anticipation, the fear and the relief... It all came flooding back in a wave and I felt myself swept out to sea.

I was crying again by the time my daughter was placed in my arms, tears of joy and released tension all in one. She had Isen's colouring and my eyes, two bright blues staring up at me from a dark face. So beautiful. So perfect.

Some women say they didn't know what love was until they had a child. I do not agree, but I will admit, I didn't understand what I would feel until I saw my daughter for the first time. My resolve cracked. My excuses felt like fragile things, weakening with every little movement the child made. A little piece of me and Isen merged together and forged into something new, unique. Something the world had never seen before, a being with infinite possibility.

Hardt stood from the chair he had found, walking over to my bed. He looked ill, but then passing out will do that to a person, and I'm fairly certain he threw up also. My bed sheets were a mess, twisted up around my legs and stained with blood, and I know full well I didn't look much better. But I didn't care right then. I turned my daughter around to face Hardt and she looked up at her uncle. I'm told children can't really see that early in their life, but Hardt would make an impressive blur, especially to a child. I handed her to Hardt then and it took a lot of willpower to do so. All I wanted to do was hold her and never let go. She was mine, and I loved her with a fierceness that went beyond words or reason.

"She's beautiful," Hardt said, his voice choked. "What's her name?"

I smiled, despite the exhaustion. "Kento. After my mother." I don't remember my mother very well, but she had brought me into the world and raised me for six years. The least I could do was carry on her name. Hardt must have said the name a dozen times as he held her. I wonder if, even then, he knew the decision I had made. I wonder if he held my daughter so long because he was trying to etch her little face into his memory.

We are all born into this world innocent. Free of greed, or anger, or grief. I wasn't free; I was drowning. I didn't want to pass that onto my daughter. I am the weapon. I broke everything I touched, corrupted it. Infected it with my rage and my sorrow. Ssserakis whispered in my ear, the truth I already knew. The longer the child stayed with me the more likely I would be to destroy the life I had created.

The midwife checked over both myself and Kento and then set about instructing me on feeding the child. Eventually she left and I braved my feet. Despite the wobble in my legs I felt lighter than I had in months. I tired quickly and retreated to a nearby chair. I think I fell asleep with Kento cradled in my arms. A perfect memory of a perfect little creature.

CHAPTER TWENTY ONE

I LIKEN A NEW-BORN TO A CHUBBY LITTLE face connected to an arse, as everything they do concerns one or the other. Despite this, there is nothing that can bring joy to a household quite like a child. No bard's song has ever been quite so beautiful as a baby's laugh, and no monster's cry has ever been as horrifying as a baby's howl.

Of the next three days I remember little save for feeding Kento, cleaning her, rocking her to sleep, and being woken by her shrill cries, demanding and desperate all at once. You might think I'd resent her for it, for taking over my life so completely in so short a time. I'd be lying if I said I didn't feel some measure of frustration, but the truth is I relished every moment spent with my daughter. Even when she woke me up, just minutes after I finally dropped off to sleep, I ached to see her face again. There is a strange addiction there, to have someone so completely dependent

upon you that they cannot live without you. I'll wager the
shine wears off after a while, though.

Hardt was good with the child and Kento seemed to
like him, far more than she did Tamura, for a certainty. She
cried whenever the crazy old man went near her. I think
that hurt his feelings somewhat, though he'd never admit
it. Imiko was all smiles and stupid noises, blowing whistles
through her mouth and crossing her eyes. Despite that,
she never once held Kento, and anytime there was work or
cleaning to be done the thief vanished without a trace.

Eventually the time came. The consequences of my
decision. Silva knocked at the door to our house. She didn't
usually knock, but then she wasn't usually there on business.
She had her notebook with her that day, the one where
she kept all the favours owed to her. I opened the door to
find her standing there, the sun lighting her from behind,
making her hair glow like molten gold. Kento was in my
arms, wriggling as she passed her morning feeding. For a
moment Silva just stared at me and I stared back. There was
compassion in her eyes, a true understanding of what I was
doing and how much it would cost me.

You have no idea of what it will cost. Ssserakis was angry.
Angry at me for the decision I made.

"I'm only going to ask you this once, Eska. Are
you sure?" Silva never second guessed me, no matter my
decision. And only once did she try to change my mind.

I tried to speak, to say *yes*, but Kento was gurgling in
my arms, pawing at my dress and staring at me. The words
stuck in my throat, so I just nodded once and blinked away
tears.

Hardt arrived home just as I was leaving with Silva,
Kento wrapped up in a swaddle and held against my chest

by a sash. He grinned at me as he waved a finger in the child's face, and I returned a dead stare. I lied to him then, told him we were just going for a walk, to give Kento her first introduction to the city of her birth. I lied because I knew he would try to talk me out of my decision and I needed no help in doubting myself. Hardt loved the child; he saw her as a final link to the brother he'd lost down in the ruined Djinn city. He would have argued, fought against the decision. But in the end Kento was *my* daughter, the father already nine months dead; it was *my* decision to make. I wasn't ready to be a mother. I have never quite been ready to be a mother.

Coward! I wanted to argue with the horror but could not find the words. It can be hard to argue against the truth.

Silva could see my turmoil. I think she sought to distract me, chatting about everything and nothing all at once. She told me about the shortage of nuts after our recent stop at Hattain. Apparently the tahren are quite partial to a variety of nuts and many of Ro'shan's supplies came from Hattain, but the entire region had recently suffered from a drought and nuts were scarce. She also told me we were nearing Isha again and Ro'shan would pass over Terrelan within the month. It would mark the first full orbit since I had climbed my way up to Ro'shan. That should probably have been a cause for celebration, but I couldn't bring myself to feel happy. I didn't deserve it.

The Terrelans will be waiting for you. That child is your only protection.

I hissed at the horror to be silent and Kento waved a chubby hand at my face.

I didn't even realise where Silva was taking me until we stopped. When I looked up from the little sleeping face of

my daughter, I found an entrance to one of the great arches
that rose from the city and crossed in the centre of Ro'shan.
I think the look of surprise on my face was what made Silva
smile.

"It's a rare thing, giving up a child," she said. "My
mother has asked to meet you first."

"The Rand wants to meet me?" I will admit it took a
moment for it to sink in. Back then the Rand and the Djinn
were little more than stories I had read in bard's tales and
most of those were fraught with inconsistencies. Some
depicted the Rand as monstrosities of flesh and wood and
water all fused together and somehow alive despite the
madness. Others painted them as sirens, beautiful maidens
that caused everyone to fall in love with them. Yet others still
had them as giants, almost terran in proportion, but with
skin that glowed like metal left in a forge. As far as I knew
back then, there was only one consistency throughout all
the stories I had read or been told and that was that all Rand
were female. And all Djinn were male.

"Surrogate parents have been found, Eska. They are
not terran, but they will treat the child with love…"

"Not terran?" I was holding back fresh tears. My guts
twisted and I thought I might vomit. I hated myself, but I
knew it was the right decision. It had to be. I couldn't allow
my daughter to share my fate. We are, all of us, marred by
scars, plagued by the faults and insecurities laid upon us by
our pasts. We are drowning in history, both good and bad,
and we cannot help but drag our children down with us. But
they deserve better than that, better than us. Kento was a
little version of me and Isen, unmarked by my scars, unable
to comprehend the flaws I would pass onto her. I am the
weapon, but I would not, *could not*, allow her to share in my

guilt.

More lies. You can't allow her to get in your way.

The horror spoke the truth, a part of it at least. I could not give up my fight any more than I could convince my enemies to let me go. I had no choice but to give my daughter up. I would only bring pain into her innocent little life, pass on the scars carved into my soul. Bring my enemies down upon her little head. Our children deserve better than us. Kento deserved better than me.

Silva shook her head. "That is as much as I can tell you. My mother wants to meet you first. If she agrees to your request, you'll leave the child with her and never see her again." I didn't realise it at the time, but Silva never referred to Kento by name, only ever as *the child*. I think she did it to keep distance.

I nodded, though I really wanted to do the other thing, and Silva led me inside the arch. There is a platform inside each arch that seems to move under its own power. At another time it might have fascinated me to attempt to discover how it worked, but I couldn't tear my eyes from the little girl watching me, gurgling. Blue eyes so like my own. A tear fell onto Kento's face. She started to cry. A noise that rent my heart in two. I wiped it away quickly and danced about the platform, rocking her gently until she quieted once more. Silva watched me all the while.

Ro'shan's palace lies high above the city, yet the platform took only minutes to reach the top of the arch. It slowed to a stop and there was a doorway, light streaming in through it. Silva led the way again and we walked through white halls, decorated with treasures and statues I now know as ancient and valuable beyond money. On one side there were no windows, only a large balcony that ended in a sudden drop to the streets below. From there I could see out across all Ro'shan and even see to the far edge of the floating mountain. Beyond that lay the fathomless blue of the ocean. We were nearing Isha and it was the height of summer there, blue skies and a blazing sun for much of it.

Giving up the child will kill you. Keeping it will kill her. Such a decision to make. Ssserakis' tone mocked me.

"Just… leave me alone," I said, my voice breaking on the words.

Silva stared at me with an odd frown, but she didn't ask who I was talking to.

I had a wild urge to turn back, keep Kento and flee back to Isha. I could make my way to Keshin, where I was born. Perhaps my parents and brother were still alive, maybe they even remembered me, though I had been gone for so long. I could settle down there, make a life for myself and for my daughter. Weave baskets and raise the child. It was a wild urge, and a fleeting one. I could never be happy there with so much left undone. With so many enemies left alive. All of them actually. Besides, I was sure Prena Neralis had already considered I might return to my childhood home. I knew there was nothing waiting for me there but a short thrust of cold steel. And my daughter would die with her mother. She had only once chance to live and I was taking it. I had to believe I was making the right choice. The only choice.

I had stopped to stare out of the balcony. I felt a gentle squeeze of my hand and came out of my reverie to find Silva next to me. She didn't rush me, nor ask me again if I really wanted to go through with it. She didn't say anything, just stood there next to me, holding my hand until I felt ready to move on. I don't think I've ever appreciated any friend quite so much as right then, not even Josef's support throughout our years at the academy came close to the silent company of Silva as I struggled to overcome my doubts. I don't know how long we stood there, hand in hand staring out over the city, my daughter asleep against my chest. Long enough for my resolve to strengthen. Long enough for Ssserakis to remind me of the drop below our feet. A little thrill of fear to feed the horror inside.

We moved on, Silva leading the way again, and I found the palace of Ro'shan to be quite empty. Whether that was because of its size or because the only people who stayed there were the Rand and her children, I don't know. I was far too preoccupied. For once, my curiosity was quiet, squashed by the dread apprehension that I was feeling.

Silva led me to the throne room, a large open area made of the same white bone as the rest of the palace. It was mostly empty save for a red carpet leading up to a throne that could easily have seated ten of me. There was an older man standing to one side of the throne, his hair grey and face stony, robes long and elegant and blue trimmed with gold. I did not recognise him. There were several doorways leading from the hall, each one tall enough to admit a giant. No matter which of those doorways I looked at, I saw Isen's bloody face staring back at me from the shadows. You might not think he could look so accusing given the ruin Josef had left of him, but he managed it. I turned away from the visions of Isen and found Silva watching me.

"Who is he?" I hated how weak and broken my voice sounded then.

"That is my brother, Gol. He always looks that serious. He was even worse when I was growing up. I just wanted to play, but he always made us do our work first. A real taskmaster."

"I can hear you just fine, Silva." Gol's voice suited his severe appearance; hard and rough like grinding rock, but with an oddly regal quality.

Silva leaned in close to me and spoke in a whisper. "Softer than he likes to admit though. He used to bring me and Coby sweet pastries when we were young."

Gol just watched us. He had unnerving eyes, all grey without a hint of real colour to them.

Silva gave my hand one final squeeze then let go and approached the throne, standing on the opposite side to her brother. I found myself feeling very alone in front of that empty throne, my daughter swaddled against my chest. I felt like turning around and running. I have never dealt well with being left alone. I draw strength from those around me, from my friends. Bereft of them, I am lost. Weakened. Right then, I had only the horror for company. I stood there, rooted to the spot, and waited for the Rand.

I was still waiting when a monster slithered into the hall. I recoiled when I first saw it, clutching at the child against my chest and backing up first one step then the other. One hand fell to my side, to where I kept my Kinemancy Source, but it wasn't there. I had taken to leaving it at home, hidden and safe, so the temptation to use it would be less. But now every instinct I had was telling me I needed it to protect Kento, though I doubted one Source would be enough to even hurt such a creature. It stood at maybe thrice the size of Hardt, and that was before you took into account the long tail trailing behind it, so like a garn's. The lower half of its torso, if you could call it that, was covered in a short fuzz of fur, like a pahht. It had six arms, each one always moving, twisting one way, then the other. It took a moment for me to realise that in the palm of each hand was a single eye, cat's eyes like pahht. I think what made the creature most disturbing was its head. A terran head, for the most part, though many times larger than any terran I had ever seen, with red hair like the dying embers of a fire. But that head had no eyes, just flat skin where they ought to be. The creature was disgusting and fascinating all at once, like some sort of fusion of all the people of Ovaeris.

And you call me a monster. This thing is what nightmares dream of.

Both Gol and Silva bowed as the creature slithered quickly towards the throne. Only a moment later I finally knew what I was looking at. The monster before me was the Rand. I must admit the first thought to cross my mind was to wonder how such a thing could be a mother to Silva. Then I dropped to my knees, awestruck and completely unsure of myself. I will say this for a certainty, never drop to your knees no matter how plush the rug beneath you might look. It will hurt.

Stand up! Do not kneel before this thing. We are better than that.

"Well, at least she knows how to show obeisance." I must admit I expected the Rand's voice to sound a lot like Ssserakis for some reason, a hissing noise as though a snake had learned to speak. Far from it, her voice was rich and silky, almost dusky. She stopped in front of the throne and her tail coiled around her. Hands twitched my way, eyeballs focusing on me. I saw both Gol and Silva stand from their bows, though neither spoke. Silva sent a brief smile my way and I will admit it helped to bolster my courage. I climbed back to my feet, anger at my foolishness lending me strength. I knelt before no one; not emperor, not god.

Ssserakis was right. We were better than that!

"Why do you have a throne?" I have found that sometimes the most innocent of questions, especially those with little relevance, can often do a lot to release tension, and I was feeling quite tense. I think Kento picked up on it in that way that children can; she started to cry a little and I immediately rocked her against my chest.

The Rand laughed, her hair shaking with it. A fiery mane like Imiko's, only it seemed so horribly out of place on such a monster's head. "A throne gives the impression of royalty, authority, regardless of whether I sit on it or not." She reared up on her tail and spread all six of her arms wide. "Do I impress you, terran?" Every time the Rand spoke, I could see rows of sharp teeth in her mouth.

"I have a name," I all but growled it at the monster in front of me. I think back now, and I must admit I'm half amazed the Rand didn't kill me there and then. I think perhaps she would have had she known the trouble I would cause her. But as powerful as the gods are, the future is beyond even them and I was just an impertinent terran, more useful alive and cowed than dead.

In a burst of speed, the Rand uncoiled and slithered forwards, towering over me. It took a lot of effort not to retreat. "And I should learn it? Why?"

I tried to glance towards Silva, but the Rand was too big, too close. She filled my vision. I felt Kento start to squirm and she let out a wail, of discomfort, or terror, I don't know which. I do know it stirred something in me, a need to protect her no matter the odds. It was enough to break me out of my mindless fear. Just like down in the Pit, my first encounter with Ssserakis, I felt the terror pass, and with it went the paralysis.

Fear is a strange thing. I have seen it in so many different forms. I have discovered a smell, a taste. Ssserakis fed off fear, turned it into strength and that strength leaked into me. The horror often scared me, whenever it was hungry, and I soon discovered that, more often than not, anger lies in the wake of fear. I found it then, too, facing a monster out of legend, a god. As the fear of her washed away, I felt a red-hot anger take its place. The room around me darkened with it, a cold prickling across my skin.

It was Ssserakis' power, working through me, that brought on the unnatural darkness. And the horror was pleased that I had unwittingly brought it about. It was not the first time I used it, nor would it be the last. Each time before, the other person trapped in the dark with me felt fear, but there was none coming from the Rand. She watched me, an amused smile playing on her lips, hands darting around, viewing me from different angles. As always, the darkness vanished quickly, fading away as light regained its rightful place.

Still so weak, Ssserakis said mournfully. There were limits to how much the horror could affect the world through me.

"Interesting," the Rand said with a toothy smile, pulling back and settling down onto her coiled tail. Behind her I could see Silva frowning. "And what is your name then, terran? So, I might remember it."

I'm sad to say I had to cough to find my voice. It's hard not to be at least a little humbled in front of a creature like that. The Rand are, after all, immortal and considered by most to be gods. She had probably seen the birth of my race and she would likely be witness to the death of it too. "Eskara Helsene." Kento was still wailing in my arms and I went back to rocking her gently from side to side.

"And this is the child you wish to give away?" The Rand did not need to shout, despite Kento's cries, her voice seemed to carry over the noise. I noticed she had a single hand twisted around, the eye in the palm staring back towards her own children.

I nodded. "Her name is Kento."

"May I hold her?" the Rand asked, extending a single hand toward me. I looked at that hand, Kento would fit inside the palm with space to spare. The eyeball embedded in the skin, turned towards me, watching.

That thing will kill her. You give your daughter to a monster. To her death!

It takes a lot of willpower to put your hand inside a monster's mouth, and I can tell you from personal experience it takes even more to put your child into a monster's hands. I will admit I hesitated, but in the end, I had already made my decision and I trusted that Silva would not have brought me here just to watch my daughter die. I placed Kento, still wailing, into the outstretched hand and watched as the Rand waved another hand over the top of my child. I would be lying if I said it was comfortable. I felt my legs shaking and my resolve cracking and all the while Ssserakis was whispering doom in the back of my mind. I fed it well with my fear that day.

Strange to realise it now, but Kento stopped crying. Maybe she, too, was in awe of the Rand as it held her.

"A strong name," the Rand said eventually, lowering her hand so I could take back my daughter. I all but snatched Kento back into my arms. Once I had, the Rand slithered back towards the throne and settled into a coil before it. "My daughter has explained the terms? You will leave the child

here and never see her again. You will not know where she
has gone or who she belongs to. It will be as though you
never had a daughter."

I nodded my agreement. But I didn't agree, not really.
I knew then that even if I never saw Kento again, I had a
daughter. That was something no one could take from me.

"Then leave her and go, Eskara Helsene," the Rand
said. All six of her hands turned to face me, all six of her eyes
focused on me. I held the complete attention of a god.

I hesitated. I don't think anyone could think less of
me for that. I looked down into the face of Kento one last
time. A baby's face is a strange thing; to an adult it can look
as though a hundred emotions are passing across that face in
an instant, yet the reality is the child is probably just trying
to pass gas. Whichever one it was, I felt my heart break and
new tears spring forth all over again. But I am the weapon,
and all a weapon can do is cut, hurt, kill. She watched me all
the while as I put her down on the red carpet and took a step
back. Then she started to cry again, and my world shattered.

Leaving Kento there, crying for her mother, her wail
echoing around that empty hall is the hardest thing I have
ever done. I thought my tears would never stop. I turned
and fled from that place and it took every bit of willpower
I had not to run. Isen stared at me from a nearby shadow,
his ruined face accusing me of deserting the one good thing
either of us ever did. He wasn't wrong.

Silva found me sitting on the balcony overlooking
the city, my legs dangling off the precipice. I thought of
throwing myself over the edge. I wanted to. I was so close.
Lesray Alderson's greatest legacy lies in my contemplation
of suicide. The call of the void, its siren song lulling me once

again. I was staring out at the city, but not seeing any of it; my eyes and mind unfocused. I couldn't help but dream of the possibilities of Kento's life, of what she might become and what she might do now, and I wouldn't be there. I hated myself, and I wanted that hate to end.

Silva sat next to me on that balcony, shoulder to shoulder. She was always a good hand taller than me and it showed whenever we sat next to each other. She didn't say anything, just sat there with me. Sometimes a silent shoulder to cry on is all the support you could ask for. I was still leaning against Silva's shoulder when the tears finally dried up. I think something inside of me went hard then. Like a surgeon cauterising a wound—yes, I still remember some of my medical studies from the academy—I cauterised the memory of Kento. Or at least I tried.

We walked back to my house and I was glad Silva came with me, I was still in something of a daze. I'm certain that without a guide I would have wandered the streets of Ro'shan like an untethered ghost with no purpose or direction. The others were all inside, laughing and sitting down to a bowl of cold stew and fresh bread. Hardt was wearing a flush as though he had recently been at work, but Tamura was still rubbing sleep from his eyes. Imiko was grinning as she told a story. Judging from the laughter it must have been funny, but I don't remember a word of it.

Silva walked me in and we both sat down at our little table. The room went silent as all three of my friends realised I had no child with me. I didn't trust myself to use the right words, but Silva was there and she told the others of my choice, of what I had done.

Hardt was the first to respond and it was not favourable. He shouted, accused, stopped just short of threatening. I have never seen him angrier. I look back now and the sight of Hardt enraged was terrifying, but I didn't feel it then. I didn't feel anything but numb. Even Ssserakis retreated from that void inside of me. I think that was where Hardt's mistrust of Silva came from. He blamed her for the choice I made. His rage should have been directed where it belonged. Silva stood her ground even as Hardt shouted, his big hands balled into fists. She wasn't scared, not at all. I felt more fear coming from Imiko than Silva.

By the time Hardt finished shouting, Imiko had vanished. I didn't even see her leave. His anger gave way to sadness and he stormed from our house in a torrent of growls and slammed doors. That only left Tamura. He looked older suddenly, as though my decision had added ten years to him, and I know just how that feels. He looked at me then and for the first time since we had met, I felt he was disappointed with me. It stung. Even in my numbness I felt his disappointment like a fist crushing the air from my lungs. He said, *Trees die when cut off from their roots.* And with that he stood, let out a ragged breath and left the same way Hardt did, only without the slamming door.

I found myself alone with Silva again. There were three bowls of mostly untouched stew left on the table. It's strange to think of it, but less than a year earlier none of us would have dreamed of leaving a bowl of food uneaten. Priorities change with circumstances. Silva stayed with me a while longer, but she wisely left before any of the others returned. I was just glad they did return. In my eyes, I had just lost a child, I don't think I could have coped with losing my family as well.

CHAPTER TWENTY TWO

I THREW MYSELF BACK INTO THE TRAINING I had started when we left the Pit, only this time I went at it without hesitation. I held nothing back. I became a creature of fury with a razor-sharp purpose to become stronger. It was my anger I was channelling. Not my anger at Terrelan for destroying Orran, nor my anger at Josef for betraying me, not even my anger at Ssserakis for subtlety undermining me every day with whispers in the back of my mind. It was my anger at myself. I was so certain I had done the right thing by giving up my daughter, and I hated myself for making the decision. Hardt stopped holding back as well, and I quickly discovered just how powerful he really was. I think his own anger over my decision made him a harsher tutor. He didn't understand why I had done it. He couldn't understand. I had nothing to offer Kento but pain, and the sins of her mother, a life lived on the run. She would be safer away from me. And I hoped she would be happier too. I think he searched for Kento a little. I sometimes wonder what he might have done had he found her. I wonder what I might have done.

Each day I rose before the sun and began training just like Hardt had instructed, exercises designed to build muscle and stamina. I was already sweaty and tired by the time Hardt joined me and picked up where we had left off, teaching me how to move my feet and how to throw a punch. Finally, I impressed him with the speed at which I improved, and I think that went a long way to repairing the relationship between us. But I had hurt him, far more than I even realised, and the pain he felt bled into our sparring. I came off worse for it, and he often left me bleeding.

I trained with Tamura again as well. Whether the old man had forgiven my decision or just forgotten Kento ever existed, I don't know, but Tamura acted no differently towards me. That, I think, was far worse than the anger Hardt showed. I embraced the pain Hardt dealt, knowing full well I deserved it, but Tamura's indifference left me bitter for reasons I couldn't understand. He, too, taught me how to move. He taught me how to breathe and how to use an opponent's own strength against them. In many ways his teachings were the opposite of Hardt's. Hardt taught me how to be stone, Tamura taught me how to be water. I tried my best to marry the two teachings into one, but when darkness and light mingle all you get is shadows of their former glory.

I took to swallowing my Kinemancy Source every day, re-adjusting myself to forcing it down, to living with magic sitting in my stomach, at my beck and call. It was uncomfortable at first. It had been long over a year since I had last spent significant time with a Source inside. Uncomfortable, but empowering. My body soon remembered the feeling of Kinemancy, and I felt powerful for the first time in so long. I hated giving it up each night, but there was no sense in pushing my limits to rejection.

Isha almost snuck up on me, I'd forgotten how close we were to our homeland. Just two weeks after I had given away my daughter, the great anchor dropped, scarring the earth once more. We were much further west this time, deep into the lands that used to be Orran. I never did learn how the Rand controls Ro'shan's orbit around its sister city of Do'shan. One more mystery of her magic, I suppose. Gods can do almost anything they wish when they set their mind to it. They can create life, they can make mountains fly, of course they can make those same flying mountains move wherever they want.

Silva was busy with her official city business, and Hardt had not yet forgiven me far enough for social niceties, so I approached the limits of Ro'shan alone. It is a daunting thing looking down at the ground from so high up, knowing that a single slip could end it all. I felt a wave of vertigo and swallowed it down, sidling closer and closer to the edge. I will admit I felt that sudden call of the void, the urge to throw myself over the precipice and watch the ground rush towards me. Maybe it was all about the thrill of knowing that I could, that I had the power to end it all right then and there. All that pain, anger, and sorrow gone in an instant. Unless the tahren priests of Azakbarn are right and there is something after death. Or maybe the garn who believe those who die are reborn into future generations. I have never met one who questioned that belief. On the other hand, if you ask a dozen terrans what they believe, you will likely receive

a dozen different answers. The same can be said of the
pahht, though many of their cities still bear shrines to dead
Rand.

Far below me, lit by the midday summer sun, was a
ruin. A city that had once been great, reduced to nothing but
burnt out husks, shattered stone, and ghosts. I recognised
many of the scars that ruined city bore, they were the marks
of Sourcerers duking it out. Great rents in the earth, stone
twisted beyond natural shapes, earth so blackened by fire
that even two years after the fact nature refused to reclaim
it. There is nothing quite like the devastation magic can
cause, nor the scale upon which it can act. There are other
lasting effects of battles involving magic, often things that
were invisible to the naked eye, but a person can feel them
if they get too close. That was why the city was still a ruin.
That was why no one tried to rebuild or even scavenge the
debris. In fact, there was no settlement within sight of the
ruins. It must have been a truly devastating battle. But that
wasn't surprising to me; the ruins I was staring down at
were that of Picarr, and on the western side of that city the
Orran Academy of Magic had once stood. Now all that stood
on that western side were broken slabs of stone and the
occasional sparks of lightning racing between the wreckage.

I couldn't stop a lump from forming in my throat, or
the tears welling in my eyes. My home, for most of my life
lay in a wreckage below. Almost everything I had ever done,
most of my memories both good and bad, and there was
nothing left of them. I had known Picarr was sacked by the
advancing Terrelan army, reports had come in while Josef
and I were preparing our last defence at Lanfall. But hearing
about it and seeing the devastation and ruins that are left
of the place you thought of as home for so long, are two

different things. A fresh wave of sorrow washed over me
and I couldn't control it. I staggered and very nearly pitched
over the edge. I had to throw myself backwards with a blast
of kinetic energy and there I sprawled in the grass.

When I returned to our little house in Ro'shan, I
found Silva waiting for me. She hadn't been there long, but it
was enough to have Hardt glaring. I was later told he all but
threatened her to find the location of Kento. Silva told him
nothing. I wonder if Hardt's anger scared her as much as it
did me, or if she knew how safe she was from him? She was
wearing a tight brown shift and wooden clogs, plain attire
by anyone's standards, but she made them look elegant. She
took my arm and led me into our little garden where I grew
Spiceweed and Tamura grew tea. Given that I rarely let a
day pass without swallowing down my Kinemancy Source,
I thought it best to grow my own supply of Spiceweed. I
have since learned the herb has a variety of different strains
and some are not nearly as harsh as others. The one I grew
up on Ro'shan tasted of liquorish, which was not altogether
unpleasant. At least for the few moments before the vile
retching began.

"How are you, Eska? I'm sure it can't be easy,
being back here." Pleasantries. I've never liked starting a
conversation with pleasantries. I much prefer people to
speak their minds directly, so we waste less time. That being
said, I was never opposed to anything that kept Silva close
for longer. She had already seen me at my worst, burning
with shame and sorrow and grief, and one shuffle away
from giving in to Lesray Alderson's suggestion. I was
determined she would soon see me at my best as well.

"It's fine." I shook my head at her. It should have
been all the indication she needed that I didn't want to talk

about it.

"It's not a weakness to admit pain, Eska. We all feel it. In fact, it's far easier to hide your feelings, than it is to admit to them…"

"I said I'm fine."

Silva didn't let it go. "And you don't strike me as the type of person to take the easy way." She was smiling at me in that disarming way she had. "Though I suppose it shouldn't surprise me."

"What does that mean?"

Silva sat up straighter, her smiles gone and her eyes piercing. "I'm not here to judge you. But I am willing to listen. We're back in Isha, or over it at least, and I suppose you spent some time in that city below us. I like to think we're friends, and friends tell each other how they're feeling."

I snorted. It wasn't very polite, but then I have never been that. I was taught manners at the academy, that much is true, but I was also brought up to be a weapon that Orran could point at its enemies. Social etiquette was not nearly as important as knowing how to burn people to ash. In my defence I excelled at the latter.

"You're not going to give up, are you?"

Silva shook her head. "I'm relentless, and I have the patience of a glacier. You might as well just give in now and tell me how you're feeling. It will save us both the time and effort of an argument." She smiled again.

I heard Ssserakis laugh in the back of my mind. *Secrets she can use against you. One more* friend *to betray you. Just like Josef did. And then you'll have to kill her, just like you did Josef.*

Maybe it was the horror's whispering, or Silva's pushing. Maybe it was just because I wanted to let her in, even a little. But I opened up then. I opened myself up and to my surprise anger came flooding out.

"You want to know how I feel? Imagine you were torn away from here for two years. You were locked in a gaol full of the very worst Terrelan has to offer. Beaten, whipped, tortured, betrayed. And even when you escape, life isn't the same anymore. You're hunted and stabbed." I'm not sure when fresh tears started tracking their way down my cheeks, but I was crying. "You give up… everything. And then, finally, *finally* you make it back home, only it's not there anymore. It's a ruin. Everything you knew growing up is gone. Everyone you knew is dead. The people who taught you. The people you liked. The ones you hated. Everyone. Everything. Gone."

Silva didn't say a word. I think she knew I'd freeze up if she did. But into that damnable silence I couldn't help but throw myself, every bit of me. All Silva did was sit in silence and I tripped over myself to get my pain out. I'll never know how she did that.

"There's nothing left of my past but memories of anger, and pain, and more anger." I think I may have listed my grief then. I told Silva about many of the tutors; Bell's kindness, Elsteth's calm confidence in my abilities even when I was sure something was beyond me. The way Zemmeten used to start each lesson with a basket of fruit—I loved his lessons. Stories came flooding out of me and Silva listened to them all.

For a long while we sat in silence. It was oddly comfortable, considering how much of myself I just revealed to her. I glanced up and saw Isen standing in the shadow of our house, dead eyes watching me with an accusation I didn't understand.

"It's been an emotional day," I admitted after a while, my voice breaking. I felt foolish. I had just ranted at the woman, poured out my grief and anger. "Do you think we could just forget that whole outburst?"

Silva laughed. "I'm afraid not. But then it's quite endearing when you stop hiding inside yourself and actually *be* yourself."

I shot her a look. I was aiming for contempt, but I think I must have missed the mark a little because she just smiled at me. Then the smile dropped, and I knew whatever was coming next, I wouldn't like.

"I have some bad news, Eska. We're over Isha again and last time we were here you admitted to war crimes against the Terrelan empire."

Ssserakis laughed inside my head. The horror didn't need words to remind me that it had told me this would happen. Silva was about to betray me.

I snorted. Just six months after admitting to the crimes Terrelan placed at my feet, and I already considered myself an idiot for my actions. "A moment of madness. I just wanted to distance Hardt and Tamura from my crime. Or at least from the accusations levelled against me."

"You admitted to the crimes, Eska. In front of Coby and myself, Ro'shan officials. And also in front of Prena Neralis, a Terrelan official. Now, while I would like to hope she has forgotten about you... I doubt it. And the condition of your asylum was based upon your being with child. Your daughter has been born and is gone. I'm afraid your asylum is over."

Betrayal. After everything, you are nothing to her but a mark in her book.

I felt the cold inside more keenly than before. I felt

myself go hard with it. Brittle. Ready to shatter. How could she do it? How could Silva turn me over to my enemies after everything I had shown her of myself? I made ready to fight, though I had no idea who against. Silva? I could never fight against her. Prena might be chasing me, but we had only just arrived and it would take time for her to catch up with Ro'shan. It didn't matter. I felt ready to fight. I wanted to fight. I just needed an enemy. Something... someone to hurt.

She sells you out to your enemies, and just as you were getting close to her. The world darkened around me. *They always betray you when you get close. You can't lie to me. This betrayal hurts even more because you wanted her to like you, to trust you. You wanted her to love you.*

I screamed inside my own head. I didn't know if it would work or not, whether Ssserakis would hear me, or if the ancient horror would even care. I wanted it to shut up, so I imagined myself screaming at it. It seemed to work, though I had the feeling I would end up paying for it later. When I opened my eyes, I realised I had screwed my face up and Silva was on her feet, watching me with the curiosity of a rabbit unsure if it has just encountered a predator. The day brightened around me as the unnatural darkness fled.

I looked away and surged to my feet. "Sorry, I..."

"I have a solution, Eska. Though I'm not sure you'll like it." Silva stood at a distance, wary and tense.

I let out a bitter laugh. "If you tell me to get pregnant again, I think I'd rather face the executioner." A poor attempt at humour.

"No. I'm offering you a job. My mother is offering you a job. Starting immediately. As a city official you would be protected, no matter the crimes the Terrelans lay at your feet."

"I'll take it!" Over eagerness has ever been one of my flaws. I had yet to even learn what the job would entail, but I knew I needed the protection it would afford. I wasn't ready to stand against Terrelan alone. I wasn't strong enough.

Silva let out a little sigh. "My mother has need of a relic hunter. Someone she can send to the ground to search for items she wishes to be retrieved. Items she believes too powerful to be left lying around for others to find. It is part of her responsibility to the world, as the last of the Rand. To protect it, and all of you, from the artefacts left over from her war with the Djinn."

If she hadn't already sold me on the prospect with the offer of protection, her mention of power would certainly have sealed the deal. I was already wondering how many of those powerful artefacts I could claim for myself, to turn their forces on my enemies. Perhaps Silva and her mother would have found someone more suitable, had they known what I was planning to do once I had the strength to back up my threats.

"Why not send you or Coby?" I asked. "Why would she need me for that?"

"Because you're expendable." I must admit I had not even noticed Hardt standing nearby, eavesdropping on our conversation. For such a big man, he could move silently when he wanted to. I felt an irrational anger at him, as though he were intruding on something private, intimate. But his accusation warranted an answer and I turned my harsh stare on Silva.

She lied to me. "Not at all," she said with a shake of her head. "And, in fact, my sister Coby will be accompanying you most of the time. She is the most well suited of my siblings for the task. Stronger than she looks, and she's never met a situation she couldn't blend into." I had met Coby only the once on my first day on Ro'shan, but she had stood out like a broken nose. I wondered what it would be like to spend time with a pahht, and a daughter of the Rand, one who wasn't Silva. I'd be lying if I said I wasn't looking forward to it. Not many people who know Coby would admit to looking forward to spending time with her.

"So, she's not expendable?" Hardt pressed. He was relentless when the mood took him, and overly protective of me, even after I had given up his niece.

Silva shook her head. "What Eska is, is a Sourcerer. And they are valuable even to my mother."

I don't like being talked over. It feels like a measure of disrespect, as though I'm still a child and others are arguing over what I should do, or think, or be. "What Eska is," I said, my voice harsh even to my own ears, "is sitting right here. Well able to hear and talk to both of you." Silva bowed her head and apologised, but Hardt just crossed his arms and leaned against the outer wall of our little home, his eyes sharp.

"That's why we're here, isn't it?" I said. "Over the ruins of Picarr. There are no other cities nearby. No one to trade with."

"You might be surprised." Silva smiled. "By tomorrow morning there will be carts and merchants swarming towards us. But they will not go near the city ruins. It has a foul reputation since the war. Covered in traps and haunted by things not of this world."

And there it was. They needed someone who could navigate the magical traps left behind, avoid the rifts in reality, and do battle with creatures from the Other World. They needed a Sourcerer trained in battle, and they had a

powerful one in me. I could only hope they would give me
the tools I needed to perform the task.

HOME! Ssserakis screamed in my mind, reminding
me once again that I had promised to send the horror back to
the Other World just as soon as I had an Impomancy Source
inside of me. I flinched at the noise in my head, and I'm
certain both Hardt and Silva saw it.

"Are you well?" Silva asked, her brows drawing
together in a frown that made her more beautiful.

I ignored the question. "When do I head down?"

"Right away. Coby has already been down on the
ground to scout, poking around a little, but she won't get too
close to the ruins until you arrive."

"I'm going too." Hardt's voice was a gravelly rumble.

Silva opened her mouth to speak, but Hardt cut her
off. "I'm coming, Eska. And I'd bet the crazy old man will
too." He turned dark eyes on Silva. "Don't try to stop us."

"I wouldn't dream of it. The flyer will be leaving at
midday." She pointed south to where the sun would be. We
had a couple of hours at most. "Don't be late."

As soon as Silva was gone, I stood, determined to
get myself ready. I owned little, but I had taken to wearing
a dress during most days, and that simply wouldn't work
where we were going. I would change into the clothes I
trained in, a sturdy pair of trousers and a shirt to match,
a leather jerkin over the top. It was not true armour, but it
might provide some protection. As I moved past Hardt. I
stopped, unable to hold my tongue.

"You don't have to be so abrasive towards her all the
time." The words were out of my mouth before I could stop
them.

He just laughed at me, some of his good humour

showing around his eyes. "Well, isn't that the river calling the sea wet."

I levelled a punch at his arm and he threw one right back. As always, I caught the worse end of that trade.

CHAPTER TWENTY THREE

JOSEF

Ro'shan is back. Death received word it is passing over western Terrelan and we're following. We've recruited a Portamancer to make certain we get there before it leaves. And once we're there, Death will board Ro'shan and bring Eska back. I still can't believe she had a child. Or I suppose has a child by now. Eska, a mother? It just doesn't sound right. It must be Isen's. They were always watching each other down in the Pit, always finding reasons to be close. She fawned over him. She protected him even as she pushed me away. And I killed him. I killed the father of her child. I wonder if she hates me for that? I shouldn't care. I don't care. She can hate me. Soon we'll find her, and Death will throw her back into the Pit. Let her spend the rest of her life where she left me to die.

Even after months, the others don't like me. I hear them

making fun of me, croaking out noises that mimic my own. I wish I could speak so I could tell them just what I think of them. Urkol is a brute. He's as ugly as a spotty arse. I can write that here. I know he can't read. I left a few pages near him to test. He barely looked at them before committing them to the fire. It was a shame to use such good paper for nothing but fuel, but now I know I can write whatever I want and that stupid, ugly, mud fucker won't know. Unless Tine reads them to him. But I don't think he will. Tine can read, I know that for sure, but he doesn't have the time. As soon as we stop for the night, he pulls the cover from his shield and polishes it. For hours and hours on end he polishes it. He sleeps for scant few hours a night, and I can see the toll it takes on him.

Books at the academy library were quite clear on the effects of sleep deprivation. It's bad for most people, worse for Sourcerers. Tine shows all the signs; bleary eyes, sudden starts, mumbling to himself. Anyone would think he's mad. He doesn't look after himself like he used to, either. I don't remember the last time I saw him shave and he smells worse than I did down in the Pit. Death should say something. I know she's noticed, but every time I see her watching him, she just looks sad.

I caught a glimpse of Tine's shield a few days ago. He guards it jealously, covering it up when anyone goes near and staring at them until they walk away. But I can move quietly and I snuck close. I saw… I'm not sure what I saw in that reflection. It was me, but it was like a dream. I looked into the mirrored surface and I saw a vision of light pouring out of my stomach. I don't know what it meant, but Tine caught me looking and backhanded me so hard it felt like my teeth were loose for days. I think he would have gone further, kicked me, maybe even grabbed his axe, but Death was there in an instant with a single word and Tine stopped. I saw fear behind his madness, just for moment, and then he turned away, covering up his shield and holding it close.

Urkol just laughed, not at Tine, but at me sprawled on the floor. He holds his hammer in almost the same high regard as Tine does his shield. And Death, her sword. There is something strange there. Maybe they think I'm too stupid to figure it out, but I've been with them for months and I've pieced the truth together bit by bit. They are three of the Knights Lunar. Three wielders of the ten weapons that fell when our moons collided millennia ago. I had heard rumours, even down in the Pit, that the Terrelan Emperor had collected the ten weapons for the first time since they were found. Now I believe it to be true. The emperor has re-forged the Knights Lunar and I travel with three of them. I wonder where the other seven are?

It all makes sense when I think of it. Tine's shield is no ordinary kite shield; it is Madness, named for the effect it had on the first Orran emperor, Tanus Per Orran. The fool was the first to start the war with his neighbours, back when Isha was split into a hundred little kingdoms, the first to call himself an emperor. He used the shield to do it. Not only on the battlefield, mesmerising his enemies with glimpses of their future, then striking a killing blow. He also searched the visions it showed him endlessly, always looking for the next place to strike, the next move to make. But that shield and the futures it shows are a curse as much as a gift. They drove him mad, seeing enemies every step of the way and forcing him to see his own deaths over and over again; by his enemies' hands, by his allies' hands, some say he even saw his own son kill him over and over again. But none of those futures were true. He made them false. Tanus became paralysed by the possibilities he saw in that shield. Where once it had showed him the way, it showed him so many paths he couldn't choose one. The more paths it showed him, the more he looked into the shield, trying to find the right one. Eventually, Tanus' son found his father dead, his wrists cut open and his blood washing the shield. That was why it was locked away in the Orran Academy of Magic, behind a locked door with no lock. It's already working its curse once more.

Tine shows all the signs of the madness the shield is named for. How long before he starts to believe one of us is trying to kill him? How long before he acts? Maybe I can escape his suspicion. Maybe I'm not important enough. After all, only Death really speaks to me and she treats me like a servant. I was one of the most powerful Sourcerers in the Orran army, and now I fetch water, brush down horses, and stir the stew. I think I prefer it this way. A life without the constant training and war. Without the killing. But I think I'd trade it all back for a Source, just one to sit in my stomach and rid me of the relentless, gnawing hunger.

The others are stirring. I've already packed away the camp and I can see the Portamancer's horse on the trail behind us. We'll be away soon. I'm coming, Eska. In Death's wake, I'm coming for you.

CHAPTER TWENTY FOUR

THERE IS AN AREA OF RO'SHAN KNOWN AS Craghold where bits of the mountain long ago started to crumble and fall away. Metal struts were driven deep into the side of the rock and a massive wooden pier was built. It is upon that pier that the flyers sit, Ro'shan's own little fleet of flying ships; its only real way to and from the surface of the world below. I, of course, do not count climbing the great chain and for good reason, only the truly foolish even attempt such a thing. I had seen the docks before, having spent quite some time around them trying to reason out how the flyers worked, but I had never been out on the piers or stepped a single foot onto one of the flyers. It was a lack I was about to change. There would be no climbing the chain for me this time.

Silva was waiting for us by the flyer, dressed in a more serviceable shift than I had ever seen on her, though still dazzling and elegant by comparison to anything I had ever worn. Several pahht loaded crates onto the flyer and then crowded on board. It appeared we weren't going down alone. A tall terran woman stood next to Silva and wore a look as sour as wine left out for too long. She was as dark as Tamura, with eyes bluer than my own, and had thick braids of hair reaching down to the small of her back. I had never seen her before, but she seemed familiar with Silva. I approached with caution.

"Eska, Hardt, Tamura," Silva greeted us all with a smile and then gestured to the woman next to her. "This is my sister Coby."

It's fair to say I was a little confused. I had met Coby once. I had been locked in a cell and a little delirious from both pain and exhaustion, not to mention a bleeding hole in my shoulder, but my memory served me well enough to remember that Coby was pahht, not terran. I think my look of shock and confusion was rather obvious. Coby let out a savage laugh and then turned, striding up the gangplank onto the flyer.

Tamura, never one to pass up the opportunity for laughter, joined in and followed Coby up onto the flyer as though it wasn't a marvel of wood, metal, and magic. "I may wear many clothes, but I am still me," he said with a giggle.

Hardt did not seem so easily persuaded. "What is she?"

Silva shrugged. "Coby is Coby. Take your eye from her for just a moment and she will be someone else, but still Coby. I'll explain on the way down, we should have an hour or so before we reach the outskirts of the city."

"You're coming with us?" Again, that eagerness in my voice I couldn't quite withhold.

How else would she betray you? She needs to be close to drive the knife between your ribs. Or perhaps it's all just a ploy to get you back down on the ground where she can abandon you to your enemies.

I tried my best to ignore Ssserakis, but it is a lot like ignoring yourself. The horror was relentless and always knew just where to prod to draw forth my fears.

"Only to the ground," Silva said. "There will be merchants coming soon and all trade deals must be negotiated with a city official in attendance."

"Only way the Rand makes sure to get her full cut," said a richly dressed pahht as he strolled past us and up the gangplank. The pahht have a way of speaking the terran tongue that makes it sound almost musical and this one was no exception.

"Must I remind you that the Rand is my mother, Eivful?"

"How could I ever forget, most glorious Silva? After all, you have her eyes, though thankfully not as many of them." Eivful barred his teeth in an expression I've since come to understand is the pahht equivalent of a smile.

There was a second flyer being readied and I saw several tahren climb aboard, and even a garn slithering up the plank and down into the hold. Despite my months on Ro'shan I had had very little interaction with any of the garn. They were still very much a fascinating mystery to me. Almost slug-like in appearance, the garn don't so much have arms as fleshy tentacles that can extend or shrink back into their bodies. They have eyes, though they are little more than shining pits in what I consider to be a face, and mouths that are more like gaping holes leading down into their bodies. They are as alien and wondrous as the mur. And they smell. I don't mean to be disrespectful, but the secretions they leave—and they leave a lot of secretions—are offensive to me. I'm told it's quite insulting to point that out.

"Shall we get under way? Coby will give us all grief if we delay any further." Silva said, gesturing to the flyer.

"I think I'd a prefer a real boat," Hardt said as he walked up the gangplank. "Better than climbing a chain, I guess."

Silva stopped me as I made to board, a hand held up in front of my chest. There was something in that hand, something small and almost spherical. Something that caught the light and hinted at power. A new Source. I felt the urge to snatch at it, to cram it into my mouth and swallow it down. I already had one Source sitting in my stomach and it did much to relieve the hunger, but power is addictive like that. Some always leads to a desire for more, and more leads to yet more still. Power is a road with no end. At least not for me.

"An Arcmancy Source." Silva took my hand, her touch warm and soft and sent a thrill through me that had nothing to do with the magic I now held. "From my mother. She's only loaning it to you, so don't lose it."

"Little chance of that." I wasted no time popping the Source in my mouth and swallowing it down. It was larger than I was used to, and I had to stop myself from gagging, but the desire for power won out. I felt a new energy inside, almost too much of it, as though my limbs struggled to keep still. I raised my hand and rubbed my fingers together, sparks of lightning crackling between them. "How did you know my attunement?"

"I didn't. But my mother knew the moment she looked at you. Given the condition of the ruins down there, she thought that particular magic might be useful to you."

Silva took my hand again and didn't even flinch at the spark that shocked us both. She led me up the gangplank and onto the flyer where Coby was waiting, a harsh look in her eyes. Within moments the ropes were tied away and the propeller above started up until it was so loud I could hear little else. Then the flyer was pushed away from Ro'shan and for a terrible, lurching moment we dropped, but it soon steadied into a gentle swirling descent, like leaves on the wind.

I stood up on deck for a while, near the bow to be out of Coby's way as she operated the flyer. I call the flyers small, but in truth they are quite large, far larger than our little home up on Ro'shan. The flyers are built to carry cargo and have large hulls. The deck itself is often crowded with those making certain everything runs smoothly. I wanted to look at the system that turned the propeller, to figure out what made it work, but I did not dare get close or interfere, not when we were so high up that even a moment without power could send us dropping to our deaths. Eventually the noise of the propeller was too much and I trudged down below, where I found Hardt and Tamura and Silva, and much more surprisingly, Imiko.

The thief had stowed away without anyone noticing. She grinned at me from the gloom and I knew just how pleased she was with herself at my shock. I tried to hide it and ignored her, refusing to ask how she got on board, or why. It was a petty victory really, but Imiko often brought out my pettiness. I'm told sisters are often like that, and I had started to consider her a little sister, one that I never wanted. I approached Silva and slumped down against the wall next to her. I could feel the thrum of the propeller through my back. It was both reassuring and disconcerting all at once.

"What are you? Really?" I asked Silva. It was perhaps not the best time for it; there is nothing in the way of privacy aboard a flyer and, though many of the pahht were up on deck, I could see a few were down in the hold with us. But the noise of the flyer was oppressive and I hoped our conversation wouldn't travel much further than each other's ears. "I've heard people call you Aspect."

With neither beds, nor chairs on our little flyer, Silva and I were sitting on the floor, leaning against each other shoulder to shoulder. It was comfortable and exciting all at once.

"People should be more circumspect." There was hesitation in her voice, but I was sick of hesitation and misdirection. I wanted the truth.

Ssserakis laughed at that, a vindictive mirth full of mocking. *This creature is of the Rand. They don't know how to tell the truth.*

"That's not an answer," I said, ignoring the horror inside.

"Can't it be enough that I look terran? I sound terran. I feel terran."

"No. It's like a bard playing the first two notes of song then getting up and leaving." I heard her smile. I didn't need to turn my head and see it; I already knew exactly what it would look like. I took a deep breath and prepared myself to ask the dangerous question. "Are you Rand?"

"Yes." At her admittance I felt my heart skip a beat for some reason. "No. A little bit. Maybe."

When you ask someone a direct question, the same question you have asked them dozens of times before, and they are purposefully, maddeningly vague, it starts to get a little tiresome. I tensed and moved away from her just a little and she sighed. I hoped, tricked myself into believing Silva was evading my question because the others were nearby. Because it was something she would tell me and me alone.

Or because she doesn't want you to know the truth. Because it's too horrible. Because if you knew what you were sitting next to you would fear it even more than you do me.

"I wasn't born like you, Eska," Silva said. I glanced to find her staring at me and quickly turned away in case my obvious interest convinced her to stop. "I was... created. My mother took a piece of herself, an aspect of herself, and with it she created me. She calls us her children and we call her mother, but we are a part of her. Separate, individual, but still a part of her. Some of us are terran. Some of us are pahht. Coby is something else, though she certainly likes to look terran most of the time. I think that's because of me. We're twins, of a fashion, created together. We each of us had childhoods. We grew, were raised. We each have had time to discover ourselves; who we are. Who I am. What I want from my life."

Silva fell silent and I heard her let out a soft sigh. I leaned back in, once again resting my shoulder against hers, providing what scant comfort I could. Even then, I had the feeling that it was far harder for her to reveal her true nature than it appeared. I had questions still, dozens of them, maybe more. I didn't entirely understand. I failed to see the purpose behind the Aspects. But then it is difficult to see the truth behind the lies when so many of the facts are hidden. And she was lying to me then even as she told me the truth.

"What aspect are you?" I couldn't help myself. I needed to know more.

"I don't know. That's part of my purpose, to discover what I am. When I die, all that I am becomes part of my mother again. So, in discovering what I am, I help her understand herself better."

I felt I was closer to the truth and further away all at once. "So, the Rand removed a part of herself and turned it into you, but she has no idea what part of herself she removed?"

The silence again. This time I waited. *It takes time to construct a believable lie.*

"Yes."

"Does she control you?"

"No." Silva let out a ragged laugh. I think she might have been crying, but I didn't want to look; I knew if I did, I wouldn't be able to continue questioning her. Her tears would break me. "But she asks things of us and none of us have ever refused her. Well, there was… She is our mother and we are part of her. Why would we refuse her?"

I could think of a hundred reasons. These days I can think of even more. Have I mentioned how much I hate the Rand? Trust me when I tell you I have good reason. I thought it better to change the subject slightly, rather than argue. I didn't want to argue with Silva. I wanted us to stay as we were; close and comfortable.

"What did you mean when you said Coby is something else?" I could see the shine from Tamura's eyes, watching us. I could see Hardt staring as well. Whether they could hear us over the sound of the propeller above and the grinding of gears, I don't know.

Silva let out a moan. "She'll hate me even more for telling you. Each of us is given a gift when our mother creates us; something unique that only we have or can do, a power of our mother, given to one of us. Coby was given the gift of being everyone and no one all at once. It is a glamour of sorts. When you look at her you see what she wants you to see. She can appear as male or female, pahht or terran or tahren. I don't think I've ever seen her take on the guise of a garn, but it must be possible. But no matter how many of her faces you might have seen, she cannot show you her real one, and yet every time she looks in a mirror she can see nothing else."

"Sounds like a curse as much as a gift."

I felt Silva nod. "All gifts are also curses, Eska. I gave you the gift of Arcmancy and yet if you hold onto it for too long it will kill you."

We both fell silent then. Maybe I should have left it at that. Maybe if my curiosity had let me, I wouldn't have pushed for the rest of the truth. Maybe if I hadn't known Silva's gift, things might have turned out differently for us all. But there is no point in second guessing myself so far into the past. I am what I am, and I asked what I asked. And I have done what I have done.

"What is your gift?"

"When I look at a person, I sometimes get glimpses of who they really are underneath all the masks we wear and the lies we shroud ourselves in," Silva said without hesitation.

You can't trust a person who sees the real you. Perhaps you should ask her if she sees you or me.

Some answers only pose more questions and sometimes it seemed like Silva only gave those sorts of answers. Regardless, it had me quite intrigued.

"What do you see in Imiko?" The little thief had vanished again, though whether she was skulking around the shadows of the hold, or up on deck annoying Coby, I didn't know. I hoped it was the latter.

Silva laughed. "I'm not your personal crystal ball into your friends' minds, Eska."

There are ways in which a person can say *no* when what they actually mean is *ask me again*. Silva knew how curious I could be, and I knew she would answer me eventually. We were dancing, though I didn't know the steps. "What if I asked nicely?"

"Do you even know how to ask nicely?"

"No. But back at the academy my tutors used to say the word *please* had something to do with it." I flashed her a grin. "Please?"

Again, Silva laughed, falling silent for a moment before answering. "In Imiko I see a girl chasing the spirit of adventure, her name forever written on the horizon. Always looking for trouble that can't be fixed, and she forces herself to move on before comfort sets in. Most people in her life are just shadows to her, things to hide behind before moving on."

"Is that what we are to her? Just a shield from the trouble she gets herself into?" I knew there was a reason I never liked Imiko. Just a shame it wasn't the whole truth, but then Silva never told the whole truth.

"I don't know. You'd have to ask her that yourself. I only see what I see, Eska. Sometimes the visions are clear, sometimes not."

I was angry, tensing at the thought that Imiko might be using us. I was also dancing around the real question I wanted to ask Silva.

"What do you see in Hardt?" I knew he was watching us, listening. I half expected him to stop Silva from answering, but sometimes we need someone else to look into our soul to shed light on the things long hidden. Sometimes others can see things in us that we cannot. Or will not.

"I see a man surrounded by a storm. He stands in the eye, clinging to the calmness of it, refusing to move lest he be swept up into the torrent. But the storm is moving, the eye is moving, and the more he stays still the closer the chaos gets."

I looked up at Hardt then and saw him staring not at Silva, but at me. There was a hard look to him, his face drawn in sharp lines. I think Hardt was tired of struggling so hard to resist the storm. I wondered why he refused it so. I saw him down in the ruined Djinn city. I saw what he could do, what he had done to the Damned. I had also seen what the violence had done to him. The Damned are monsters, little more than soulless beasts and killing them had caused Hardt so much grief. I sometimes wonder if Silva failed to mention the woman standing beside Hardt in the centre of that storm, slowly pushing him towards the edge.

"What about Tamura?" The old man giggled when I asked. I was still trying to work up the courage to ask the real question.

"In Tamura I see a man surrounded by mirrors each one reflecting only himself. Every one of the mirrors is cracked and along those cracks are reflections of who he used to be, his past leaking out along lines. But he is stuck there, trapped by the mirrors. They are somehow more real than the rest of him. And a shadow, something great and terrible and dead for longer than any of us have been alive."

I half expected Tamura to say something then, some pearl of wisdom hidden behind madness. But he said nothing, just stared at us, a smile on his lips and at the corner of his eyes. Again, I tried to summon the courage to ask Silva what she saw in me and again I failed. I'm not sure if it's because I was too afraid to find out, or too afraid to ask her to look. We settled into a comfortable silence then and rode out the rest of the trip that way. I have rarely felt more content.

CHAPTER TWENTY FIVE

IT'S FAIR TO SAY THAT PICARR HAD CHANGED a little since I had last been there. I remembered a vibrant city, expansive and alive. Even towards the outskirts there was never a lull in the activity; homes and shops, people and animals, guards and thieves, all moving about their daily lives. It was a farming town for the most part, with plenty of arable land to the east, some of the only Orran land to allow crops to grow.

When I was just eight years old Josef and I ventured out into the streets of Picarr for the first time since arriving at the academy. We were both foolish, but I was also awed by the hive of activity that was the city proper. You have to remember, I spent my first six years in a forest village with just two dozen families as company, a hectic day was seeing more than five people. We roamed the streets and soon found ourselves quite lost. When we asked a candlemaker how to get back to the academy, she scoffed at us and told us to go peddle our lies somewhere else. I suppose she took us for thieves rather than students. Eventually we found a kindly guard, a man with grey hair spilling out from under an ill-fitting helmet, and he took us back. I thought of it as my first adventure since leaving Keshin. Back then everything seemed like an adventure. The world seems so much bigger through the eyes of a child, and so much smaller once the innocence washes off.

Picarr was once a thriving city, supported by farmland, and made important by the academy. Tens of thousands of people all huddled together in their homes against the forces of nature. Now it was tens of thousands of graves all buried beneath that they thought would protect them. It is hard to look upon such destruction and not feel the devastation. I have caused it myself in other places, other cities, but never one I knew so well. Never one that birthed so many memories. Never one that housed so many people I knew. All gone. Alice, a kind baker who sold Josef and I sweet pies for half the normal price. Serra, the old lady with a walking stick as sharp as her tongue. Brogue, the half deaf blacksmith who seemed to be always fitting new shoes to horses. I wonder if any of them got out alive. No. It is not the terran way to flee a city on the verge of destruction, but instead to hunker down and hope the walls protect us. They were all dead, and standing there, looking into that mass grave, I saw the faint wisps of their ghosts.

"By the moons," Imiko said. "Are those what I think they are?"

"You can see them too?" I asked. We were on the outskirts of the city, where some of the buildings still stood. Deserted homes in severe disrepair. I could feel my skin prickling and knew all too well there was still magic in the air. It does that, hangs around, leaves echoes of itself. Magic never truly fades from the world.

"Of course I can see them!" Imiko hissed. "There's a bunch of ghosts floating about, poking at the ruins. Who couldn't see them?"

I could taste her fear, not just hers but Hardt's as well. I drank it in and felt myself grow strong with the power Ssserakis fed me. "They can't harm you. They have no purpose, no master." I took the first step inside the city limits, joining the cracked road that led further in. "Why was Necromancy used here? It has it's purposes, but it's almost worthless when fighting other Sourcerers."

"But they're ghosts!" Imiko shouted.

Coby snorted and followed me onto the road, her steps hesitant. I could feel her fear, but it wasn't due to the ghosts that drifted about. Coby was scared of something else and I wondered why she was following so closely in my footsteps. Tamura joined the road next, and Hardt after that. The big man had his gauntlets hanging from his belt and I was glad he thought to bring them. If Silva was right and Sourcerers had summoned monsters from the Other World which were now inside the city, it was quite possible we would need his strength and skill. Some creatures, like Hellions, tend to roam the world once they are set free from their bondage. Others, like Garlkin, prefer to burrow into the earth and wait for prey to come to them. I have seen a Garlkin ambush. One moment the ground is still, packed dirt and grass, and the next it erupts with enough force to snap bones. Ten spindly legs, sharp as steel, pierce flesh and crush prey before it ultimately ends in a mouth full of rasping teeth. It does not look a pleasant way to die.

We picked through the outskirts of the city ruins slowly, carefully, measuring every step and watching each shadow, peering around every corner as though all the horrors of the Other World might come screaming out at any moment. Ghosts drifted around us, ignoring us for the most part. Imiko soon found she had quite a following of the ethereal wisps, and they crowded around her like flies to rotten meat. At first, she panicked, swatting at them and mewling. Coby laughed and I will admit I almost joined in until I felt the terror pulsing off Imiko in waves.

That one is an endless supply of fear. I can see why you keep her close. Ssserakis' thought disgusted me, not for the horror's nature, I couldn't fault it that, but for the implication that I only kept Imiko around to feed Ssserakis her fear. I found a deep well of compassion along with that disgust. For all else Imiko might be, she was family.

"They're drawn to your fear, Imiko." I turned to the girl and walked through one of the ghosts, putting my hands on her shoulders and staring into her eyes just as Hardt had done with me so many times. An anchor to the world, pulling her back into herself. Her gaze flitted about for a few moments, but eventually locked on mine. "They can't harm you, but they are drawn to your fear."

"You know about this stuff." Her voice was quiet and pleading. "Can't you make them go away. Please." One of the ghosts drifted close and Imiko squeaked, a new wave of fear rolling off her, drawing yet more ghosts. We had quite the gathering, dozens of spectres and more arriving all the time. Panic and terror brought tears to her eyes and I felt it as my own.

"She has a point, Eska." Hardt's voice held a tremble to it I hadn't heard since we climbed the great chain. "This is a little unnerving."

I turned to him but kept my hands on Imiko's shoulders. "Don't you start, Hardt. You're too big and old to be scared by a few harmless ghosts."

Coby laughed. She was busy playing with one of the ghosts, poking holes in its form and watching bits of it float away like smoke on a breeze.

"Imiko." I pulled her gaze back to mine and held it. "We can do this without you. Maybe you should run back to Silva."

The little thief shook her head. "I'm staying."

"Then I need you to calm yourself. Here…" I snatched her arm with my hand and dragged her towards one of the ghosts. She tried to resist, pulling against me, but the terror flowing out of her was making me strong and my grip was iron. I waved her hand through one of the spectres, its form scattering. For just a moment her fear turned to blind panic, and then lessened a little.

"I didn't feel anything."

"Because there's nothing there to feel. All these things are just memories of people who used to live here. They're not real. They can't touch us, or see us, or interact with the world in any way. They just float here, tethered to the place they died and drawn to the fear of anyone who comes close." I let go of Imiko's arm and she pulled it back, hugging herself tightly, but her fear wasn't as strong as before. Her eyes still darted from one ghost to the next, but the panic was gone.

Tamura took a bite out of one of the ghosts, scattering its form with his lunge. "Tastes bitter. Like a love lost before its time to blossom."

"You just ate a ghost, old man," Hardt shook his head.

His gauntlets were on his hands, balled into tight fists, ready for a fight.

"I don't understand why they're here," I said as I scattered one of the ghosts only for it to reform a few paces distant. "Sourcerers wouldn't have fought with Necromancy, ghosts are pointless. Yet they drift around us, forming everywhere."

Ssserakis laughed. *There's only one Necromancer here. These pitiful apparitions are your doing.*

"They can't be," I said. "I haven't so much as tasted a Necromancy Source in half a decade." The ghosts were the result of some sort of residual magic, I was sure, but no Necromancy I knew of could leave such a strong impression on the world, causing the ghosts of an entire city to rise and mill endlessly about the ruins.

"Can't be what?" Hardt asked and it took me a moment to remember he hadn't heard Ssserakis' lie.

"Nothing," I said quickly. "It's nothing."

"Can we move on?" Coby said with a bored tone. "This is why I didn't want to bring you tourists. Bloody terrans."

"Are you alright?" I asked Imiko, ignoring Coby. The girl nodded; her eyes still frantic but the panic gone. I turned back towards the city, taking my place at the head of the group once more.

I couldn't help but notice that Coby had changed slightly, her skin a little lighter, her hair darker, and she was shorter than before, matching my height. Silva had said Coby could change her skin, make herself appear to others as she pleased. I wondered then if she could mimic others, if she could fool people into thinking she was me. I could imagine it was quite a useful skill to have, and a dangerous one in the wrong hands.

The throng of ghosts lessened, but they did not disperse entirely, we accrued quite the entourage following in our wake, drawn by Imiko's fear. We walked through empty streets, strewn with rubble and discarded belongings. Here an upturned cart missing a single wheel. There a basket, its contents long since rotted away to nothing. Blood stains, weathered and faint, but still there. We saw buildings reduced to nothing but hewn stone, and others all but whole, doors and windows forced and hanging at odd angles. Everywhere in the ruined city of Picarr we saw evidence of a battle hard fought. Weapons and armour littered the streets, some clean and some bloodied. We saw shields rent in two, and others burned to blackened husks. Everywhere we looked we saw ghosts, and wherever they mingled we saw wreckage and ruin. The one thing we did not see, was bodies. It had been almost two years, and the last thing I expected was fresh corpses littering the streets, but we saw none, fresh or otherwise. There were no remains at all, no bones or rotted carcases. Armour, rent and stained brown with old blood, but no sign of the body it had tried to protect.

Hardt was the first to broach the mystery. He poked at a breastplate with his foot, rocking it back and forth. A Far Spider crawled out, disturbed from its webbing, and the big man leapt away from the little beast. It hissed, back legs scraping across its abdomen, and then faded away. I have never liked Far Spiders. No creature should be able to phase to another location without the use of a portal, least of all something the size of my fist with venom that can phase a person's limbs out of existence. "What could have done this?" Hardt asked. "So much death and not a single body.

Where are the bones? The army couldn't have collected all the bodies yet left the city like this."

"Wars are like flipped coins." Tamura said. I believe that was another of Belmoroes teachings; two sides and only one winner. I would argue that wars have no winners, no matter the outcome.

"Old man…"

"Ghouls did this," Coby said. "Look around you, terran. Both armies fought here, and neither one walked away from it. Some idiot Sourcerer brought an army of Ghouls across. Probably died and lost control. They've been here ever since, years of scavenging off the dead."

"Ghouls?" Imiko's voice was a timid squeak and I noticed more ghosts started drifting towards us.

"Corpse eaters from the Other World," I said. "They look worse than they are." I'll admit that was a complete lie, but I was trying to reassure my friend. In truth, Ghouls are just as bad as they look, and they look like death given form. "They almost look like terrans, I guess. Two arms and legs, one head. But they never stop growing, the oldest ones can be a bit bigger than Hardt."

I heard Ssserakis laugh in my mind. *You have never seen an old Ghoul. Brakunus is old enough to eat an abban in a single bite.*

I ignored the ancient horror. I should have listened. "Some walk upright, others on all fours. Their skin is a milky grey and glistens like morning dew, but it's rubbery to the touch and tough as old leather." We were still walking, picking our way through the streets towards the academy. I tricked myself into ignoring the scrabbling noises I heard, pretending it was rats, or just my imagination. "And they have no eyes, only holes in their faces that we might consider a nose, and a mouth full of sharp teeth for tearing flesh." I had never brought a Ghoul through from the Other World, I preferred creatures like Hellions than monsters such as Ghouls. They were easier to control, but I had read extensively on the subject.

"They sound horrible," Imiko squeaked.

"Well, they are monsters from the Other World." I glanced back and smiled at her. "They're not so bad, really. Not when you consider the other things in that world. But if we do see any, try to stay away from their claws. Sharp enough to do that." I pointed at a shield that had two large gouges ripped away from the wood. Imiko crept closer to Hardt and we continued.

As we passed the shattered remains of Braggart's Tower, we saw our first evidence of a magic bubble. The tower had fallen and not evenly, it looked as though something had blasted apart its southern side, and the tower had collapsed that way. Huge chunks of rubble lay strewn about, some of the stone broken, other bits scorched black. But at the bottom of the tower was a man, frozen only moments before his death. One arm was raised high, as if to shield against the huge blocks of stone above him, frozen in time with the Sourcerer. His other arm hung limp by his side, drops of blood pooling at his fingernails, one fat droplet paused mid-way to the ground. He knelt there, an arrow piercing the meat of his thigh. Dust hung in the air around him. He was dead. Or at least past saving. A Sourcerer on the edge of desperation, clutching at one final chance to save his own life. A bubble of our world ripped out of time. Some might consider it a work of art, a picture of a man in an eternal struggle against that which hunts us all: death.

"You shimmered blue like that when you... back

underground with Josef," Hardt said as we all stopped
to consider the scene. Even the ghosts drifted clear of the
bubble.

"He's a Chronomancer. For some reason time
is blue." I shrugged at him, unable to offer any sort of
explanation. I still can't offer any explanation for that, but all
Chronomancers shimmer blue when they use the magic.

"Can you free him?" Coby asked, pacing around the
frozen man, keeping her distance.

"He'd die," I said. "The falling stone would crush him
the moment time unfroze." I saw no reason to risk such a
thing.

Coby snorted. "He's as good as dead already. And he
has a Source."

I just shook my head. "Without another
Chronomancer he'll stay like that forever. Don't get too
close." I picked up a small stone and tossed it towards the
man, a few feet away from him the stone just stopped and
hung there.

The light was failing by the time we reached the
walls of the Orran Academy of Magic. I say walls, but there
really wasn't much left of them. Shards of rock and twisted
metal littered the courtyard where I had trained. Lightning
crackled around the stone, appearing as if from nowhere and
striking in an instant. I stared at a spot where a large oak tree
stood and remembered climbing it to leap over the wall and
escape into the city during the night. The tree was burning
from the inside. A gash had ripped through the trunk and
flames licked out of it, dancing red, yellow, and orange, but
never managing to consume the wood.

"How long has it been like that, do you think?" Hardt
asked. I had no answer for him. Magic did strange things to

the world when it clashed, and I couldn't shake the feeling
the tree had been burning that way since the city fell years
ago.

My skin prickled and it felt like I was being watched.
That crawling sensation on the back of the neck. Imiko felt it
too. She had the same sensitivity to magic I did, though she
is no Sourcerer. I could see her shifting foot to foot, nervous
like an animal about to bolt for freedom.

"What is it we're looking for?" I asked Coby.
Now that I was there, back at the academy, I wanted to
be somewhere else. Anywhere else. So close to so many
memories, I felt grief bubbling up, threatening to engulf me.

"A crown made of fire," she said, eyes locked on the
burning tree. "That looks like a good place to start."

The Crown of Vainfold. I had seen it before of course,
in the same room as the shield that showed me glimpses of
my future, and the same room as the sword with metal that
seemed to boil. The sword that Prena Neralis now carried.
Just the thought of that sword made my shoulder ache
where the blade had parted my flesh. The thought of paying
her back in kind did wonders for my temperament.

*That crown is a monster worse than any I could show you
from my world.*

"How did something like that end up in a tree?"
Imiko asked.

Tamura laughed at that. "How does a painting end up
on a wall? How does an onion end up in soup?"

"Someone puts them there?" Imiko asked, clearly
unsure of her answer.

Tamura sketched a low bow to the little thief. "Wise
beyond years."

The compliment certainly seemed to improve Imiko's

mood, and she nudged me in the ribs with a bony finger. "Hear that? I'm wise. What are you?"

"Vicious." I barely spared the girl a glance and let the threat hang between us. I should probably remind you that our first encounter ended with me on the ground and her fist in my face. I liked to think I had grown since then, both stronger and more skilled. That said, I didn't really fancy trying my luck against Imiko again. For a start she might have beaten me a second time and I'm not sure my pride could have taken it. There's also the fact that the girl was growing on me like a fungus I couldn't get rid of no matter how many times I tried to wash it away. She grinned at me and I felt my own mouth tugging into a smile.

"Why would anyone hide something like that in a tree?" Hardt asked. None of us had dared step foot onto the academy grounds yet. There were bolts of lightning flashing between blocks of stone and a feeling about the place, something menacing and savage. Like violence on the edge of eruption, simmering and waiting for a chance to inflect itself upon the world.

"Because it was chaos," Coby said. She had a look on her face like she had just smelled something rotten, nose screwed up and eyes cold and hard. "A Vibromancer set off an alarm when the fighting started, and it wailed in and out like a pulsing torrent of noise. You can't imagine how annoying that is. The city was burning, fire and smoke everywhere made it hard to see. And the screams! Why do you terrans always scream when you die? It's not like that will stop it. The noise doesn't ward off death, you'll still die. You just annoy those around you on the way out."

"Such compassion," Hardt growled.

"Fuck you, terran." Coby snarled back. "It was

a pitched battle, Orran Sourcerers fighting through the streets as they retreated towards the academy. Soldiers and Sourcerers, from both Polasia and Terrelan, beating them back. It was almost a good day's work, so many of you primitive terrans killed. But the noise..." Coby trailed off and shook her head.

"You were here?" I asked.

Coby gave me a withering look. "My mother wanted someone in the vanguard. The academy held plenty of powerful items and she wanted them secured before the looters could get to them. So, she sent me. And I failed." Again, the sour twist to her mouth. As much as I have always hated Coby, I can't deny her loyalty to her mother. She saw her failure as a slight against her own purpose, her reason for living. Her mother ordered her to do something and she failed, and now she was back to try again. Persistence and determination are two enviable qualities in a person, I see them in myself often. Perhaps that is why I clashed with Coby again and again, we were too similar in many ways. Then again, I think it more likely she just hated me for my relationship with her sister. For my part, I hated her because she's a heartless bitch who believes herself to be better than everyone. I don't need reminding of the irony.

"This place was a killing ground," Coby continued with a smile. "You think the rest of the city was scarred from the battle? Terrans died here in the hundreds. Sourcerers, young and old, stood atop a building where that rubble is now, and rained down ten flavours of death. Some idiot brought a Kathon through from the Other World. Have you ever seen a Kathon? As big as a house and armour harder than steel. It was crushing soldiers with claws while spraying others with something that made their skin melt."

Coby paused for a moment. "Far too strong a monster for some idiot terran Sourcerer who thinks she's bigger than she is just because of a taste of real power." I couldn't help but feel the jab was somehow aimed at me. It seemed quite unfair, given that I wasn't at the battle of Picarr and I had never summoned a Kathon. They were on the banned list for a reason.

Minions. Servants. The cowering wretch thinks our beasts of burden are monsters. Ssserakis laughed bitterly.

I must admit, I stopped listening to Coby's account of the battle. It's not that it wasn't important, but that Ssserakis had said *our*.

The ancient horror laughed in my mind. *Did you think I was the only one? By now the others will have claimed my city as their own. All my servants and my power stripped from me. I must return to reclaim what is mine. SEND ME HOME!* I winced at the shout and pulled my attention back to Coby.

"...the Geomancers collapsed the buildings and some dumb salt-kissing Sourcerer decided to summon an Arcstorm. Burned the fool up from the inside, but... Well, you can see for yourself." As if on cue, a lightning bolt ripped through the wreckage in front of us, striking stones and making the air crackle with its power. "This is why you stupid fucking terrans shouldn't mess around with magic you don't understand." She snorted and turned her back on me.

You might think Coby had a special hatred for terrans, but you would be wrong. She hated everyone, regardless of race or gender. I didn't realise then just how deep that hatred ran, how ingrained it was into her very being. I have thought of it often; what aspect Coby represents within her mother. To others, I can see why they would think it is her hatred, but I still remember what Silva told me about her sister. I think Coby is the Rand's insecurity, and she cloaks herself in deception and hatred to hide her true self.

That being said, she wasn't wrong about the Sourcerer who summoned an Arcstorm. Localised bursts of lightning striking randomly with lethal amounts of energy. I summoned one at the Fall of Orran, the very last battle of the war. It turned an entire squadron of Terrelan soldiers to nothing but ash and smoking breastplates in mere minutes. But that one had been only a fraction of the size of the one we faced down in Picarr. There is no way to dissipate an Arcstorm, at least not as far as I know. Some will wear themselves out, lightning striking until the power runs dry and leaves an odd void in its place where magic can no longer be used. Others draw on something deeper and more powerful and never stop. There is a place out in the Polasian desert that has been plagued by such lightning for as long as terrans have lived there. The sand hangs in the air, charged, and some areas of the dunes have been turned to glass. It covers an expansive area, and no one who has ventured inside has ever returned. Well, almost no one. I had no idea of the size or power of the Arcstorm left there in the rubble of the academy, but given that it had been raging for at least two years I suspected it had tapped into a power I could only dream of.

"I'm going in," I announced before I could think better of the bad idea. "I'll need someone to run to the burning tree and pull the crown out. Assuming it's actually there."

It was clear from the pinched look on Hardt's face he was not taken by the plan. The lightning crackled around the tree every few seconds and scorched the stone where it struck. "What are you going to do?"

I set my sight on the centre of the ruined courtyard, where much of the stone was blackened from scorching magical bolts. "I'm going to face the storm."

CHAPTER TWENTY SIX

JOSEF

The Portamancer is too tired to take us any further. Death used him mercilessly and he is so exhausted I had to shove the Spiceweed into his mouth. His skin is already starting to show the signs of Source rejection. He bleeds from his nose and ears, and he has that same peculiarity that all Portamancer's show when they have overused their magic. When I looked into his eyes, I could see all the places we have been today. I could see all the way back to Juntorrow where we started. We have travelled half the continent of Isha in a matter of a few hours, and he is too spent to take us any further. But he doesn't need to. Ro'shan hangs in the sky above us, a hulking monstrosity of rock and magic. Is Eska up there? Or is she down in the ruined city below? That's the question Death just asked me. I know Eska better than anyone, so where would she be?

The ruins. Of course she'd be in the ruins. Eska is a power-

hungry bitch, always has been. All Sourcerers know the hunger, but Eska is the only one I've ever known who likes it. Even with her stomach full of Sources she always wanted more. Yes, she'd be in the ruins, picking over the bones of the academy. Of our past.

Why? Death wants to know why. Because there is magic buried in the academy. Magic most people won't know to look for. There were secrets there, things the tutors didn't want anyone to know. Things we only know because Eska went digging and found them. Things like... I can't remember. I had it, and then my mind went blank.

We're leaving now. Leaving the Portamancer behind and heading out into the city. Even Death looks apprehensive at the thought, but she shows no fear. Tine is different though. He keeps glancing at his shield and mumbling something. I'm going to edge closer and see if I can hear him.

"It's here. It's here. It's here." He just keeps repeating those two words. What is here?

CHAPTER TWENTY SEVEN

TREPIDATION IS BOTH A TERRIBLE AND wonderful thing. I stepped into that wreckage of a courtyard, past crumbling walls and the twisted black iron that had once been a gate, beautifully crafted with a symbol for each of the known schools of Sourcery. I held my hands out and braced myself, fear and excitement rising with each step. I knew it was coming. I *knew* it was coming. I had that feeling in my stomach. A fluttery feeling, as though my guts were full of writhing eels. I heard a crack, lightning jumping between two slabs of stone, each many times as large as I, but the bolts ignored me. That wouldn't do. I wasn't there to be ignored. I've never been one to be ignored. I was there to draw attention to me, to force the lightning to strike at me and no one else. It's entirely possible I hadn't thought my actions through.

I stepped over a flagstone splashed with blood long

since dried to a flaky brown. Still, the lightning arced around me. Still, the magic ignored me. I saw lightning flash from deep within, striking blocks of stone and trailing sparks until finally cracking close to the burning tree. Further and further into that courtyard I went until I could see shards of glass scattered amongst the broken stone. I knew then that I was standing by the dormitory. It was gone, nothing but a giant mound of rubble long since collapsed in on itself. I looked up at a building that was no longer there. I had slept in there for ten years of my life. I remembered so clearly the way my old bed would creak whenever I rolled to the left. I knew the scratched marks in the mettle of the frame of that bed, both the ones I had put there, and those that predated my existence. I knew the walk from the girls' rooms to the boys'. I knew every groaning floorboard, and every shadowed nook to hide in. Even now, years later, I know with a certainty I could make that walk blind. From my bed to Josef's. So many memories, both good and bad. I like to think mostly good. I had a hard childhood, almost torturous at times at the hands of tutors, but I was warm and I never went hungry, and I had Josef beside me. A true sibling with a bond that went deeper than blood ever could have.

All gone.

The building I had grown up in, nothing but cracked stone and shattered glass. The bed I had slept in, nothing but twisted metal bent and broken beyond any fathomable shape. The floorboards and nooks, buried and burned to ash. The brother who had been my rock and anchor for all my life, dead and far behind me.

All gone.

I felt anger then, not sadness. I know I should have grieved for everything I had lost. But instead I raged at everything that had been taken from me. And I laid all that anger, all that hate at the feet of the Terrelan emperor. Right where it fucking belonged.

The lightning needed some convincing, and I was in just the state of mind to help it along. I wanted to feel it strike me. Odd to realise it now, but I did, and not just because I needed to draw it to me. I wanted to feel the pain of it, the heat of it, the sharp bite of it. Perhaps it was the punishment I thought I deserved, or perhaps the sight of a place I had once called home, wrecked beyond recognition made me desire to hurt just as those who had died there hurt. I can't say for certain. I held my arms out wide and drew on the Arcmancy Source inside, rubbing my fingers together I created tiny sparks of lightning. And it was all the invitation the magic around me needed.

I screamed, between the pain and pleasure of it, as bolts of lightning ripped from the stone around me and struck.

There was a joy in creation that was entirely unrivalled by anything else Maratik, the Breaking, had ever experienced. He often spoke of it to his brothers, but the other Djinn didn't understand. They maintained that it was the role of the Rand to create, to bring about the new. The role of the Djinn was to preserve the old, or at least only to alter it slightly so its original purpose was retained. Time and time again, Maratik had tried to express his joy. He pointed to their cities, Ro'shan and Do'shan and Mo'shan and Uo'shan. The other Djinn didn't agree. They claimed the cities were alterations, a mountain made to fly was not a new creation. Only the Rand created.

It was almost enough to send Maratik mad. How could he convince his brothers that the Djinn were not so limited? They could create from nothing, bring about whatever they desired, rather than just changing what already existed. Together they had the power to do anything. And perhaps that really was the truth, Maratik considered. They were not limited to altering Ovaeris. There was more they could do. More they could create.

Maratik went back to his brothers, full of excitement. His form crackled with the energy of it and a storm trailed in his wake, drawn by his power. His brothers waited in the world of the Djinn, a place they had created for themselves and a place the Rand could not reach. A place between earth and sky and water. A place where the wind howled, the rock rumbled, the water roiled, and the fire burned. It was proof. The proof Maratik needed all along. He would convince them all with his excitement, with his joy, with their world, and they would join him. Maratik was certain of it now. The Djinn would create something even the Rand could never dream of.

The Djinn's memories flashed through my mind so fast I struggled to comprehend them, and I had no time to ruminate on the experience.

My scream was something primal, something that belied my size and tore through the entire city, echoing around until it wrapped the ruins in a shroud of noisy agony. My eyes glowed as though the blue of them were somehow lit from the inside. I knew none of it. The lightning did not strike just the once, the magic was not so kind as that, it latched on and emptied itself into me, trying to tear my body apart with its force. Bolts struck my hands, but they did not stop at blackening my fingertips. Lightning wreathed my arms, burning away my sleeves and travelling up to spark at my face. I felt it all over, until I was sure I was burning. I tasted lightning as it travelled through me and erupted from my mouth, blistering my lips. Perhaps you would like to know what lightning tastes of? Well it tastes of fire. And don't ask what fire tastes of because you do not want to know.

I was unable to move. I couldn't break free. I was trapped there in that agony, a prisoner of the Arcstorm as it refocused itself with me at its centre. Unable to move, unable to feel anything but the pain, unable to think much past my own foolishness and knowing that I was going to die there. How arrogant I was to believe I was a match for such a force of magic, to believe I could wield and control something that no other Sourcerer ever had. A true Arcstorm is a Source unleashed, all the magic, all the power, all the life of that Source cracked open and inflicted upon part of the world. We Sourcerers can use the magic of a Source, we access a small portion of its power, letting it leak out into us where we can use it to our own ends. It hurts us. All Sourcerers are damaged by the magic we use and if we use it too long, or access too much of it, it will kill us. I thought I had created an Arcstorm at the fall of Orran, but I was wrong, a small lightning storm is all I had ever set free. A true Arcstorm is created when a Sourcerer unleashes and is consumed by the Arcmancy Source they hold inside. I wasn't just standing at the centre of a lightning storm; I was standing on a Sourcerer's grave. I was bearing the raw destructive power of their sacrifice. And in that moment, I knew the feel of that lightning. I'd felt the touch of it before. Tutor Elsteth had died here. She who taught me everything I knew about Arcmancy had sacrificed her own life here years ago to create a storm that would protect the secrets buried beneath us. I hated her for that decision, even as I respected her conviction. The academy's secrets were just that, and for a good reason. Even with all the tutors dead, it was important those secrets stayed buried.

I suppose we are lucky Hardt did not try to save me from the storm that held me in its fiery grasp. He would have died; I knew it for a certainty. The sheer amount of power coursing through me was enough to kill a man, even one of his size, a thousand times over. Maybe more. Definitely more. Only my magic stopped it from killing me. I can't even describe how, really. An Arcmancer accesses the Source, draws the lightning out of it to inflict upon the world. But I wasn't doing that, I was drawing lightning into me. The Source inside of me was absorbing it. I was absorbing it. Nowhere in any of the books I had read, and in none of the teachings of the tutors, had such a thing been mentioned. But, as I have said, what the tutors and the books did *not* know about Sources far eclipses what they *did* know. We were all just children playing with a power we couldn't hope to understand.

It burns. Even Ssserakis sounded strained. The horror shrank down inside of me, but it couldn't hide from the storm. Neither of us could. We both felt the pain of it and the scream that tore from my lips belonged to us both. It was killing us both. The academy might have forged into a weapon, but even weapons can break.

The others stared at me, witnessing my agony, and unable to do anything to stop it. I hated them a little for that. The sooner they ventured into the courtyard and found the damned crown, the sooner I could try to figure out how to stop the storm before it consumed me, and it was consuming me. I could feel the skin on my arms smoking and my fingers were blackened and cracked. The pain was surreal. I have endured torture, both down in the Pit and later in my life in the emperor's Red Cells. Those tortures were meant to break me. They were designed to break me. Some of them came close, some of them even worked, but most of them fell far short of the agony imposed by standing in the centre of that storm.

Coby was the first to break out of her stupor and she gave Imiko a solid push in the back so the thief stumbled into the courtyard. She froze there, wincing as she no doubt expected lightning to rip from the stone around her and fry her from within. Such foolishness. It was as though they couldn't see me just a short distance away, drawing all the magic to me, caught in a cocoon of lightning. It was everywhere, tearing free from the stone and air around me, forking in and striking my arms.

Tamura was with Imiko in moments, walking alongside her, wearing a broad smile. I couldn't hear the words over the crackle of the Arcmancy, but I could see the utter confusion on Imiko's face. She was ever to join in with his laughter, but never one for deciphering his words. I don't think she had the patience or learning for it, and it often took a working knowledge of the histories to decrypt Tamura's riddles.

I smelled burning hair, it has quite a distinctive flavour that is entirely unpleasant. There was nothing I could do, even if my head was on fire, I was caught, held rigid by the lightning running through my veins. I didn't even know how to free myself once Imiko had the crown. That thought drove me to a panic, but even that I couldn't act upon.

The thief and the old man reached the tree and stopped, staring into the flames licking out from the cracked trunk. There seemed to be some discussion, probably over which of them should try to retrieve it. I should mention

I was still screaming, my voice unnaturally loud. I wasn't breathing. I screamed for an eternity and didn't draw a single breath. I suppose I must have, but I couldn't think past the agony. Eventually Imiko thrust her hand into the burning crack and held it there for a while before pulling it out entirely unscathed, as though the flames didn't even touch her. Tamura turned to me with a wide grin that quickly faltered when he saw me. I was still caught in the lightning, my mouth open and screaming. The skin on my hands was black and blistered, blood boiling as it seeped from my broken flesh. My arms were scorched by the lightning licking at me, and magic tore out of my mouth along with the scream, jagged bolts of bright light. I was dying, being slowly torn apart by the magic I could neither absorb nor contain. There was simply too much power there. I was caught in the Arcstorm, I couldn't even warn my friends of the Ghouls creeping through the ruined city behind them.

Ghouls are scavengers, corpse eaters, but they are not above making the corpses before eating them. Some Impomancers favour summoning Ghouls for the intelligence they possess, far more than Hellions or Khark Hounds who are beasts and nothing more. Ghouls are devious, if not smart. They are excellent at moving quietly, and striking swiftly, and with claws that can shred metal. It is their intelligence that has always made me steer clear of summoning Ghouls. If I lose control of a Khark Hound, it is one more beast running around the world. A very dangerous beast, but still a beast. If I lose control of a Ghoul, there is a murderous monster on the loose, one that will not balk at sneaking into a house and taking a child from their bed in the middle of the night. I would not willingly unleash such evil on the world.

I saw movement all over the ruins of the city, creeping through the wreckage and stalking closer to the academy grounds. No doubt they were drawn by my scream. Responsibility for my friends' deaths would be one more travesty in my growing list. That I would be forced to watch them torn apart and eaten while the Arcstorm consumed me, filled me with helplessness.

All because you're too weak to stop it. Ssserakis' voice in my head was strained and in pain. *Take control of the storm!*

I couldn't let it happen. I couldn't see another one of my friends die in a ruined city. I couldn't leave another body behind to be eaten by monsters that crept along in the dark. I saw Isen watching me from the shadows, standing close to his brother. His face, once so handsome and full of life, was a wreckage of broken skin and bone. Even with only one eye left to him, he somehow managed to accuse me with his stare. I knew the ghost was Ssserakis' doing, but I couldn't help the guilt that threatened to swallow me. Isen was right. I let him die, and I left him behind. I gave away our child, the last piece of him that both I and Hardt possessed. And now I was going to just stand by while his brother was slaughtered. Now I was going to do nothing, even while surrounded by so much power.

I did the only thing I could think of. I drew upon the power of my Arcmancy Source. Somehow, somehow the pain intensified. I can't describe it. I have never felt anything like it, before or since. It was as though I was being ripped apart piece by piece, my very makeup being shredded, while also burning. Instead of directing the lightning towards the Arcmancy Source inside, I drew on power from the Source and let that power mingle with the storm inside of me. I

found I could move. I took a single step forwards, bracing
myself and pointed my arm towards the city, where Hardt
and Coby still stood. Where the Ghouls were sneaking up
behind them. Coby froze, but Hardt took the initiative,
grabbing her and throwing them both to the side.

I redirected the power of the Arcstorm.

Lightning ripped out of me, tearing through the
courtyard, bolts splitting off and licking at the ground. My
skin blackened further and further up my arm, blisters
rising and bursting, but I didn't stop. I redirected the magic,
pulling it into me through one arm and releasing from the
other. Memories of tutor Elsteth flooded me, not just my
own memories, but hers as well. I saw flashes of her youth,
of her family, of her children. But those memories were part
of the storm, they didn't stay with me but passed through
as I channelled the magic. It struck the wreckage beyond the
academy and the Arcstorm burst into new life, a frenzy of
lightning bolts striking everywhere, and at everything. The
Ghouls were roasted as the magic tore through them; dozens
of them killed in an instant.

And then it was gone. The Arcstorm still raged, more
violently than ever, no longer over the academy grounds,
but just outside of it. I collapsed, boneless and in an agony I
don't want to remember. I did it. I saved my friends, but at
such a cost. The lightning had done its terrible work on me.
My arms were charred, skin blackened and weeping. Ruined
beyond saving. I couldn't move my hands, couldn't feel
anything but the pain. I had seen burns that severe before,
but never on anyone who survived. I knew with a sickening
certainty that not even a Biomancer could save me.

CHAPTER TWENTY EIGHT

I WAS IN SO MUCH PAIN I COULDN'T EVEN lose consciousness. The agony served as an anchor, keeping me attached to the world. I fucking hated it. I was dying, and in such pain, the sooner I got around to it, the better. But Hardt wasn't about to let me die so easily. The big Terrelan has saved my life more times than I care to count, and often when I've already given up on it myself. He rushed to my side, heedless of the storm that had so recently consumed the area. His face told me everything I already knew; the burned wreckage of my arms was far too severe. Still he plastered on a weak smile.

"It's not so bad."

You're dying. It did not escape my notice that Ssserakis had not included itself in the statement.

I tried to laugh, but I think I just whimpered instead. "You're usually a much better liar." My voice was

a wretched croak. I was shaking, trembling from shock
and everything else. It was about all the movement I could
manage.

"There has to be something we can do." There were
tears in Hardt's eyes. The tears of someone who refuses to
except the inevitable.

"Looks like I finally get to sacrifice my life for yours."
Again, I tried the laugh and failed. "I've been trying for a
while now."

"A physician, a Biomancer. Something. Coby, can the
Rand save her?"

I saw Coby staring at me, a look of disgust on her
face. "Why would she?"

Hardt stood, squaring up to the smaller woman. "Can
your mother save her?"

Coby didn't even blink, but she did shrug, then
turned away. "You have it?"

"One crown of flames," Imiko said, her voice
trembling. "It's not even hot. And how am I holding fire?"
She looked at me. "What's wrong with your eyes?"

Hardt crouched down again and helped me sit with a
strong hand on my back. I didn't tell him that I could feel the
burns there as well, stretching between my shoulders, the
skin blackened to crackling. Imiko and Tamura were close
by, concern on their faces. Imiko held the Crown of Vainfold
in her hands, the flames dancing in the shape of a circlet
with three peaks at the front.

"We need to get Eska back to Ro'shan before... The
Rand sent her on this quest, she can damn well deal with the
consequences." Hardt sounded very demanding, but I could
feel his fear. Even with Ssserakis leaking its strength into me,
I knew it was too late.

Idiot terran! Now how am I supposed to find a way home?

"Sorry," the word tumbled from blistered lips. No one asked who it was directed at.

Coby snorted and turned towards the city.

"Don't you want the crown?" Imiko asked.

Coby glanced back at the girl and the fire she held. "You hold onto it for now. Don't wear it. You won't like what it does to you."

If anything, Imiko only looked more worried, but she kept the crown in both hands. "What is wrong with your eyes, Eska?"

Hardt just shook his head at Imiko. "We need to get her back to Ro'shan." He turned to me. "Silva will convince her mother to help you." Desperation. We all knew the Rand had no reason to help me.

Still shaking, I nodded. Agony had become my life, killing me and yet it was the only thing keeping me tethered to the world. "Best hurry," I sputtered and tasted blood.

Tamura was there beside me in a moment, his eyes on me and full of something like wonder. "The fury of the storm held inside."

Our trip back through the city was something of a blur to me. Awash in a sea of torment, I could barely keep my mind focused on putting one foot in front of the other. Hardt offered to carry me, but I wouldn't let him. I couldn't force him to carry the guilt of watching me die in his arms. I decided I would walk until I couldn't. I suppose in some way I thought it fitting that I die in Picarr, where I had spent most of my life. I cradled my charred arms to my chest, unable to feel them past the pain. Unable to even move what was left of my fingers. The mere sight of them sickened me, those charred lumps of meat.

We retraced our steps as best we could but skirted the relocated Arcstorm as it raged amidst its new home. The smoking remains of the Ghouls were a stark reminder of how deadly that storm was to anyone who entered it. The smoking remains of my arms were another reminder, and an even more urgent one. Coby refused to hold the crown and refused to lead the way. I thought nothing of it at the time, distracted as I was, but I think she feared any traps that might have been left behind. She poked Tamura into walking ahead of everyone and the crazy old man led us happily. I glanced at the crown in Imiko's hands time and time again. There was something to it, something about it. It called to me like a Source; begging, demanding to be used. Promising power untold. Too little too late, I suppose. Imiko glanced at me often, always looking away the moment our gazes met. I wanted to ask her what she saw in my eyes, but I couldn't find the energy.

I've always wondered why my past has such an unwavering habit of catching up to me at the worst places and times. It is relentless in that way. Down in the ruined Djinn city, Josef caught up with me just as we were making our escape. It cost him his life, and that of Isen's as well. And there, in the ruined city of Picarr, Prena Neralis caught up with me yet again. We were, once more, passing the collapsing ruins of Braggart's Tower, skirting the edge of the bubble of frozen time, and then she was there. Tall and perfect, her uniform unruffled despite our surroundings. A slain Ghoul lay at her feet, its guts oozing into the dead city, her sword slick with black ichor. Behind her stood her two minions; the old man with the shield, and the giant who looked like he enjoyed pain. And behind them all stood Josef. I knew it was Ssserakis, showing me a vision of

the brother I had killed, but the horror had never worn his
ghost before and I felt my heart skip at the sight of Josef.
For a moment, just a single moment, I let myself believe he
was still alive. For just a moment, I felt relief. But it was a
lie. I was fooling myself and I knew it. Reality rushed in as
quickly as my false relief had, and I knew it was Ssserakis,
watching me as he did through the eyes of Isen and all the
others I had killed.

He's here to betray you again.

"Oh wonderful." Coby's voice dripped with sarcasm.
"More terrans."

"If you don't like us, why make yourself look like
us?" Hardt asked as he stepped in front of me. Always trying
to protect me, even when he's the one who really needs
protecting.

"This skin is convenient. For the moment." Coby took
a step forward and raised her voice. "What do you want,
terran?"

Prena kicked the body of the Ghoul aside. Despite
having just slaughtered one of the monsters, there was no
stain on her uniform. Her plate gleamed golden, shining
even in the dim light of the afternoon. "We're here for Eskara
Helsene," Prena said in that brusque accent of hers. "Unless
you are claiming she is again with…"

Coby threw up her hands and stepped aside. "She's
all yours. This way, thief, and bring the crown." She took a
few steps away from me, but none of the others followed.
Coby turned back, incredulous. "Last chance, thief. Follow
me and bring the crown, or I will pick you up and carry
you."

Imiko looked torn. She was never a fighter, not really.
She hated conflict as much as I revelled in it. Coby was

offering her a way out, and I agreed she should take it. Not just her, but all of them.

"Go." My voice was broken, a wet crackle barely audible even to my own scorched ears. "All of you."

Hardt turned to me with that severe look he got, the one that said he thought me a fool and he was about to argue. As I've pointed out, he likes to make excuses for my decisions after they're made, but that doesn't mean he agrees with them.

"Look at me, Hardt. I'm already fucking dead." I held up my hands between us. They were ruined. A mess of cracked and weeping skin, charred almost to ash. And the pain… I will admit, I wanted it to be over. I wanted the pain to be gone and there was only one way I could see to end it. Of course, that didn't mean I was going to go out without a fight. I couldn't draw on the Sources inside my stomach, I was too weary for that, but the crown promised power. And I have always been relentless in my pursuit of power.

"The Rand…" Hardt's voice faltered as he looked at me. He knew the truth; he just didn't want to admit it.

"Give me the crown," I rasped, my voice painful and bloody.

"No!" Coby's voice was a savage hiss. "The crown belongs to my mother."

I turned a savage grin on the Aspect and felt a new wound open up on my chin as my skin split there. "You can take it off my fucking corpse."

Imiko glanced between us, briefly, then rushed forwards and dumped the crown in my waiting arms before retreating. I expected to feel heat from it, even past the wreckage of my hands, but there was nothing. It weighed a little, but not as much as you might expect given what it

contained. Hardt and Tamura lingered. We had come so far
together and now they didn't want to leave me. There were
tears in Hardt's eyes. I have been the cause of so many tears
in my lifetime, usually shed by those I love most.

Hardt stepped close, a big hand resting lightly on
my shoulder. I tried not to wince at the extra pain his touch
caused. "I'll find Kento." He nodded to me, then turned
away, his shoulders slumped as he went.

And only Tamura remained. The crazy old man bit his
lip as he looked at me and a smile ghosted across his face.
"In the ashes we find embers. Waiting for more to burn. You
can't beat him, but you can win." And then he too turned
from me. They didn't look back to watch my last stand. I
think it would have been too painful for them. Only Coby
stayed behind, her eyes fixed on the crown in my hands. I
think she would have rushed in and taken it had she dared.
But she was too scared of the crown, and that only made me
believe in its power even more.

I stepped forwards, past the bubble of frozen time and
away from Braggart's Tower. Prena watched me, her eyes
narrowed into slits, and glanced over towards my friends
regularly. She didn't trust they wouldn't come back to try
and save me. There was no saving me. Her two minions
spread out, surrounding me. And Ssserakis watched me
through Josef's eyes. The horror was muttering something I
couldn't hear, pity written across its hateful face. Of all the
faces it could wear, it chose Josef's. I hated it for that, yet it
seemed somehow fitting.

"Do you accept your judgement?" Prena asked, her
sword held ready in long, slender fingers.

I shook my head and kept trudging forwards, one
agonising step after another, a mad cackle escaping my

cracked lips.

"You die today, Eskara Helsene," Prena said, dropping into a battle-ready stance. Her armour was enchanted against magic, designed to absorb and deflect a variety of Sourceries. But I couldn't use the Sources inside my stomach. I had only one hand left to play. I could only don the crown and hope its power would let me go out fighting.

My cackle turned into a bellowing laugh, blood spraying from my lips. No doubt they all thought me bloody well mad. But then I think the shield bearer had me beat in that. He had moved around behind me and even over my laughter I heard him muttering. "This is it. This is it! The end. All the ends."

Prena faltered, glancing past me to her minion. "What end, Tine? Get control of yourself."

I stopped and turned, trying to keep both Prena and the giant in view as I glanced behind at the man with the shield. It was hard work given they had me surrounded and every time I moved my neck I felt fresh wounds open in my skin, weeping something fouler than blood.

"The end. All ends." The old man with the shield was raving, his eyes wild. "There is no future past this point. All of them. All of the futures lead here and then… I'll show you." He reached over his shield, grabbed hold of the cloth covering it and whipped it away.

I had seen that shield before, up in the locked room of the academy. Along with the crown I held, and the sword Prena wielded, they had been treasured and locked away. I had seen things in that shield, visions of the future. Some had come to pass, others hadn't. I saw another vision then. All it took was a moment, a brief glance into the mirrored surface of the shield as the old man pulled the cloth away.

I saw myself at the head of a great army. Men and monsters together, standing side by side against numbers beyond counting. I stood straight and strong, a flowing overcoat, black as shadow, blowing in the breeze, and in my hands were the outlines of swords wreathed in crackling green lightning. Fire rained down on a battlefield that twisted from the all the magic clashing there.

I tore my gaze away from the shield just in time to see the giant advancing towards me at a run, his hammer raised for a swing. I saw Prena's eyes go wide, but she wasn't looking at me. She was staring past me, towards the old man with the shield. Even as her giant advanced, Prena turned into a sprint away from me.

Don't do it! Ssserakis knew my intentions and the horror pleaded with me for any other course.

I raised the Crown of Vainfold in my cracked, blackened hands, and placed the dancing flames atop my head.

CHAPTER TWENTY NINE

I LEFT MY BODY BEHIND, AND I WAS GLAD
of it. Isha and Terrelan and Picarr and the fight and my
body and the pain. I left it all behind and found myself
somewhere else. An open landscape, black and red like
the skin on my arms, stretched out before me. Barren rock
pitted with bubbling lava and plumes of flames that shot
into the air before splashing back down onto the ground.
To my left I saw a mountain rising up, a volcano spewing
forth magma and smoke. To my right I saw a castle, glowing
red as though made from fire. But it wasn't, it was made
from glass, lava pulsing behind the walls. Above me was an
orange sky, gloomy but well lit. There were no clouds and
there was no sun, but the world was light enough to see.
When I turned around, I found a patch of flame, burning in
the shape of a person, watching me. At least I think it was
watching me. It had no eyes; no features of any kind save for

the frantic dancing of flame.

"Hello?" I croaked the word. My voice still felt like I was dragging it over a razor.

The flames jerked a little and the voice that reached my ears sounded like a large hearth burning high on a winter's eve. "You must be the one wearing my crown. Welcome to my little world. I'm afraid it's not very hospitable to your kind." The flames fell silent and I got the distinct impression they were distracted.

"Where am I?"

"I just told you. You are in my world. It's not as large as the one you're used to. What you see is pretty much it."

It was a maddeningly vague answer. "Am I inside the crown?"

The flames shifted, drawing a little closer to me. I could feel the heat of them, and I realised then that I felt warm. Not just on my broken, blistered skin, but all the way through. I felt warm like I hadn't since Ssserakis had first possessed me.

"Yes and no. No and yes. You wouldn't understand. You creatures have such primitive intelligence, even after they changed you."

I bristled, as I ever have when someone questions my intelligence. "Try me."

"Very well. You are in what I like to call a pocket realm. It exists both inside, and outside of the world you know. It is mine in its entirety. Every bit of it was designed and brought into creation by my will. It exists within my crown, but also entirely outside of everything you know as the world."

The flames were right. I didn't understand. I assumed the crown was some sort of portal, but that was far from the truth. And it didn't answer the question of where I really was. "And you're Vainfold?"

"Yes." The flames dipped into what I assumed was a bow, it was oddly mocking.

I took the opportunity to check over my body. It was not like visiting the Other World; my body was there. I could move and touch myself; I could feel the pain of pinching my cheek. My burns still hurt, but the pain seemed a distant thing; unimportant. I was neither ethereal, nor dreaming. I looked inside for Ssserakis and found nothing but a void where the horror should have been. It didn't answer when I called it, and I felt nothing of its presence. I was alone, empty, terrified. I was so used to the horror's presence, it's company. It tormented me, yes, it was a curse, but it was always there. I relied upon it. I hate being alone. I have always hated being alone. Ssserakis saved me from ever feeling that. It was my secret passenger. My company when all others left me. Gone. I felt abandoned.

"What are you?" I asked, trying to focus my thoughts away from the emptiness.

The flames shifted angrily. "How quickly you creatures forget your masters. I am Djinn."

I shook my head at that, so certain of myself. "The Djinn are all dead."

"Are we?"

I shrugged. "It's a widely accepted fact."

The flames laughed at me. "And there you prove your ignorance, creature. It cannot be a fact for it is not true. A fact must be a truth, backed up with reason, logic, and proof. What you claim to be an accepted fact is actually a widely accepted rumour, conjecture. A falsehood. The Djinn cannot all be dead, for I am not dead." Again, the flames drew closer, the heat of them scorching my already blackened skin. "And I'm not the only one. In fact, there are more of us left than there are Rand. I believe that means we won."

I didn't believe the flames. Everything we had been taught back at the academy about history told us the Djinn were all dead, and the only survivor of their war with the Rand, a war between gods, was Silva's mother. "You're a little small to be a Djinn."

Again, the laugh. "Would you prefer a towering inferno?" The flames grew, swirling around and around until a massive vortex of fire blasted the land beneath our feet. It was so hot I couldn't help but back away, shielding my face with blackened hands. Two fiery arms reached out of that maddening whirlwind of flames. In one hand, lava bubbled up and dripped away to reveal a giant sword, red as blood and dripping something foul and black. In the other hand, a hammer shimmered to life from the flames, and at the centre of the hammer blazed a light so bright I couldn't look at it. "Do I impress you now, little terran?" The voice no longer sounded like a crackling hearth, but more like a forest fire, wild and out of control, mesmerising in its danger. I'd be lying if I said I wasn't impressed. I was also fairly convinced that the creature was in fact a Djinn.

The Djinn raised both sword and hammer high, and then brought them crashing down around me. The hammer sent chunks of rock leaping from the earth, and molten magma started forming beneath it. The sword drove point first into the ground and sat there smoking. I backed away another step, awe and fear warring within me. Over the years I have found it important, when dealing with Djinn or Rand, not to make them angry. Even weakened they are terrible creatures with power beyond reckoning.

Unfortunately, I have a habit of not taking my own advice and I've never met a Rand or Djinn I didn't eventually make my enemy. I'm really quite good at pissing people off.

From the bottom of the vortex, where the fire touched the earth, stepped the smaller figure of flames. The vortex slowed and faded away as though on a strong wind, and the smaller flames walked towards me. The hammer and sword remained, embedded in the ground. "You little creatures are so easy to impress." The voice was back to a warmly crackling hearth, full of good humour.

"So, if you're still alive, why not show yourself like the Rand? Why let everyone think you're dead?"

"Because I'm trapped. I suppose I might as well educate you as long as you're here. Tell me, little terran. What do you know of the war between Rand and Djinn?" There was an intensity to the question. The Djinn was just waiting for me to prove my ignorance once again. I didn't disappoint.

"You were once like gods, living in harmony…"

The flames laughed at me; the interruption obvious. I was starting to realise this Djinn loved the sound of its own voice. More than that, I think it loved having a rapt audience. "You little creatures have an odd concept of harmony. Does the sea live in harmony with the land? Does *fire* live in harmony with water? Does light live in harmony with dark? We tolerated the Rand and they embarrassed us, deceived us. They tried to destroy what we created. They sought to seed our world with parasites. And eventually, even after we tried to make peace, they made a mockery of us. Harmony? Hatred! Opposition! War!" With each word the flames grew brighter and hotter until I had to back away and shield my face.

"But you created the world together?"

The laughter that burst forth was like a volcano erupting. Great plumes of fire shot into the air around us. "The world you know was there long before the Djinn and Rand, and we are as bound by its laws as you are. Different laws, but they exist all the same. It is those laws that doomed both our people."

"What does that mean?" I had to shout to be heard over the roaring fire of the creature.

The flames shrunk down again, the anger there simmering to a festering hatred. "Continue your story, little terran."

I thought back to all the history books I had read, all the bard tales of crafty warriors tricking Djinn, and princes begging boons from Rand. They all seemed so inadequate now I was confronted with a creature they all claimed long dead. But then, there are always rumours. Back at the academy, I had heard the Iron Legion had found a Djinn and bested it in some manner. I couldn't help but wonder if that Djinn was Vainfold? Had Prince Loran donned the crown before me? Had he stood where I did at that moment, matching wills with a god? If so, how had he beaten it?

"You started the war." I paused, expecting the Djinn to argue and grow enraged once more, but the creature stayed silent save the flames of its form dancing away. "No one knows why. I've heard it said it was for vengeance over a lost life. Some people say it was to seize control of the world for yourselves. Others say it was a war for the lives of the rest of us; terran, pahht, garn. The only thing all the stories agree on is that the Djinn started the war and lost it."

The Djinn was silent for a while and I got the feeling its attention was elsewhere. I wondered where else it might be, trapped inside the crown with me. "We struck the first blow," the flames said eventually. "But the Rand started the war. We asked them for a favour, and they twisted it into an insult. It was our way of pursuing peace, an attempt to create something together. Something to rival the birth of your world. Something new. Something different. Something of both of us, Djinn and Rand. They made mockery of our venture and gave birth to a slight. We knew then, there would be no peace between us. There could be no harmony. There would be war. We struck first, killing one of them. Her name was Yuestethan, the Light, and until her death we didn't even know if we *could* die."

I felt an itch deep within my chest, as though something was scratching away behind my ribs, but I ignored it, determined to learn the truth of the Djinn's war with the Rand. It was curiosity, but also something else. I wanted to know the secret. I wanted to know what no one in the world knew. A truth that was mine and mine alone, unless I chose to share it.

"For every one of them we killed, one of our own fell. They struck back, killing us even as we killed them. For your kind with your meaningless lives, generations passed. Terrans huddled behind their walls of stone while the land shook with our war."

"I've seen the scars your war left on the world," I said.

The flames laughed, a bitter crackling of dying embers. "No, you haven't. Our war left no scars. It reshaped Ovaeris. Eventually some of us started to tire of the war. We saw how it must end, in mutual destruction. The Rand saw it too, of course, and they made their own plans. For us, some of us, we tried to escape the cycle. And so, my crown came into being. I created this place, a realm outside of the world, to escape the laws your world imposed upon us. I fled here, escaping the fighting and devious machinations of the Rand. I wasn't the only one. Keratoll, the Learned, made his home within a book. Geneus, the Guiding Light, fled into a lamp. Aerolis, the Changing, was the boldest of us and made his home deep in the heart of Do'shan, binding the city to his whim."

"And you, Vainfold, chose a crown of fire?"

The flames laughed and grew to a blistering radiance. "Vainfold, the Eternal. And the crown was made of wood before I made it the home of my realm."

"And yet the war is over. Centuries old. Everyone believes the Djinn lost. Everyone thinks you're all dead. So why not leave?" Again, I was shouting over the roaring flames.

"Because I can't. I am trapped here. The power of Djinn is shared and bolstered between us all. As more of us perished, our power waned. I tried to leave once the war was over, but I no longer have the power to tear myself free of this prison I created. I am stuck here for eternity." The flames turned towards me and grew intense. "But thanks to you I again have my measure of freedom. And with your body I will finish what we started so long ago and carve the last of the Rand from the world."

I felt the itching grow stronger and clutched at my chest, wincing through the discomfort and pain. "What do you mean?"

The flames laughed, like a roaring fire fed too much fuel. "Your mind is here, little terran, but your body is still there, my crown sitting upon your head. It belongs to me now. I must remember to feed it. The last body died after just a few days because it weakened so."

I tried to wake up. To flee back to my body, but I couldn't. I didn't know how. Panic started to set in. I think I can be excused that, at least to some degree. Wounded beyond repair and on the verge of death, I may be, but my body was mine. The thought of the Djinn walking around in my skin made me feel ill. What destruction it might cause in my name? What damage might it do to those I loved? Not just my friends; Hardt, Tamura, Imiko. Silva. No, not just them. The Djinn meant to take the war to Ro'shan, to kill the Rand. And Kento was somewhere up in that city. My daughter, lost to me she might be, was still my daughter, and I wasn't about to let the Djinn harm her. I couldn't. I couldn't die knowing that a god would use my body to destroy the thing I loved most. I had to stop it. Somehow I had to take back control.

The itching grew stronger still, turning into a cold lance of pain. I staggered forwards, closing on the flames of the Djinn regardless of the heat. "No!" I shouted at it, clutching at my chest. "I won't let you…" The pain grew so intense I collapsed onto my knees, struggling to breathe. I had failed. I was dying.

My shadow grew beneath me, turning pitch black and pooling like water around my legs. Then the pain eased as that pool of shadow separated from me and coalesced into something ancient and horrific.

CHAPTER THIRTY

"NIGHTMARE!" THE DJINN SOMEHOW MADE that word a damning accusation.

Ssserakis rose from the shadow, a formless black that seemed so out of place in the fiery landscape. The horror didn't so much take a shape as it did convulse, as though it couldn't decide on its appearance. I will admit to both relief and joy at seeing Ssserakis. The horror tormented me relentlessly, poking at my fears to feed itself, reacting to my anger to scare others, but I had missed it. Missed its company, its cold reassurance. It's strength.

The flames of the Djinn grew in intensity until I could feel the heat of them even half a dozen paces away. "Deceitful abomination, you are not welcome here. Leave this place."

Ssserakis seemed to bubble and I could feel its anger as clearly my own. We were connected again, our shadows mingling into one inky substance that seemed far too real to be shadow. *This body is mine, Djinn. I have claimed it. You are not welcome here.*

The Djinn started to swirl and grow once more into the whirling vortex of fire. "I will purge your existence, as we should have done the instant of your creation." Its voice grew louder as the vortex swelled in size. A blaze. A roaring inferno. A fire long since past any hope of control.

Ssserakis laughed, cold as ice and carrying all the menace of an assassin's blade. *You have grown weaker, Djinn, and I have grown stronger than the Rand ever dreamed.*

I have never been very good at standing by while others decide my fate. I stepped forward, placing myself between the two monsters. "This body is *mine*! And neither of you are welcome in it. I may be on the verge of death, but I will see you both cast out before I let you hurt anyone with my hands." I must admit, I had no idea how to back up my threat. Trapped inside the crown, I didn't have access to the Sources inside my stomach, and I doubted punching a tornado of fire would do much but make the burned wreckage of my hands even worse. Besides, what good would it do beating the Djinn there? We needed to find a way back to my body.

A great arm burst out of the Djinn and a hand gripped hold of the sword still embedded in the ground. Another erupted and took hold of the hammer. Ssserakis turned to me, inky shadow roiling in anticipation.

You have been pushed out, Eskara. The Djinn fills your body with fire and covers the world in flames. I had a sudden vision of my body, wearing the Crown of Vainfold, surrounded by the burning ruins of Picarr. The flames were spreading, growing stronger and hotter every moment as the

Djinn pushed more and more of its power into my failing body. *But I am the link you need. I have clawed my way past his defences. Neither of us can reclaim your corpse by ourselves, but together…*

The horror was right. Even channelling so much of its power through my real body, the Djinn was too strong for us. It was, after all, a god. A diminished god, but still a god. It wrenched its fiery sword from the ground, preparing to swing and end both of us.

Ssserakis knew the moment I agreed even without words. The inky shadow rushed over me, into me, filling me and surrounding me in a blackness that was in no way dark. Tendrils shot out of my right hand even as the Djinn's sword fell, wrapped around the blade and hardened, stopping the sword dead, and in that moment, I saw something in the vortex of fire. I don't know how exactly, but I saw it hesitate. I saw the Djinn doubt itself. A god showing weakness.

The shadow continued to bubble around me, flowing out of my skin, surrounding me and lifting me up. I found myself held in a cocoon of darkness that responded to my will. And more than that, I felt the power of the Sources inside of me once more. The bridge Ssserakis created between my world and this one let my power cross over. Arcmancy and Kinemancy and freezing shadows, all fuelled by the fear I had been feeding Ssserakis for months. I didn't know if it would be enough to beat the Djinn, but I did know that I had no other choice. No other chance. In order to reclaim what was left of my body, in order to protect Ro'shan and the child I had abandoned there, I had to fight a god of fire. I couldn't afford to lose. For Kento's sake, I would cast the god out of me.

The Djinn pulled on its sword, ripping the blade free

of our shadowy grasp, at the same time raising the hammer high above. The shadow form was clumsy to move, slow and sluggish, so we raised an arm, forming a shield of kinetic energy just in time to block the hammer blow. As far as we were aware, such a thing had never been done with Kinemancy before, a physical shield formed of energy that we could hold onto. But we had no time to appreciate the discovery. With our other hand we sent jagged black spikes shooting from the writhing shadow pool below us. They pierced into the heart of the fire storm and we drew on the Arcmancy Source to send lightning bolting along them. If the attack did any damage to the Djinn we couldn't tell. The swirling fire ate away at the shadowy spikes until they faded into the light, and the magma dripping from the hammer was eating away at the kinetic shield.

The Djinn thrust with its sword and we lurched to the side away from the blow, the shadow cocoon around us absorbing the force and wrapping around the blade, holding it tight. But that, too, played into the Djinn's hand. The fiery vortex drew closer, burning brighter and hotter than before. Our shadows were pulled apart by the flames, ripped from our form to scatter and fade to nothing. We screamed from the searing pain of the blaze and willed the icy shadows to erupt around us, pushing back the vortex and freezing the magma forming beneath us.

Like hundreds of grasping hands, we willed the shadows to reach out of the black pool, snatching at the Djinn, clinging to its arms and its weapons, freezing whatever they could. We heard the Djinn howl and it drew back for a moment, pulling back its sword and then cutting away all the shadows with a single blazing slash. The hammer followed the sword again, crashing down upon us once more. We raised both hands just in time and enveloped the weapon in a mass of inky darkness, slowing the blow just before it crushed our body at the centre of the shadow. I could feel the heat of the magma dripping from the hammer, eating into our shadows even as we tried to freeze it.

Let me handle the defence. Do what you do best, Eskara. Be the weapon. Attack!

I took Ssserakis' advice to heart. Before, we had been acting as one, the horror's full power given over to my direction. But I was still learning that power, what I could do with it, and how. I had little time to learn anything when most of my attention was given over to stopping the Djinn from crushing us to burning embers. I gave up the defence and let Ssserakis shield us as best it could. I attacked!

I willed jagged shadowy spikes to thrust out from the pool beneath us and pierced the vortex in a hundred places, then I sent a Kinetic burst out through each spike and detonated them all. Thousands of icy shards ripped through the mass of swirling fire. I wasn't sure whether the Djinn was inside the vortex or whether it *was* the vortex, but I could see no other target, so I bent every bit of power I could muster upon it. The Djinn swung for us again, the sword trailing a light so bright it hurt to look at. I ignored the strike and trusted Ssserakis to protect us, and the ancient horror kept up its part of the bargain, blocking the sword even as I sent bolts of freezing lightning into the heart of the vortex.

The Djinn staggered, the vortex falling backwards, and I saw it slow. For a moment, just a single moment, I let myself believe we were winning. In a battle, those moments are the most dangerous thing a person can feel. The terror of a falling sword, the pain of lanced rib, the pride of a blow well struck; those are things a warrior should let themselves feel. It is good to be scared, for it keeps us pushing past our limits. The pain is useful, it lets us know where our weak points are. Pride spurs us onto more of the same, forever chasing the next good strike. But the belief that you are winning… The moment you let yourself think that, is the moment you forget to expect the next attack. And more often than not, it is that attack which will decide the outcome of the battle.

I felt the ground shake beneath us and the cocoon of darkness around me tightened a mere moment before plumes of molten magma shot up around us. The scream wasn't mine. I wish it had been mine. A part of me had always believed Ssserakis indomitable; beyond pain and defeat. The horror's cry of agony proved that wrong, and my moment of belief that we could win turned to a damning certainty we would lose. Our shadowy body was burned away in a rush of fire. In panic, I willed a mass of shadow to extend behind us and pulled our body away from the erupting column of flames. I hadn't known I could do that; I thought our inky body clumsy, but the truth was I just had no idea how to use it. It was ungainly, that was true, a dark blob of pulsating shadow, but it was fast when we needed it to be, but it could only move along the shadows we sent out. I determined not to be caught by the same attack a second time and sent out shadowy tendrils in every direction, waiting for the moment we needed to relocate to a better position.

The Djinn came at us again and once more we traded blows. I couldn't tell if anything I did hurt the creature; every time I disrupted the vortex, even a little, it came back blazing hotter and swirling faster than before. For our part I could feel us weakening. It wasn't just Ssserakis either, there is a limit to the amount of power a Sourcerer can draw from a Source, a limit before the body starts to reject the Source, and I was drawing that power from a body that was a world away. We dodged the Djinn's attacks as often as we blocked them now, and twice I backed us away then threw long range shadowy whips at the vortex, trying to sheer into the heart of the storm.

What are you doing, Eskara? We are outmatched. We can't hope to kill this thing here, and you're burning through my strength too quickly. It is the Djinn's will that holds us here, I burrowed through it once when it was distracted, but its walls are set tighter. Distract it again and I will carry us both back to your real body. I could hear the weary frustration in Ssserakis' words, and I could feel the way every movement was getting harder and slower. We were failing fast and the Djinn only seemed to be growing stronger.

Ssserakis was right. All my attacks were accomplishing was making the Djinn focus more strongly on us when what I really needed to do was distract it. We couldn't hope to beat such a creature in a realm of its own making; a realm where the very world around us responded to its will. A thought occurred to me, a plan forming in my mind, and I glanced backwards to see the castle of glass and fire. The Djinn's home within its home. The grin I let slip out was malevolent, one of a child revelling in thoughts of kicking over another's tower of blocks. I sent out a mass of tendrils snaking along the cracked ground until they reached the Djinn's home, then I pulled us along them. It is quite disorientating moving so fast and I felt a moment of dizziness

The Djinn paused, uncertain for a moment. Perhaps it believed I was laying some sort of trap. It was all the hesitation I needed. I launched hundreds of thick shadowy lashes out towards the castle, gripping hold of every bit of it I could. The heat pulsing within the veins of the structure made Ssserakis hiss in pain, but the freezing shadow held. I augmented the horror's strength with my own Kinemancy, and we pulled on the bones of the castle.

Too late, the Djinn realised what we were doing. It sank down into the ground and raised up nearby in a jet of fire, but by then the glass holding the fire in had started to crack. With a final ear-splitting crash, a large section of the building shattered, molten fire rushing out of it. Vainfold roared in anger and swatted us aside with its hammer before rushing to the castle and bending its will on reforming it. A distraction, and all Ssserakis needed. I felt my consciousness tugged away from the world and my vision started to fade. Victory. No. We hadn't won, we had lost. The thought was a bitter one. We were running away, beaten and bloody. One more failure laid at my feet.

Something grabbed hold of me. It was nothing substantial, nothing I can truly explain, but the Djinn gripped hold of my consciousness somehow, and I felt myself tugged between two forces. Ssserakis desperately pulling me back to my real body, and Vainfold refusing to let me go; one blazing, hot as a sun, the other freezing cold as an icy death. But it was too late for the Djinn, Ssserakis was aided by my body's own gravity and I felt myself slipping from that world of fire.

Far from anger or annoyance, I felt the Djinn laughing at me. "I will remember your name, Eskara Helsene." My entire life was nothing but an instant to a creature as old as Vainfold. It could wait for as long as it needed for another body foolish enough to don the crown. Of course, whether it remembered my name of not was no matter to me. I may have escaped the Djinn's clutches, but even that was a hollow victory. All I had to look forward to was pain, and a body so riddled with injury I'd be lucky if I survived past the day.

CHAPTER
THIRTY ONE

I TORE THE CROWN FROM MY HEAD BEFORE I even opened my eyes, let it drop to the ground without so much as a clatter. What sound does fire make when it falls? Then I awoke to a ruined city bathed in flame. It awed me to think of how much power the Djinn must have pushed through me to scorch the ground and burn stone. How could stone burn? Everywhere I looked, there were patches of flames licking the sky, molten rock, earth twisted into violent shapes. Even the clouds had drawn away from the city, spiralling around themselves as they were pushed by the force the Djinn had let loose. And it caused all of that while fighting Ssserakis and I, keeping us locked inside the crown. It was my first real taste of the power the Djinn and Rand possess, but far from my last.

I took in the full destruction Vainfold had wrought through me. A city bathed in flame, stretching as far as I could see. I did not think I had been in the crown for that long. I was shocked, there's no doubt about that, but there was something else too. I felt a hunger stir inside. I wanted to possess that kind of power, but I would not make myself slave to a Djinn to obtain it.

Ro'shan still hung in the sky, distant and dominating the horizon, untouched by Vainfold's flame. The relief that surged through me at that brought tears to my eyes. My daughter was safe. Kento was safe. A laugh broke free from my lips and the tears I shed ran freely down my cheeks.

The bubble of frozen time by the burning remains of Braggart's Tower had a new resident. The old man with the shield was frozen there, tumbling backwards as if he had fallen, his shield held out in front of him, a wild-eyed look on his face. Flames ringed the man, some in the moment of vanishing, and others just beginning to take hold of his clothing. In the reflection of his shield I saw a vast tornado of fire doing battle against an inky amorphous mass of tendrils and shadow.

Where do you think I got the idea? Ssserakis sounded diminished. The horror had expended too much of its power doing battle with the Djinn, and I knew with a certainty it would be a long time before it was strong enough to aid me again. A long time, and a lot of fear.

That was when I noticed that the pain was gone. Strange that it took so long for that to sink in. I looked down at my hands, expecting to find them blackened and weeping, ruined beyond any sort of use. But they weren't. The skin covering my hands and arms was new, fresh and raw to the touch, unblemished by exposure to the elements, but healed all the same. I reached up and touched the back of my neck, wincing at the feeling of such raw contact, but the burns were gone. The pain was gone. I quickly touched my cheek to find the wound Prig had given me, the ugly torn scar from a whip lash poorly treated, was still there. I'm honestly not certain if I was happy about that or not. A part of me would have loved the last evidence of Prig's torture scoured from my flesh, but another part of me wanted the scar. Wanted the reminder of the forge that had hammered me into what I was.

I turned away from the frozen scene, a Chronomancer caught on the very edge of death, unable to escape the falling rocks, unable to escape his own eternal prison. At least now he had some company. The grey haired Terrelan soldier caught in a moment, not of panic, but of resolute acceptance, as though he had known it would end this way all along. Perhaps most fitting was the shield the old man held. A shield made to show people glimpses of possible futures, now locked in a moment of the past. A young woman wreathed in shadow, doing battle against a fiery god; the last thing it would show to anyone. I felt a stab of pride at that.

A girl stood nearby, a shimmer around her like a heat haze. She couldn't have been more than six years old, pretty and pristine despite all the ruins and fire. She was terran, dark skin and smouldering eyes too old for such youth. I took her for a ghost, perhaps one of those lost when Picarr was sacked, and somehow with a will strong enough to keep her old form, but that was just my exhausted mind playing tricks on me. And I was exhausted. Body and mind almost too weary to go on. I could feel the shakes too. I was on the verge of rejection and would need to retch up my Sources before I created a second Arcstorm with my corpse at the centre of it.

"Are you *you* again?" The moment the girl spoke I recognised her voice.

"Coby?" My determination to remain upright fled with the last of my strength and my legs gave way beneath me, depositing me hard onto my knees. It is no wonder my knees ache these days, considering the punishment they received in my youth. Though in truth, it is not just my knees. What I wouldn't give to have even a taste of immortality, though I suppose Tamura would argue it a curse, forever trapped in the body of an old man.

Behind the girl, a patch of burning rubble shifted, a slab of stone pushed aside, causing a cascade of pebbles. Prena's brutish companion lurched to his feet from that patch of rubble. He was in a bad way, his face burned on the left side and his chest a mass of sores where the breast plate had heated and seared its way into his skin. His hair was all but gone, both on his head and face, and his left eye was swollen shut and weeping blood. But still he dragged that hammer up with him. I know the weapon now as I didn't then. It is called Shatter, and is one of the ten weapons that fell when our moons collided. It is said that one swing of that hammer can break anything. The one-eyed glare the man sent my way was enough to convince me he wanted to test the weapon's abilities on me. And I knew with a certainty that neither myself, nor Ssserakis had enough strength to stop him. We were, both of us, spent.

The man screamed a bloody roar and lurched into a run, dragging his hammer behind him. His eye was locked on me and filled with enough hate to drown the Pit with rage. As he drew close, he pulled the hammer up, swinging it around in such a way I was certain he meant to crush my skull with it. Twenty paces away, then ten, and all I could do was watch my death approach for the… Honestly, I'm not sure how many times I almost died that day. Far too many. There is an important lesson there; never overstep your limits. Know how far you can push yourself, how strong you are and how much punishment you can take. Also, don't walk into cities ruined by a magical battle without the proper precautions. Perhaps I should also add never trying to redirect an Arcstorm or doing battle with a Djinn. A lot of lessons I should have learned that day.

Coby stepped into the path of the hammer-wielding giant. Such a small girl, fearlessly facing off against such a large man. He should have crushed her underfoot. Barrelled her down and barely broken his stride. But Coby is more than she appears no matter which skin she might be wearing. She stopped the man with a single punch. A tiny fist and yet the giant stopped as though he'd run into a wall. The seared remains of his golden breastplate crumpled in from the force of the strike. The man stumbled backwards a single step, dropped his hammer, gasped for one last breath, and then fell backwards with a crash. He lay still amongst the rubble, one more ghost in a ruin full of them.

I knelt there too, almost as stunned as the giant who had just been punched. My mind worked to comprehend what I had seen, but I think it may have been a little overtaxed. Coby turned towards me. "You are you again?"

I nodded mutely, unable to summon words.

"Good. Stupid sun-sniffing terrans. Pick up the crown, and don't put it on again, you fucking idiot. Follow me." She turned and started away, her little legs struggling to clamber over a collapsed section of wall.

I glanced down at the crown beside me. The flames leapt and danced almost joyously. I imagined Vainfold staring out at me from the depths of those flames, willing me to don the crown once more and set his fires loose upon the world. I snatched the crown up with my right hand and lurched back to my feet. When I saw Coby again, she was wearing a new skin, a gangly terran woman with hair as short as a boy's, wearing a serviceable pair of trousers and a tunic to match. Where the young girl had struggled over the rocks, this new skin Coby wore stepped fearlessly. But I noticed the path she trod as the same one we had used earlier. Coby was retracing her steps rather than exploring new ground.

No one was waiting for us when I stumbled out of the city limits. I suppose it had been a vain hope to think the others might have stopped there, hoping I would make it out. I had said goodbye and told them I was already dead. And I had meant it. Of course they didn't wait for me. I should have just counted myself lucky that Prena wasn't waiting there. She had turned tail and ran the moment I donned the crown. The way she was staring past me, I think she saw something in the shield, a glimpse of her future, the city bathed in fire. It was too much to hope that the flames had caught her. I wasn't that lucky. I knew she was still alive and I was certain I had not yet seen the last of her. Coby didn't slow her pace, but when I looked away, she changed her skin once more, taking the guise of a stunning terran woman with perfect charcoal skin and dark eyes that seemed to have no end to their depth. I staggered alongside her, my feet dragging with every step. It wasn't far to the flyers and I would be damned before I turned up to the reunion, stumbling along behind Coby like a dog on a leash.

There is something wonderful about unabashed joy. That childlike glee that blasts all other thought from a

person's mind. It writes their feelings across their face in
such a way that it spreads, infects all those around them. I
have seen it time and time again. I have felt my own gloomy
spirits soar with a single smile from a child, or a raucous
laugh so genuine it pulled the same from my own lips.
I have seen hostility turn to instant friendship all for the
price of a well-timed joke and the grin that accompanied
it. It was that joy on Hardt's face that had me weeping, not
tears of sadness, but of happiness. I don't think I've ever
been so happy to be alive. The big man lurched into a run
the moment he saw me, barrelling towards me at a speed
that belied his size. I felt some trepidation, partly because of
the giant running towards me, and partly because I had so
recently said goodbye to my friends. I had so recently put
them through the turmoil of accepting my death, and yet
here I was. Alive. That turmoil didn't matter to Hardt, or to
Tamura, or even to Imiko. They were just so glad to see me
again. Silva, I think, was less certain. I saw the tears on her
face, the way she turned away from me. Then Hardt scooped
me up into a hug so tight I felt my bones creak.

    I let Vainfold's crown drop from my fingers and lost
myself in that embrace. In the comfort of it, the protection
I felt inside the iron circle of Hardt's arms, the relief and
joy of seeing him alive again, and the love he felt for me.
Not a romantic love, never that, not between Hardt and
I. It was the love of family, of a friendship forged in the
heat of something so few would understand, so few could
understand. We had not known each other long, not really,
but we had been through so much together. We had endured
so much together. I had put Hardt through such pain, and
yet he stood by me, and each time he refused to hate me
for my decisions and actions, it made our bond that much

stronger. It made it that much more difficult for me to hate myself.

I heard Coby snort, disgust so plain it was impossible to mistake. "Don't forget the crown." She stalked away. I think the display of affection hurt her somehow, perhaps it was that streak of envy running through her. Perhaps it was because Silva's tears were for me and not her. There were many reasons for Coby to hate me and I think she struggled to decide on just one.

Tamura danced around us like the ground was on fire, unable to keep still for more than a moment. He jumbled out a cascade of words and I heard few of them. "Like Lunize after the Hundredth Step. Renewed." When Hardt finally put me down, Tamura rushed forward and held up my arm, running calloused fingers across the smooth skin there. I swayed on my feet, barely able to keep standing once I was bereft of Hardt's support. Eventually Tamura looked up from my arms and met my eyes, holding my gaze. "The second Augury." I thought nothing of his words at the time, lost in the moment and struggling just to stay conscious. I felt something from Ssserakis, something more than general disgust at the joy I was feeling. The horror stirred at Tamura's words. Seeing signs in them only the ancient could know.

"You're healed!" Imiko made it sound like an accusation and Hardt took a step back, the joy on his face turning to shock as though he had only just realised I was no longer a charred wreckage of a woman. "There's still something wrong with your eyes."

"How?" Hardt's words were choked by the relief and I could see tears in his eyes.

I didn't answer him. Partly because I had no answers

to give, and partly because I looked past him, towards the flyers. Coby and Silva were standing together, arguing over something. The aggression was clear, but only from Coby. Silva kept glancing my way and I saw both relief and regret on her face. A part of me ached at that, for I knew whatever it was they were arguing about, I was the cause. They both quieted when we approached and Silva smiled at me. Not the joyous smile of a child, nor the genuine warmth of an adult. Silva smiled a thief's smile, a guilty smile, a smile to hide the truth. I see it now in my memories as I didn't then. Or perhaps I am simply jaded by what came after. I can't be sure. But I do know I was happy to see her again, and I believe that feeling, at least, was returned in full.

Silva did not give me time to speak. Even as I was trying to think of something to say, she stepped forward, placed her hands on my cheeks, and kissed me. I found myself in the centre of a tempest, a chaotic whirl of emotions tearing me apart. I didn't know how to feel. I didn't know how I should feel, how I wanted to feel. Her lips were soft, warm, tingling with something like lightning, though perhaps that came from me. My body shook from exhaustion and grew hot from her touch. The tornado melted away and in its wake I was left with only myself, a scared young woman as confused as I was rapt. By the moons above, her lips were so soft.

When finally, Silva broke contact and pulled away, I felt as though she sucked the breath from my body. I let out a ragged gasp and felt my legs wobble. I think only sheer determination, my body acting of its own will, allowed me to lock my knees before I fell. Silva blushed, a warm pink spreading across her cheeks. Never, not in all my years on this world, nor any of my years in the other one, have I seen something so beautiful. I forgot to breathe.

Our eyes met and I saw surprise on Silva's face, shock turning to a smile. "There's lightning in your eyes, Eska."

CHAPTER THIRTY TWO

JOSEF

No. I didn't know about the crown, I swear.

I've seen it once before. It was kept in the academy, next to the sword you wield, and the shield.

It wasn't Pyromancy.

Because all Sourcery starts with the Sourcerer. It comes from the Sourcerer. A Pyromancer can throw balls of fire, or create walls of ice, but it has to come from them. When Eska put on that crown the flames just sprang to life around her. There was no genesis for it. It was magic, it must be, but not of a kind I have seen before. It was not Sourcery.

I think Death is angry. It's hard to tell, she keeps it all so tight, so bottled up. She reminds me of Eska in that way.

I saw her. In Picarr, or at least what is left of Picarr. She looked unwell. No, that's not quite right. She looked dead. How is it that I'm the one who almost died? I'm the one who had his throat cut. I'm the one who suffers still, unable to say even a word. And yet she looked worse. How is it fair that I should hate her, but all I want is to rush to her side and heal her wounds? I wonder if she died in that inferno? Her arms were blackened like smouldering logs on a fire. Her hair burned away almost to the scalp. The pain. I know her. I know her face. I know what her pain looks like.

Eska is alive. I know it. I can feel it. My oldest friend. The one I both love and hate. She is alive and I don't know if I'm happy or not. Would I prefer to see her dead? Yes! I think. She is a blight. A black mark upon the world, and an infection that crawls inside of me. She's always been that way, pulling me into trouble, making me care for her when hurt. Just like the time she took it too far with Lesray. I had to sit at her bedside for days nursing her back to health. She doesn't even realise she started that fight. Or the time she dragged me down into the cellar and… I can't remember. I had it. The memory. Now it's gone.

I was twelve, I think. Eska had one more doorway to explore. One more of the five we were warned to never open. It was guarded by traps, but she could feel them and guided us around them. Then there was the door, dark and... There was light spilling out from under it. The sounds of animals rattling their cages. And then nothing. I can't remember. We were punished afterwards, I remember that. Actually, Eska was punished. She took full responsibility. I remember the look in her eyes so clearly. Was it pity? Was she truly sorry for dragging me down there? What happened beyond that door and why can't I remember?

Urkol is back, but he's in a bad way. How is he still walking? How is he still dragging that hammer? The ghosts are trailing him, vapid forms drifting alone behind him like they sense his death. They're thinner here at the city limits, most of them fading away before they reach this little derelict hut of ours, but they gather around him like scavengers waiting for a wounded animal to die. Will they welcome him? Will they pull his spirit from his body as it starts to grow cold? Will they tear at his memories, pulling him apart until all that is left is a vague impression just like them?

No. I can't save him. He's dying.

The burns are too extensive. I could clean and bind the cut above his eye, but the real problem is his chest. The breastplate has been seared into his skin, and this looks like an impact wound. The metal has been broken inward, digging into the flesh around his stomach. From the looks of it, the metal is both killing him, and the only thing keeping him alive. Perhaps if we could get him back to a city, where the physicians have real tools but...

Biomancy? If I had a Source I might be able to, but his wounds are so extensive. I don't know how he's not already dead.

Of course, I would try. No matter who he is, or what he might have done, I would always try.

CHAPTER THIRTY THREE

MAKING MISTAKES IS EASY, ADMITTING THEM is hard, correcting them harder still. I have made a great many mistakes in my life, some small and others grand. I have even made one mistake that may yet see the world brought to ruin. I admit to them all freely, a small measure of my desire to take responsibility for my actions. I will also admit that I am truly terrible at correcting my mistakes, and much better at compounding the issue with yet more mistakes. On the flyer, as it climbed its way steadily upwards towards Ro'shan, I admitted to myself that I had made a mistake, and I could see only one way to correct it.

Silva sat across from me in the hold. A number of goods had changed hands down on the ground, and even more coin. We were now quite cramped, barrels and boxes lashed down in every spare spot. Hardt didn't even try to fit himself into such confines, but simply shook his head and climbed back on deck where Imiko and Tamura guarded the crown. But Silva and I found space. I was wedged in between two crates, contemplating my life. Considering the kiss and how it made me feel. But my mind kept wandering back to something. Something I had felt while fighting the Djinn. My determination to defeat Vainfold had come not from a desire to save my own life, but from an imperative need to protect. I had felt the terror so strongly when the Djinn had said it wanted to see Ro'shan burn. The idea of the flying city in flames, my daughter somewhere amongst it, brought something out of me I hadn't even known was there. The need, the desire, the will to protect the one life I loved above all others. That thought had stolen my breath, frozen the blood in my veins all while lighting a fire so hot in me it burned away all doubt. I made a mistake. Not just any mistake, but the worst mistake in a short lifetime full of them.

I had given away my daughter because I believed I could not protect her from my enemies, from those who sought to crush me, and I thought Kento would be caught up in the consequences of my actions. A daughter murdered for the sins of her mother. But I had proven that false. I could protect her. I had protected her. I had fought Vainfold, a Djinn, a god, to keep her safe. I may not have won the fight, but I had succeeded. I had protected my daughter. And I would do so again and again. I would fight to protect her no matter how many times I needed to. Keeping her safe was more important than my revenge, and it was that I would use to drive me onward.

"I have a favour to ask." Those words, the first I had spoken since Silva kissed me, hung heavy in the air between us. It suddenly dawned on me that it was a terrible way to start the conversation. We should have discussed what had happened first, but it was too late to take back, and I didn't want to. My resolve was set, and I wanted to give myself no chance to waver.

"Anything." Silva's little book was in her hands in an instant. We were friends, and something else besides, but she never passed up an opportunity to collect a favour, no matter who was offering it. I wanted to see inside that book. I wanted to know how many powerful people owed Silva favours. And I wanted to know how many I owed her. By my count it was already four and I was on the verge of asking for my fifth.

Hesitation breeds doubt. "I want to find my daughter. I want her back."

Some silences are louder than a scream. This one was deafening. Silva said nothing and in that void, I heard the propellers whirring above, the creaking of ropes and cargo as it shifted and resettled, my own breathing tight and stuttering. In that silence, I heard Silva's heart break. And in her words just a moment later, I felt my own shatter to join it.

"Ask me for something else, Eska." Silva closed her book and tucked it away into a pocket of her dress. There was a grim finality in that. "Ask me for anything else."

I didn't. I couldn't. Asking for something else would have made a lie of my request, made a lie of the pain I felt knowing I would never see Kento again. There was always that between us, Silva and I, no matter close we got, no matter how entwined our lives became. No matter how much we came to love and rely upon each other, there was always Kento. Silva knew where my daughter was and refused to tell me. All infections start small.

We passed the rest of the journey in deafening silence.
I didn't go up on deck, it would have felt too much like
running away. Isen watched me from a dark corner, perched
on a crate, his one remaining eye fixed accusingly on me, but
Ssserakis said nothing through the wraith. Only watched
me. It wasn't fear the horror stirred within me though, it was
disgust.

Have you ever been so tired, so exhausted down to
your very bones, you are unable to sleep? That was how I
felt. I knew I needed to rest. I wanted to. I wanted to close
my eyes and find the dark oblivion of unconsciousness, and
I knew Ssserakis would not bother me there. The horror was
exhausted as well, depleted. It needed fear like I needed
food, but had not the energy left to provoke it. But I could
not find sleep, even closing my eyes led to nothing but a
dull aching of my senses. I just wanted to sleep. Sometimes,
the only way to truly rest is to simply keep going until your
body just stops. So, I kept going.

When the flyer docked Silva pulled me up out of the
crevice I had wedged myself into. She apologised then, and
I accepted it. Strange how you can accept an apology for a
thing, but never accept the wrong done in order to require
one. I was wearing a weary smile by the time we reached
land. Silva had a large wooden box pulled up and I placed
Vainfold's crown inside before any of Ro'shan's inhabitants
could see it. It did not escape my notice that neither she, nor
Coby would touch the crown. And even in my exhaustion I
noticed Tamura keeping a wary distance from it.

It would have pleased me then if my part of the day
was done. Imiko floated the idea of a tavern and few stiff
drinks to toast the failing light and a job well done. I must
admit, the idea was appealing. With a drink or two in front

of me I'd even happily have accepted Coby as a companion, not that she'd ever lower herself to drinking with terrans. But Silva shook her head at the idea and within moments we were on our way to the palace, to an audience with the Rand herself. I was in no state for such a meeting, but there are some summons one simply does not ignore.

The tiredness made the trip through the city laborious at best. Hardt carried the box containing the crown, holding it at arm's length as though the contents might burn through the wood at any moment. Coby led the way, wearing the skin of a male pahht and stalking along the streets with a menacing look. She drew quite a few stares from passers-by, and I think that was the point. Though perhaps I drew even more, people staring at me then quickly glancing away when I met their eyes. My gaze has always been quite piercing, but now it held the flashing of a storm behind it. I was trying to ignore it, but the Arcstorm was a part of me now. I had somehow absorbed some of its fury and its lightning crackled in my eyes.

The rest of us followed Coby. Well, except Imiko. I could not tell you when the little thief left us, only that at some point I noticed she was gone. It has always been her way. I felt new strength seeping into my limbs as we passed through the busiest part of the city. Ro'shan never slept, and many would argue that dusk was its busiest time, especially with an influx of goods from the world below. The populace was a buzzing hive of activity, and I have long since discovered that any living city generates a lot of fear. Most people wouldn't notice it, but to me it was intoxicating. A general miasma of unfocused fear rose up and Sserakis drank it in, growing stronger by the moment. I hadn't realised just how weak the horror had been until

it started to swell within me once more. Until the strength
that bled out from it loaned me new confidence to each step
I took. By the time we reached the palace I almost felt a new
person, the cobwebs blown away and my mind sharp again.
It had not done away with the exhaustion, but like a burst of
adrenaline, it helped me move past the weariness. And I felt
I would need to be alert and attentive for my meeting with
the Rand.

I tried to send the others away when we got to the
root of the palace, before we ventured up the arches, but
neither Hardt nor Tamura would have any of it. Hardt
smiled at me, he'd been doing that a lot since I walked out of
Picarr miraculously still alive, and told me it was likely his
one chance to see a Rand and he was not going to pass up
that chance. Tamura slapped his face once with each hand
and pointed a long finger up to the nest above, where the
arches met and the palace hung above the city.

"Longer than a life, shorter than a life. The pariah
returns to the pinnacle." I had no idea what the crazy old
man meant by that, but it certainly seemed like he wasn't
about to turn away. We crammed ourselves into the arch and
ascended towards my second meeting with the Rand.

I don't think I have ever seen Hardt as excited as
he was that day. Giddy as a child with their first view of
the wider world. He couldn't seem to stop grinning and
shifted from foot to foot as though each one itched too
much to keep still. He made Tamura seem positively glacial
by comparison, and the old man only ever really stopped
moving when he was fighting someone. I blame Hardt for
the nervous apprehension I felt, his restlessness spilt out
of him and I found myself rolling the tension out of my
shoulders. Coby watched us both, a sneer of disgust on

her pahht face. Disgust is the one expression I have never mistaken on a pahht, perhaps because they tend to do it so well, a slight curling of the lips, revealing just a few teeth.

Mezula was waiting for us. The Rand was coiled in front of her throne, seemingly in deep conversation with Gol who stood rigid as stone beside her. Silva often claimed Gol was far softer at heart than his severe appearance made him seem. I can't help but feel she lied about that. There was nothing soft about Gol, even his eyes were two hard chips of icy steel with a glare that could match my own.

"You return." I might have imagined it, but there seemed to be a small measure of surprise in the Rand's voice. No, I didn't imagine it. She didn't expect me to survive the ruins of Picarr. Luckily for me, I have made a lifetime of discarding expectations, much to the disappointment of those wielding them. The Rand waved her hands about, the eyes embedded in her palms flicking unblinking gazes over all of us.

Coby didn't break her stride, nor look back to us, but walked over to her mother and then collapsed onto the throne behind her, draping one long leg over the arm of the giant chair. I couldn't say when it had happened, but she seemed taller, broader, large enough not to seem tiny ensconced there. Silva stayed by my side and I felt her squeeze my hand gently, just for a moment, and then the touch was gone. I took a lot of courage and solace from that brief contact, knowing that she was there to support me. Tamura stood beside me also, a wry smile on his face that I didn't understand at the time. Hardt, however, was frozen to the spot a few paces behind us, his mouth open and the box forgotten in his hands. I turned around and approached him; he didn't even seem to notice when I plucked the box from

his grasp. He certainly noticed the savage kick I delivered to
his shins, and promptly regained at least a few of his senses.
I can't blame him, really. He stood there confronted by a
creature our people believed to be a god. I might have been
right beside him, but I had met her once before and found
her more monstrous than godlike. As I turned again and
approached Mezula with the box, I noticed Silva and Tamura
shifting away from me.

It is not an easy thing, walking close to a monster.
Every sense I had rebelled at the idea and I felt Ssserakis
shifting inside. If the horror were a dog, I would say the
close proximity made its hackles rise. To me it felt as though
the air grew thick around the Rand, my throat closing so
tight it was difficult to breathe. My legs shook with every
step and I struggled to look at her, feeling some strange need
to keep my eyes cast down to the floor. I fought against that
desire and kept my gaze locked on her face, though it held
no eyes. A few paces away, I crouched down and placed the
box on the ground, flipping open the lid to reveal Vainfold's
crown burning within.

"Now there is a thing I have never seen before,"
Mezula said, ignoring the crown for the moment. All
her eyes were staring at me. A grin stretched across her
monstrous face. I cannot see the flashing storm in my eyes.
To my own vision, nothing changed. But I have spent some
time studying it in a mirror and I must admit it is quite
striking. And I can always feel it, the Arcstorm inside. It is
a roiling fury of motion and power. I will not try to blame
it for any of my rash decisions, but it certainly has never
helped my temperament.

Unlike her children, Mezula was not afraid to touch
the crown. The short brown fur on her serpentine body

seemed to ripple as she reached into the box and plucked the crown from its wooden confines. She placed it on the flat of one hand and passed another hand around it, her eyes looking at it from so many different angles. A sharp toothed grin split the Rand's face with something like hunger, and for just a moment I thought she meant to swallow the flames.

"Hello, my old nemesis," Mezula said as she lifted the crown up towards her face, hands still passing around it in a dizzying blur of activity. It seemed all else in the room had been forgotten, and we all stood like statues as we watched the Rand and Djinn meet for the first time in an age. Maybe I imagined it, but the flames of the crown seemed to flair a little brighter.

"Can it see you?" All else in the throne room might have been forgotten, but I wasn't willing to be. I had risked everything to retrieve Vainfold's crown, and very nearly lost everything. I wasn't about to let that achievement be overshadowed.

One of Mezula's hands flicked my way, the eye staring at me from the palm. "Oh yes." Again, that toothy grin. "He can see me. He knows who bested him."

Us! Ssserakis hissed inside of me and I very nearly repeated it out loud. Mezula took the credit for our achievement. Not that we truly bested him so much as barely escaped with our lives.

"May I see the crown once more?" I asked.

Mezula slowly turned the crown towards me and I stared at it. I imagined Vainfold watching from within his fiery world, his last words to me, the promise that he would remember my name echoing all around. Then I flicked him the most obscene gesture I knew.

Mezula laughed and drew the crown away from me. "I almost have you all now, Vainfold."

"Why are your children afraid of the crown?" I knew I would not get a straight answer from Silva, and Coby was even less likely to humour me, but I thought perhaps the Rand herself might answer my questions. I thought I had earned answers. I've always had an arrogant streak that allows me to make demands of even the most powerful, gods or not.

Mezula's hands twisted, one to each of her children; Silva, Coby, and Gol, and one more looking past me, over shoulder, where Tamura stood. I followed the gaze of that eye and found the crazy old man waving at the hand.

"Bits and pieces everywhere. All littering the ground. Pick one up and…" Tamura gasped. "There you are."

When I turned my attention back to Mezula, her hands were moving again, one placing the crown carefully back in its box, while the others continued that waving dance as her eyes looked all around the room. "Because my Aspects are wise enough to know what the Djinn would do to them if he had even the barest whisper of a chance. Vainfold was a bitter flame even before war brought he and his brothers to ruin. Fire does nothing but consume if not kept in check and Vainfold *is* fire. His brothers wanted to raise the world up, build structures to inspire awe and shape the landscape into their myriad images. All Vainfold ever wanted to do was burn." Mezula turned away from me, carrying the closed box with her. "And nothing burns better than life."

I couldn't help but feel I was dismissed and I felt something like bitter pride rise up in me. I had almost died retrieving the crown, and Mezula had not even thanked me.

I felt the need to remind her what I had done for her. "What will you do with him now?"

A dark laugh rumbled around the throne room, filling all the empty air with its sinister tone. "Do with him? I will do nothing with Vainfold. He will sit in his box, watching wooden walls for the rest of eternity. A far greater punishment than any you might imagine, to be surrounded by something that should so easily burn at a whim, but instead keeps him locked away. The world will vanish from his sight and he will vanish from its memory. A fitting end for Vainfold, the Eternal. Why do you ask, Sourcerer?"

"She wore the crown," Coby said lazily, still lounging on the throne.

Mezula stopped slithering away and turned back towards me, all her hands snapping my way, six huge eyes watching me. Gol stepped forward for the first time, his stern face hard, eyes narrowed in suspicion. More slowly than before, the Rand approached me. All her eyes but one was fixed upon me, the last one pointing off deeper into the throne room. I glanced in that direction and saw one of the hunters I had murdered in the Forest of Ten watching me from the shadows. I wondered if Mezula could see the apparition, could see Ssserakis as it appeared to me, or if there were something over there I couldn't see. Perhaps the horror was trying to warn me of something? I braced myself, ready to stir my weighty limbs into action. I had already retched up my Sources and had no chance of swallowing them down again so soon. I readied myself for something, even knowing there was nothing I could do.

"There is a storm in your eyes. You wore the crown?" Mezula asked.

Not knowing where to direct my gaze, I stared up

into that eyeless face and nodded. "I thought I'd see how it sat. All queens should have a crown."

The Rand did not stop until she towered over me and all I could smell was a strange stink halfway between reptilian and musty fur. Hands moved all around me, unblinking eyes boring into me. "Did you meet the Djinn?"

Again, I nodded. "I met him. We had… a disagreement."

"Over what?"

"Who should have control of my body. He made a few valid points, but I didn't like his agenda, so I kicked him the fuck out."

There was something like scepticism on her face. "You wrestled control back from Vainfold?"

I found Silva beside me once more, her hand squeezing mine. "I told you she was special, Mother."

"The second Augury," Tamura said with a laugh. He had said the same down on the ground and I still had no idea what he meant. One of Mezula's eyes turned his way and she slithered past me, bearing down on the crazy old Terrelan.

"Tamura il Raither," the Rand said, her voice hard as sharpened steel and with a similar edge. "Pariah."

Tamura waved, showing no fear in the face of such a monster. "Hello."

"I should show you the quick way from my city, but you are all that is left of my most cherished sister. What do you know of Auguries, Aspect?"

Tamura let out a friendly laugh and folded up, crossing his legs and sinking down onto his arse like he often did when he was about to tell a story. He was silent for a few moments, and then launched into the tale. Even

Ssserakis listened to the old man's words, I could feel the ancient horror's concentration.

"War is a dangerous thing, and none more so than a war between family. They are vicious and unrestrained. Eons of resentment built up, and built up, and built up, and finally it broke like waves ravaging the beach. Families know best how to hurt each other. Brothers and sisters knowing their weaknesses, exploiting them. A horrible thing, war between family. On one side the Rand, life itself, the power to create, to give birth, to see something new brought into the world. Creators, fore bearers. Gods." Tamura paused and bowed his head before the monster in front of him. When he looked up, he shot me a wink. I have always wondered how the old man could be so precise and eloquent when telling a story, yet so fractured and puzzling the rest of the time.

"On the other side, the Djinn. Rock and stone, water and sky, the power to shape the very world we stand upon. Designs to mould the course of history. Cities, oceans, flying mountains; such wonders the world would never have seen if not for such unending creativity. Moulders and shapers. Gods.

"The war that scarred the world. For when gods clash, it is those below that suffer most. The pahht took sides first, begging protection from the Rand, but at what cost?" Tamura paused and stared up at Mezula. "You know best what changes were wrought upon them. A people twisted to fit a new image." Tamura shook his head. "So much history lost. The old must ever make way for the new.

"The tahren fled underground where they believed they would be safe from the conflict above, but darkness is never truly safe." He paused again, glancing my way. "Is it? Down there they found their own war to fight. The garn fought the war on both sides, brother against brother, and countless died, but such is the garn way. That was the start of a war without end, a raging fire that continues, even now. Perhaps the garn are fated to wipe themselves out, or perhaps they are wise enough to know there is simply no other way. No world could support their numbers if they turned away from their war.

"Beneath the waves, oceans and seas the world over, the mur fought as well. Not for one side or another, but against the powers unleashed when gods clash. After all, when the wardens are busy fighting each other, the prisoners want to escape."

Tamura swivelled himself around to look at Hardt and I. "And that leaves the terrans. Wanting no part in such destruction, they fled the cities made for them, leaving behind all the Djinn had built. They fled to the desert and the jungle, the plains and the ice, the mountains and even the sea. The terrans fled all over the world and started new cities. They built new empires, heedless of the war that still raged all around them. An ant hill kicked over is rebuilt stronger than before.

"The war made suffering a worldwide pastime. Men, women, and children of all civilisations lived with death just a step away. People like to say it as an enclosed event, *the war between the Rand and the Djinn*, but it was never such a thing. It lasted for centuries. Millenia. It rages still, the War Eternal. But time dulls all edges, no matter how sharp they might once have been, and history is remembered only for as long as it is relevant. But when they clashed... A battle between a single Rand and Djinn could make mountains tremble, cities fall. A war so devastating even the moons took solace in each other's arms and wept tears of metal."

Mezula shifted. "But what of the Auguries, Aspect? What do you know? What did Raither know? What knowledge did my sister leave to you?"

Tamura looked up into the huge eyeless face of the Rand and grinned. "Everything. Too much of everything. Too much to hold. Too much to know."

I felt a big hand on my shoulder and glanced up at Hardt. "What is this? Tamura is one of them?"

All I could do was shrug. I turned to Silva, but she had no answers, her attention fixed upon Tamura sitting before Mezula's towering form.

"The Auguries, Aspect. Tell me!" Some threats are given, not by what is said, by the way it is said. I have often found those threats to be all the more dangerous.

"Mezula," Tamura said with a grin, "the Impatient." He giggled and held up three fingers on his right hand. "Mother saw the truth long before you. Before any of you. A path of mutual destruction with no end but the end. But she also saw the Aspects for what they were, a beginning. The beginning of something new. Something the world had never seen before." Tamura leaned away from the Rand and grinned at me. "Through the Aspects, Sourcery was born." I realised then the story he was telling was for my benefit, not Mezula's.

"The Auguries were Mother's prediction. Prophecy, if such a thing exists. An end to the war. A true end, not this interlude you play at."

"An end? The death of the Djinn." One of Mezula's hands twirled around so the eye was staring at me. "Three Auguries. What did Raither predict?"

"One is the fusion of both life and death. A coin flipped and landing on both sides at once. Two is the renewal. A reforging into something the same, yet different. Three is the unity of purpose. Two forces acting together for an uncommon goal." Tamura lowered all three of his fingers and nodded, folding his arms against his chest.

"You dare mock me, Aspect?" Mezula asked, her voice menacing.

"Not at all. You asked. I answer. Not all are answers and expected or desired, yet they exist all the same."

"She was as good as dead," Coby said, still lounging on the throne. "Idiot terran walked into the centre of an Arcstorm. She should be dead. She looked dead. Then she put the crown on her head and her wounds healed in the flames."

Tamura shook his head. "The young know not the value of a word. Djinn can't heal, Biomancy is the realm of the Rand. Djinn can only renew."

"Renewal?" Another one of Mezula's hands turned my way, eye focused on me. The Rand reared back from Tamura and the crazy old Terrelan shuffled backwards, a wary look on his face. Mezula slithered towards the throne. "All of you go. I wish to talk to the Sourcerer alone."

CHAPTER THIRTY FOUR

I HAD NEVER BEFORE BEEN THE SUBJECT OF a prophecy. I understood little of what was going on, but I gathered enough of the bits together to realise I was in a position of power. I had something the Rand wanted, or perhaps it is more accurate to say; I was something the Rand wanted. That gave me leverage, a stake in the game, and I was determined to use it to my advantage. Even if I had to bluff my way to victory.

This creature is no more trustworthy than the Djinn. Ssserakis' warning fell on deaf ears. That's an odd turn of phrase considering the horror spoke within my mind, but the sentiment is no less relevant. I could smell the offer of power long before the Rand laid it on the table.

"I want to see my daughter." The words were out of my mouth as soon as the last of Mezula's children had left the room. Silva glanced back at me many times as she went, something unreadable in her eyes, but her mother had ordered her away and she could never disobey her.

The Rand settled down on the coil of her tail, resting in front of the throne, hands moving around to watch all corners of the room. "That would be the cost of your help? You ask it before you even know what I want."

I have always been impetuous. I wonder how many times I've gotten myself in trouble because I speak before I think, and because I speak before I listen. "It doesn't matter what you want. I'll do it, but I want my daughter back."

The Rand's breath hissed through her teeth. "Ask for something else, terran. Your daughter is no longer within my power to give."

"What does that mean?" Fear rose up in me so strongly I should have felt Ssserakis' pleasure. Instead all I felt from it was distance, silence, a strange tension.

"It means that I cannot give to you what I do not possess." There was anger in her voice, Mezula was not used to having her authority questioned. "Ask for something else."

The daughter is dead. There was an odd sadness to Ssserakis' words. It resonated within me. But I wouldn't believe. I couldn't believe it.

"Is she alive? Is Kento still alive?" I couldn't help the panic rising in me.

The Rand said nothing. I saw Isen watching me from the shadow of her throne and I could swear there was a sadness along with his usual accusation. Even with Ssserakis leaking power into me I felt my legs wobble. Mezula cocked her head and then waved a hand, I heard a grating noise behind me and when I turned, I saw a stool growing out of the bone of the floor. "You look tired, terran. Perhaps you would like to sit down."

A tide of grief rose up, threatening to engulf me, crash over my head, drown me and carry me out to sea. Silva may have helped me deal with my grief over losing Josef, but I had been steadfastly ignoring the pain of giving away Kento. It was easier that way, than to face the consequences of the decision I made. I had to push it back down. Force the tide to recede. Neither Mezula nor Silva had said Kento was dead, only that she was beyond their power. I clung to those words like a poorly constructed raft. I knew the implications of their words. I knew what they were trying to tell me, softening the blow of a dead child with bandied words, but I wouldn't hear it. I couldn't hear it. I couldn't take what I knew that truth would do to me. If Kento was truly gone, if my giving her up had led to her death, it would destroy me. So, I did what I have always done when confronted with grief, I ran from it.

I turned back to the Rand and wiped the tears from my eyes, staring up at her. "I have a name." I ignored the stool.

Mezula laughed, a loud noise that echoed around the throne room, like a cacophony of bells all ringing out of time. "I like you, Eskara. Perhaps my daughter is right about you. We should start again. Tell me, how were you able to defeat Vainfold?"

I considered telling her the truth. *If you mention me neither of us will make it out of this room alive.* There was something to Ssserakis' voice. Panic? I had felt it from the horror only once before, and recently, in our battle with Vainfold. I was slowly piecing things together, fragments of the truth let slip by creatures ancient enough to know to horde their knowledge. But it was time for that to change. I

made a promise there and then that Ssserakis and I would
be having a long conversation soon. For as long as the horror
was sharing my body, it was time it started sharing what it
knew as well.

"I didn't defeat Vainfold. I escaped him. He was
distracted, trying to force his fire into my body, my real body.
I made him talk, asked him questions. And then I destroyed
his castle."

"How?"

I shook my head as though the answer were obvious.
"With Kinemancy. I just blasted it apart."

There was hesitation in Mezula's reply, perhaps even
suspicion. "How did you draw upon on your Source in his
world?"

*Careful, Eskara. This is not one of your friends so easily
fooled by your lies.*

"No differently than I do in this world. I just drew
on the power of it. Vainfold was quite angry, but it took all
his concentration to reshape his castle and in that moment I
escaped."

"How?"

I had to think about that for a moment. My story
was flimsy without the involvement of Ssserakis, but then
that was what Mezula was looking for. A prophesied one,
someone able to do things that no one else could. As I have
said, I am no stranger to bluffing. "There is a gravity to our
bodies," I said slowly. "I didn't know it until I was forced
out of mine. But there's a pull that wanted me to return. I
followed it, held onto it and dragged myself from Vainfold's
crown, back into my body. And then removed the crown
before he could try to wrestle control back."

One of Mezula's hands shifted, the eye staring down

at the wooden box containing the crown, but all other eyes were on me. "Why did you wear the crown in the first place?"

I shook my head. "No. You've had a question, now it's my turn."

Mezula grinned, showing row upon row of pointed teeth. I took it for an invitation.

"Tamura said the Aspects gave rise to Sourcery. What did he mean by that?" I don't know why it was so important to me. Perhaps because I wanted to know my own nature, where I had come from.

"The Aspects were to be our legacy. When my sisters and I realised the war would consume us, we created children and gave parts of ourselves to those children. We didn't realise the consequences it would have. Even as my sisters died, their Aspects went out into the world and found lives for their own. They found love. They had families. They lived and they died as any other mortal might. Curiously, when two Aspect bloodlines converged, a Sourcerer is born. Someone who can wield crystallised magic. I assure you; it was never our intention to create Sourcerers. But such a valuable mistake in the end."

I was more than a little stunned. If what Mezula said was true, it meant my ancestors were Aspects. It meant I was a descendant of the Rand. I thought back to the academy, to all the tutors and students I knew there. I thought of Josef and Tammy, tutor Elsteth and tutor Bell, even Lesray and the Iron Legion. All descendants of the Rand. I couldn't help but wonder how many of them knew, but the answer to that was obvious. No one knew. One of the closest kept secrets of our world and Mezula had offered it to me like a scrap of a much larger meal. And it was. I knew with a certainty there was so much more she wasn't telling me.

You have no idea. The Rand and Djinn both deal with half-truths, lies, and deception. She is blinding you with one revelation while hiding another.

I let Ssserakis' words wash over me, my mind still reeling. My parents were not Sourcerers. They had never even seen a Source or the magic it contained. My mother was a basket weaver, my father an herb gatherer. They had cried when I was taken. I could see it now as I couldn't then. They didn't understand. But each of them must have carried the bloodline from an Aspect, each of them was related to the Rand, and when their lines crossed in their children… A thought struck me then; my brother. Not Josef, who I had always considered a brother of my soul, but Renuin, the brother of my blood.

I'm not sure how long I stood there, considering all the implications of that revelation. My mind raced down paths that threw my whole life into a different light. Foolishness. Nothing had changed, not really. Mezula had told me a secret, and there I was thinking it changed everything. And that was exactly what the Rand had hoped, to throw me off guard.

I never did return to Keshin to find out if Renuin was indeed a Sourcerer like myself. The fear of it was too great. The possibility of seeing my parents again, of them not recognising the woman I had become. The knowledge that even if they did recognise me, they could never understand the things I have done in my life. The reasons for them. No doubt they have heard my name, if they still live, and they know my deeds well. There is no context that can excuse them, and any excuses I gave would be just that. Easier for them to pretend their daughter is dead, than to face the monster she made herself into. It is, and always has been, fear that keeps me from returning to my family home. And it is one fear I don't think I shall ever overcome.

"Why did you wear Vainfold's crown?" Mezula's voice was soft, coaxing. Perhaps that was why I answered without hesitation.

"Because I had no other choice. I was dying. The Arcstorm had done too much damage. But I wasn't going to die without a fight. I could feel the power in the crown, the promise of making my ending a fiery one. So, I put it on, hoping to take Prena Neralis with me. I think the bitch still got away."

"You didn't know Vainfold would renew your flesh?"

I let out a savage snort. "I didn't even know he was in the crown until I met him. I thought all the Djinn were dead."

"And when you did realise, you decided to break free why?"

"Because Vainfold told me what he had planned. He wanted to burn Ro'shan from the sky and I couldn't allow it. I had to protect Kento…" I paused. Just mentioning my daughter snapped me out of my shock. It was all so pointless. I had fought back Vainfold for nothing. Kento was… No. I pushed the thought down, unwilling to let it take hold. Once more, I turned from my grief and ran. I realised I was answering Mezula's questions without hesitation.

And you think I'm insidious.

"What is this all about?" I asked.

Again, the Rand showed me her toothy smile. "I am trying to decide whether you are telling me the truth, or whether you are in league with Vainfold. If you are telling the truth, then my daughter is right and there is something special about you. That would make you useful. If you are lying and Vainfold has somehow convinced you of his misguided quest for vengeance, then you are dangerous."

"Can't I be both? Useful and dangerous."

"Oh, I hope so."

She hides the truth of what she has lost. Ssserakis' words were almost true, but Mezula had given it away, not lost it.

"You can't see it, can you?" I asked and was glad to see a flash of annoyance pass across her features. It was strange upon a face with no eyes. "Silva says she can see inside a person; past the masks they wear. She said you gave her that gift. But you can't do it anymore, can you? What you give to your Aspects you lose for yourself. That's why all the stories could never decide on how the Rand appeared, because you can change your appearance, but you're stuck in that form because you gave the ability to Coby."

"Very clever." There was a threat in those words, something about the way they were said. I'd seen past enough of her lies and deception to find some truth. Perhaps the smallest of the truths she hid. If only I had seen the rest of them.

I ignored the threat, I was already pulling on another thread and seeing where it led. "And Tamura is an Aspect. What did his Rand give to him?"

"Her immortality." Mezula's voice tinged with sadness. "Raither was ever the most compassionate of us all. The devastation the Djinn's war wreaked upon the world and our creations, upon us, was too much for her. She created a son, a legacy who would contain all her knowledge, all her insight, and gave him her immortality. A coward's way out, she took her own life rather than see through to the end the war she helped to start."

Tamura was so old even when I first met him, yet I had no idea of the truth of that statement. He has lived far longer than anyone has cause to. The things he must have seen. The things he must know. I have two theories for his scattered mind. The first is that the knowledge and wisdom of the Rand is simply too much for a terran mind to take. Raither passed on to him all she knew and, in the process, broke his mind. My other theory is that with everything he has seen, thousands of years of experience, the pain of it is what broke him. How many children could he have fathered only to watch them die, and their children after that? How many wars had he seen start and end? How many lives lost for what must seem to him as little to no point at all? Such pain and tragedy. How could his mind not have broken? There were always rumours that he was down in the Pit by his own choice, and I have come to believe them true. He knew where the Chronomancy Source would be in the ruined Djinn city. He had put it there. I think he made his way down into the Pit to look for hope. It is easy, when surrounded by the world, to see only the bad things; the injustices and the pain, the death and violence, the guilty and corrupt. But down in the Pit we were surrounded by those things; I think that made it easier for him to see the glimmers of hope. Because down in the Pit we might all have been criminals, but we weren't all bad. I pity Tamura for his long life, even as I envy him for all the years I will never have.

Mezula uncoiled, slithering slowly towards me. It is strange, but I felt the need to stare up at her face, even though her eyes waved around me on long limbed arms. The smell of fur and scale filled my nose once again and I couldn't help my lip curling at the stink. Ssserakis drew back inside of me, as though hiding itself from the Rand's gaze. Perhaps I would do the same if I came face to face with my maker.

"Raither predicted you would come, Eskara. She gave us the Auguries, signs to look for. You are the end to something we started millennia ago. Something we were unable to finish. It has shaped the world as you know it." Two of the Rand's hands lowered down in front of my face. They were huge, each four or five times the size of my own, and the eyes embedded in the palms were more pahht than terran; they watched me, unblinking. "You are the end to the War Eternal."

"Because Tamura thinks I satisfied the second Augury, the Renewal? What about the first and third?"

The Rand's hands started moving again and she turned and slithered away, one eye remaining on me all the while. "Prophecies are never exact things, Eskara. You have fulfilled one, who is to say you haven't already fulfilled the others or will not later in your short life. You are the most likely candidate I have ever seen, and my daughter sees something in you. I am willing to take a chance on you."

"To do what? What is it you want me to do?"

"I want you to go to Do'shan and kill Aerolis. He is the last of the free Djinn. I have trapped him there in his decaying city for so many years, but to do so I bind myself here to Ro'shan. I cannot leave my palace, and he cannot leave his prison. At least I had the foresight to lock Do'shan in place."

I have been called arrogant once or twice in my life, and I will admit to it. I often believe myself more capable than I am. There is a hunger running through me that craves

power and renown, it is true. I was still young, but already
I had commanded magics that put me at the head an army.
I had fought against numbers that far outweighed my
own. I had not only survived the tortures of the Pit, I had
done the impossible, and escaped it. I survived bringing an
Abomination across from the Other World, and to this very
day that accomplishment, or perhaps mistake, has never
been replicated. But even in the arrogance of my youth, I
knew an impossible task when it was set before me.

"How could I hope to kill a Djinn? I barely survived
against Vainfold."

"You view your victory in a harsh light, Eskara. You
battled against Vainfold inside his world. By your own
admission you drew on magic that should have been locked
to you. You slipped away from his grasp. You clashed with a
Djinn and won, whether you realise it or not. Next time you
will do more than just win. You will kill Aerolis. Do it. Set
me free and I shall grant you anything within my power to
give."

Take it!

"I can't..."

"You can." Mezula slithered forwards once more,
towering over me and fixing me with all six of her eyes.
"I am so certain of it; I will send one of my daughters to
accompany you."

It is a heady feeling having the unwavering
confidence of a god. Maybe if I had been older or wiser I
would have seen through her compliments and promises.
Maybe if my desire for power hadn't been so great, I
wouldn't have been blinded to the truth. If I wasn't running
away from the possibility of my daughter's death, I might
not have sought my own so readily. Maybe I would have

thought to ask more questions, had Ssserakis not been urging me to take the offer. The horror had done nothing but warn me both about Vainfold and Mezula, but now it demanded I accept her task. I know why. It wanted me to ask for an Impomancy Source. Ssserakis saw this as its way home, and all it needed to do was throw me to the wolves.

"What is it you want, Eskara?" Mezula's voice was soft and insidious.

With Kento beyond my reach, there was only one thing I wanted. My passion for it had not diminished no matter how far behind me I put the Pit. "I want the power to take revenge on everyone who put me down in the Pit. I want to destroy Terrelan and kill the emperor." It is somewhat strange to think of it now, but I had set myself against the man, sworn to bring about his death. The emperor had done the same, and he had sent his most dangerous warrior to kill me. We had never met, yet both of us had set ourselves on a path of conflict with the other that could never end until one of us was victorious.

"You will need power, allies, an army," Mezula said in that soft voice of hers. "I can give you all three. Do we have a deal?"

There was a saying in Orran; *"Never make a deal with a Djinn"*. It was most often uttered when trading with merchants, especially when one wants to steal a customer from another, but I think it came from somewhere more relevant. The truth is, the Rand should have been included in that statement, as well. Neither the Djinn nor the Rand are to be trusted, but that was a lesson I had yet to learn.

I nodded, and for the first time since leaving the Pit I felt as though I had made progress. "We have a deal."

I am the weapon. The mantra the academy drilled

into me. They had always intended me to be a weapon used against the Terrelan Empire, but what if I was more? What if I could be more? What if, instead of being a weapon used by one empire against another, I was a weapon to be used against a God?

CHAPTER THIRTY FIVE

JOSEF

Urkol is alive, thanks to me. I'm not sure if he deserves to live, but that's not my choice to make. I could save him, so I did. I know where Death found the Biomancy Source. She went to the traders from Ro'shan and purchased it. I can't imagine how much she must have paid. Is Urkol's life really worth so much? What is the going rate for a life? In the Pit it was nothing. Scabs murdered over a single spoonful of gruel, others because their foreman was in a bad mood. Up here, on the surface, life seems more precious somehow.

Eska must not have been there. I know Death well enough to know she wouldn't have come back so quickly if she had the chance to kill Eska. I've have seen Death's brutality. The way she callously blinded Yorin, her merciless use of the Portamancer. He is yet to recover, even with the Source no longer in his gut. Early stages of Source rejection, his mind is scattered throughout a dozen places and in his eyes, I can see each of them as clearly as when I was there. I don't think Death knew how much danger she put us all in by pushing the Portamancer so. We could easily all have been lost in the space between portals, or with that last step we could have found ourselves back in Juntorrow where we started. Even worse we could have found ourselves scattered. I wonder if I should tell her just how dangerous portals are, especially with a Sourcerer so close to rejection.

I must write this. I have to put my thoughts down on paper. Speaking a thought or writing it down makes it more substantial somehow, and I can't speak. I think I might have to burn the page after writing it. I need to see the words, but I can't let anyone else see them. Not until I know what they mean.

The Biomancy Source did something to me. I didn't have it for long. Death stood over me the entire time, watching as I removed the crushed and broken metal from Urkol's skin and forced the flesh beneath to heal. There was little I could do for the burns; they weren't severe enough and will heal in time. Biomancy can heal flesh, kill disease, but wounds leave scars and Urkol will have many of them. I don't know how he even survived as long as he did. He was near the centre of that torrent of fire Eska unleashed. There were some wounds I could nothing about, not without surgeon's tools and a team of physicians to help me. On his left pectoral the metal of his breastplate was heated to such a degree it fused with the flesh beneath. The act of removing it might well kill him. I've done what I can and he lives. He will live. But with the extent of his injuries, I'm not certain saving his life was a kindness.

But that is all what I did with the Source, not what it did to me. For months now, I have been remembering, and also not, a time when Eska and I dug too deep into the mysteries of the academy. Something we shouldn't have seen. The doorway, black as night with jagged yellow light escaping from beneath. The noises within, animals rattling cages, a desperate plea from a voice no longer terran. And every time we approach that door, my mind went blank, as though I fainted. As though the memory just wasn't there. I know how it was done. A master Impomancer, one far beyond anything I ever saw Eska do, altered our memories. Eska always focused on the Other World, on what Impomancy could bring across. But that magic is more than just a bridge between the two worlds, it is the power of control, of giving orders to things. We were ordered to forget what lay beyond that door. What we saw and what happened to us. We were ordered to forget the truth buried beneath the academy. And we did. Both of us. Eska doesn't know, I'm sure of it. Because if she did know she wouldn't forgive him. She'd have hunted Prince Loran to the end of the world.

I was scared. More than scared. I was terrified. I would have turned and ran if not for Eska determined to explore every secret the academy had to hide. One more misadventure she dragged me into. The door was unlocked and Eska inched it open with no regard for what might lie beyond. Dim yellow light from a hanging lantern cast everything in long shadows, and to each side of the door there were cages. Sturdy things of wrought iron designed to hold monsters. They lined the walls to either side of the door, creating a corridor of caged beasts. Only they weren't all beasts.

I recognised some of them. There were two root hounds, one male and one female, caged next to each other but separated by bars. The male lay on the cold stone, mewling. Its legs twitched and the scales on its back were a dull grey. It was going through a malting, trying to shed, but it didn't have the energy to rub its way free of the dead skin. The female growled, chewing at the bars between them with flat teeth designed to pulp grass. It was painful

*to see, but the least of the mistreatment down there. Eska wanted
to set the beasts free. She ran over and pulled at the cage doors, but
even a grown man the size of Urkol couldn't have opened those
cages without a key, and we were but children. There was an abban
calf, a female with mangy fur and horns just starting to grow in. It
watched us walk past without a sound, slitted eyes so sad it hurt to
see.*

*The further we went the more horrible the conditions. Some
of the animals had clearly been kept there for a long time. Some
still raged at the confines, snarling at us as we passed and rattling
the cage doors. One creature, almost terran in appearance but
with long hairy arms and a mouth full of chattering serrated teeth,
reached for us, snatching just short of Eska's skirt. Its eyes were
pitch black pits of nothing and it crushed itself against the bars,
trying desperately to reach us. I tried to pull Eska back, but she has
always been as stubborn as falling rock and fearless. She forged on,
past more and more cages. More and more beasts.*

*There were many creatures I didn't recognise, but Eska
did. A young Khark Hound from the Other World in one cage.
Sharp spines on its back and legs bristled as we approached and
its face was a twisted mass of bone and teeth, as though its flesh
just couldn't stretch far enough to cover its muzzle. Why is it
everything in the Other World is a nightmare given form? I
forget what they were all called. I stopped looking, even as Eska
continued to name them. For as much as she has always been
drawn to the creatures of that world, I have always been disgusted
by them. They serve purposes only ever fulfilled by war.*

*Only at the very last cage, before the corridor emptied out
into a well-lit room beyond, did Eska agree it was time for us to
run. By then it was too late, both for us and for Barrow.*

*He had been there on our very first day at the academy,
a student no older than myself. Both Eska and I had played with*

him, ate with him, learned with him, and lived with him. He used to tell me jokes he heard from the adults, dirty limericks and tall tales. A natural storyteller. What we saw in that cage could barely be called a terran. He was filthy, dishevelled in a way none of us had ever been down in the Pit. Like an animal caged so long it no longer recognises it should not roll around in its own faeces. Barrow pressed dirty hands to his ears and clawed at his scalp with cracked, bloody fingernails. His eyes were wrecked, weeping pits. Yet I heard something past the whine in his voice. He muttered about the light, the endless burning light.

Barrow always had an unfortunate pairing of attunements, both Vibromancy and Photomancy. He was not the first Sourcerer to be driven mad by the horrors of light and sound that we others just don't see or hear. But he'd always been so careful about it. I spoke to him many times about the danger and he had showed me his research, endlessly reading books, accounts by other Sourcerers. He'd even done the numbers, calculating how far he could push each school and how long it would take him to recover. I have never known anyone quite as obsessed by their research, nor anyone so careful with how they used their Sources. I didn't think of it then, consumed as I was by my pity and the need to rescue him. I thought if I could just get him to the infirmary, I could save him, maybe use my Sourcery to heal his wounds. But Barrow was beyond saving. I didn't know what had been done to him. I didn't know what lay through the door at the end of the corridor. I... I still don't.

It's coming back to me. But slowly. Something happened to us beyond that doorway. It happened to both of us. It changed us. What happened to us?

CHAPTER THIRTY SIX

LIFE UP ON RO'SHAN HAD ALREADY SEEN ME pitted against one Djinn, and my deal with the Rand put me on a collision course with another. The last of the free Djinn, though freedom seemed an odd choice of words. I wasn't clear on the details, but Mezula claimed she had trapped the last Djinn on Do'shan by trapping herself on Ro'shan. I assumed there was some magic at play I couldn't begin to understand. In truth it was the natural laws of our world I didn't understand. Ignorance can make even the mundane seem like magic.

Negotiating with Mezula took some time and I think I acquitted myself in those negotiations quite well. The Rand agreed I needed time, that I was not ready to assault Do'shan nor confront the Djinn she kept trapped there. Time not just to recover from the exertions, but to prepare and train myself. Do'shan was not just some uninhabited ruin. Aerolis had been busy in his incarceration, summoning creatures to his floating city, enslaving them, and preparing for his inevitable confrontation with Mezula's own forces. Mezula said the city was a fortress, built like a labyrinth and housing monsters. She granted me time to train myself and prepare, and money to purchase the services of those I would need. I couldn't take an army, there weren't enough flyers and they couldn't support that kind of weight, but I would need more than just myself and the determination to succeed. That sort of determination can take a person far, but when up against the odds, outnumbered and outpowered, it is wise to level the playing field as much as you're able.

With time to train and money to recruit anyone foolhardy enough to join me, I still needed something else from Mezula. Sources. I couldn't hope to fight the Djinn without power, and to that the Rand agreed. I asked for the Arcmancy Source I had already been given, Pyromancy, and Portamancy. Ssserakis was not pleased. The horror raged at me for some time, plaguing my days and curdling my nights with dreams of betrayal. I woke from one dream where Hardt was choking the life from me, his big hands wrapped around my throat, squeezing. I will admit I found it quite difficult to look at the big Terrelan for a couple of days after that particular nightmare. Ssserakis wanted me to ask for an Impomancy Source, to finally make good on my promise to send it home. I justified my actions by pointing out that I couldn't hope to beat the Djinn without the horror's help. For Ssserakis to help itself, it first had to help me, and then we would both get what we wanted. I'm not sure which of us was more naive for believing my placation. The truth that I was hiding so vehemently, was that I had no idea how to send the horror home. Even with an Impomancy Source, I still had no clue.

Ro'shan stayed anchored over Picarr for close to a week, an extended stay by the city's usual pattern. It was far away from any living, breathing town, and Silva wanted to allow ample time for merchants to reach us from nearby settlements. Ro'shan was a trade city first and foremost, and many of the supplies the people needed simply couldn't be procured in any way other than trade. I did not see her much for those days, she spent so much of her time either down on the ground far below, or coordinating with the city's merchants. It was her job, both as ambassador and bureaucrat, to make certain trade was fair and everyone had their chance. I've always wondered if that little book of favours she kept detailed any special permissions granted to those she dealt with. Just how many people owed Silva, I will never know. I certainly owed her more than I care to admit. I missed her. We hadn't had a chance to talk, and honestly, I wasn't sure talking was what I wanted from her. But I missed her. Silva's absence that week made my life a doubt-soaked agony that I struggled to understand. It was not unlike my pining for Isen before we had slept together down in the Pit, but then, it was also not that much like it either. That is the strange thing about love, it is never the same twice. Each time it is a brand-new mystery to explore. Each time involves new dangers, pitfalls, and rewards.

Hardt and Tamura argued about whether I should go along with the Rand's request, as though the choice belonged to either of them. Hardt pointed out that it was likely to be quite dangerous; he should have known that would spur me on rather than deter me. I think he knew if he came along, he would have to fight, to bloody his hands once more. We all knew he would not let me go alone. He

told me he was still looking for Kento, but that nobody
seemed to know anything of a terran babe anywhere in
the city. I didn't have the heart to tell him my suspicion,
and I couldn't face admitting it to myself. That didn't stop
Ssserakis from whispering the truth to me. My child, my
daughter, the little piece of me I had created, nurtured, and
abandoned was dead. I yearned to see her face again, to hold
her close, to feel the life I had made. But Mezula and Silva
had both all but admitted it, she was gone. As long as I never
forced them to tell me the truth, I could pretend. It was a
grief I simply wasn't ready to face. No parent is ever ready
to face that kind of anguish, and those who claim otherwise
are fucking lying.

Tamura encouraged me to go to Do'shan. He said
nothing about the Auguries or his mother, and when pressed
he either babbled nonsense or changed the subject. That was
maddening; to know that he had so many of the answers I
still sought, and yet either couldn't or wouldn't share them.
He liked to tell me that *'Time makes students of us all.'*, and
I suppose he was right in so many ways. Of course, time
is a luxury ill-afforded us in our youth. I find it somewhat
ironic that the older I get and the fewer years I have left to
me, the more patient I become. Perhaps that is just because
I understand the world so much better and realise that it
works on its own schedule and no amount of impatience will
change that. Perhaps because I realise now that the changes
I wrought upon the world did not necessarily alter it for the
better, and if I had taken more time to stop and consider my
actions and their consequences, I might have done things
differently. Probably not. Impulsiveness is one of the many
things I'm known for, and even grey hairs and wrinkled skin
have done little to cure me of that. In the end there was no

question over whether Tamura would come with me, but
he told me in no uncertain terms that I was not ready. And
when Tamura is direct, it is worth taking note.

Imiko was a different matter altogether. She laughed
when she heard of my plan, and gave Tamura a queer look
when she learned his true nature. I don't think she entirely
believed us, but then she fled rather than meeting the Rand.
She called me a fool and worse, claiming I would find
nothing on Do'shan but an early grave. But I saw past her
bluster this time. Imiko would argue right up until we left,
and then we would find her accompanying us all the same.
She has played many roles in her life; thief, assassin, spy,
foster mother, but to me Imiko will always be the little sister
I never wanted. That doesn't mean I'm not secretly glad to
have her.

I had no idea how to recruit the others I needed.
Warriors, I would certainly require for any assault to be
successful, but Ro'shan had none. It was a trading city which
flew hundreds of feet above the ground. No other nation in
all Ovaeris could hope to make any sort of military move
against Mezula's city, and if they did somehow manage it,
they would find the golems more than willing to show them
the error of their ways. It would also be helpful to have a
Sourcerer or two to back me up. I was confident in my own
strength, but when fighting a god, it is wise to bring other
targets to draw their ire.

Unfortunately, the only other Sourcerers on
Ro'shan were tradesman. Ingomancers who used their
magic to shape metal, blacksmiths and nothing more. I
met an Augmancer who had developed a way to draw
enchantments on crop seeds to increase yield. A Biomancer
who made house calls to those residents of Ro'shan who fell

sick. Everywhere I looked up on Ro'shan, I found Sourcerers who had never even considered using their magic for battle. It made for a stark contrast, for I had no idea how to use my own Sourcery for anything but. The Orran Academy of Magic had trained me to be a weapon with a single purpose: to kill. I thought all Sourcerers were trained to fight, but up on Ro'shan, I found that only terrans forced their Sourcerers into that role.

Perhaps it was because all of Isha had been at war for generations. Before there was only Orran and Terrelan, there had been dozens of smaller kingdoms, each fighting amongst themselves for dominance. We were a continent of people who had never known anything but war, so our culture had developed a way to find Sourcerers and put them to their most destructive use. To make people into weapons. But I think it is more than just our history that forged us into such a way of thinking. Polasia sits across an ocean from Isha, a desert kingdom rich in mineral mines and with a tradition of trade far more than one of war. Yet still they train their Sourcerers to fight. I think, perhaps, it is terran nature to find the most destructive purpose in everything, and then refine it until it is as much a danger to those who wield it, as it is to those caught in its way.

All this is to say, I spent three days searching Ro'shan, speaking to Sourcerers, and enquiring after mercenaries, and I found no one willing or able to help with my cause. I did, however, develop a new appreciation for the sheer size of the city and its warren of streets and alleyways. Not to mention how clean the tahren managed to keep the place. By the darkening evening I was feeling quite disappointed, so much so a ludicrous thought popped into my head. I knew a place full of fighters. A place where some of the most dangerous people in all Terrelan were kept. They were guarded by a few hundred soldiers, it was true, but the Pit was an army waiting for freedom, and purpose. It was a foolish thought, dreamed up by a desperate mind. The soldiers were one thing, but Deko and his thugs were also not likely to let me walk in and take away all the prisoners. And any who were left down there were unlikely to trust me after the riot I started. A stupid thought destined for failure, but at least I knew where it had come from.

I spotted Horralain easily, towering over the residents of Ro'shan and pushing them aside as he strode through the crowded street. We were in the artisans' section of the city and surrounded by workshops. I had just come from an Ingomancer who had told me in no uncertain terms that he would never work for a warmongering terran, and it put me in a foul mood. I was determined to drink away that mood and listen to one of Tamura's stories of the world gone by.

We saw each other at the same time. A familiar face, but certainly not a friendly one. Twice the giant had tried to strangle me, and my voice still held a slight croak from the damage he had done, yet I didn't hate him, nor try to think of a way to kill him. I think that shows how I was growing as a person, or possibly how desperate I was. Horralain was not nearly so magnanimous; he charged me with a roar, pushing a pahht couple aside and nearly trampling a tahren as it scrambled out of his way.

Many small animals have a strange instinct; in the presence of a large predator they freeze rather than run. I suppose there is some logic behind it, playing dead and hoping the predator was only looking for the kill and not a meal, perhaps. I think it is indecision that roots them to the spot, despite the promise of death bearing down

on them. Horralain was as tall as Hardt and perhaps just
slightly broader, a towering mass of muscle and unpleasant
disposition. His skin was so pale it was pasty, and his hair
hung down around his face in greasy clumps. He no longer
wore the prison rags of the Pit, but instead a patchy leather
vest and trousers that looked too small for his meaty legs.
And everywhere he was smudged with a dark oil. I knew
with a sudden certainty he had also climbed the great chain
that anchored Ro'shan to the ground, and I knew from
experience how difficult a challenge that was, and Horralain
had done it alone by the looks of him. I froze in the path of
that marauding giant, indecision rather than fear freezing
me to the spot.

Crush him!

Out of time and only moments from being trampled,
I reacted, throwing up my hands and drawing on the magic
inside. I created a shield of kinetic energy, barely visible but
for the purple shimmer in the air in front of me. I hadn't
even known such a thing was possible, but then I had done
the same thing while trapped inside Vainfold's crown.
I had no time to consider the implications as Horralain
crashed into the shield, rebounding and sending us both
sprawling on the clean street. The energy of that charge
had to go somewhere, and though I believe most of it had
been reflected back on the charging Terrelan, I still received
enough of the force to remind me of the difference between
our sizes.

I was the first back on my feet and facing Horralain
even as he shook the confusion from his head and lurched
upright. I crouched, settling onto the balls of my feet just
as Hardt taught me, ready to move. Horralain growled
and swung for me. I ducked under the fist and stepped

away from the follow up. It was in that scuffle that I finally realised Hardt and Tamura's training had truly paid off. Down in the Pit, I had thought Horralain swift in a way that truly belied his size, but in reality I had just been slow. Now I saw his attacks as if I were infused with Chronomancy, and I found my body strong enough to move away from them with ease. I revelled in it, enjoying the ability to flow away from his strikes so easily. We had quite an audience too, the citizens of Ro'shan drawing close to watch a slight woman dodging away from a clumsy giant; some laughed while others glanced around, worried. Spectacles such as the one we created are prime occasions for thieves, though they must be careful. The distraction allows pockets to be picked easily, but it's important to flee before the authorities arrive.

Arrogance is so very often the mother of mistakes, and I was feeling quite arrogant as I dodged around punches and leapt over lunges. Horralain turned his lunge into a leap and threw himself at me. There was little I could do about that, all the speed in the world can't help you when a man three times your weight lands on top of you. Joy at my body's ability to move quickly turned to fear and horror as I realised that Horralain had won. He thrashed out wildly, one massive fist hitting me in the shoulder and another just barely missing my face. I hoped punching the street hurt him, but Horralain didn't show any pain. I don't think I ever saw the man show pain, perhaps he simply couldn't feel it.

I will admit, I panicked. I'm not one to give over to such instinct, but I think I can be forgiven it once or twice in my life. Lying there, crushed to the street, with a giant pinning me down and raining fists upon me, my panic rose in an instant, and I released it along with a kinetic blast. It was unfocused, a wave of force I threw out in every direction. It cracked the stones beneath me, scattered the crowd of citizens watching, none of whom had tried to help me, I might mention, and threw Horralain into the air.

I was scared. The crowd were scared. Everybody but Horralain was scared. Ssserakis drank in the fear with glee and I felt its strength leak into my limbs. *This is how it feels to rule, Eskara. Make them bow down and worship you. Make them fear you.* I won't deny the heady feeling. The thrill and the odd pride that I could make so many people cower in terror. I like to think it was Ssserakis, more than myself, but I can't be sure. I have been a queen but once in my life and my reign was certainly one of fear.

Despite the pain from being crushed to the ground and punched, I rose onto my feet fluidly. The air crackled around me, strange as I had not swallowed the Arcmancy Source that day, and I felt the storm within. I felt the rage of it flashing behind my eyes, the chaotic tempest inside driving me to action. Little bolts of lightning sparked to life around me, licking at the ground and rippling along my arms and legs.

Horralain groaned. He had landed about a dozen feet away, blood leaking from his nose and his arms scraped raw in places. He struggled to rise, first to his knees and then he got a foot beneath him. I stopped his resistance there, drawing on my Kinemancy Source and flattening him back to the ground with a wave of force. Not enough to kill, not even enough to injure him any further, but enough to knock him back down. Again, the giant struggled to his knees and again I knocked him to the ground. Three more times he tried, and three more times I showed him why a Sourcerer is not to be trifled with. I could have killed him. I had killed before with Kinemancy. The old hunter from the Forest of

Ten watched me from the shadows of a nearby tannery. I could have killed Horralain, crushed his chest with a stronger kinetic blast, shattered bones and ruptured organs. I could have killed him. A younger me, the Eska forged by war and her time in the Pit, would have. I like to think I was a little wiser than that Eska.

"Why, Horralain?" I shouted the words. I didn't need to, the storm I felt was only inside, energy left over from the Arcstorm maybe, but the blood was rushing through my ears so I shouted over it. "Why do you keep trying to kill me?"

The giant Terrelan struggled onto his hands and knees, breathing heavily and dripping blood onto the cold stone of the street below. Some of the nearby tahren and pahht fled, probably seeking refuge or possibly fetching the golems to stop the fight. Golems are quite effective at breaking up fights, though they lack restraint and those being broken up often find themselves broken. Others nearby stayed, though they had backed away from us. I think that is something all the races of Ovaeris share, a draw to the dramatic, a need to stop and stare at spectacle. Horralain's shoulders slumped and he sat back on bent knees. Sweat dripped from him along with the blood and there was a weariness to his eyes along with the anger smouldering in them. Anger, I realised, not hate.

"Deko's orders," Horralain said between great heaving breaths.

"You're following the orders of a dead man," I said, taking a step forward. I kept my hand raised, ready to buffet the giant with another kinetic blast if he renewed his resistance.

"Huh?" There was true confusion on Horralain's face,

as though the concept were somehow beyond him.

"Deko is dead." Can it truly be a lie if I wasn't certain one way or another? I could have said Deko was alive with as much degree of certainty. It was surely possible the thug was dead. I think it would still class as a lie and it served my purpose to tell it. "The overseer had him killed for letting me escape. You're following the orders of a ghost. And even if he were still alive, you have no need to do what he says anymore. You're free. You made it out of the Pit, the same as I did. It's madness that you'd chase me all over Isha…"

"What do I do then?" His words were slurred slightly, his mouth worked at them slowly. Had he always spoken like that? I had never heard him much more than grunt down in the Pit.

"Whatever you want to do. Just stop trying to kill me."

"What if I want to go back? Deko said don't come back without you."

It was my turn for confusion. "To the Pit? You want to go back to that prison?"

Horralain, a hulking brute of a man on his knees, nodded slowly. I think that was when I learned even he could feel fear, but not fear of pain or injury. It wasn't me he feared, even after I used Sourcery to beat him down to the ground. He feared the freedom. The idea of being trapped in the outside world. He wanted the simplicity of the Pit, where things made sense to him. Protect Deko, do as he says, use brute strength to intimidate the scabs, eat, sleep, repeat. It was the world that scared Horralain, because he had no idea how to deal with it.

"What do I do if Deko is dead? Where do I go?"

Belmorose wrote that an ally is only one common

cause away from an enemy. I have always believed the reverse must also be true. There was no hatred of me in Horralain, no desire to see me dead other than that Deko had given him. I couldn't give the man back to the Pit, I couldn't send him there. But I could give him a different purpose. All I had to do was give him what he wanted.

"Follow me," I said, finally lowering my hand and releasing the kinetic tension. "I'll give you orders, tell you what to do. I'll see you housed and fed. And all you have to do is follow me like you did Deko. Do as I say."

Horralain frowned and looked at me, then nodded.

I heard Ssserakis laugh. *Your first minion.*

Horralain was not a smart man. He had trouble learning many basic concepts and I soon learned he often kept quiet so not to reveal his dim wit. I think, perhaps, it was a defence mechanism on his part, no doubt he had been mocked mercilessly in his youth for having such troubles. But for all that lack of wit, he was one of the strongest people I have ever known, perhaps even more so than Hardt. Speaking of my friend, it is fair to say he was not pleased with my decision to recruit Horralain. For years, he had been the thuggish right hand of Deko, and no doubt both Hardt and Isen had suffered due to him, but I ignored Hardt's protests. Three times Horralain tried to kill me in his life, and three times he failed. He also saved my life once, and I count that a balance paid in full.

CHAPTER THIRTY SEVEN

ON THE SIXTH DAY, ANCHORED ABOVE PICARR, I caught a fleeting glimpse of Silva as she supervised the loading of the latest cargo onto the flyers and negotiated with the merchants over whatever it is merchants quibble over. The price of nuts or something, I suppose. I wasn't even sure why I had made my way to Craghold; I had no reason to be there. At least, I had no official reason to be there. I was there to see Silva, and in that regard, I succeeded. Six days of negotiating, cajoling, overseeing, and interacting with every merchant on Ro'shan, and many of those from Terrelan; and yet Silva seemed energised. There was a lightness to her step and a warm flush of colour in her cheeks. This was what Silva enjoyed, the social interactions between peoples, learning names and prying details.

She once likened negotiating to gambling, a pastime I certainly enjoy and have gotten quite good at over the years.

My aggression in the game of Trust aside, I am very good
at watching players for their weaknesses. Silva told me that
negotiating was no different. Half of the game was making
friends with the opponent, learning their names, the names
of their children, where they live, and how they get on with
their mother. Inconsequential details, or so it would seem
to me, but Silva deemed them vital, not just for the trade
at hand, but for all those down the line. Her little book of
favours is not filled with names by accident. One visit she
might learn that a merchant's father suffers from gout, and
the next she would deliver a small pot of ointment designed
to alleviate the symptoms. The first delivery might be free of
charge, a gift designed to put the merchant in her debt. The
next delivery would, of course, be extravagantly expensive,
but Silva would offer it at a near criminal discount; further
putting the merchant in her debt.

Other times Silva would take what she had learned
from subtle enquiries and use them while negotiating prices.
I have always been amazed by how easy it is to throw a
person off their game with words alone. Down in the Pit I
used deceitful tactics as often as not, bluffing when I should
have been cautious, and underplaying even the most brutal
of hands. Other times, I would lose on purpose, giving away
things I neither wanted nor needed, and then only when the
item I desired was on offer would I play the game to win. It
was often the way down in the Pit. If you wanted something,
you had to pretend you wanted anything else. Scabs
instinctively held on to what they thought was valuable,
even when they could trade it for so much more than it was
worth. I watched Silva negotiate once or twice, and I can say
this for a certainty, I would not want to gamble against her.

I caught her eye that day, loitering near the docks of

Craghold with no purpose but to see her. She smiled at me over the crowded dockworkers and my heart skipped. Then she went back to her discussion with a pahht merchant who was wearing more jewellery on his hands than I had seen in my entire life. I lingered for a while, watching Silva. Long enough for Ssserakis to take notice.

See how little you matter? The Aspect does not even spare you time for a word. You are nothing to her but another name in her book. I didn't want that to be true, but the horror's words stuck with me. Surely if I meant as much to Silva as she did to me, she would find the time, if only a fleeting moment or two. I felt like a fool, vulnerable in a way I'd not felt since Isen down in the ruined city. I fled from Craghold. No, that's not true. I fled from Silva rather than face her indifference.

I had a plan that day, a task that required both space and privacy. Twice now, I had done something with Kinemancy I had not thought possible. The tutors at the academy taught me to throw out kinetic blasts in arcs, bolts, and plumes. To the more advanced students, they taught the ability to express pressure, a constant kinetic push, though I had never qualified to be classed as advanced. What they had never taught any of us was a kinetic shield. From that very first time, trapped inside the Djinn's crown, I had known it was a different form of Kinemancy. The shield I created was not some push, or even pressure, it was a solid thing formed of kinetic energy. I felt the force of Vainfold's hammer strike the shield, and instead of breaking it, that force was absorbed by it, strengthening it. At first, I thought it a peculiarity of that place, of Vainfold's personal world, but I had done it again as Horralain tried to kill me. The shield I created that time was slightly different, most of the force of Horralain's charge had rebounded back upon him;

I had only received enough to knock me onto my arse, but the giant Terrelan had been thrown backwards. The only problem was I had no idea how I had done it either time. It was a new skill I intended to learn, but Kinemancy can be a truly destructive magic, so space and privacy were of paramount importance.

The lake up on Ro'shan is neither large nor deep. It can be walked around in just a single hour or waded across with only wet knees to show for it. I was never truly sure of the purpose of that lake. Everything up on Ro'shan seemed sculpted to the Rand's purpose. The city was made of bone, grown from a monster that slept inside the mountain's core. Mezula could make the bone grow or crumble at a whim. Due to that, I believe that monster was linked to her somehow. I think, perhaps, it was another of her Aspects, created specifically for the purpose of growing her own city, but I have no proof of that, and I very much doubt Mezula would deem to satisfy my curiosity. The forest served a purpose in that the trees grew unnaturally fast, a seedling blooming into an ancient in a matter of weeks. I spent some time in that forest and I am not exaggerating when I say you can actually watch the trees grow. They are felled regularly to keep the forest in check, and to supply the city with a constant surplus of wood. The lake, however, seems to serve no purpose. It has a stock of fish, but they are small and never caught. Its waters shimmer a clear crystal blue, dazzling in even the barest sunlight, but people do not drink from it. I wonder if the point of it is the spectacle. In that lake, Mezula has created one of the most serene scenes Ovaeris has ever witnessed. I only visited the lake twice, but both times I certainly disturbed the tranquillity.

There were no other visitors to the lake that day and

I found a long patch of grass to settle into. The sky was overcast, grey clouds above threatening to wet us all, but hesitating. Clouds like that are a Meteomancer's dream, but it is not one of my attunements. It is important while playing with Kinemancy to think about footwork, pushing out a kinetic blast without being properly braced can lead to serious injuries, or sometimes death-defying leaps. I planted my feet, a wide stance with one foot forward and the other firmly rooted. I thought about the shield I hoped to create, then drew on the Source and pushed out with both my hands. I did not form a kinetic shield on that try, nor on the eight subsequent attempts. I did, however, cause some wonderful ripples in the water, managing to scare a few fish. Not exactly my intention, but at least my efforts amused someone. Ssserakis laughed inside my head.

How can you hope to defeat a Djinn when you cannot even master your own purpose? It had a point, I suppose.

"Fuck you!" I swore. "Either help or shut up."

"What you do matters, though you may not see how." Tamura said. I hadn't even noticed him approach. Whether he heard me talking to my horror, I don't know.

"And what is it I'm doing?" I asked a little more testily than I intended. Frustration at not mastering something, I was used to, but I had managed to create a shield twice when I needed it and now I couldn't even fathom how I had done it.

"Making ripples." Tamura walked over to the lake and crouched down near the shore, splashing a hand in the water. Then he stood up and pointed towards the centre of the lake. "See how far the consequences reach?"

The implications were somewhat lost on me. But Tamura was right. Even the smallest of our actions can have far reaching consequences, and I was committing myself to killing a god. It's safe to say I hadn't thought of what that might mean to the rest of the world. Kill one god and set another free. Wipe out the Djinn once and for all, and once more unleash the Rand upon the world. All I really saw was a way to bolster my own power, to finally set my feet upon the path of vengeance.

"What I'm trying to do is form a shield. I did it earlier, but now I can't seem to do anything but push," I said grumpily.

"The wind needs no help from you."

"Very helpful, Tamura."

Tamura giggled and shook his head. "Would you like a drink?"

"I'm not thirsty."

"Water maybe? Here." He dipped both hands in the lake and pulled them out, water rolling off his fingers. "Oh dear." He tried again to the same result. The third time he cupped his hands, forming a bowl, and when he raised his hands from the lake, he kept hold of the water. Tamura walked towards me his hands still cupped, water sloshing about in the recess. "How can you hope to hold something so fleeting as water, without first giving it something to fill?" He opened his hands and splashed water on my shoes, then he set to giggling once more and I couldn't help but join in. Wet feet seemed a low price to pay for sage advice.

I tried again, this time pushing the kinetic energy out in the shape of a shield. I scared a few more fish, I think, but I was no more successful in achieving my goal. With a growl of frustration, I pushed a concentrated blast at the water, a purple haze sending large splashes skittering across the rippling surface. I definitely scared some fish with that.

Tamura shook his head. "Think of the shape you wish to fill. Do not push at it. Fill it."

A shape came to mind, the kite shield I had first seen at the academy, the very one that was now frozen in a timeless bubble down in Picarr. I closed my eyes and imagined that exact shape, the way the edges curved outward just slightly, the thickness of the metal, the leather straps affixed to the back of it to secure it to the wielder's arm. Then, instead of pushing kinetic energy into the shape, I let it seep out of me, drawing on the Source in my stomach and letting it flow along my body up into my arm where I let it go.

When I opened my eyes, I held a shimmering purple kite shield on my right arm. It mostly matched the shield called Madness, but almost twice the size. It should have weighed more than I was able to lift, but it was weightless upon my arm. When I moved, the shield moved with me. I turned to Tamura to find him grinning, a small stone in hand. He launched it at me and the stone hit my shield without a sound. Its momentum arrested, it then dropped to the ground. I let out a whoop of joy, thinking I had mastered a new technique. *Mastered* was a strong word to use, and an incorrect one. I think I realised this the moment I also realised my shield was getting brighter, the purple haze of its outline growing in intensity.

Tamura took a step backwards. "An overfilled skin goes..."

The shield on my arm popped. Perhaps that does not really conjure the correct image. It burst apart, the kinetic energy buffeted me so hard I slapped myself in the face with my hand and fell sprawling in the grass, all to the furious giggling of Tamura. I did not let the accident dampen my spirits. I did it! I had created a shield of magic. I just had to learn to stop filling the shape once it was made.

"Belmorose said some victories are worth the loss, and few victories come without failure." Tamura extended a hand and pulled me to my feet. "Of course, shields are the easiest form of kinetic arms. Or… Well, maybe a club. Or a hammer. Staffs are simple as well. Though anything with an edge is far more complex."

"What? You knew this was possible before?" It's fair to say that made my victory sour a little. I thought I was discovering something new. A new technique no Kinemancer had ever thought of before. The truth is that new ideas are far rarer than you might believe. Most are just alterations on existing concepts. This is even more true when it comes to Sourcery. The Rand and Djinn were using magic for millennia before terrans even crawled out of the dark.

"Of course," Tamura said with a nod, then started off towards the city. I hurried after him.

"Can you teach me?"

"Can you learn?"

As we walked through the city, Tamura started humming. It was a tune I had heard him sing before, and I knew there were words that went with it, but I couldn't remember them. Perhaps I was just distracted. I noticed people looking at me strangely. I may never have been very good at determining pahht or tahren facial expressions, but it is hard to miss eyes turning your way and following you, and people looking away whenever you meet their gaze. It was also hard to miss the fear I inspired within so many of those I caught staring. It wasn't the first time it had happened lately, ever since I had returned from Picarr I noticed people watching me.

Enemies in every shadow. They see your power and fear you. You must nurture that fear but keep a wary eye for betrayal.

"Have you noticed people are staring?" I asked Tamura. I think I was looking for confirmation that it wasn't all in my head.

"Have you looked in a mirror recently?" The crazy old Aspect said with a shake of his head. I hadn't. I often avoided mirrors for days or weeks on end. I was never sure who I would find looking back at me. Would I see myself or Ssserakis or someone else? Would I even recognise the woman I had become? It was more than just the unnatural ageing from Chronomancy, and more than the renewal Vainfold had forced upon my body. What I was scared of, the thing that really made me avoid my own reflection, was seeing echoes of my daughter. Of being reminded of her in my own features.

"Mezula was right about you," Tamura continued. "There is a storm in your eyes."

I tried to ignore it. I couldn't see how such a thing was possible, I hadn't swallowed the Arcmancy Source since Picarr. But I approached a shop window and stared at my reflection, and Tamura was right. Even days after absorbing the Arcstorm my eyes flashed, jagged forks of lightning sparking in them. And not just once or twice, but constantly. The fury of an Arcstorm raged in my eyes, even without the Source in my stomach. I wondered what that meant, how such a thing was possible, but I had no answers. Ssserakis was quiet on the subject, and when I asked Tamura about it, he simply shrugged and said, *'What would be the fun in knowing?'*.

Tamura led me to the tavern he frequented, *Hakreem mo Tahn*. I had no idea what it meant then, and I am just as ignorant now, though Tamura assured me it was a humorous name in pahht. After a year of both his business and his stories, they knew him well and the owner and many of the patrons knew him by name. They never made any mention of his half-crazed ramblings, and never refused him a drink even if he had not the money to pay for it. His stories drew people from all over Ro'shan and Tamura had long since taken over from the local minstrel as the tavern's main attraction. They knew of me as well. After all, I had been drunk there on more than one occasion, but it was mostly as Silva and Tamura's friend. I might have the Djinn and the Rand and the emperor of Terrelan remembering my name, but in that little tavern I was no more important than any other midday drinker. Perhaps even less so as I didn't have any coin to pay for my drink.

With only a couple of words in pahht, Tamura led me out the back door of the tavern, through a small kitchen where the smell of stewing broth assaulted my senses and left my mouth watering. There was a small courtyard out the back of that tavern, with barrels stacked high and lashed against the building. A table and some chairs were set up there and a pahht chef was busy chopping away at a bucket of horn root, slicing each of the yellow tubers into thin sections before depositing them in another bucket. Tamura spoke to the chef and he laughed, shaking his head. He finished the horn root he was chopping, then set down his knife, wiped his hands on his apron, and walked back into the kitchen, barely sparing me a glance.

"What are we doing here, Tamura?" I asked, frustration may have crept its way into my voice.

"Me? Teaching. You? Complaining. Sit." Tamura collapsed into one of the chairs and picked up the chef's knife, he then reached into the bucket and pulled out a particularly knobby root and placed it on the wooden board, then started peeling it.

I sat with a sigh and reached for the second knife; Tamura was faster as he snatched it away. "Consider the knife. The shape and size, longer on the blunt, curved on the edge. A comfortable handle. Consider the edge. Thinner and thinner and thinner until it parts the skin." He finished peeling the horn root and set to slicing it into small sections, occasionally popping one in his mouth and chewing. Uncooked horn root tastes somewhere between nothing and mud, yet Tamura seemed to relish it.

I took the hint. He had given the basics, the fundamentals of how to form kinetic arms. He had told me what was possible, and now he intended to force me to practice. Admittedly, he was throwing me in as deep as it got. Why build myself up to forming a knife, possibly one of the most difficult kinetic arms to manifest? He could have started me with simpler forms, but honestly that is not Tamura's way. He may have more patience than a marsh cat on the hunt, but he was never one for simple challenges. Despite this, I went to his task with a passion. I imagined the knife over and over again and filled it with kinetic energy, and every time I formed a blunt instrument far more capable of crushing than cutting. That's not to say such a tool could not have a purpose, but it was not the task I had been set. Still, I took solace in the fact that forming kinetic objects was getting easier with every attempt.

Somewhere into my second hour of mangling horn roots, Imiko sauntered into the courtyard carrying three mugs of ale. She set them down on the table and sank down to sit cross-legged on the ground. "Why are you mashing things?"

"Mostly for fun." I said as I crushed the skin of
another tuber. I dismissed the attempt at a kinetic knife with
a puff of purple haze as the energy dissipated. I had honestly
lost track of just how many attempts I'd had at it by then.
"How did you know we were here?"

Imiko reached up to the table and grabbed a mug,
blowing on the froth. "The owner told me. He said the crazy
old man is in the back playing with food."

Tamura laughed. "One is preparing food, the other is
playing with food." He sent a cheeky glance my way then
paused to drink a mouthful of ale, heedless of the white
froth it left in his patchy moustache.

"What kind of witch can't even chop a few
vegetables?" Imiko grinned at me, softening the insult.

"The type who was trained to make people explode
and set cities on fire. And they're not vegetables."

"So, you finally admit you're a witch?"

I glared at her.

"Oooh, scary eyes." Imiko knocked back a mouthful
of ale and grinned at me. "Can I play?"

I was busy forming a new kinetic knife. I didn't need
to try peeling a new root, I already knew the edge was dull
as a starless night. "Of course." I launched the kinetic knife
at Imiko and watched her panic. The knife burst apart as
soon as it left my hand, the magic maintaining its form
breaking down and the kinetic energy dissipating. By the
time it reached Imiko it was as little more than a puff of force
that set her fringe swaying.

We talked while we worked, all three of us peeling
and chopping. Well, Imiko and Tamura peeled and chopped,
I continued to mash and crush. The one time I actually

thought I was making progress, my kinetic knife sliding
down into the horn root, I lost my concentration in my
excitement. The knife burst apart and the tuber exploded
in my hands, showering me in chunks. It might have been
embarrassing, but there was nobody but my friends around
to see it, and all three of us were soon lost in a giggling fit.
Despite my failure, that afternoon was the most fun I'd
had in a long time. It did much to bolster my spirits. It is
somewhat surprising to me. Imiko and I have faced down
seven types of death together, we have fought and we cried
together, we have had to rely upon each other and trust each
other. But no matter what else we had been through before,
and what we were yet to face, I think that afternoon, peeling
horn roots, helped forge our friendship. That being said,
there were still plenty of times I have wished we had never
met.

Suffice to say, I did not master kinetic arms that day.
Or the one after, or the ten after that. It was weeks before I
managed to form a sharp kinetic knife, and months before
I learned to bring a true Sourceblade into existence. That
is my name for them, not Tamura's. He called them all
kinetic arms, but I felt I needed to differentiate between the
various forms. There were shields, hammers, and axes, but
I found I was always drawn to the shape of a sword. So, I
named them Sourceblades and I practised endlessly, forming
different shapes and sizes. I spent days researching different
weaponry, visiting blacksmiths to see what they had to
offer, and then copying the styles. Eventually, I learned to
form a variety of different Sourceblades at will, taking only
moments to go from empty handed to wielding a blade as
sharp as any terran hands had ever forged. But no matter
how many Sourceblades I formed; I still had no idea how to

really use one. For that I needed a new tutor. One who could teach me swordplay.

CHAPTER THIRTY EIGHT

MY NIGHTS BELONGED TO SSSERAKIS, AND THE horror did an excellent job of making me fear sleep. Night by night, it introduced me to the monsters of its home, some I knew from the Encyclopaedia Otheria, and many more I had never even heard of. These days I have multiple copies of that tome in my personal library. I have a sixth edition, first copied mere years before I became a student at the academy, and I have my own personal copy of the book. When I look at all the additions I have made over the years, the alterations and corrections, I realise I have rewritten roughly seventy percent of the encyclopaedia, and my personal copy is without a doubt the most comprehensive guide to the Other World terran eyes have ever seen.

Yet not all the things Ssserakis showed me terrified me. Some were more intriguing, at least to my curious mind. One time, the horror showed me a colony of creatures

living on an endlessly rocky plain, scavenging in the cracks
between those rocks for plants and insects. The fact that
there were insects in the world was curious enough to my
eyes, but I suppose it makes sense. How else could things
thrive there without a stable ecosystem to support them?
Even more curious to me, was that I recognised so many
of the insects. Recluse beetles and scavenger ants, horned
wasps and thunder flies, they are all as common in Ovaeris
as the Other World. I think, perhaps, if I had considered
it more, I might have realised then that there is more
connecting the two worlds than we ever realised.

The colony Ssserakis took me to held many
individuals, all clothed in patchy robes. They huddled
together in tents, and as we drifted closer I thought I was
looking at terrans. Just for a moment, I thought a colony of
my own people had somehow found their way to the Other
World and survived all the horrors and monsters that call it
home. But no. They were monsters, more like the Damned
than terrans. Their faces were warped masks, warty and foul
to look at. Teeth grew at all angles from their mouths, sharp
and yellowing, or brown. Each of the creatures had one arm
ending in single curving talon, and one arm ending in a
hand with six fingers. Yet still, they were the most terran-like
monsters from that world I had ever seen, even more so than
the imps that toiled endlessly underground to fashion new
networks of tunnels.

There was a large figure in that colony, towering over
the creatures and presiding over them like a king over his
little empire. I say little because that colony was only a few
hundred individuals, but Ssserakis assured me there were
dozens of colonies just like it, and they all bowed down to
their king. He was as tall as Hardt, yet wiry where my friend

was all brawn, yet there was a feeling of strength to the king;
something I couldn't quite place. I knew, without a doubt, he
was beyond any mortal I had ever known. He looked terran
for the most part, two arms and legs, a single head, entirely
bald. His face though, that was a twisted mass of flesh, as
though someone had taken all his skin and stirred it into a
whirlpool of pitted, pallid flesh. His eyes were beady and
glowed with a malevolent red light, and his mouth was a
gaping maw opening into an abyss of serrated teeth. From
a distance, this little king might pass as terran, especially
wearing a brown suit of tanned leather, but up close there
was no mistaking the monster.

We approached, I on bare feet and Ssserakis an
inky mass beside me, connected to me by my shadow. The
horror took on a vaguely terran shape, but moved strangely,
convulsing over itself rather than walking. *Do not speak.* The
ancient horror said as we passed through the king's little
colony of minions.

I snorted. "Have you ever known anyone to say that
to me with any success?"

*I keep my existence a secret from your friends. It is time for
you to repay the favour.* There was anger buried somewhere in
that hissing voice. *Or would you like Hardt to see the darkness
you carry inside? Perhaps I should reveal myself to Imiko?*

I gritted my teeth. Ssserakis was right. For the most
part it had kept itself secret, hiding inside of me, in the
dark corners of my body and soul. The few times it had
manifested had been due to my influence, my anger calling
upon the power Ssserakis could wield. All the horror asked
for right then was a return of the favour, and I could grant it
that much at least.

The little monsters in their robes turned to us as we

passed, bowing their heads and whispering in a language that was just beyond my recognition, yet sounded so familiar. The king watched us approach. He stood before a fire, the wood burning there smelled more like flesh, and I saw the back of his hands were set with shards of razor-sharp bone. Of all the monsters, horrors, and creatures of the Other World I had seen, that king was perhaps the strangest, for he was so very terran in so many ways.

"Is that really you, Ssserakis?" the king asked, his voice crackling over the words like shells broken beneath the feet.

It has been long, Kekran.

"All the others thought you were dead. Your fortress abandoned, your minions scattered, your lands unprotected. There was some talk that Brakunus might have eaten you."

I was ignored. I hate being ignored.

Not eaten, nor dead. Taken. A Sourcerer from the other world, the most powerful I have ever seen.

Kekan's beady red eyes flicked my way and I felt suddenly small and weak. There was power in that look, the same sort of strength I felt from Ssserakis. In that moment I knew I was sitting in on a conversation between monsters who were ancient, powerful, and knowledgeable beyond mortal ken. The king's eyes moved back to Ssserakis' inky form.

"This?" Kekran asked

No. Ssserakis laughed. *This is my current body. I wear it for now because it has promised me a way home. Do not be fooled by its frail appearance. It is stronger than even it knows. We bested Vainfold together.* I could tell Ssserakis thought Kekran should be impressed by that, but the monster kept silent.

I held up my end. I kept my silent promise, by

keeping my mouth shut, but Ssserakis could hear my thoughts and I made damned sure the horror heard me when I told it that I have a name.

It is called Eskara.

Judging by the bellowing laugh that erupted from Kekran, something amused the monster. "You actually learned one of your hosts' names? Perhaps the others were right about you, Ssserakis. You have grown weak."

I felt the anger then. No, anger isn't quite the right term. Rage. Furious, blinding rage. Seething so cold I felt my heart had turned to ice in my chest. The inky darkness of Ssserakis seemed to swell beside me, drawing more and more of my shadow into itself it grew until it towered over both myself and Kekran. The little robed creatures scurried away, yelping in alarm and hiding in tents. Yet Kekran stood there, arms crossed, unmoving. I sensed fear all around us, flowing from the monsters and feeding Ssserakis, but Kekran held no fear. Whatever that creature truly was, I knew with a certainty that it never knew fear.

Do I appear weak to you, Kekran?

"Yes." The king turned his gaze from Ssserakis and picked up a large branch, feeding it to the fire. I realised then why the fire smelled of burning flesh. It was no tree they were feeding it, but the bony arms of a Creaker. "The Ssserakis I knew wouldn't come to me and posture. It would have smothered the land like a blanket of darkness, drawing fear from us all. Your lands are gone, taken by those who thought you dead. Your minions are gone, scattered and fallen under new influence. Your strength is gone, Ssserakis. And you are not even really here. How do you even appear to me like this?"

I felt Ssserakis brooding, a dark mood settling across

us both. *It is a quirk of my host. She is able to cross over even without a Source.* I had always thought it was Ssserakis who brought my consciousness across, but if the horror was telling the truth, then it was simply guiding me while we were there. I didn't understand, there was no way a Sourcerer could cross into the Other World without an Impomancy Source. It was unheard of.

You have not claimed any of my lands?

"Of course not. The others might believe you dead, and Brakunus might well claim to have eaten you…"

Arrogant ghoul! I will show it what its fear looks like. I will make it beg me to stop.

"But I always believed you would be back. Besides, I have no wish to involve myself in the fighting of the others. Last time I tried; the serpent took one of my arms." Kekran made a fist of his right hand. The flesh did look different, and the arm was shorter, as though it was from a different creature entirely.

But you took one of its eyes.

Kekran nodded. "A mighty battle. But I still lost. I don't pick fights I can't win any more."

You won't help me take back my lands then?

"No. But I won't stand in your way, Ssserakis." Kekran snorted. "It is all just words. You are not here." He nodded towards me. "And your host is fading." He was right about that. My body was fading from sight. I was becoming incorporeal, like most Sourcerers who visit the Other World. But it was more than that. I could feel myself slipping back to Ovaeris, the gravity of my body calling to me.

I will be back.

"This Sourcerer," Kekran said, his words growing

distant as though shouted across an endless chasm. "The one
who captured you, dragged you over. The dangerous one.
Does it still live?"

Yes.

I woke in a cold sweat, bed sheets tangled around my
legs. It was not a cold night, yet I felt a chill inside. I drew
a little on my Pyromancy Source and let the fire of it warm
me. I had taken to sleeping with my Sources in my stomach,
all four of them. I was trying to re-accustom myself with the
feeling of having them in me. It is not comfortable carrying
Sources, they sit heavy in the gut and some Sourcerers say
they give them gas, though I have never seen any proof of
that myself. Still, I liken it to the middle stages of pregnancy.
You can feel something inside, pressing at times, and moving
at others. Certainly not comfortable, but well worth it for the
power carrying Sources gives.

I could feel Ssserakis sulking. Odd that. Such
a powerful, ancient creature, one who had brought
civilisations to heel and was old enough to have seen my
people crawl out from the dark caves we once called home,
yet it was sulking like a child with its favourite toy taken
away. A figure stood in my room, back in the far corner and
shrouded in the shadows that pooled there. Even so, I knew
it to be the huntsman from the Forest of Ten. I never even
knew the man's name. I couldn't decide why Ssserakis was
sulking inside my soul, and still watching me from the eyes
of a dead man, but it was all a little too much to take. Our
brief time in the Other World had raised as many questions
as it had answered, and I was in no mood to be scared by an
apparition just so my passenger could feel strong for a while.

"Who was it? The Sourcerer who took you from the

Other World?" I asked aloud. I knew I could make Ssserakis
hear me by asking the question in my mind, but I wanted
to speak it. Maybe it had something to do with hearing my
own voice somehow making the conversation feel more real,
less like I was imagining the horror possessing me.

A man. Terran.

"You don't know his name?"

*Your lives are brief flickers of light in the darkness. They
pass so quickly, there is little point to learning one name from
another. He was a man, a Sourcerer. He pulled me from my world
and tried to dominate me, to control me. He was not expecting a
will to match his own. I escaped his prison and fled. I was new to
the world and unsure of how much of my power had crossed over.
Less than I would have liked, certainly. But your hateful sun was
too bright. It burned my body to mere wisps.*

"That's why you were in the Pit? You fled there to
escape the sun?"

*Coincidence, but a grateful one. To escape the sun, I fled
into one of your kind. A terran who couldn't understand my
existence. He blamed others for what he couldn't see and struck
out at those close to him. He killed and killed and killed. And the
fear he fed me was delicious. But others caught up with him and
put him in chains, dragged him underground and forgot about
him. He kept killing down there, always saying the voices made
him do it. I never told him to kill anyone.* I could feel Ssserakis'
amusement. *A simple mind with no idea how to make others fear
without pain, without threat, without death. The little king took
notice and killed my host, setting me free. But it was no matter.
The fear down there could have kept me sustained for eternity. And
the darkness was as comfortable as any place in this world of yours.*

*But even there, underground, the light of your world hurt.
It is everywhere. It seeps through the rock and shines out of your*

eyes. I must return home. I must take back what has been stolen.

It was the most Ssserakis had ever said to me in one go. I decided to ask the horror some questions while I had its attention.

"Can I take your form again? Like we did inside Vainfold's crown?"

No. The rules there were different, more like those of home. Taking form here is difficult, straining. But I am not powerless. My window was open and moonlight poured through, casting my shadow on the bed. I saw it move, then. I saw tendrils of darkness worm their way out of my shadow. It seemed to change consistency, becoming less incorporeal and more like thick tar, spreading unnaturally far. A mad grin stretched impossibly wide, across my shadow's face, as though the moonlight passed right through me. And then it was back to normal, as though I hadn't just witnessed Ssserakis making a mockery of my shadow.

I can draw on fear and lend you strength. I can sap the warmth from around you and give your shadow form, but I cannot assume my form. Not here.

It was something, at least. I had a better idea of what I might be capable of with Ssserakis lending its strength to mine. Perhaps even more useful would be the knowledge such an ancient creature could provide, assuming I could keep it communicating with me.

But I must be fed. I cannot help you without power, and for that I need the fear of others.

I had other questions I wanted to ask, many others, but there was one that had been there ever since we had left the Pit. "Why do you appear to me as people I have killed? Why stand there watching me through the hunter's eyes, and yet speak to me inside my head?"

A few moments of silence were damning. *I have nothing to do with your apparitions.*

I snorted "You're telling me you're not watching me from his eyes? Over there in the corner. The huntsman I killed in the Forest of Ten." I stood from the bed and approached the figure standing in the shadow. It was the closest I had ever got to one of the spectres and I winced at the guilt I felt. He was a tall man, and broad. He had been strong in life, but he seemed somewhat diminished in death. His ribs looked buckled and blood leaked out of his mouth, drying to brown on his bearded chin. There was damning accusation in his eyes.

I am not your conscience, Eskara. The ghosts you see are of your own making.

I don't know how exactly, but I knew truth when I heard it from Ssserakis. The ancient horror could see them too, but they were not its doing. "Then how is he here? Why do they keep appearing?" I reached out and passed a hand through the ethereal form of the hunter. Like stirring mist, my hand disturbed the apparition, but its form quickly resolved. There was nothing but pain and hate in those dead eyes.

Only one of us is a Necromancer. I know as little of Sources as you know of my home.

"I'm no Necromancer. I haven't even tasted a Source since they determined I was attuned to it. The academy didn't even teach it as a school."

Excuses. These shades are your doing, not mine.

Truth is a prison. One that sits behind us our entire lives, just waiting for us to step inside its barred domain. I have heard people say that the truth can set you free. Somewhat ironically, that's a bloody lie. The truth locks you in, determines a set way of thinking, of feeling, of believing. The truth is the opposite of freedom. Lies, on the other hand, can be whatever we want them to be. Lies can free us from a burden that truth would bury us with. Lies can ease a pain that truth would cause to rot and fester. Lies can make a point, where truth would just expose us for the hypocrites we are, a lesson all parents know well. The world is founded on lie, upon lie, upon lie. But the truth is always there, just waiting for an opportunity to tear down everything we have built.

Ssserakis was telling the truth that night, and I could find no lies to spare me the confusion and pain. The ghosts were my doing, somehow. I was, entirely without design, bringing about my own haunting. I had no idea how I was doing it, and the ancient horror was my only confidant in the matter. I couldn't tell any of the others about Ssserakis, and I certainly couldn't tell them I was a Necromancer who was bringing back the dead as spirits to haunt me. How could I possibly explain to Hardt that even in death his brother found no rest because I was somehow responsible for raising him as a ghost to follow me around all my life. I was already responsible for Isen's death, the truth that I was also responsible for his continued torment was too much even for me to take.

I did what many of us often do when confronted with a hard truth we'd rather not submit to: I jumped out the nearest window. Of course, I couldn't escape Ssserakis, but at least I left the ghost of the huntsman behind for a time. My window opened out into our little garden and I had to be careful not to step on my Spiceweed. It wasn't just about not wanting to damage the plants, but also that the stems came with barbed thorns and in my haste to escape my room I had not bothered to find my shoes, nor anything else, for that matter. I was standing in the garden wearing nothing but a loose white shift, but at least the fire inside of me kept the chill from my arms and legs.

Drawing in a deep breath, I blew it out through my lips and settled into the routine of stretches and poses Tamura taught me. In truth, I wanted to move, and I would happily have launched into a run, but I was not dressed for it and didn't feel like climbing back into my room while the huntsman was still there. Chased out of my home by a ghost. I wish I could say it was the last time such a thing has happened.

It is easy to get lost in that series of stretches. I don't know what time I woke, but by the time I had finished the sky was starting to lighten. As morning broke over Ro'shan, the city started to shake. The great chain was being drawn in, and it was finally time to leave Isha behind once more. I hoped that next time we floated past; I would be in a position to take the fight to the Terrelan empire. In case you have never considered the practical side of laying siege to an empire, let me be brutally honest about it. Even considering it is a daunting prospect. Back then the extent of my planning was to swear I would destroy Terrelan, I had not even thought about how I might go about it.

I was being watched. I knew it by that crawling feeling between my shoulders, there were eyes focused on me though I couldn't say where. Silva, standing by the gate to our little garden, was wearing a smile that was all appreciation. Despite the early hour, she looked energised, her golden hair almost glowing in the first rays of light, and her eyes hungry.

"Don't stop on my account. I'm enjoying the view,"

Silva said.

I wasn't sure how to feel about that. The implication was clear, she was watching me bend and stretch. Yet I felt embarrassed somehow, as though I had been caught in the act of something forbidden. I crossed my arms over my chest and looked away from her. We hadn't managed to speak since she had kissed me, not properly. I had run the conversation over in my head time and time again, trying to parse what it had meant, how it made me feel, and how she felt about me. Just like my time in the Other World, all my thoughts had only left me with more questions; questions I was determined to ask Silva the next time we spoke. But there she was, the sun just starting to rise and Ro'shan beginning to wake, and I could not find my tongue. All the things I wanted to say to her, all the questions I wanted to ask her, they all vanished. Silva knew. She saw me, saw through me, and knew my frustration and awkward embarrassment even before I did. But of course she did, looking into people's hearts was always her gift.

She walked over to my window and jumped up a little, perching on the lip. I noticed then that she had a bottle in her hand, long necked and holding something rose tinted. A fruit wine, if I wasn't mistake, and from her favourite vineyard.

"You're celebrating?" I asked, finally finding the courage to look at her again and feeling my heart skip at the sight.

"We are. Six days of trade," Silva said with a grin. "And not a single bum deal. In fact, I made some excellent new connections and secured Ro'shan with a new supplier of iron for a third less than what we are currently paying the pahht of Itexia. So, yes, I'm celebrating. I really hoped you'd join me."

I did. We sat on that windowsill and talked while we shared a bottle of wine and watched the sun rise over the city. My nerves and embarrassment both evaporated in the heat of Silva's company. I found myself laughing as she told me of a young terran merchant who had been trying to learn pahht but kept stumbling over the pronunciations so badly he almost crashed a deal at the moment of its completion. And again, at the story of a fat terran who had actually offered to purchase Coby's hand in marriage. Apparently, the mercurial Aspect had taken on the skin of a stunning Polasian man for the day, and it had gotten the female merchant rather hot and bothered. The idea of anyone trying to court Coby was enough to have me giggling and struggling to breathe past the wine I swallowed down the wrong way.

Thinking back now, I cannot tell you when it happened, nor which of us made the first move, only that we kissed again. I say again, but the time before, Silva had kissed me, the second time we kissed each other. My heart raced at the touch; my mind blank save for the feel of her. Life had never felt so joyous, and all that lay behind me and before us could be nothing but pale shadows of that moment. Sense and sensuality mixed. The smell of each other, the feel of each other, the taste of each other. I wanted her like I had never wanted anything; and the ecstasy of her lips against mine, of her body slowly moving against mine, was almost too painful to bear.

We spent the rest of the day in my room, actually we spent most of it in my bed. It passed in a blur of whispered voices, hot breaths, and lingering kisses. And more. By the time we emerged, the day had long since passed and night, once more, had its claws in the world. In some ways, you could say it was a day wasted, but a day spent in the arms of a lover is never a wasted thing. It is in moments like that, in time spent entwined with another, that even I can find new reasons to go on.

CHAPTER THIRTY NINE

WE STOPPED FOR A FEW DAYS IN POLASIA, Ro'shan anchoring itself in the ocean just off the coast. Silva explained that water anchorages were not ideal, but there was simply nowhere else to secure the city. Beyond Polasia's capital city, there was nothing but a broad expanse of desert that stretched on to forever, dotted with the occasional oasis, most of which were surrounded by smaller settlements. It was also dangerous for Ro'shan to float too far out into the desert. Somewhere out there, the sky was ripped open and a great eye stared through it, a rift caused by a battle between Djinn and Rand when they were at the height of their power. Strange things happen around that tear in the world, and once the eye focuses on you, it never looks away. No matter how far you might flee, or how deep in the earth you might hide, the eye is always watching. Proof, if ever it was needed, that there are things greater than all of us.

Silva was required on the ground once more, the most suited of all the Aspects to broker trade deals, and it was also something she loved doing. I didn't understand the thrill she got from dealing with merchants, but I didn't need to. I could happily listen to her talk about anything, and for hours. It made me happy just knowing she was happy. We were growing closer every day, and there were few nights we didn't spend together.

Belmoroes said there are three reasons for a nation to go to war. The first is power, and the second is principle. The third reason is sex. You may wonder why I bring up the matter of war while talking about my first few weeks with Silva. A new relationship is a lot like war. Two kingdoms meeting. Borders drawn up, lines in the dirt where sides should not cross. Then the testing of those borders, prodding to find the other's weaknesses. Pushing against them harder and harder to see just how far those lines can bend before they break. We tested each other's borders regularly and I will admit no one has ever managed to break them quite like Silva.

I decided to visit Polasia with Silva, having never been before. I had seen it from afar, watched the ships navigate their way around the chain and into port, glimpsed movement in the great coliseum that dominated the western edge of the city, gawked at the size of the palace and how much of it is green in a city on the edge of a desert. I wanted to see the place up close, and in no small part because I hoped to get a glimpse of one of Polasia's feared Demonships. I also hoped I might be able to find some mercenaries willing to tie their lives to mine. I was making very little headway in building myself an assault force, though it was somewhat fun watching Horralain and Hardt growl at each other every time we all came together.

The flight down to the city was somewhat disappointing in a way. Silva had little time for me, organising and instructing the Ro'shan merchants, but Imiko had decided to join me. I think the little thief was looking for fresh ground to stalk, new marks to rob. She had grown taller than I in the past few months, and gangly with it. Between her lithe shape, her hair that was the colour of dying embers, and her easy smile, she drew quite a lot of attention. Attention was something the thief in her hated, so Imiko took to wearing a heavy hood she could pull up to obscure her features. I think we made for an interesting pair. I have never been tall, but I had put on muscle and Hardt liked to describe me as compact. Imiko, on the other hand, was a good hand taller than I, and thin as a reed. My hair was dark brown, almost bordering on black, and short. Hers was long and red, so distinct that people often stopped to look. Imiko was pretty, near flawless skin and so easy with her smiles. As for me, well I have always worn my scars with pride, and I scowled at others as often as smiling. But my eyes drew the attention. The storm that raged in them had not subsided, if anything I felt it even stronger than before.

We landed at the docks. Flyers were built for land-based berths, ideally, but they could sit in water just as well, though I will admit it felt quite strange underfoot. After just a few minutes on board that bobbing flyer, I felt myself growing queasy and hurried onto dry land. Silva said goodbye with a kiss, and Imiko and I made our way into the city. We walked along the docks for a while, based solely on my desire to see a Demonship up close. I have since learned, with disturbing clarity, that it is not wise to get too close to a Demonship.

The vessel we came across was called *Ilrahadeen,* and it was a monster, in more ways than one. A huge boat with three sails, and sailors climbing all over it like ticks. You have probably never seen a Demonship. There are so few of them left, but they are horrific things. The hull is made from some sort of fusion of Golemancy and Necromancy. It is flesh, pulled from the corpses of terrans, and somehow given terrible life. It appears red, almost bloody, and has the texture of skin. But as we drew close, I saw eyes opening along the hull. They were huge things, round and unblinking, and they watched us pass.

"That's creepy," Imiko said. Fear making her voice tremble. "You think that's creepy as well? It's not just me."

I did, and not just because I saw hands reaching out of the hull and clawing at it, pulling on the eyelids and reaching for us as we passed. Ssserakis raged inside of me, hissing and speaking in some language I had never heard before. The Demonships are an affront to nature, not just the natural order of our world, but of the Other World too. They are a fusion of magics and flesh and wood and monsters. And they are dangerous. I have seen arms burst forth from the skin of one ship and grip a person, breaking bones and tearing limbs. I have seen mouths open along the hull, screaming out in pain and gnashing teeth, I have seen the Demonships eat, and it is all blood and anger. Only the Polasians know the secret of making Demonships and it is a secret that I hope will soon be lost.

Imiko pulled me away from the ship as it reached for me with dozens of clawed hands, mouths opening all along the hull, whispering something just beyond my understanding. I let the thief lead me, but kept my eyes on the ship, and it kept its eyes on me, so many eyes all tearing open from the skin of that thing, watching me.

Polasians have some odd traditions, perhaps it is part of living so close to a desert. The men all wear veils across the lower half of their faces. It is considered quite impolite for a man to show his mouth to a woman, yet most of the men also went bare chested, sweat glistening in the baking sun. Others wore loose fitting robes of myriad colours, made of silks and other materials I couldn't even name. The women wear similar robes, though often far grander, and rather than veils, they put their mouths on display with powdered makeup, coloured lips, and piercings that look as painful as they are decorative. At first, I found it quite strange, but I soon realised that it is because the women do the talking. All the talking. Polasian men are, for the most part, silent. In fact, it's quite rude for a man to speak in public, and the few times it is required, they do so in hushed voices, drawing close so no other can hear their words. I felt quite out of place in my close-fitting dress, but I would wager Imiko felt it even more in her blackened waist coat and matching trousers.

Imiko and I moved further into the city and, I will admit, I spent much of the time gawking at what I saw. Imiko was far more circumspect, but then I suppose it benefits a thief to be so. There is nothing like staring at something mundane to turn yourself into a spectacle. We were already something of an oddity, perhaps not the only Terrelans in the city, but certainly the palest. I thought my skin quite tanned until I set foot in Polasia. We saw pahht as well, quite a lot of them, some with stalls set up and others ferrying goods here and there. Polasia is a trading kingdom, like Ro'shan, and is only a short sail away from Itexia, where the pahht build their cities. There were a few tahren, mostly keeping to themselves in large groups, but not a single garn. I am told it is because they cannot stand the humidity. Polasia is a dry place. It is dusty and hot, and altogether lacking in good water supplies. The garn prefer jungles and marshes where their skin does not dry out.

"Where are we going?" I asked Imiko as we passed a tavern that looked quite enticing. There were half a dozen Polasian women sitting out front, sipping on wine from glasses that had condensation on them, they were so chilled. A group of Polasian men laboured nearby, loading up a handful of carts with crates. The women watched us pass with the eyes of competitors, one or two moving hands to the swords hanging from their belts. I needed no such obvious weaponry; my blades could be willed into life in mere moments.

"The bazaar," Imiko said without turning to look at me. I noticed she was wearing a couple of rings on her left hand, yellow gold set with large gemstones. She had not been wearing them on the flyer, nor had I ever seen her wear rings before, quite where and when she had stolen them was a mystery. "I've never been, but I hear you can buy just about anything in the grand bazaar. I'm thinking of picking up a ringlet."

"A what?"

"Little furry creatures about half the size of a tahren, with strong legs for jumping and nimble fingers. If you get one young enough you can teach them all sorts of tricks, and even a few words. Back in Yun I knew a man with one, taught me everything I know about lifting." She turned to me with a wink. "Only thing is, the ringlet was even better than he was. He'd dance and cavort, sing the odd song, sometimes juggle, and all the while the ringlet would slip through the crowd, lifting jewellery and cutting purses. He called it Burt."

It sounded quite fun. "How do you think Hardt will feel about a little beast living with us?"

Imiko snorted out a laugh. "He'll hate it. I want one even more now."

She led us unerringly onward towards the bazaar, seeming to know the way despite never having stepped foot in Polasia before. When I asked her about it, Imiko told me she had studied the city from above, both up on Ro'shan and on the way down on the flyer. I never even thought of taking special note of the city layout, and was more than a little glad I had Imiko at my side to guide me, though more than once she seemed to vanish, leaving me all alone, only to reappear a minute later with a heavier purse, or a new piece of jewellery. She even handed me pair of crystal blue earrings after one such disappearance, claiming they would help to bring out the lightning in my eyes. I had to admit to her I did not have my ears pierced, but by the time we left Polasia, I did. I wore those earrings for the first time for Silva, and she agreed they did bring out the flashing of my eyes.

The grand bazaar in Polasia is a churning mass of flesh and goods. The smell is cloying, a dizzying mixture of sweat and spice and food and dung. The noise is so abrasive, I struggled to hear myself think, I even struggled to hear Ssserakis' excitement about the fear it drank in. I had to shout to be heard, and all the while the sun beats down upon everyone, baking them all into a miasma of anger, fear, and frustration. Imiko loved it there, finding so many opportunities to snatch a bit of wealth from deal hunters and fleecers alike. It is important, in any marketplace, to keep

a wary eye on your possessions, but not too wary an eye
unless you want to tell the thieves where to look.

"You there. Lady with the flashing eyes." We were
barely even inside the limits of the bazaar before I found
myself accosted. A large Polasian woman with lips as red
as blood and skin as dark as mud waved at me. I made the
foolish mistake of eye contact with her and she launched
into a speech as she pranced back and forth on a slightly
raised wooden platform. "A woman like you, so beautiful
and distinguished, you must be tired of carrying luggage.
All Terrelans love their luggage. I have just what you need."
She slapped the Polasian man standing next to her on the
arse. "Firm and strong."

"We should go," Imiko said, pulling on my arm. She
was right about that. Never engage with the merchants of
the great bazaar unless you are willing to buy, for they are
relentless in chasing the sale.

"Yes, yes. Firm and strong. Would you like to feel?
This one can carry all the luggage you need, wherever you
need to go. See the arms? Strong. Bulging. Fed three times
a day all his life. Good meals. Strong meals. Lots of fibre,
hmm. See the back? Straight as a pole. Trained to stand.
Hours, days, stand for as long as you need. Always straight.
Always strong."

The torrent of words was dizzying, but even more
incredulous was that the man just stood there while the
woman tried to auction him off like a prize abban.

I shook my head. "I have no luggage." My second
mistake. By replying to the woman, I indicated that I was
interested in the sale. I didn't even realise it, but I had started
haggling.

"No luggage. No problem. Many uses, a man like

this." The woman kept speaking, barely pausing to breathe. The man just stood there, dark eyes staring ahead, his mouth covered by a thick green veil. "Good breeding stock. See this?" The woman stepped closer to the man and pulled his robe apart in the middle, exposing him. I'm ashamed to say I blushed and looked down at the ground. The woman probably had a good laugh about that later, talking to her friends about the embarrassed Terrelan blushing at the sight of a cock.

"You like, yes?" The woman continued. "Big. Good breeding stock. Serve you well and often. Just sixteen golden rems, that's twenty-two golden broms in Terrelan coin. I do the math for you. A service, yes?"

Imiko snorted. "Rems are worth less than broms, not more. And I doubt he's worth that anyway."

"Your maid speaks true, glorious lady," the woman continued. "He is not worth that, but so much more. I am offering him to you at a steal. I make a loss, but you look like you need the breeding stock, yes? He will give you fine children, and many of them."

Again, Imiko snorted. "You call that big? I've seen boys in Terrelan with bigger cocks."

The man reacted a little then, his eyes flicking to Imiko for just a moment, and then away.

"If this is so, perhaps we can trade instead. My stock for yours. You get a man; I get a boy. Show me the boy."

"We should go," I said, realising a few other nearby merchants had stopped to watch. This time it was me pulling on Imiko's arm.

"Ten golden rems," the woman shouted after us. "You can even try before you buy."

A few other merchants tried to show us their wares,

but by then I had the knack of pushing into the crowd as Imiko and I forced our way further into the bazaar. "I don't think anyone has ever called me *lady* before." I had to lean in close to Imiko to make her hear me.

"No one has ever called me *maid* before either," Imiko said with a laugh. "She probably has no idea what a Terrelan woman of consequence actually looks like."

I was wearing a dress, sky blue and reaching past my knees, but it certainly wasn't an expensive one, and I had never seen any *lady* wear serviceable work boots like mine. Imiko, on the other hand, was wearing faded black trousers and a baggy blouse to hide her spoils, a dark waistcoat over the top. She was also hooded and bedecked in jewellery while I wore none. I admit, we made for a strange pair and I can't imagine anyone truly mistaking us for nobility. But the merchants of Polasia will take a sale wherever they can find one. I learned my lesson quickly that day, not to engage unless I was prepared to buy. Never accept the first offer, nor the second, nor even the third. I was starting to see why Silva likened negotiations to a battle.

We spent some time shopping in the bazaar. Imiko spent her wealth freely, happily trading stolen items for anything she desired. I had some coin on me, Polasian silver rems for the most part, but most of my wealth was in promises of credit from Ro'shan. I would not spend that frivolously, but if I saw anything I truly needed, I knew Silva would cover the cost on her mother's behalf. I had a small ink stamp to certify any writs of payment due. We tried some sort of fried lizard on a stick, and I must admit the spices made it quite good, though it was somewhat troublesome to eat, and I later found a couple of greasy stains on my dress. Imiko found the ringlet she wanted, a tiny thing, all fur, grasping hands, and big round eyes. The merchant told us it was as young as they could be separated from their mothers and just the right age to start training. Imiko poked it a bit and laughed as it grasped hold of her of her fingers and started trying to suckle. She haggled the merchant down to five golden rems and three silver, then rounded it up to six golden if the merchant delivered the little beast and its cage to the Ro'shan flyer at the docks. She paid out of a purse I hadn't seen her steal, and the merchant sent his boy running off to deliver the little beast. Imiko named it Kazh, and the creature almost never left her side.

As much as Imiko infuriated me at times, I always enjoyed spending time with her. We had fun together, and I always felt like I could be myself around her. She has an infectious sort of joviality that spreads to those around her. Rarely have I laughed so genuinely as when we stalked markets, remarking on all those around us. But there was a flightiness to Imiko, one she could never overcome. She hated open conflict and vanished whenever it reared its head. I teased the truth of it out of her once, when we were three bottles into a night at a tavern. Imiko's father was not a pleasant man, and he often beat her mother for little to no reason at all. It is an upbringing many Terrelans share. The endemic violence of men against their wives is a blight upon that society. My own father was never anything but loving to his family; I suppose I was lucky for that. Imiko's mother could always tell when her father was about to get violent and she would bid Imiko to hide, and hide she did. Imiko was hiding the final time it happened when her father beat her mother to death. She was hiding when the city guard arrived to march her father away in chains. She was hiding when the city lord appropriated the house and sold it off for his own gain. And she was still hiding when a new family moved into her home. That was how she learned to steal, to survive while hidden amongst people who didn't even know she existed. I think Imiko has been hiding ever since, and in my shadow, she found the perfect place to disappear from the world.

There is a training ground in Polasia full of swarthy warrior types aiming to test themselves against each before signing up to coliseum bouts. Imiko claimed to know the way, and after we had found her a ringlet, she was in a pleasant enough mood to lead me there. But just as we were leaving the bazaar, I recognised a voice, one I thought long dead. I felt my throat tighten and hope burst to life inside as I searched the crowd nearby for the owner of it. And there, standing in front of a fruit cart, inspecting a bushel of apples, stood a greying man with a faded red robe and the face of a kindly grandfather. Prince Loran Tow Orran, the Iron Legion.

"My prince." I was perhaps a little overzealous. I went down on one knee in front of him; I had never done that the previous times we had met. I think that was when Imiko vanished, unwilling to stand with me in the centre of that attention. And I certainly piqued the curiosity of the bazaar. All around me people stopped to stare, whispering to each other, some even laughed but I ignored them all, my attention fixed on the prince in front of me.

"Oh dear," prince Loran said as he glanced over his shoulder at me. He was wrinkled far beyond his thirty odd years, his age unnaturally accelerated just as my own had been but to a far worse degree. The Orran Empire had used his abilities mercilessly during the war and it had taken an awful toll upon his body, inflicting ancient skin and bones upon an otherwise young man. Still, he bore those extra years well. Short grey hair and wrinkles did nothing to hide his royal lineage and the old man who stood before me was as handsome as the younger man I had met on my very first day at the academy. When we are young, we believe that age decays beauty, and after a prime few years everything is deterioration. But the older I get, the more I have started to realise that age only accentuates. Skin may wrinkle and hair may grey, but there is wisdom to be seen in those lines, experience to be drawn from the drained colour. No. Age may wither some, but in many others, it is truly sexy.

"I'm afraid you're quite wrong, my dear. I'm not a prince of anything." Loran turned around and graced me with a sad smile.

KILL HIM! The maelstrom of noise and rage Ssserakis unleashed inside staggered me and I collapsed sideways so I was sprawled in the bazaar walkway. I struggled to find my thoughts in that chaos and failed. Prince Loran crossed the distance between us and called for others to stand back. He reached down and helped me stand with a strong hand on my arm. All the while I heard and felt Ssserakis going mad inside of me, like a newly caged animal dashing itself against the bars over and over again. Stunned, I stood with the prince slowly and stared into his face, still trying to find my thoughts, find myself, amidst the chaos inside me.

"I've never seen eyes like yours before, my dear." The prince kept hold of my arm, escorting me out of the way so the rest of the bazaar could go about its business. "They flash like lightning. It's quite magnificent."

In my dizzied haze I saw my shadow start to move, curling forwards to surround the prince, the inky blackness writhing as sharp tendrils formed within. I pulled my fragmented awareness back together and locked Ssserakis inside. My body was mine. The horror was a passenger, a parasite. I gave it a home within me, but I would not allow it to take control. I would not give it another chance like it had down in the Pit, the day it had almost used me to kill Josef. I felt the horror's rage at my assertion of will, and I weathered the storm as it spat at me again and again in a language I could never understand.

"You look familiar, young lady," Prince Loran was saying. His dark eyes seemed to almost twinkle, and in those depths, I found the youth that the rest of his body hid so well. "From the academy?"

I nodded. "Eska. Um. Eskara Helsene, my prince." We were out of the way now, tucked beside the fruit vendor's cart, and, though there were still a few stares pointed my way, most of the bazaar was continuing about its business. Ssserakis finally quieted its rage and lapsed into a sullen sulk, but I could feel its anger simmering inside of me and I could hear its whispers to *kill him* repeated over and over again.

The prince narrowed his dark eyes at me, perhaps wondering how much I remembered of him. "Of course. You were friends with young Josef Yenhelm. How is he?"

"Dead." I blurted the word and my voice cracked a little on it. Perhaps it was finding the man I used to worship as a hero was still alive, or perhaps it was the boiling anger of Ssserakis inside, but I was struggling to properly master myself. "We were sent to the Pit after Orran fell. I... He died there."

"I see." Prince Loran bowed his head and nodded. "A true loss. I always had high hopes for the Yenhelm boy, much as I did for you."

"You're alive?" It was not the most eloquent way for me to form the question, but I have always had trouble finding the right words when also dealing with shock.

"I am? Let me check." Prince Loran patted at his chest, then placed two fingers at the side of his neck, and finally poked a finger inside his mouth. When he withdrew the finger, he was smiling. "I do appear to be alive. It shouldn't be that surprising, really, I don't remember ever dying. I have come close once or twice though. I should tell you about my time up on..."

"We received reports of your death." Oh, how I wish I hadn't interrupted him then. I would have loved to have heard what he was about to tell me. "Before the Fall of Orran. You were sent out at the head of our largest force. No one made it back alive. How are you alive?"

"Oh that? Well, that's probably because I defected." He smiled at me, the lines of his face making him seem a harmless old man.

I will say it now as I didn't see it then. He was so jovial and carefree; I missed the deception. I should have listened to Ssserakis when the horror bid me kill the prince. The Iron Legion had never been harmless. Generations of selective breeding topped with the most dedicated training any Sourcerer had ever received. I like to think I am powerful; I am attuned to six different schools of Sourcery and I can hold five in my stomach at one time. The Iron Legion made me look like a common village witch. Attuned to eleven of the twenty-two schools, and the reports I read back at the academy said he could hold no less than eight Sources at once. The reports understated his abilities. A kindly old man, indeed. The Iron Legion was the most powerful Sourcerer Ovaeris had ever known, even in his youth, and age only makes us stronger.

"But you're an Orran. Your brother is dead. You're the last Orran." I searched his face for any sign of reaction, but all I saw there was a disarming smile. "You are Orran. The rebellion."

He laughed. "No. There is no rebellion, Eskara. And I am no longer a prince or an Orran. I'm just Loran now. Simple Loran. You see, the Terrelan emperor is far more shrewd than my brother gave him credit for. I suppose he must have had spies close to me. He saw what I wanted and he offered it to me. Sent an emissary to me the night before the battle and made me an offer. All the resources I could need to continue my research, and none of the rules the Orran Academy imposed upon me. And all I had to do was not fight. I assure you; some offers are too good to refuse."

"What research? What could possibly be worth sacrificing your kingdom for?"

Again, the laugh. "What is a kingdom worth, Eskara? It is just land and responsibility. I never wanted that, and in truth my brother had very little idea of what to do with it other than wage war. There are far more important things in the world than owning a part of it. Perhaps once you realise that, I'll tell you about my research. Maybe then you'll be ready. But not now. Even with all the rumours about you, you're not there yet." He stepped aside and started past me, pausing for a moment. "It really is a shame about Yenhelm. I had high hopes for the Biomancer." The Iron Legion shook his head and started walking again.

Kill him, Eskara! Ssserakis tried again, screaming inside me. *That hateful creature dragged me from my home. We can stop him now before his plans unfurl. His back is turned. KILL HIM!*

"What plans?" I asked. But Ssserakis had no answer for me, only the damning certainty that they would see both of our worlds in ruin. As prince Loran vanished into the crowd, my chance to stop him before the world suffered was lost.

In the prince's wake Imiko reappeared, stepping through the crowd right where Loran had disappeared into it. She glanced back at him once and then approached me cautiously, as though I were some wild animal that might bite for no reason at all.

"Old flame?" she asked, a little too lightly for my liking.

I was feeling quite beside myself, confused and angry all at once. I couldn't understand why the prince wanted no part of my fight against the Terrelans. I think I was also angry at his betrayal, but that anger could have been Ssserakis'. It was often difficult to tell our emotions apart.

"Thanks for backing me up," I said with venom.

Imiko held up her hands and smiled. "Oh, I was around, watching. I'm no good in the thick of things, I work better from the shadows." She grinned at me and thumbed towards the exit of the bazaar. "We still going to shop for some mercenaries?"

I nodded to that, already wondering if it might help my state of mind if I could find someone to spar against. There is little that can clear a mind quite like violence, and my mind was a whirl that needed focus.

By the time we reached the sparring grounds the light was starting to wane, casting the city in long shadows and a dusty yellow light. I liked it. It suited my mood as it flipped between anger and melancholy. Isen stalked me from those shadows, his ruined face a constant reminder of what violence can bring. It didn't stop me. I couldn't let it. I needed to find help, people to help me commit violence up on Do'shan. I was in a rather savage state of mind.

"No place for young ladies," said a lounging pahht man at the gate. "The coliseum is further on. Plenty of muscle for you to ogle there." One glare from the storm behind my eyes convinced him not to stand in our way and we continued into the sparring grounds.

It was, itself, a small coliseum, though the ring around the grounds had no place for seating. Several weapon racks lined the walls here and there, and the sand covering the ground was bloody in many places. Half a dozen small scuffles were taking place, ranging from duels, to outnumbered fights, to one all out brawl at the far side. They were mostly Polasian women, I noticed, and they fought in a style of combat that made their bodies seem to flow around the weapons they held. Even Tamura is impressed by the Polasian fighting style. I noticed a few pahht as well, scrapping with each other, though they seemed to put little effort into the bouts. There were also several Polasian men, bared chested and oiled so their muscles gleamed in the waning light. All of them wore veils over their mouths and none of them carried any weapons.

"It is a thing of beauty, watching the men wrestle. Just wait. Soon they will writhe together, like eels in a bag." I turned to find a pahht woman lounging in a chair beside the entrance. A gourd hung from a string tied around her wrist and as I watched she flipped it up into her hand and swigged at the contents before letting out a grateful sound that was all pleasure. Her fur was a charcoal black, short where on many pahht it is long, and she had a grey dusting of hairs around her mouth and ears. She wore loose cotton trousers, a leather jerkin cut off at the shoulder and a hood to match, hiding much of her face in deep shadow. But her eyes twinkled in the dim light and I saw the gleam of white canines. I noticed, too, that there were a couple of curved swords sitting sheathed at the base of the chair. A warrior, then, but judging by the smell of booze that rolled off of her, she was not in the grounds to fight.

"Who…"

"Here they go. Watch." I turned back to the sparring grounds to see two of the Polasian men step forward, and then bow to each other. Then they locked arms and within moments they were writhing together on the sandy ground, each trying to manoeuvre the other into a hold of some sort. "Wouldn't you just love to be in the middle of that embrace?" The pahht woman let out a drunken giggle that went on for far too long.

The other Polasian men cheered behind their veils, and some of the other people sparring stopped to watch. I noticed a small throng of Polasian women, each of them armed with swords or axes, watching with clear interest. The bout ended with one man on top of the other, bending his arm painfully behind his back. The man on the floor bashed at the sand with his free hand and the two competitors parted, bowing to each other after they both had their feet.

Imiko had her bottom lip between her teeth and a hungry look on her face. When she noticed me, she quickly looked away. "That was impressive, um, fighting."

Again, the pahht woman giggled. "Polasian men do not fight. They slap each other and make it look good. A show for the women. You want to see a fight, look over there." She pointed to where two Polasian women were circling each other, swords drawn. When they clashed it was to the ring of steel, and I barely managed to follow the series of blows they traded.

"Fighting." Again, the woman pointed at the Polasian women, then shifted her wavering finger towards the men. "Foreplay. I prefer to watch the latter. It is more fun."

I took a step closer to the woman. "What's your name?"

"Ishtar, of the Rolling Hills." She waved the hand with the gourd attached in a way that was almost regal.

"Eskara." After a few moments of her piercing gaze I realised she wanted more. "Of Keshin."

"Ahh. Sounds like a wonderful place."

"I wouldn't know. I haven't been back there in a very long time."

Ishtar bared her teeth. It is important to realise that, with the pahht, smiles and snarls look very similar. "That's what homelands are for. To remember fondly, and never see again. And you?"

Imiko shrugged. "Imiko, of Yun."

"I have been to Yun," Ishtar said jovially. "It smells of fish."

"And that's the nicest thing you can say about it," Imiko agreed with a nod of her head.

"So, what is it that brings Eskara, of Keshin and Imiko, of Yun to these grounds? Come to watch the boys play with each other? Or is there more to you than the eye sees?"

"Why do the men fight without weapons?" I asked.

Ishtar swigged from her gourd and let it drop, wriggling even deeper into the depths of her lounging chair. "Polasian men are not allowed swords. They would only hurt themselves with sharp things. Some are allowed spears, I think, but not these. These are for slapping each other and looking pretty. They play at fighting, then go back to their mistresses to give them children. Or perhaps their mistresses are already here, fighting like women. I do not know. I do not keep track of people who live in palaces."

Imiko let out a sigh. "Why shouldn't men fight? They're stronger than women."

Ishtar turned her twinkling eyes on Imiko. "Strength serves only the purpose it is given. Skill and wisdom provide the purpose. Those who fight with their arms lose. Those who fight with their heads win. I suppose the women of this place think they have better heads. Who am I to argue?"

"What about you?" I asked. "I see you have swords. Do you fight?"

Ishtar let out that drunken giggle again. "If only, Eskara, of Keshin. None of my troop will fight me, they know better." She waved a hand towards the group of ten pahht sparring in one of the larger areas of the grounds.

"But you can fight?"

Ishtar didn't answer that with words, only a shrewd glare.

"Show me."

"I don't fight on demand, Eskara, of Keshin. No. No, wait. For free. I don't fight on demand, for free. Yes, that's right."

I turned to Imiko. "Give her one of your rings. She had this one valued, it's worth three gold rems." The thief grumbled but handed over one of her stolen rings. Ishtar turned it around in her fingers, squinting at it, then tucked it into a pocket and rocked herself forward, scooping up her swords. She towered over me by a good hand and a half, and I could see the muscle beneath her fur. Ishtar moved with natural grace that convinced me of her skill long before I watched her fight.

"Watch closely, Eskara, of Keshin. You are likely to miss what you wish to see."

Ishtar walked not towards her own people, but to the Polasian women sparring with their bladed weapons. She interrupted their duel with a bow and flourish and though I didn't hear what was said, there was little time spared before both Polasians saluted Ishtar and surrounded her. It's fair to say the bout was short. Ishtar was outnumbered, and I had been able to smell the alcohol on her from half a dozen paces. Even so, the woman didn't even draw her swords. She put both Polasians on their arses twice over using sheathed weapons and made it look easy. I hate to admit it, but I did miss a lot of what I paid for in that fight. I saw her win, but I could not tell you how, only that she appeared faster and stronger than both her opponents, and even numbers could not sway the fight in their favour. She bowed once more to her opponents, then swaggered her way towards us, still swaying from the drink.

"You did that while drunk?" Imiko asked, a touch of awe in her voice I could not blame her for.

"I am drinking," Ishtar said with a snort. "I am not drunk. Yet. Later, for certain I will be drunk, moons willing. Especially if I can find anyone in that coliseum to fight with me. It is hard to find a challenger with a reputation like mine." I must admit I do not agree with that sentiment. I have always found my reputation, no matter how dark or deadly, only serves to recruit me more enemies.

"Are you a pit fighter or a mercenary?" I asked.

"There is little difference with no one to fight."

"If you're a mercenary, I have an offer for you. You and your troops."

Ishtar laughed. "We are not cheap, Eskara, of Keshin. Your little ring bought you a fight. How much do you think my whole troop costs?" She slumped back down into her chair and raised her gourd to her lips, swigging down a mouthful then frowning as she found it empty.

"I'm sure I can afford your services, Ishtar, of the Rolling Hills. I represent the Rand in this." I pointed towards Ro'shan, hanging in the air just south of the city, filling the skyline. "And I assure you she has deep pockets."

Ishtar's eyes twinkled again within the depths of her hood. Greed can make fools of even the wisest. "What sort of work is this?"

I stepped forward, close enough so she had to tilt her head to look up at me. "For a few months it will involve nothing but sitting on your arses, and a bit of teaching me how to fight."

"You don't know how to fight?" Ishtar said with a laugh.

"I know how punch and kick. But I don't know how to fight with a blade."

"Ha! You know how to slap with the boys. I did think it strange a lady in a dress turning up here without even a sword."

It was my turn to grin. It was my turn to impress. "Oh, I have a sword." I drew on my Kinemancy and formed a Sourceblade in my right hand, the same size and length as Ishtar's own weapons. It glowed with a hazy purple light from the kinetic energy I filled it with.

"Huh." Ishtar sat up in her chair and reached out a hand, poking at the blade and then pinning it between strong fingers. "Now there is something I have never seen before."

"No one has." I cannot deny the pride that crept into my voice. "It's something only I can do." I released the shape of the blade and the energy within burst apart, puffing against the fur of Ishtar's arm. "Come with me and I promise to show you plenty of things you've never seen before. And I'll pay you, obviously."

Again, the twinkle in her eyes. Her whiskers twitched too; Ishtar's whiskers had a habit of twitching when she was excited. She rose to her feet, again towering over me, and nodded. "Tell me more about this offer, Eskara, of Keshin." I opened my mouth to speak but she held up a finger. "Ah. Over a drink. Or many drinks. There is a tavern nearby, and it is your round."

I had her, my sword tutor and mercenary rolled into one. A better bargain I have rarely struck. For the price of a bit of wonder and a few promises, I had secured one of the most accomplished warriors Ovaeris had ever seen. I'm not about to claim Ishtar's deeds compare with those of the heroes of old; ancient Brinta and her battle against the Seven Forgelords is a tale the bards tell even to this day. Even hundreds of years buried, the message of her greatest adventure remains: even the mightiest of armies can be overcome by a well-placed word. The ten trials of the mercenary company, the Wyvern's Claw, has books written on it by no less than four different authors, each telling the tribulations in a different way, but they are all telling us that camaraderie and trust can salvage almost any situation. Ishtar already had songs written about her, but few could claim to contain any message other than *Do not screw with Ishtar, of the Rolling Hills*. Her loyalty only ever stretched as far as my coin, or at least my promise of riches, but it was worth its weight in gold.

By the time I assaulted Do'shan, I was ready. I could fight, with hand, blade, and magic. I had followers: my friends who would stay with me no matter what, my mercenaries who were bought and paid for, and Horralain who would protect me as viciously as he had Deko. What I was missing, what I have always been missing, was knowledge. So much of the truth was hidden from me. It had to be. Mezula and Silva both knew if they had but told me the truth, I would have torn Ro'shan from the sky long before I dared set foot on Do'shan.

CHAPTER FORTY

JOSEF

Healer, page, servant. Life has become meaningless save for the work Death gives me. I'm neither trusted nor liked. Each day Eska eludes us, Death only treats me with more hostility, as though it is somehow my fault. Why are people so quick to blame their failures on others?

I am given the Biomancy Source only when one of her knights needs healing, and then made to retch it up as soon as my work is done. I am monitored at all times. Even now, sitting by the fire, writing this. Even with the music in the tavern and the beer flowing freely. Even with the contests of strength and arms going on around us, one of them watches me. I have been with Death for over a year, and still they treat me like an enemy in their midst. I have done nothing to warrant it. I have been good. I have been loyal. I am Death's servant. Yet still, I'm nothing but an Orran to them.

"We're all Terrelans now." It's a popular saying these days. Everywhere we go I hear it. It's not true. We who used to be Orrans are treated differently. I hear other things said, by Death and her Knights of Ten: "True Terrelans." It's not just them. I've been to Juntorrow. I've suffered through the emperor's presence. He does not look kindly on those of us from the Orran side of his empire. And the way he looked at me... More than two years after the Fall of Orran, and I'm still referred to as one of the last of the Orran Sourcerers. Just me, and Eska. The hatred in the emperor's eyes was terrifying. For me, he had nothing but disgust, but for Eska there was true hatred there. He spoke openly of how he wants her to suffer. Death has orders now. All other duties aside, she is to find Eska and bring her to the emperor in chains. I don't know what he plans to do with her, but it will be painful. Can I let it happen? I don't know if I hate Eska or love her anymore. But can I let them have her? Can I stop it? Do I want to?

There is a spy. Someone close to Eska maybe, I don't know who. They've been sending information to Death. And now we know where she is going. Eska is on her way to Do'shan, the second flying city. But why? There's nothing there but monsters and ruins. She must know something we don't. There must be something worth leaving the sanctuary of Ro'shan for. And here we are, waiting. Death and three of her knights. A small army at her back, with three Sourcerers; Temmet, Rurin, and Pilk. I hate them. They watch me write, mock my lack of voice. I caught Temmet going through my things the other day, looking for the pages I write my thoughts upon. He'll never find them. Sometimes I burn them, my thoughts turned to ash. Other times I leave them behind, a page tucked into a hollow of a tree branch, like treasure hidden away for some lucky soul to one day find. I never keep them on me. I have no voice, but my thoughts are dangerous. Dangerous to me, and to Eska. I will never let them read my thoughts. Perhaps I'll hide this page. There's a loose floorboard below my chair, I could pry it up just a little and slide the paper in. Maybe one day someone might find it.

I like to think all the thoughts I've left around Terrelan might one day be collected. A historian collecting all the shattered fragments that I've left behind, all the little pieces of me. I'm so alone. I like to think that one day someone will join me on this journey. They'll read through all the things I've written, and I won't be alone anymore. I'll never have been alone. Just one person reading them, and they'll have been with me the entire time. It's about the only comfort I have left.

This is my first time anywhere in the world other than Isha. I have discovered I don't much like ships. They rock endlessly and down in the belly of the beast you can hear the water sloshing against the wooden hull. It's unnerving. I like this place even less. Rolshh is a savage continent full of lumbering beasts that look upon terrans as a small snack. At first, I thought the monsters here were dragged over from the Other World, but Temmet is an Impomancer and I heard him telling Death that they are native creatures. I didn't think our world had anything so large. Some of them stand at twenty times as tall as a terran, giant things that walk on two legs, with huge mouths. We saw one the other day, stalking the nearby jungle, and I could see the blood of a fresh kill dripping from its beard. We hear them constantly, roaring to each other, crashing through trees. At least they don't come near the city. I think maybe the walls keep them out. Or maybe it's the patrols. Something keeps them away and I'm glad of it. The eight-legged monsters are even worse. They are nightmares given form, scuttling through the trees and singing to each other in voices that are almost terran. No wonder Rolshh is barely inhabited, it seems everything in this damned continent wants to kill us.

Do'shan hangs in the sky like a dark stain filling the eastern horizon. Four great chains run down from the mountain, sunk deep into the earth nearby. They are larger than the chain that anchor's Ro'shan, each link many times the size of a house. I do not know what creature could have built them, but they were not made to retract into the flying mountain, they were made to anchor it to the world for all eternity. The locals say the chains are unbreakable, and they've had generations to test the theory. No picks can chip them, no fire can melt them, no hammer can dent them. Whatever magic keeps them unbroken doesn't seem to stop nature. I see moss growing all along the links, vines crawling up them. I swear I've even seen creatures upon them, a group of some sort trekking up the links to reach the remains of the city atop it. But it is hard to be sure. At that distance, the eyes play tricks on you. With enough distance, even monsters look like ants.

We're going up tomorrow. Pilk is scared. I hear her complaining about how portals are dangerous at that distance even for one or two people. She's sending half an army through. No doubt Death and her knights will go first, using portals gets more dangerous the more people that go through. Those of us towards the end are just as likely to find ourselves in oblivion as our true destination. I hope we all find that the portal leads nowhere.

I'm sorry, Eska.

I want to put that down on paper. I want it recorded. In case we arrive tomorrow and... In case Death wins. I want someone to know I'm sorry. I want whoever finds this scrap of me to know I never wanted any of this.

CHAPTER FORTY ONE

A FEW MONTHS AFTER OUR STOP IN POLASIA, I felt I was ready to take the fight to the Djinn on Do'shan. Ready to match power and skill against a god. Rolshh reminded me a lot of home; my first home, Keshin. Dense trees reaching up into the sky, creating a canopy so thick some of the smaller creatures could walk along it. No doubt there would be some treacherous footing, but I imagine the view was spectacular. Our view was better. Two flyers, one large enough to carry the bulk of our force and our supplies, the other smaller to carry our landing force. Of course, I put myself on the smaller one. I intended to be one of the first of us to set foot on Do'shan.

I saw the trees rustle far below and caught sight of some great tail swishing back and forth, just a glimpse and then it was gone, obscured by the green mass. Ishtar told me tales of Rolshh, of the monsters that stalked its jungles and mountain ranges. By their size they were monsters truly, and even Ssserakis had a kernel of respect for the beasts. Other stories Ishtar told were of riches hidden in abandoned cities, and temples built to the worship of dead gods, Rand or Djinn, who had not survived their war. She also told me tales of strange pygmy creatures that stole the faces of terrans and pahht alike, but I think those were lies. Then again, perhaps she was referring to the Damned; they exist all over Ovaeris, hiding in the dark places where most civilised folk fear to tread.

We passed a town far below, so small it looked like a brown stain amidst a sea of green. I asked its name and Ishtar only shrugged, asking why it mattered. I had no answer at the time, but I think I would now. Names matter. Names of people, names of places. It is through naming a thing that we give it meaning and value. Would anyone notice if a nameless town in the middle of the jungle was suddenly gone? But give that same settlement a name and suddenly it is a place where people live. Put it on a map and it becomes a permanent fixture. Have a queen claim it, and it becomes property to be defended at all costs.

A single name, just six letters, can hold more meaning than the sum of its parts. People see a terran walking through their town and they do not spare her a second glance, just one more face in an endless sea of them. Give that terran a name, Eskara, and reactions change. Suddenly people know who they're looking at, years of reputation and tavern tales have new meaning. An abstract terror, almost thought to be a myth, becomes real. In knowing that six letter name, the city goes from safe, to under threat. *The Corpse Queen is real, alive, she walks among us, and in her footsteps, ruin will follow.* But in truth, what has changed? I am the same person, whether people know my name or not. The city is no less safe than it was just for the knowing of my name. And I still just want to purchase a basket of fruit, whether people tremble at my passing or not. Our actions may be what defines us, but it is our names that bear the consequences.

The sun was waning, but our moons were on the rise. Lursa was dominant in the sky, but not by much, and her light bathed us all in a sallow blue glow. Rolshh is a warm continent, the temperatures ranging from pleasant to unbearably hot, but this high up, it was cold. A sharp chill hung in the air and I huddled into my winter coat, letting the heat from my Pyromancy Source keep my core warm. My breath misted in front of me and I could see frost clinging to the hanging strands of my hair. Ishtar and her pahht mercenaries looked even less pleased at the cold, and I saw frosty dustings on the fur around their mouths.

"Ro'shan is not so cold," Ishtar said with a grumble. Her right hand brushed against the gourd hanging from her belt, but she resisted its temptation. That was quite unlike her, I wondered if my sword tutor was perhaps nervous. We had spent months together and she rarely hesitated to swig from it.

"The air around it is," I said. "But the Rand keeps the city pleasant somehow." I could see snowy mountains in the far distance, and on the south side of Do'shan there was a frozen waterfall, caught in the moment of streaming from the flying mountain. It appeared whatever magic or system Mezula used to keep Ro'shan a verdant paradise did not exist up on its sister city.

"I do not like snow. Or ice," Ishtar said and her voice seemed to tremble from the cold. "That looks both snowy and icy. You are not paying us enough for such frigid conditions."

I laughed at that. "With the amount I'm paying you, you could have bought some warmer clothing instead of more booze."

"You terrans rely far too much on your warm clothing. It is all because you wish you had more hair."

"You're the one complaining about the cold."

"I complain about many things. It keeps me warm."

I cocked an eyebrow at Ishtar and she bared her teeth at me, her eyes twinkling in the depths of her hood. She sighed. "A good student would sacrifice her lovely warm coat to keep her master warm."

"You think I'm a good student?" I asked, already knowing the answer.

"No. You are a terrible student. But your coat would make you a better one."

"I'm happy with terrible." That was a lie. I will never be happy with being terrible at anything.

The flyer started to rise, the operator twisting whatever control it was he used to steer the thing, and the propeller above us whirring even faster and louder. I still knew little about our transports, but I had guessed the source of their power. Kinemancy can do amazing things and I wondered where the Source was attached, and how large it was, for that was the only way I could see how the contraptions were powered. Behind us, the larger flyer started to rise as well, though more slowly, struggling against its much heavier load. Most of Ishtar's troops were in that flyer, along with Silva and Tamura and Imiko, and most of our supplies as well. Hardt and Horralain joined Ishtar and I, and we would form the boarding party, landing first in order to secure space for the larger flyer to land. We weren't sure what to expect on Do'shan, but Mezula claimed the city was not so much ruins, as it was a fortress, and a heavily occupied one at that.

Do'shan really is as large as its sister, though the mountaintop certainly wasn't as flat. As we rose to become level with it, I could see the city spread out across the entire mountain. Huge buildings of multiple levels lay in various states of dilapidation. Streets wound through the city in a maddening maze of circles. And in the middle of that city sat a solid black sphere, dwarfing all the buildings around it. It was a curious sight and I could guess where we would find the Djinn.

Seven satellite islands orbited the main land mass of Do'shan. Some were large islands, populated by green trees that could withstand the cold. Others were barren shards of rock, long since crumbled away from the mountain but still held in whatever magic kept it afloat.

Higher we rose, and higher still, and I could swear the temperature dropped until even Ssserakis noted the cold. I glanced back to the operator, but he seemed unconcerned by the temperature. The man had thought to bring thick padded gloves and I envied him for that foresight. Horralain stood nearby, staring off towards the city, ice in both his beard and hair. He noticed me and grunted. "Looks like the city next to the Pit." His voice was slow as he measured each word, or perhaps made certain in his head each one was the right meaning.

"Djinn city," Hardt said through chattering teeth. He hugged himself with big arms and danced on the spot. It would have made for a comical sight if not for the razor tension in the air.

He was right. Ro'shan was a city made by the Rand.
She had sculpted it from the bones of some great monster
that lived in the centre of the mountain. The buildings
were organic things, possessed of flowing lines and natural
curves. Everything in Ro'shan spoke of life. Do'shan couldn't
have been more different. The buildings were bizarre shapes,
bending outward and then in again in hard angles. There
was an oddly uniform nature to the layout of the city and if
I let my focus drift, I could see some underlying pattern that
dictated the flow of the streets. It was not natural; it was all
built by design.

*The Djinn shape everything to their will. To their sense
of aesthetic. You have seen this city before, Eskara. I have shown
it to you.* Ssserakis was right. The city was the same layout,
the buildings the same shape. Ssserakis had once owned a
city just like this, but in the Other World. The possibilities
blossomed, questions rolling around my head. Did that
mean the Djinn had been to the Other World? Had they
shaped it like they did Ovaeris, or had they come from the
Other World, and brought the architecture across?

"The Djinn built your city," I said, lowering my voice
so nobody could hear me over the whirring of the propeller.
But Ssserakis could hear me, the horror didn't need the
sound of my voice to know my thoughts.

*The Djinn built everything in my world. They were its
architects. We were their greatest disappointment.*

"Stop this thing," Ishtar snapped in a harsh voice and
turned on the operator. "Take us no closer."

The operator turned some dials and pulled a lever.
I left him to his ministrations and joined Ishtar at the front
of the flyer. She had a viewing glass in her hand, raised and
pointed towards the city. I tried squinting, but eyes alone

have their limitations. I'm told a well-trained Photomancer can see for miles in the clearest of details, but then I've never known a Photomancer who wasn't eventually driven mad by their magic.

"What is it? We can't board the city from here," I said.

Ishtar let out a low growl. "You pay me to be a mercenary, not a corpse." She handed me the viewing glass. "Look towards the rooftops."

I will admit, I had no idea what I was looking at or for. I stared through the viewing glass and saw shapes, some of them possibly moved, others might have been shadows. Whatever Ishtar saw eluded my poorer eyesight and I ground my teeth in frustration. So close, and yet one more delay.

"Your people call them machines of war," Ishtar said.

Hardt joined us at the front of the flyer and squinted. He was shivering from the cold and wearing a frown as deep as my own. "What types?"

"Does it matter?" Ishtar snatched the viewing glass from me and stared through it once more.

"Conventional war machines might struggle to hit us. Catapults don't have the accuracy against moving targets and ballista won't do enough damage unless they hit the propeller," Hardt said. "Source weaponry is a different matter."

Ishtar lowered the viewing glass and glanced at Hardt. "You seem surprisingly knowledgeable on the matter."

Hardt smiled. "Tamura has had me reading Belmoroes' Treaty on War."

Ishtar gasped. "A terran who can read. Next, you'll be telling me that your people bathe also. I do not know the

name of the thing." She squinted through the viewing glass.
"It is a wheel, lying on its side, connected to some sort of
platform, I think. The wheel has many spokes, each one with
something like a rock sitting on it. I have never seen a thing
like this before."

"A Ringan," Hardt said. "Powered by a Kinemancy
Source, they spin at terrifying speeds, just like the propeller
keeping us flying. There'll be a lever near the machine and
when it's pulled the discs, not rocks, start releasing, straight
forward. If they have us targeted right, just one salvo will
tear through the flyer and everyone on board."

"The hull is strong," I said. "It withstands…"

"Not tough enough," Hardt said. "Those things can
punch through stone walls. We might not even be out of
range now. Are they manned?"

"Yes. Little figures in robes swarm around it. I think
they know we are coming," Ishtar said, watching through
the viewing glass.

"Is it just the one of these, uh, Ringan?" I asked.

Ishtar shook her head. "Of those, I see at least five.
There are others. One looks like a fork, and I see lightning
sparking between the prongs." She glanced at me. "Looks
just like your eyes when they flash, hmm?"

"Arc Biters," Hardt said. "Moons damned Source
weaponry. They take less time to operate than the Ringans
and they're more manoeuvrable but have a shorter range.
How will arc lightning react to the wood of the ship?"

I shrugged. "It will likely set us on fire."

"At least we'll be warm," Ishtar said. "You there, man
at the controls, circle the island. No closer than this. We shall
find a less dangerous place to approach, maybe."

After an hour of circling the mountain, we had not

even seen a quarter of it, but Ishtar still ordered the flyer to a halt. She pointed to an area where grass had poked its way through the rocky earth and two buildings nearby had collapsed into nothing but rubble. Beyond that small clearing, the city started, dozens of buildings springing up. It was about as far away from the centre of the city as could be, but Ishtar claimed it to be the best landing spot we had seen so far, and said we were best beginning the assault before the light of day. The moons were bright, but at least the slight gloom obscured us a little.

"Why not land further in, take us all the way to the sphere?" I asked.

Ishtar sighed. "Terrible student. You learn nothing. Here we can land with maybe two machines pointed our way. Further in, there will be many from all over, all aimed at us. We must make land and disable those nearby, let the other flyer deposit its load. Then we regroup and make towards the centre. Best plan. Only plan."

Horralain let out a grumble behind us but said nothing. I knew that sound and knew it meant he wasn't happy, but the big man wouldn't say anything for fear he might sound stupid. In many ways I envied that about Horralain. I have never been able to hold my tongue, no matter how stupid it might make me sound or the trouble it gets me into.

"How do *we* make the landing without getting shot down?" Hardt asked. Ishtar snapped her jaws shut and went back to staring through the viewing glass.

"Take us down," I ordered the operator. "Below the land line. We'll rise up as close to the edge as possible, and those of us going will jump off. Then drop the flyer back down and wait for the all clear. We'll make our assault and take out the closest machines to allow the rest of our force to land."

Ishtar glanced at me, eyes twinkling in the depths of her hood as she considered. "It could work. Assuming they don't react quickly enough to target us."

"We'll have a lot of open ground to cross before we find the cover of the buildings," Hardt said.

"Then you'll just have to trust me to protect you until you reach them," I said with a confidence I didn't truly feel. I have often found that bravado will convince others to action long before any true trust in my abilities.

You lead your friends to their deaths. Why not just push them over the side now?

"Not helping," I hissed under my breath. Ssserakis chuckled in my mind.

The operator set the flyer to start descending and flashed a signal to the other vessel to hold position. Ishtar took hold of my arm and turned me to face her. "You are a terrible student and a slow learner. So, tell me, Eskara, can you do this? Can you defend us long enough to cross such a killing field?"

"First you insult her and then doubt her?" Hardt shook his head. "If Eska says she can do it, she can do it." He pinned me with a stare. "You've pulled us through worse." If I had, I certainly couldn't remember when.

"I was not talking to you, overgrown terran." Ishtar dismissed Hardt with a hiss. "Opinions are like children. Those who have them want them to be special, rarely realising they are just as dumb and ugly as all the others."

"And what about your opinion?" I said it to avoid her question.

Ishtar shrugged. Her clawed hand was still on my

arm, an uncomfortable pressure given her grip was like iron. "I don't have children. Tell me if you can do this, student? I will not throw my life before these machines for nothing."

We sank below the land line, dropping far enough that we would be out of sight of any up on Do'shan. Then the operator levelled the flyer off and started it on the approach towards the mountain. I pulled my arm away from Ishtar, ignoring the painful scratches she left, and held her gaze. "Stay behind me and stay close."

I walked to the rear of the flyer, stopping briefly by the operator. He was a stout man, short but swarthy. Silva had hand picked him, claiming he knew the flyers like no other. "Just keep going," I said. "Get them up on the land, close enough to jump across, then drop back down out of range. Don't take any risks." He nodded to me and I continued to the aft railing, stepping up onto it. It's quite dizzying staring down at the ground so far below. A fall like that could take minutes, watching the earth rush towards you, knowing there is nothing you can do to stop it. I heard the call of the void once more, Lesray Alderson's lingering *gift* to me, the unshakable desire to end it all. To be free of the pain, the exhaustion, the endless struggle. To be nothing.

"What are you doing, Eska?" Hardt asked, close by. I didn't turn to look at him.

The flyer was rising, closing in towards the edge where the city would open before us. Where the machines of war would have sight of us. "Stick to the plan, Hardt." I grinned at him over my shoulder, my eyes flashing with the storm I held inside. "Trust me." If there are two more insidious and destructive words in our language, I do not know them.

Drawing in a deep breath, I whispered the academy's

mantra to myself. "I am the weapon." Then I stepped over the side of the flyer into the abyss below.

CHAPTER
FORTY TWO

FOR A FEW SECONDS I DROPPED LIKE A STONE, gravity dragging me downward so quickly I felt my hair flapping about my ears and my stomach lurching inside of me. The fear I felt was a jolt of pure terror and Ssserakis drank it in, lending my limbs new strength. I heard Hardt's voice above me, words lost to the roar of the wind. None of it mattered. My course was set, my will in motion. All that was left was to follow through with it. I drew on my Sources and snapped open a portal below me. There is a feeling to passing through a portal, only one in a hundred feel it, but too many have noted it to be pure fancy. For just a moment, the briefest flicker of an instant, you are nowhere; you don't exist. Portals are tears in the fabric of our world leading to another tear; and passing through them is dangerous. I'm not talking of the possibility of simply not emerging from the other side, though that is certainly a worry. I'm talking about the feeling of being watched by something far larger than us. For a moment, as I pass through portals, I feel that something's eyes upon me. I believe it is the same eye that watches through the great tear out in the Polasian desert. I do not know what that thing is, or where it is, but I believe that all portals pass through its world, even as they lead back into ours.

Gravity shifted as I re-emerged from the other side up on Do'shan. I had been falling, but now I was rising through the air in an arc that deposited me on the ground, running in front of where our flyer would appear. I slid to a halt and threw up my arms. A purple haze formed in front of me, a huge kinetic shield twice as tall as I and many times as wide. It took a lot of energy to fill that shield, and moment after terrifying moment passed. I knew if those waiting for us in the city decided to choose that moment to loose their weapons upon me, my shield would not hold. In truth I wasn't sure it would hold even once I had it fully erected, but I was running on pure fucking bravado at that point. What a spectacle I must have made to those watching from our second flyer. Silva and Tamura and the others, watching me jump into nothing but frigid air and deadly drop, only to vanish and reappear on land, shield already forming.

The first few arrows struck before my shield was fully formed. I was, perhaps, quite lucky that none of them were on target. Two of the three hit my shield and dropped, their momentum robbed. The third passed through a thin section of the shield and hit the ground a few paces to my left. I ignored the danger and concentrated on filling my shield with kinetic energy. I could already form a Sourceblade in mere moments, but the shield was huge, large enough to protect the flyer as it rose behind me.

I heard the *whir* of the propeller and then boots hitting the ground behind me. Hardt was the first to reach me and was quickly followed by Horralain and then Ishtar. On a distant rooftop, I saw one of the Ringan's shift slightly, even as the flyer started to back away and descend. I rushed forward two steps and went down on one knee, my shield held up before me, a shimmering mass of purple energy. It is fortunate that kinetic arms do not weigh as much as their physical counterparts, all four of us together wouldn't have been able to hold aloft a shield so large. Hardt knelt with me, a huge hand on each of my shoulders, lending whatever support he could. I was glad of it. The Ringan finished turning and released its ammunition in a devastating volley.

I have seen the discs of a Ringan cause untold damage. I have seen one cut through a man in full armour, ripping him apart so his legs fell one way and his torso the other. Hardt was not exaggerating when he said they can punch through stone walls. They are one of the most destructive devices I have ever seen, and I suppose I should be glad they have a limited number of uses. There's only so many times a Ringan can be spun up before it rips itself apart in an explosion of wood, metal, and stone. I tell you this now so you know well the power of the machines. They are Kinemancy Sources unleashed, the force pushed into stone and thrown at a target. They are also worryingly accurate.

The first of the discs hit my shield and I felt the impact up my arms. I wonder if the bones might have shattered, but for the strength pounded into them from months of holding the marker down in the Pit. Hardt grunted behind me and gripped my shoulders tighter. There was no respite. Disc after disc after disc spun through the killing field before us at such speeds I couldn't see them, only feel their impacts. Twelve of them, I think, each one shattering against my shield. I was screaming from the pain in my arms by the time the bombardment stopped.

"Up, terrible student. We must move before they reload." Ishtar's clawed hand gripped me under my arm and hauled me to my feet. It took a moment for my senses to return.

The killing field stretched out before us. The occasional arrow flitted through the sky, but I barely felt the impacts against my shield. The Ringan took time to reload, needing to slow to a stop before new discs could be fitting into their housing. The flyer dropped out of sight behind us and Horralain and Hardt stepped up beside me.

"Keep behind the shield until we reach the buildings then split off and destroy as many machines as you can." It was all the warning I gave before lurching into a run, my shield held up before me. Ssserakis laughed, not a malevolent sound, but one of glee. The horror could feel the fear around us; and it fed well.

The first of the Arc Biters turned our way as we reached the buildings of the city. I saw the prongs of the fork crackling with energy and had no idea how it would react against my kinetic shield. I had a feeling it would not go well. I released the shield in a rush of kinetic energy that blasted the ground around us, then drew on my Arcmancy Source and summoned lightning to my fingers. It is a strange phenomenon, but Arcmancy attracts. By summoning lightning of my own, I drew the Arc Biter's attack from Hardt to myself. And just like the Arcstorm down in Picarr, I drew the energy inside of me.

Visions flooded me. Perhaps that is not the right term

for them. Memories, I think, though not my own. Just like
the Arcstorm had been tutor Elsteth's death throes, the
energy somehow tainted by her memories, so too was this
lightning laced with the recollections of another.

*Jagran, the Swift, raced through the sky, soaring between
clouds. Lightning trailed in his wake, crackling out in an endless
series of branching forks. Onward and onward he raced, but he
already knew he was too late. The fastest of all the Djinn, even he
could not arrive fast enough to save his brother. The joy of riding
the sky was robbed from him this day, replaced by the anxious fear
of failure.*

*Creatures watched from below, insignificant and mindless.
The Rand called these ones terrans, an altered form of the beasts
who called the darkness home. They stared up at Jagran and
watched in wonder as he lit the night sky with his luminescent
form. They fell to their knees and threw up their arms in worship.
Whatever the Rand had done to them, at least they understood how
small and worthless they were. At least they placed their worship
where it was due, instead of gnawing on the bones of their own
dead and worshipping nothing but the darkness.*

*The sky bristled with energy at Jagran's passing and
a storm followed him. A great storm. The greatest he had ever
summoned. And he would unleash it upon the Rand. Upon his
brother's murderers.*

*An unparalleled storm raged around the battlefield.
Lightning ripped from the sky in a dozen different places, arcing
down to strike the earth. Wind whipped in every direction
possible, and great swirling vortexes formed, scouring the ground
and tearing up the homes of the creatures that lived there. The
Rand thought to shield themselves with their own creations, the*

whimpering pahht, another species raised up from the dirt to worship their betters. They mattered nothing to Jagran. Their lives were as worthless as they were short. They died in the hundreds as they rushed to protect their creators. But nothing they could do could harm Jagran. He was fury. He was energy. He was the storm.

Floods ravaged the land, wind tore the living and dead both into the sky, lightning blazed, setting the world on fire. And still, the Rand hid from Jagran. Cowards! But then the Rand had always been cowardly. They made mockery of his brothers and called their insults pranks. Jokes that harmed none. But the Djinn had created something wonderful, something unique, something that stood alone as a true testament to their power. And the Rand had filled it with their mockery.

A laugh floated up to Jagran, somehow navigating the storm and sounding over the tumult. It was clear to him. Echoing around him as crystal. The Rand mocked him even now, even as he vented his rage upon them. He would show them the fruits of their mockery. He would tear the very earth asunder to find them!

The storm died around Jagran; its fury spent. The winds trailed away, the rains stopped falling, the clouds thinned to show blue sky above. And Jagran realised his folly. Only once the storm was vented did the Rand show themselves, slithering from the ground, rising from the rushing waters, emerging from their hiding places. It was a trap. Half a dozen of the hateful sisters rose up on wings of bone and surrounded Jagran. Even as swift as he was, the fastest of all his brothers, he was too exhausted to run.

The Rand fell upon him, tearing away at his crackling form with talons and teeth and sucking his life away. He had no fight left to visit upon them and they knew it. But even in death, Jagran seized victory. Even as the last threads of his consciousness

*crumbled away, locked inside his crystal coffin, he saw Elesis, the
Growing, join him in death.*

It was over in an instant. The memories of a Djinn.
Jagran, the Swift's final moments, rushed through me and I
saw it all, experienced it all. His hatred of the Rand sparked
something inside of me. My own anger and hatred sat
dormant for too long, covered over by my love of Silva, my
pain at the loss of Kento. I felt the hatred rekindle; embers
brought back to life by experiencing Jagran's final moments.

Lightning sparked between my hands. I had absorbed
the Arc Biter's discharge, and its energy raged inside of
me. It needed a way out, and I had a target. Robed figures
watched us from the rooftops, some wielding bows and
others swords. There were dozens of them, crowding
around and readying to pounce down on us. I unleashed the
lightning upon them, sending bolts of jagged energy arcing
from my fingertips, setting the rooftops ablaze.

Ssserakis laughed. *Make them fear us!* And I bloody
well did.

The others split off, even Hardt, rushing into the
buildings where they could fight our enemies hand to hand.
I'd be lying if I said I didn't worry for them, but Ishtar was
a true master with a blade, Horralain was a monster who
didn't feel pain, and Hardt… Well, Hardt let go. Just like
he had down in the ruined Djinn city, fighting against the
Damned, Hardt stepped into the storm that surrounded him
and let the violence take him. Perhaps it is wrong to say he
stepped into the storm willingly. It was the second time since
we had met that I pushed him into it. It took him a long time
to find his way out.

With a Sourceblade in one hand and Pyromancy in

the other, I made my way into the maze of Do'shan's streets. Enemies lurked in darkened doorways, but their cover did not shield them from me, I could see it as plainly as day. They were pahht, only also not. At least not like any of the pahht I had already encountered. I think it is more fitting to say that the creatures we found on Do'shan were as to pahht, what the Damned are to terrans. Primitive, unintelligent, savage. They wore ragged robes and moved on all fours, only rising onto their back feet to strike. Their weapons were crude things, jagged strips of metal with cloth wrapping for handles, stone axe heads mounted on sticks. It should have seemed stranger to me than it did, that their weapons were so primitive, yet they operated some of the most sophisticated war machines anyone in Ovaeris had ever seen. I should have realised then that there was more going on than the surface revealed.

We made them fear us, Ssserakis and I. I was no master swordswoman like Ishtar, but my training had progressed far enough that I was more than a little dangerous with Sourceblade in hand. I left bodies in my wake, sliced, stabbed, and bleeding into the cracked streets of Do'shan. I was ruthless, sending plumes of flame into doorways and burning the enemies that hid within. Ssserakis coiled around me, warping my shadow and making me appear a monster. By the time I was done, I was a monster. I killed without mercy, justifying murder by the tips of the swords pointed my way. We called them enemies, but I would wager they named us similar. Perhaps invaders.

By the time I made my way back to open ground, I had the blood of more than a dozen of the creatures on my hands. Some I had killed by blade, others by fire. I should have been feeling tired and sick to my stomach, but I was energised. It wasn't just the strength seeping into me from Ssserakis, I felt the thrill of battle. It is an odd thing to name it, but accurate enough. The joy of a well-placed sword stroke, the pride of an enemy dead when you still stand, the energy of living so close to the edge where each moment is someone's last. It was the first time I had felt the thrill of battle so keenly, and I was not prepared. This is how Hardt feels every time he loses himself in battle. His woes and cares vanish amidst the flood of violence and fear. I think I understood the big Terrelan a lot better after that day.

Ishtar was waiting for me in the dark doorway of one of the buildings. I saw her eyes gleaming in the darkness and she bared her teeth as I drew close. There was fresh blood on her leather jerkin, but I doubted it was hers. "How many did you kill, terrible student?"

I shrugged. "More than you." A baseless claim, but Ishtar grinned at me all the same. "You don't mind us killing them? They are your people."

My sword tutor hissed at that, stepping out of the doorway to join me. "They are not my people. These are Ferals. Barely more than beasts. See the way their fur is matted and dirty. Some even have mange. They care not for themselves because they have not the wit to. These things are no more pahht than your Damned are terrans. Besides, with the fortune you are paying me, I would not mind killing my own brother."

"You have a brother?" Despite all the time I spent with Ishtar, I knew very little about her other than her skill with a sword and her love of strong spirits.

"No."

Horralain was the next to appear. The axe in his hand was dripping red and his dark eyes almost glowed with malice.

Fear swirls around this one. It clings to him. Magnificent.

The big criminal said nothing as he walked past us and sat with his back against a nearby building. He pulled a cloth from a pocket and set to wiping down his axe. I watched Horralain for a while, but he paid me no notice. I was giving him what he wanted: the chance to cause death, and freedom from the moral consequences of his actions, and he was happy with it.

I waited for Hardt, stomach churning from his absence, but he did not appear. I heard him weeping, I think. Crying for the violence that had swept him up once more. Ishtar heard it too, I'm sure of that, her ears were always much sharper than my own, but she said nothing of it. Perhaps she understood better than any of us, a career mercenary like herself must have felt the grief of so much death at least once.

"We should signal the others that it is safe to land," Ishtar said. "I find myself thirsty and our supplies are on board." She cocked a lopsided baring of her teeth at me. I knew the look well, she was waiting, expecting me to hop to her suggestion.

I walked a few paces forwards, raised my right hand to the air, and sent a plume of green fire shooting up into the sky. A pre-determined signal that it was safe to bring the larger flyer in to land. The fat bottomed ship hung motionless for a few more moments and then tilted slightly, lurching forwards towards the open ground on Do'shan. I turned back to Ishtar to find her staring at Horralain.

"What?" I asked as I approached.

Ishtar bared her teeth again. "I am imagining him naked. It is a pleasant sight, so long as I ignore the face. Big terran man, have you ever thought of wearing a mask?"

Horralain looked up from his axe and frowned, his dark eyes filled with an anger I recognised. His mouth worked as though he was making certain to form the words before saying them. "Fuck you, cat."

Most pahht I have met in my life bristle at the insult. I have seen brawls started over that single word, but Ishtar took most things, including insults, in her stride. "I am sure we would both have much fun, big ugly terran, but alas there is not time. Perhaps once this thing is done, I will teach you what it is to be a man in Polasia."

Horralain frowned, biting his lip as he tried to worry out the meaning in Ishtar's words. I decided to step in before he figured out exactly what she meant. "Just ignore her, Horralain. Ishtar isn't happy unless she has someone to provoke."

"This is not true. I am always happy. I am just happier when—"

To my left I saw something fly through the sky. I turned just in time to see discs from a Ringan crash into the larger flyer. Whole sections of the vessel were torn away, half the hold broke apart, spilling our supplies into the sky below, and I was powerless to stop it. Disc after disc after disc ripped into the flimsy construct that was carrying so many of my friends. I cannot truly describe it, the fear I felt. Silva and Tamura and Imiko. Each of the discs that struck the flyer was one more chance they were dead. No magic I held could save them. No power I had earned, nor knowledge I had learned. There was nothing I could do but watch. Bodies fell into the void. Some screamed, some didn't.

As the last of the Ringan ammunition ripped away at the hold, the flyer started to list. The propeller still turned even more quickly than before; the rudder had been torn away along with so much of the hold. The flyer tilted forwards towards Do'shan and began to pick up speed.

"Cannot you do anything, Eskara?" Ishtar asked, urgency in her voice. "You have portal magic, no?"

I shook my head, shock stealing the air from my lungs. "I don't have the range or precision." It was only part of the problem. Portamancy has never been a speciality of mine. I struggle to send myself through a portal, let alone others. All we could do was watch as the flyer careened forward, passing overhead trailing debris and smoke. Ishtar leapt to the side of one of the nearby buildings, scrambling up the wall. I released a kinetic blast downward, propelling myself upwards and beat her to the rooftop by mere moments. We both arrived just in time to see the flyer crash down in the city, far away from our position. Dust, broken wood, and stone thrown everywhere in the impact. I struggled to see how any of my friends could survive it. I felt tears on my cheeks, but couldn't blink them away. I was frozen, staring at the spot where the flyer had crashed down.

CHAPTER FORTY THREE

SHOCK CAN DO HORRIBLE THINGS TO A
person. It closes off the rational mind and forces bad
decisions. I was already quite proficient at making poor
decisions even without shock, so you can possibly imagine
how I reacted to seeing my friends die. A wiser woman
might have run off in their direction to search for survivors,
take charge of the situation, and rally those we had left.
Instead, I turned on Ishtar and grabbed her by the collar.

"You said it was safe to bring them in!" I shouted at
my sword tutor.

Blame is a fool's game. There are no winners save
for those not playing. Friendships that have lasted entire
lifetimes can be lost on a single hand of blame. Worse yet,
you don't even have to agree to play, anyone can drag you
into a hand even against your will. I don't think I could have
chosen a worse opponent to play against than Ishtar.

"You said you destroyed all the Ringans!" I pushed
Ishtar backwards until she was at the edge of the rooftop.

Very slowly, Ishtar reached up with clawed hands
and gripped hold of my own. For a moment we struggled
against each other, but she was stronger than I and had far
better knowledge of how to break a person's hold. Within
moments I had let go of her collar and found both my arms
twisted unnaturally. A moment later, Ishtar had me on my
knees, hissing in pain.

"Do not mistake my fondness of you for blindness,
Eskara. Your big terran pets may let you vent yourself upon
them, but I will not. Ever." Ishtar didn't point out that it was
as much my fault as hers that we failed to clear all the war
machines. We were all to blame. And that is the ultimate
truth of playing a hand of blame. Regardless of who you
drag into the hand with you, you always end up playing
against yourself.

Ishtar released me and I rocketed back to my feet,
staring up into her twinkling eyes. Despite her strength and
will, even Ishtar struggled to meet the storm in my eyes for
long. She shook her head and turned away, already looking
for a way down to the street.

"Eska?" Hardt's voice from below. I approached the
edge of the roof and saw my friend looking strangely savage.
His face was long and drawn, but there wasn't sadness in
those lines, only determination. I noticed his hands were
stained red around the metal knuckles he wore. "What
happened?"

"The second flyer crashed," I said, pointing in the
direction of the impact. "We didn't clear all the Ringans." I
ran out of words and shook my head. They were dead. Dead
because of my mistake.

"Terrible student," Ishtar said as she reached the ground. "Stop moping. This is the right word? Moping?"

Hardt nodded, and then turned his attention to me. "Are there any survivors?"

"How would we know from here?" Ishtar asked. "Come. Someone must take charge and the terrible student is too busy crying and trying to throw me off rooftops."

I looked towards the dust rising from the crash site and tried to judge the distance. We could probably reach it quickly at a jog, assuming we weren't waylaid. Of course, I could reach it much sooner with a series of portals. I snapped one open in front of me, leading to another rooftop in the distance. Just as I was about to step through, the portal flickered, and for a moment it showed not the rooftop I was aiming for, but somewhere else. Somewhere dark and alien. Still, I considered the risk.

No! You will not drag me with you to oblivion, Eskara.

The thought of Tamura and Imiko lying injured in the flyer crossed my mind. A conjured image of Silva lying there, bruised and blooded, trapped by debris, dying alone. Again, the portal flickered showing that other place. There are places where magic works strangely, usually sites of devastating battle where forces beyond comprehension once clashed. Do'shan is one of those places. Or perhaps it was just because I had drawn the attention of whatever thing it was that looked through the great tear.

"It's worth the risk." I'm not sure if I said it for my benefit or Ssserakis'. I think I was trying to convince us both, or maybe just trying to justify my actions. I all but threw myself through the portal before either of us could stop me.

Time is about perception. Rather than being a linear thing, it relies entirely upon the observation of those experiencing it. From one standpoint, time continues while you are asleep, and yet hours can pass by in what appears to be but a moment. I *lost* time in that portal. The moons were high in the night sky when I stepped through, yet when I emerged, they were but pale shadows in a bright blue sky, the sun rising above the eastern horizon. I stumbled to a halt on the rooftop and felt myself trembling, not from the cold, but from a feeling I couldn't shake. My time in that portal was much like a dream, fading as soon as I woke, but leaving behind an impression, a feeling. Dread, I think. Not the fear that Ssserakis liked to inflict upon me, but dread. A certain knowledge that something great and terrible was going to happen, or perhaps already was happening. I stood in front of that portal, struggling to comprehend what I had just experienced, struggling to remember it. Then I felt something behind me, reaching out of the portal, clawing its way from whatever void had trapped it. I snapped the portal shut, turned and stumbled, falling on my arse and scrambling away towards the edge of the rooftop. But there was nothing there.

"What just happened?" I asked Ssserakis. "Where were we? How long were we there?" I don't know why I assumed the horror would have the answers when I did not. Silence greeted me. It was not a true silence, there were the sounds of the city all around me. Wind howled through the streets carrying with it snatched words or noises I could not place. But more, there was a silence within me. Ssserakis wasn't there. I couldn't feel the horror.

Is it odd that the lack of the horror scared me more than anything else I can remember? Ssserakis inflicted fear upon me daily, toying with my dreams and whispering doubts in my mind, yet there was always a truth in the ways it influenced me. I realised I had come to rely upon it, not just the strength it let seep into my limbs, but upon its advice as well. I relied on its warnings and its opinion. But most of all, I relied on the company Ssserakis offered. Ever since I had found the horror haunting the darkest depths of the Pit, I had never been alone. And as much as Ssserakis liked to scare me, I found I feared that loneliness far more.

"Ssserakis?" My voice sounded quiet and pathetic even to my own ears. I suddenly felt as though everything had been stripped away from me in a matter of minutes. First, Silva and Tamura and Imiko, their deaths all but assured. Hardt and Ishtar and even Horralain were likely gone. At the very least hours had passed and there was no telling where in the city they might be, or even if they were still alive. And now my ancient horror was gone. My passenger. My tormentor. My partner. "Ssserakis, where are you?" I tried again. I couldn't do this without the horror. I couldn't do any of it.

Panic took hold of me. I am ashamed to admit that, but I will. How can I describe what it is like to have the assurance of company for so long, to literally never be alone, only to have that assurance ripped away? I suppose it is, in some way, like a child separated from their mother. A child becomes so very used to having their mother around them at all times, always at their beck and call, always just a word or sound away. Often, as I have seen it, when they are separated, the child simply stands there, crying for what it has lost. It is a form of panic that elicits such a response, and it is that panic I felt. In my panicked state, I made one more stupid decision. I drew on the magic sitting in my stomach, and I tore open a new portal. I gave it no destination. I simply opened a hole in the world.

Something sparked to life inside of me.

Close it!

I snapped the portal shut just as the feeling of dread started to return. Ssserakis was with me once more, coiled around my soul. I could feel the ancient horror's panic mirroring my own. For a long time neither of us said anything, revelling in each other's company, in the relief of not being alone anymore. Of having my horror back.

"What happened?" I asked once my own racing heart had slowed.

You left me there. Panic and accusation warred in the horror's voice. If it were terran I would say it was on the edge of tears.

"How?"

That thing wouldn't let me leave. It tried to pick me apart, to understand me.

"What is it?"

A monster.

It's fair to say when a monster names something else such, it's a warning worth heeding. I decided it was wise not to use portals anymore. Ssserakis gave its full agreement.

Eventually I stood and got my bearings, feeling far more myself now that I had the ancient horror with me once more. We were still a hike away from the crash site and it seemed my best bet of meeting up with some of the others. Even if most of my friends hadn't survived the crash, I had to believe Hardt and Ishtar would head that way to check on them. I had to believe some of the others had survived our ill-fated assault on Do'shan.

Eyes watched me from windows and down alleyways. I could feel them, the prickling sensation walking over my skin, but every time I turned, there was no one there. At first, I thought it was my imagination, an after effect of whatever had happened during our time in the portal, but Ssserakis assured me it was no idle fancy. The feral pahht watched me. I formed a Sourceblade in my hand, just in case, and kept walking. I would be ready in case any of the creatures attacked, but that didn't mean I had to be the aggressor. Not this time. If they were willing to leave me alone, I was more than happy to be left.

I probably looked a mad thing as I stalked through those streets, carrying a shimmering purple blade and talking to the ancient horror that possessed me. Apparently, I had never been truly alone, Ssserakis had still been inside me, but much like when Vainfold had trapped my consciousness in the crown, the thing from the portal had trapped Ssserakis inside its world. The horror either couldn't or wouldn't tell me much about the experience, except that it felt as though some great hand were constantly picking at it, trying to pry strands of the horror's consciousness away from itself. There is a lesson to be learned there. Ssserakis was one of the top dogs in the Other World, feared by all and ruler of its own city state. In Ovaeris, it was just another monster to be feared and kept at a distance. Inside the portal, the ancient horror was little more than a curiosity to be prodded and examined, dissected. No matter how powerful you may think you are, there are always those more so.

The buildings were so like the architecture from the ruined Djinn city, only in reverse. Walking through those buried halls, the walls had sloped first outward and then back in, but the outside walls here sloped first towards me, then away. As I made my way through those streets, I couldn't help but remember my time there. When Isen and Josef had still been alive. As if on cue, I found Isen's ghost watching me from a nearby shadow. I told my old lover to go fuck himself, but if he heard me, he gave no indication. It dawned on me then that my other friends had not appeared to me as ghosts, and I wondered if that meant they were still alive. Hardt was probably too polite to haunt me, but I had no doubt Imiko would dedicate her unlife to making the rest of mine as miserable as possible. It was a thin hope, but I clung to it.

I had a following by the time I reached the crash site, both of the living and the dead. Isen had been joined by two of the hunters from the Forest of Ten, and my macabre audience watched me from various shadows. Of the living, several Ferals trailed along behind me. They made no aggressive moves and I was happy to leave it that way, but they seemed determined to watch me from a distance, chatting away to each other in some language I didn't know. Somewhat oddly, the Ferals walked on all fours, prowling after me much like stray dogs, but when they stopped, they stood up on their hind legs.

The crash site was a true wreckage. The flyer had torn buildings down and reduced a section of street to rubble. It had also all but collapsed under the strain. I saw half the propeller embedded in one nearby wall, and bits of the hull lying everywhere. Barrels and boxes were cracked open, the food we had brought with us strewn over the dusty streets. Some Ferals picked their way between the wreckage, snatching up whatever they could and either shoving it into their mouths or pulling it close, jealously guarding it as though it were more valuable than life itself. There were some bodies too, and I recognised them. I found Elig and Gen, Ishtar's lieutenants, and two more bodies I couldn't identify. They were crushed beneath sections of the hull and

I had not the courage to dig them out, but they were pahht, more of Ishtar's mercenaries. The flyer operator was dead as well, I found his body impaled on a broken section of railing. Six bodies, I found, and none of them belonged to my friends. None of them were Silva. The tightness in my chest released a little at that. They had survived. She had survived. For now.

"Where are they?" I shouted at the Ferals who were now surrounding me. They chatted amongst themselves, some shifting a little. With their ragged robes pulled tight against the chill in the air, they looked pathetic. Yet these creatures had operated the Ringans. They had brought the flyer down and killed at least six people. I screamed at them again, in part because I hoped some of my friends might be nearby, might hear me. In part, it was just because I wanted to vent my frustration and the nearby Ferals were the easiest targets.

They are dead, Eskara. We should head towards the centre of the city. Towards the sphere.

"Not until I know for certain." I clung to the belief that they were still alive, or their ghosts would have appeared to me. They might be injured, dying even, but unless I saw their ghosts, I would not allow myself to believe they were dead.

You won't be happy until you find their corpses? Do you really wish to see your friends dead? Mangled like that fool down in the darkness.

I couldn't help but imagine the image of Silva broken as Isen had been. Her beautiful face crushed and torn, her leg open and bleeding... "Stop it!"

Ssserakis laughed. *You have a new ghost, Eskara.*

The horror was right about that. Gen stood apart

from the others, staring down at his own corpse. He had always been kind in life, all jokes and bared teeth and free with the coin. More than a few times I had been drunk off his generosity. Now he was dead and one more figure in my ghastly retinue. I still had no idea how I was raising the ghosts, how I dragged them along behind me even years after their deaths. But if I could have, I would have gladly released Gen to find some measure of peace in his afterlife. He was more animated than my other ghosts and I wonder if that was because he was, for lack of a better term, fresher. I'm not sure how much sentience the ghosts retained, but I approached Gen and stood next to him as he stared down at his body.

"I'm sorry." My words were hollow, but I said them anyway. And I meant them.

Ssserakis laughed again. *You apologise to the dead, but not the living. They are yours. You killed them; you own them. Use them, Eskara.*

"How? They're ghosts. How can I use them? How can they help me?"

Gen looked at me then, but unlike Isen there was no accusation in his eyes. He bared his teeth at me, the pahht version of a smile and one I had come to know from him so well. Then he pointed towards a nearby building.

"What's in there?" I asked. Of course, I received no reply. There is one thing I have come to learn about ghosts over the years, they cannot speak. Most of them are barely even sentient.

It is probably a trap. Your ghosts seek to lure you into danger.

"One moment you're telling me to use them, the next that they're plotting against me." Ssserakis was doing what it always did, planting doubt and fear in my mind.

I formed a Sourceblade in hand and approached the doorway, Gen trailing after me. It was locked, but then locked doors do little against a trained Sourcerer. I could, perhaps, have been gentler, using Kinemancy to tease the lock open, but subtlety was never one of my strengths. I hit the door with a burst of kinetic energy that sent it careening into the room beyond. The Ferals behind me started chattering in what I assume were agitated voices.

"Can you watch my back?" I asked Ssserakis. The truth was, I had no idea how the horror viewed the world. Could it only see what I saw, or did it exist within my shadow? It had never seemed pertinent before, but now I was all but alone, I realised how useful it would be to know the horror's limitations. Unfortunately, all I received in reply to my question was a menacing chuckle.

Most people need to take time for their eyes to adjust to dim light, but my bond with Ssserakis gave me excellent vision even in the darkest of places. It saved my life that day. No sooner had I stepped through the doorway, then a Feral wearing a ratty robe and brandishing a crude knife launched itself at me. It was close confines, but I had chosen a short Sourceblade. I brushed aside the stab and then slashed a gaping hole in my attacker's chest. The Feral wasn't wearing any armour and the blade cut deep, it dropped to the floor whining out its final breaths. Another Feral charged me from the other side of the room and I raised a hand, summoning a plume of fire. The Feral careened from the building, screaming in pain while it burnt alive. Not a pleasant way to die. I felt no guilt at the time. That came later.

For dilapidated buildings, near abandoned streets, and a population that seemed to consist of feral pahht that were little more than beasts, the inside of the building was surprisingly clean. There was furniture, though of a type I certainly didn't recognise, and a stack of pots in one corner. Even with the wind blowing in through the door, there was no dust to disturb. I think I realised then that Do'shan was not ruins. It was a living city, so different from Ro'shan that it was almost unrecognisable, but still a city.

Gen drifted into the building, ignoring the Feral bleeding on the floor, and stopped in the centre of the room. The ghost then looked straight down at a small wooden trap door. I took the hint. Stone steps were built into the rock beneath the building and they led down into the darkness so far even my night sight couldn't penetrate it. I hesitated.

There is nothing to fear from the darkness.

"It's what might be hiding in the darkness that scares me."

Ssserakis chuckled. *We hide in the darkness, Eskara. We are what they should fear.*

With that sentiment in mind, I descended into the depths of Do'shan.

CHAPTER
FORTY FOUR

TRUTHS COME EASILY IN THE DARKNESS. I think, perhaps, that is because there is little to distract us.

Something tugged at my mind as I made my way down that staircase. It was a question I had been ignoring ever since we made the landing. A question I now knew Ssserakis had the answer to.

"You said the Djinn were the architects of your world. That they built everything in it."

Yes. They shape everything to their design. Even here, a staircase into darkness, shows the Djinn aesthetic. Ssserakis was right about that. The walls bent outward and then in again, the signature of Djinn design, though I failed to see the purpose.

"I took that to mean they had visited your world, inflicted their design upon it just like they did mine. But that's not the whole truth, is it? They didn't just build your cities and shape your landscapes. The Djinn made the Other World, didn't they?"

Ssserakis was silent for a while. Long enough that the stairwell ended and I found myself in a corridor like the ones I walked down in the ruined Djinn city. I drew on my Pyromancy Source and lit a brilliant yellow flame in my left hand, and gemstones along the walls started to glow from within. This was familiar, to myself and to Ssserakis.

The Djinn wanted to make something they could control in its entirety. For all their power and purpose, they found they were still bound by the laws of this world. So, they sought to create one beyond any laws but their own. They made my home. A reality that could bend to their will. And in that reality, they made a world, as big as this one, but without the rules that govern its existence. There is no sun, but there is still warmth and light and things still grow. There is no weather, yet the wind still howls and water still flows.

With their combined power, and a world that responded to their will, the Djinn pulled cities up from the earth far grander than any they could make here. They toyed with natural forces like gravity and forced their new world to create oddities and wonders. They made a world and turned it into their personal playground. Ssserakis fell silent for a while. *Or so we were told.*

"Because you weren't there." I continued following Gen's ghost as he drifted down the corridor. Unlike the ruined Djinn city, this one was not deserted. I glanced in the rooms I passed and saw Feral eyes peering from within, watching me. The smell of cooking meat made my nose twitch. "You didn't exist. Horrors didn't exist. The Other World was empty."

It took you long enough to figure it out.

"The Djinn created your world, but the Rand created

you."

Ssserakis' laugh was mocking. *You are so close to the truth, Eskara.*

"Then tell me."

The Rand gave me form, but they didn't create me. You did.

"What?" It's fair to say it was a confusing revelation. A true one though, in its own way.

Perhaps you have noticed that both the Rand and Djinn lack imagination? Power, they have. The will to use it, yes. And yet all they ever do with it is mimic what has come before. The Djinn created an entire reality and made it as much like this one as they could, changing only small details here and there. The Rand can create children in any form they wish, yet all their Aspects take the form of terrans or pahht or tahren. Even the forms they take. Mezula looks like all the peoples of your world crushed into one. Vainfold takes the form of fire.

"Jagran took the form of lightning. But what does that have to do with who created you?"

It has to do with the reason the war between the Rand and the Djinn started, Eskara.

"Why? What started the war?"

My shadow shifted beneath my feet and for just a moment Ssserakis was before me, an oozing inky blackness. The horror laughed at me, both within my mind and from my shadow. *Stop asking me for all the answers and figure it out yourself.*

"But you know the answers, so why not just tell me?"

Because this is more fun.

Frustration rarely leads to a clarity of thought. Ssserakis had given me just enough information to make me question everything I knew about the Rand and the Djinn and the war between them. A war that shaped Ovaeris in every way. A war that saw both peoples decimated. I tried to reason it out, based upon everything I had learned, but all I found was frustration and, judging by the mocking laughter, Ssserakis was enjoying things that way. I look back now and I think I see a different truth of it. Ssserakis was distracting me, forcing me to consider the implications of its revelation, rather than imagining my friends' deaths. It's fair to say the horror knew me all too well.

It was somewhat of a surprise when Gen's ghost stopped in front of an open doorway. He turned to me and nodded, but he didn't vanish. I glanced backwards to see my other ghosts nearby, and behind them, the glint of Feral eyes watching from the gloom. Somewhat odd to say it, but I was glad in a way. I've always performed better with an audience.

Beyond the doorway was a great cavern, much like the ones down in the ruined Djinn city, but also very different. Instead of a dozen glowing pillars reaching from floor to ceiling, there was a single pillar dominating the centre of the space. Blue veins of rock snaked their way up from the base, but it didn't connect to the roof, stopping just above eye level with the corridor I emerged from. That pillar was so large there was a settlement living on the top of it, with tents and ramshackle buildings. Trails of smoke rose up and I could smell something, even so far away. Cooking meat.

They're dead. These creatures killed your friends and are cooking them.

"No." I couldn't believe it. I wouldn't. Nobody would be so savage. An image of the Damned eating their own flashed in my mind, and Ishtar's words: The Ferals were to pahht what the Damned were to terrans.

That spark of anger flared within me once more. Only it was more than just anger, it was rage. A blinding, blazing rage that was borne of a fear I couldn't allow to be reality. To do so would have broken me.

Dozens of rope bridges bisected the cavern. Some led up to the top of the pillar at the centre, and others connected to doorways at the other side of the cavern. There were three connected to the doorway I stood in, and I chose the one that led up to the plateau and started forwards.

Your friends are dead, Eskara. These creatures killed them. Make them fear us!

The Arcstorm crackled to life around me. I don't think I summoned it, not consciously anyway, but it reacted to my rage. Lightning sparked between my fingers and ran up my arms, but it didn't burn me this time. This time it was my lightning, my storm.

At the academy we were taught never to draw from two Sources at once. The magics mixing inside a body can cause unpredictable reactions, and it speeds rejection. But I was long past my studies at the academy, past the lessons the tutors failed to teach me, and I was past caring about consequences. I drew on the fire inside and let it mingle with the lightning.

The rope bridge was wide, easily able to fit three people abreast and dipped down a little before rising up to the plateau. It was not the most stable of footing and had no guide ropes at the sides. It was little more than a series of wooden planks lashed together. I was a quarter of the way across it when the first Feral came bounding up to me. It ran on all fours and sprang up when it got close. I honestly cannot remember if that one had a weapon or not, but then I paid the creature very little attention. With my left hand

wreathed in fire and lightning, I grabbed the feral by the
throat. I am the weapon. It spasmed as lightning shocked
its body and its matted fur went up in flames in moments.
The creature screamed as I sent it careening off the side of
the rope bridge down to the cavern floor. There were others
down there, a settlement on the floor just as it was up on the
plateau. The smell of cooking meat was strong in the air. The
taste of fear was even stronger.

More Ferals rushed onto the bridge. Some from the
plateau, and others from behind. These ones definitely
carried weapons; I remember well the metal reflecting my
fire. I became the weapon. The culmination of a decade
of Sourcery training, years of sparring with Hardt and
Tamura, and months of Ishtar's brutal tutelage. Some of the
monsters I killed with fire or lightning, setting them ablaze
and kicking them into a deadly drop, and others I slew with
my sword in practised slashes and well-timed thrusts. There
is something to be said for Sourceblades, they do not dull
unless you let them. I put the fact to the test that day.

Even as the creatures dropped away from me, others
moved in to take their place. I am the weapon. The bridge
swung dangerously and my pace across it became a crawl
over the bodies I left in my wake. I could see more of the
Ferals scrambling up the side of the pillar in front of me, and
a glance behind told me they were doing the same there as
well. Hundreds of them rushing up from the cavern floor
to swarm me. Before long, I found myself surrounded,
desperately turning one way then the other to keep all my
enemies in sight. Some of the creatures bore weapons, others
just teeth and claws. Let me assure you, a wild animal is as
deadly with its natural weapons as you or I are with a blade.
Still, I edged forward towards the plateau, each step another

death. Another ghost added to my retinue. I *was* the storm, its fury and its violence. My blade, the lightning. My fire, the thunder. And the rain fell red around me.

Ssserakis revelled in the slaughter, in the fear we caused. I caused. With each moment the horror grew stronger, fed to bursting by my actions. But the Ferals did not stop coming, despite their fear. And even with the strength Ssserakis was lending me, I grew tired. Exhaustion setting in even as I lost count of the death caused by my hands. Perhaps it was a weariness of conscience rather than of body that inflicted me that day.

By the time I reached the plateau I was bloodied and numb. I had wounds on my arms, fresh gashes given to me by those who had broken past my guard, and even a large slash in my side. I could feel it bleeding. But not all the blood was mine, in fact most of it was not. The Ferals had paid a far heavier price than I. My rage left me. The thrill of battle, all but forgotten. I was exhausted from the exertion and numb from the slaughter, yet I did not stop. I dropped the fire from my left hand and brought a second Sourceblade into existence. Ishtar had taught me well, both in her favoured single sword techniques, and in the Polasian forms that favoured dual wielding. Lightning crackled along the blade in my right hand, and fire rippled along the surface of the one in my left. It became a dance of sorts, one that I knew all the steps to. I ducked and spun, leapt and twirled, stabbed and slashed, blocked and dodged. A circle of space opened around me, enemies surrounding me but unwilling to come too close for the fear I put in them. More than once I ran one of the creatures through with my Sourceblade and just let it go, forming a new one in my hand as quickly as I let go of the old. The release of kinetic energy does horrible things to a body when the blade is lodged in their flesh, bursting it open from the inside. I refused to think about the carnage of rent flesh I left behind, repeating my mantra over and over again with every death I caused.

My vision blurred, not from the exhaustion, but from the tears. I found myself screaming at the feral pahht, insults and threats merging into one. Taunts directed at the creatures I killed. I am not proud of who I became down there in the bowels of Do'shan. There is no pride to be had in the slaughter I wrought, nor the reputation I earned from it.

"Eska stop!"

Another Feral died on the sharp end of my Sourceblade.

"Eska!"

Lightning from the Arcstorm inside rushed along my blade and into another of the Ferals. I saw the creature's scream lit by the lightning burning inside of them.

"ESKARA!" Silva's scream of anguish. I turned to find the Ferals backing away from me, widening the circle of space I had earned in their blood. There, at the edge of that circle, staring at me through eyes wide with horror, was the woman I loved. Alive. She was alive!

I should have felt relief, but I didn't. I was past it. Past relief, past anger, sorrow, disgust. I was past feeling anything. I dropped to my knees. I let go of my Sourceblades and they vanished in a rush of kinetic energy and lightning sparks. The Arcstorm, too, faded, the lightning retreating behind my eyes once more. Not even the strength Ssserakis was feeding me could keep me going any longer. I was past the point of exhaustion. Spent.

"What have you done, Eska?" Silva's voice dropped to a horrified whisper. Her eyes weren't on me, but on the carnage behind me. It turns out I wasn't quite past all feeling. I felt embarrassed that she had finally seen the monster I was. Scared of what she might do now she knew the truth. Even that was fleeting.

"I came to save you." My voice sounded dispassionate even to my own ears. I no longer had the strength left for emotion. Nor the courage to face what I might find if I let it in.

"Save me?" When Silva looked at me there was too much pain and horror in her eyes. I was used to making people fear me. Enemies, friends, it didn't matter. But seeing fear on the face of the woman I loved was too much. Too much to know I had put it there. I looked away, focusing on a rock on the ground. Analysing the shape of it, mostly flat on top with three edges leading up to a point. Black. A rough surface on the side. "I didn't need saving, Eska. I was negotiating with these people."

One of the feral pahht stepped forwards, braving the circle of space between us. I heard hissed words, a language too alien for me to understand, but the threat seemed apparent. My shadow boiled around me, Ssserakis, ready to protect us. I was exhausted, but the horror was as strong as it had ever been. The Feral quickly backed away, hissing.

"Lursa's tears, Eskara. Did you do all that?" The voice was Yemin's, one of Ishtar's mercenaries. A jovial pahht who couldn't hold her liquor yet never stopped trying. I nodded without looking up. "How? What are you?" she asked.

"I am the weapon," the words whispered past my lips, the conviction gone. Even the mantra the academy had drilled into me could not stop the rising wave of guilt and grief over what I had become.

I heard crying. Mournful wails echoing around the

great cavern. I named them monsters, beasts, but the feral
pahht mourned their dead. I have never known monsters to
do that. The Ferals around me became agitated, chattering to
each other and shifting. Finally, Silva stepped into the circle
of space I had created around me, but she didn't come to me.
All I wanted was to feel her hand on my shoulder, her arms
around me, her breath stirring my hair. But she stopped
short.

"We need to leave," Silva said, her voice urgent.
"Tamura, can you help her up? Carry her if need be."

"Tamura?" I raised my head at that and saw the
crazy old Aspect smiling at me. That much, at least, I hadn't
ruined. "You're alive!" Behind him I saw Imiko, wide eyes
staring at me in horror. I couldn't blame her for that. I tried
to smile at her, but she looked away. That hurt almost as
much as Silva's rejection.

"More here than meets the eyes," Tamura said as he
hurried forwards and took me under my arms, pulling me
up onto my feet. It has always amazed me how strong the
old man is, despite appearing so fragile. "But not as much as
you. Even oceans calm eventually."

The feral pahht grew more and more agitated as Silva
and Yemin forced a path through them. Tamura kept me
upright, my left arm across his shoulders, and Imiko and
another of Ishtar's mercenaries followed behind. Everything
passed by me in a strange daze. I wasn't paying enough
attention, that much was clear, when one of the Ferals
lurched forwards and stuck me in the side with a knife.
Ssserakis was the first to react and my shadow became a
solid thing, shooting out like a thicket of blades and piercing
the Feral in a dozen different places. When my shadow
withdrew, the creature dropped to the ground, dead. I heard

Imiko squeak in alarm, but no one said anything. By then, I think, they had come to expect strange occurrences around me.

Down one of the bridges and out of the cavern, my friends hurried us along and I let myself be led. Unfortunately, the pain in my side grew worse with every step and before long we were forced to stop to remove the little knife. Imiko found us an empty room, her little ringlet scrabbling along the floor behind her, and we ducked inside. Tamura all but carried me to the far wall and then lowered me to the floor. I couldn't help but remember how we had dragged Isen along in a similar manner, down in the ruined Djinn city, and how poorly that all ended for him. His ghost stood in the corner of the room, watching me with a sad look in his one remaining eye. I hated the pity he showed me, and I hated him for showing it. I had yet to learn just how pointless it is to hate the dead.

This room was the same design as all the others, the walls curving outward and then in once more. It was empty save for a stone table in the centre and two wooden chairs that did not look as though they were designed for a terran to sit upon. Apparently feral pahht not only walked on all fours, but they rested quite differently to the normal pahht as well. A fireplace was carved into one of the walls, but it sat cold and dormant.

"I need light to look at your wounds," Silva said. She still hadn't come close enough to touch. Keeping her distance like a scared animal. Years of trust, of love, of sharing everything that I am or had, broken in an instant. One horrifying moment of realisation about my true nature. I wasn't a person. I was a weapon. Raised and trained to kill. To be a killer. How had she not seen it in me before? The darkness I harboured inside that was nothing to with Ssserakis. The anger and rage and malice. How had she not seen it? It is far easier to hide things from yourself, than it is to hide things from others.

Tamura picked up one of the chairs and dashed it against the table, breaking it apart. He threw the pieces into the fireplace and then stepped aside, waving towards me. I lazily flicked an arm that way, releasing a searing ball of flame that happily caught on the wood. Before long, we were bathed in flickering light and the gemstones set into the wall reflected it back at us. It's surprising how much light a small fire and a few of those gems can give.

"It's good to see you all. I thought you were dead." My voice was weary, laced with pain both physical and not. I tried to meet their eyes, but neither Imiko nor Silva would look at me. Worse, though, was that I could feel the fear coming from Imiko, and it was me she feared. That hurt a lot more than I thought it would.

Silva knelt by my side and looked at the knife. "If you thought we were dead, then you weren't coming to *save* us, Eska. You were there for vengeance." A damning truth spoken harshly.

Ungrateful.

"I saw the flyer go down. How did you survive?"

My question was met with a suspicious silence. *They hide something. They're lying to you. One more betrayal from those you thought you could trust.*

Silva peeled back some of my leather jerkin. It had stopped the little knife from going too deep, but it also kept the shard of metal lodged in me. "I'm going to have to pull this out then bind the wound, Eska." Silva was no Hardt, but she'd do a decent enough job.

"How did you survive the crash?" I pressed, even as Silva gripped hold of the knife's hilt.

"Not my tale to tell," Tamura said as he warmed his hands by the fire. "Even lovers have secrets."

Whose lover, do you think? Is she about to pull the knife out, or drive it in?

I caught Silva's hand on the knife and held it until she finally looked up and met my eyes. There was a hardness there I wasn't used to seeing in her. She nodded. "I saved everyone I could. Far too few of us, really."

"How?" I pressed.

Silva sighed. "I used a kinetic bubble to shield us from the crash and soften the impact."

A hundred questions flashed through my mind, but only one burst from my lips. "You're a Sourcerer?"

She's been lying to you all this time, Eskara. About this, and about so much more.

I pulled my hand away from Silva's and she took the opportunity to slide the knife free. I gasped. My side felt as though it were on fire. Or maybe like it was freezing, the two sensations are quite difficult to tell apart.

Silva dropped the knife and pulled the gash in my jerkin further apart. "I'm going to need to bind the wound... What is that?"

I had to shift to get a good look, but I could see my shadow moving. A single dark tendril reached up, dimpling my skin as it passed and threaded itself through the sides of the wound, pulling it closed like inky sutures. It was not without pain and I clenched my teeth to stop from screaming. Ssserakis closed my wound, and when the horror was done barely a drop of blood escaped.

"Thank you," I said quietly.

You're welcome.

"How did you do that, Eska?" Silva asked.

Do not let her direct your attention to me. She has been lying to you, Eskara.

I forced myself to my feet and stepped away from Silva, the pain making me clutch my side. "You're a Sourcerer?"

Tamura giggled. "Look to the source of the Source. Or Sources. Source, sauce, sores..."

Silva nodded. "All Aspects are Sourcerers. We were the first. That's how we gave rise to terran and pahht Sourcerers."

"Why?" I asked.

"Because we are the children of the Rand. Magic is a part of us. It gave birth to us." Silva sighed and tried a smile, but it seemed forced. "It's not important, Eska."

Only those with something to hide tell you their secrets do not matter.

"Why didn't you tell me?" I asked through clenched teeth.

Imiko was peeking out of the doorway, her fiery hair loose and wild, spilling over her winter coat. Yemin and the other mercenary stood guard at that same door. Tamura waited by the fireplace, rubbing his hands and watching me with a wild grin on his face. And Silva was lying to me. I knew her well enough to know the truth of it.

"Where's Hardt?" Imiko asked.

"I don't know." My worry over Hardt, Ishtar, and Horralain was something I had been desperately trying to ignore. "After the flyer crashed, I used a portal to try to get to it. Something went wrong. I haven't seen any of the others since."

"How did you find us?" Silva had her hair tied back in a tight tail, but far from making her look severe, it somehow managed to make her look more beautiful. Or perhaps that was the earnest look on her face. It was difficult to stay angry at her when she looked at me like that. I felt the icy distance melting away between us and wanted nothing more than to collapse into her arms.

"I followed Gen."

"Gen is alive?" This from Yemin, suddenly hopeful.

You're getting distracted, Eskara.

"No. Gen died in the crash." There's nothing like being distracted to forget about the secrets you're supposed to be keeping. I couldn't help but remember something I saw in Jagran's vision. Or maybe it was more something he had thought, moments before his death.

"How did you follow Gen if he was dead?" Yemin asked.

I glanced up at the mercenary. "I followed his ghost."

"Ghost?" Yemin's eyes went wild and his whiskers twitched in panic.

"Not ghosts again." Imiko visibly shuddered.

Jagran's final thoughts had been about his victory, even in death. Something about being locked in a coffin. The memory of his final moments was fuzzy, fading as fast as any dream.

"Why did you kill all those people, Eska?" Silva, still trying to distract me. There were tears in her eyes, and for one horrifying instant I couldn't tell if they were real or forced. They were real. They had to be real. She was too earnest to lie about that.

"I thought you were dead. I could smell…" I shook

my head. Even now I struggle to admit to what I thought had happened to my friends. "Besides, they aren't people. Just animals." *I am the weapon.*

"Yes, Eska. These pahht *are* people. You cannot rationalise that away just because it is an inconvenient fact." Silva was serious.

People die all the time. Conquerors kill, soldiers kill. They were the enemy and they were in our way. Weapons are not made to save lives.

I shook my head again, not wanting to admit the truth. It was all just so tiring. *I am the weapon.* "They're just like the Damned. Beasts who only know how to kill and mate. Mindless. The Damned are what happens when terrans lose their minds down in the dark, and these things are…"

"No, Eska," Silva said. "The Damned, as you call them, *are* terrans. Primitive terrans, but terrans all the same. They are what existed before…" Silva paused and looked away, gritting her teeth.

Another secret she is trying to hide. How much do you truly know of this Aspect, Eskara? How much of her does she hide, even as you bare your soul?

"Shut up!" I hissed under my breath.

Silva glanced at me and sighed. "Before the war between the Rand and the Djinn, there was a time of peace when the Djinn created cities for the people of Ovaeris to live. And my mother and her sisters altered the people of the world to live in those cities. Before that, there were no terrans, no pahht, and no tahren. There were the Damned, these people you call Ferals, and the Arns."

I glanced towards Tamura to find him watching, nodding, a knowing smile on his face.

Finally, a truth, but not the one you wanted. She is distracting you from another lie.

"Altered how?"

"They made you you," Tamura said with a flourish. "Or made us us. They made us all us all."

Silva nodded to that. "It's the truth. Increased size and intelligence, mostly. Some structural alterations. They wanted all the peoples of Ovaeris to walk upright on two legs, so they changed the pahht and tahren physiology to further that end. The Rand changed everyone that they could find, but some obviously slipped through the cracks. Afterwards, the Damned fled underground, and the Ferals into the densest jungles. Only the Arns were truly wiped out when the tahren decided to cleanse the evidence of their previous existence from the world."

"What about the garn and mur?" I asked.

Silva shook her head. "They remained unaltered. Both peoples exist today as they did then. They were already more advanced, building cities and forming communities. This city is based upon garn design, I believe. That's why the walls are shaped as they are. I suppose the Djinn found it pleasing."

No imagination. Everything they build *comes from others. Everything they create is an alteration or a mimic.*

I struggled over to the remaining chair and flopped down into it. It was not comfortable, designed for someone with four legs rather than two, but I was still so exhausted from the fight. From the slaughter. Perhaps massacre would be a more apt word. Silva was right about one thing, the Ferals were not beasts nor monsters. They were people, just trying to survive.

"They attacked me." Even I lacked the conviction to

make my words justify what I had done.

Silva sighed and knelt in front of me. "They were defending themselves, Eska. You attacked them."

"They shot down your flyer."

"They believed we were invading their city, their home. We *were* invading. They just defended themselves." Silva shook her head.

"They still killed Gen and all the others," Yemin said. "Defending themselves or not. Our people are dead, now so are theirs. I call it even."

Silva ignored the mercenary. "I was trying to negotiate with them. After the flyer crashed, they swarmed us, and I managed to convince them to take us to their leaders. But it was a struggle to make them understand me. I had hoped they would be allies, not enemies."

"I'm sorry." Those two words are some of the toughest to utter. There are times in life when we wish to say them, but so many things can get in the way. For me, the blockage is often my pride, unwilling to admit I am wrong or at fault. But I managed them then, though they were not meant for my friends. Not even for Silva. I said the words for the ghosts that I had made that day. A pitiful apology, begging for something I didn't deserve.

I felt Ssserakis' disgust as a wave of nausea. *Guilt is for the weak, Eskara. Ambition has no room for it. You wish to take revenge for everything that has been done to you? You wish to gain power and take the fight to your enemies? Scores of people will die at your feet. Armies will clash and city streets will run red. Death. That is the cost of true power. It is a price others must pay for you.*

"I am the weapon." My voice broke on the words and I found no comfort in them.

Silva took my hands in hers and I felt that familiar

excitement, that new energy tingling along my arms. When I looked up, I saw the tears that had been in her eyes were running down her cheeks. "You don't have to be. You don't have to be what they wanted you to be, what they tried to make you into."

"What am I if not the weapon?"

Silva smiled at me, that radiant smile that burned away all anger and doubt and pain. "You are Eska. And that's all you need to be." I wish I had learned that lesson then, but it is one I have struggled with my entire life.

I bent down and pressed my forehead against hers and for a moment we were both whole again. All the pain and hurt and secrets we kept slid away, and we were just two lovers locked together. Two lovers sharing one purpose. Comfort. One from the atrocities committed, and the other from atrocities witnessed. Love bridged the gap and allowed us both to find comfort in each other.

She is a Sourcerer. She has been lying to you all this time. Hiding the source of her power.

Something clicked inside. Not truly, but it was more like several puzzle pieces all suddenly falling into place. A moment of clarity where the truth was revealed to me, not by the lecturing of those who already knew it, but by my own dogged reasoning.

I pulled back from Silva and glanced over to the fireplace where Tamura was still warming his hands. I knew he, at least, wouldn't lie. "Sources are dead Rand and Djinn."

Tamura laughed and clapped his hands.

Interesting.

"You didn't know?" My words were meant for Ssserakis, but Silva shook her head in reply.

"I knew. You have stumbled on one of my mother's

best kept secrets, Eska." Silva stood up and looked
around the little room, gaze settling on Imiko and Ishtar's
mercenaries. There was a look in her eyes far darker than I
was used to seeing. "And unfortunately, you've already told
that secret to others."

Yemin and the other mercenary shrugged. Imiko
waved her hands in front of her, the ringlet clutching to her
shoulder. "I know how to keep a good secret," the little thief
said with a worried smile. "I've got buckets of secrets; you
have no idea."

Silva smiled. "Actually, I do." She turned back to
me, still perched on the uncomfortable chair. "How did you
figure it out? It couldn't just have been from Tamura's little
riddle."

"That was part of it. That, and you admitting you're a
Sourcerer because you are a child of the Rand, born of magic.
But also, from Jagran's memories." It was my turn to put a
confused look on Silva's face and her brow crinkling made
me smile. "I absorbed a blast from an Arcmancy Source
when we first landed. It came with memories of a Djinn
called Jagran, his final moments battling against the Rand.
Jagran was the storm, formed of lightning, and as he died, he
could feel his essence being trapped inside a crystal coffin.
His corpse became an Arcmancy Source."

Silva blinked at me. "You can absorb Arcmancy and
the memories of the Djinn? I thought you had just redirected
the Arcstorm in Picarr. This explains your eyes, at least."

I reached up to my eyes, an involuntary reaction.
Silva caught my hand. "They are flashing like they never
have before, Eska. A storm rages in them, lightning striking
every few seconds. It's quite beautiful."

"Um," Imiko said as she paced. "Does this mean

you have a bunch of god corpses in your stomach? That sounds gruesome." She smiled at me for a moment and I hoped my rampage hadn't caused permanent damage to our friendship.

"Do you know what this means, Eska?" Silva said, squeezing my hand. "My mother was right about you. You've already fulfilled all three of the auguries."

"What?"

"The fusion of life and death. You've absorbed an Arcstorm twice now, taken the Djinn's memories as your own. Renewal. Down in Picarr you were dying, the power of Vainfold renewed your body. And unity of purpose." Silva paused. "We both know what you carry inside, Eska."

I felt a moment of panic, partly my own, but more so from Ssserakis. *Her mother will kill us both if she finds out.*

"It's you, Eska," Silva continued. "*You* are the end to the War Eternal. Prophesied."

Ssserakis laughed bitterly. *How does it feel to carry the weight of the world on your shoulders?*

I'd be lying if I said it was a light load.

CHAPTER FORTY FIVE

THE FERALS CONTINUED TO FOLLOW US, BUT they did little else but snap at our heels. I could feel the fear rolling off them in waves, and it grew stronger every time I looked back. Perhaps they saw my eyes flashing in the darkness and it served as a dazzling reminder of what I could do. Strength returned to me as we walked, and I knew its true source. Ssserakis, fed fat by the fear, was bolstering me, replacing the energy I had expended in my fight. The horror couldn't heal my wounds though, despite sewing them closed with my shadow. I looked a ghastly sight with black sutures covering both of my arms, but I pulled my leather jerkin and winter coat close to hide them.

Tamura led us up and out, unerringly so. The old Aspect has a strange way about him when it comes to direction. Many times, I have relied upon him for that and he has never led me astray. He giggled to himself occasionally,

and at one point even proclaimed that the walls were
moving. I thought him mad at the time. Well, I've always
known Tamura to be crazier than a fang-toothed slug, but I
thought his ravings then to be just that. Now, I'm not so sure.
I think, perhaps, the walls were moving. I think the Djinn
was speeding our way.

    We talked little. I wanted to talk to Silva, but I
couldn't think of anything to say. There is a comfort in that,
as well as a fear. The fear that we had no more to say to each
other, that our relationship had nowhere else to go. The
comfort that despite the silence and the secrets between us,
we remained together. United. Strong. Love, true love, isn't
the grand gestures, the bombastic signs. True love lies in the
little things. In the comfortable silences and lingering stares.
In holding your partner at the end of a long day for no other
reason than they appear to need it. In the old woman on her
hands and knees, painstakingly cutting each single blade
of grass on her partner's grave even ten years after they're
gone. Love, true love, shows itself in myriad different,
unnoticed way. The signs are there, but they are not grand.
They are simple, often inelegant. Yet I would take a simple
sign over a grand gesture any day. I would take true love
over enthusiastic lust every time. Because I know which
one lasts, and which one burns itself to nothing but fleeting
memories and forgotten promises.

    I considered all that I had learned as we passed
through those gloomy halls and I realised something; I had
not solved the puzzle, only one part of it. Ssserakis' words
still gnawed at me. The Rand had given the horror form, but
I had created it. It made no sense. By the ancient horror's
own admittance, it had existed for thousands of years. I, on
the other hand, had existed for only eighteen. How could

I have created something millennia before I was born? The horror offered no help on the question, but I could feel its amusement as I reached for answers.

Imiko kept me amused with wry observations, the occasional whispered insult, and even a few faces pulled at the ringlet that rode on her shoulder. Her fear had mostly drained away, at least her fear of me had. I wished she hadn't come. It was her loyalty to me and her desire to be useful that had made her follow, but she was in danger here, and out of her depth. More than that, it was a pointless danger. Imiko could scrap with the best of them, I still remembered the beating I suffered during our first meeting, but she was no warrior. She had no magic of her own and shied away from fights. I couldn't shake the feeling that in coming with me, I was going to get her killed. The idea of seeing my little sister as a ghost terrified me. She hated ghosts.

By the time we emerged from the depths of Do'shan, the sun was well into waning. The last brilliant red light of the day was shining over the western horizon, making the city appear menacing. A family of Ferals hissed at us as we emerged from a trap door in what I could only imagine was their home. Silva growled some words at them, at least I think they were words, and the creatures backed away as we hurried outside. Perhaps Tamura's sense of direction was even better than I ever imagined, or perhaps the Djinn truly had been altering our path, but we emerged at the foot of the giant black sphere that dominated the centre of the city. And Hardt, Ishtar, and Horralain were there waiting for us.

I should probably be glad Hardt didn't finish the job the Ferals had started with the embrace he gave me; it certainly felt strong enough to crack bones. Rather than showing anger at my running off and leaving them behind, there was nothing but relief on his face as he enfolded me in a crushing hug. I'd be lying if I said I didn't let out a squeak of pure alarm, but I was grateful for it all the same. It is reassuring to know that the big Terrelan will always be there for me no matter what I've been through, or what I have done. When he pulled away from me, Hardt looked down into my eyes and I saw his face drop. The smile replaced by something like pity.

"What did you do, Eska? By Lursa, what have you made yourself into?"

He must have seen it in my eyes. Recognised the pain mirrored in them. We were both guilty of atrocities, of losing ourselves in the battle. Of killing without regard. We were both stained a red that went deeper than our skin. I didn't need to answer him, and Hardt didn't need to know the specifics. He pulled me into a tight hug once more and I cried silent tears into his shoulder. In case you're wondering, you can always tell when someone is crying without sound; they shake uncontrollably from the effort of holding it in.

There are more pressing matters than indulging your self-destructive whims, Eskara. We must find a way inside the sphere.

I pulled away from Hardt and he let me go. The sphere was behind Hardt and it dominated my view. It was huge, so large it would have taken up half the great cavern down below. It seemed to be embedded in the rock around it and the city curved unnaturally when it drew close, as though the streets and buildings were being sucked slowly into the blackness. Horralain was nearby, poking through rubble as though searching for something.

"Have you tried to enter yet?" I asked.

Hardt nodded. "That thing is solid. Horralain even

broke his axe trying to get in. There might be a doorway somewhere, but it will take us a while to search for it. It's not easy to traverse around it. There's… a gravity to it. A pull, a draw. Something… I don't know, but it sure feels magical."

"One hundred?" Ishtar's voice, loud and clearly directed towards me. "You really slew one hundred of these feral beasts by your own hand?" Yemin was nearby and had obviously been recounting my slaughter down below.

I shook my head sadly. "I think it was more like fifty."

It could have been a thousand if you had stopped resisting me.

"No," said Yemin. "It was closer to a hundred."

Ishtar shrugged. "Perhaps you are not such a terrible student after all. Come. Look. Look. We have a new problem." She sounded far too cheery for someone discovering problems.

The land rose up unnaturally around the sphere and it created a rise that looked down on the rest of the city. Ishtar pointed towards the southern edge and handed her viewing glass to me. I squinted through it and could just about make out figures swarming in towards the city. As I watched, a portal opened and more of the figures stepped through.

"The Terrelan army has arrived," Ishtar said, her teeth bared.

"You're sure they're Terrelans?" Hardt asked.

"No," Ishtar let out a sigh. "I am a terrible mercenary who does not know how to identify flags and uniforms."

Hardt joined us and I felt a big hand rest upon my shoulder. I felt quite reassured by that. "Never leave me alone with this woman ever again, Eska. She's insufferable."

"You were not alone," Ishtar said, baring her teeth again in that smile of hers. "You had the other big Terrelan man with you." She glanced at me, eyes twinkling. "They both seemed quite intimidated by me."

I ignored her attempts at humour. "Do you see any different uniforms down there? Gold plate, red on black." If anyone could spot them, it would be Ishtar.

"Some. Not many."

I felt Hardt's grip on my shoulder tighten. "Prena Neralis?"

I nodded, exhaustion making my shoulders slump. "Fucking bitch follows me wherever I go. How did she know we're here? How did she catch up with us?" Of all the enemies I have collected over the years, Prena Neralis is perhaps the most dogged. She would have hunted me all the way to the Other World if she could.

Betrayal. Someone here is working for the enemy. Ssserakis' insidious fear mongering sounded a little too plausible for my liking. I wondered at who it might be. Ishtar and her mercenaries were the most obvious choice, but my sword tutor had no love for the Terrelans. Horralain, maybe, though I wasn't certain he had the wit to plan a betrayal and keep it secret. My eyes slid to Silva, suspicion blooming in my mind. I shook it away. Silva would never betray me.

She already has. Her lies show her true colours.

"I have always found it quite amazing how enemies can dog my steps," Ishtar said. "They follow like jilted lovers, and much to the same purpose. So, not-so-terrible student, should we find a way inside this… thing? Or shall we prepare to meet the Terrelans head on?" If the thought of clashing with a couple of hundred Terrelan soldiers scared Ishtar at all, she did not show it. For my own part, I was more than a little worried. If Prena was down there, I knew she wouldn't be alone. Others of the Knights of Ten would be with her, and she would have Sourcerers too. It was a battle we were not ready for, especially still reeling from our losses as we were.

"I came here to fight a Djinn, not the Terrelans," I said, trying my best to sound as confident as I could. We had time, hours maybe before Prena and her forces reached us.

Approaching the sphere, I held out a hand. It really did have an odd gravity to it. The surface was cool to the touch, but not cold. I thought that more than a little strange given the icy temperature of the city. Smooth like polished stone, but there was no reflection within its depths. It was almost as though it drank in the light and refused to let any escape. I was just about to ask Silva and Tamura about it, when a large doorway opened in the sphere, wide enough for two of us to walk abreast and so tall even Horralain wouldn't have to duck.

One thing I have come to learn over the years, is that if someone invites an assassin into their home, the chances are they are prepared for the attempt. Unfortunately, that was a lesson I had yet to learn. I stepped through the opening before my better judgement could assert itself.

This place is strange. The rules are not quite right.

Ssserakis was certainly right about that. Outside the sphere, night had been setting in, the last rays of sun disappearing and the moons looming high and bright above. Inside the sphere, it was bright as a summer's day, yet when I looked up, I could see the black wall of the sphere all around. There was light, but no sun. The city had disappeared too. No more buildings or streets or feral pahht. I stood on a dirt road with gleaming white pillars on either side which led to a large amphitheatre built of onyx, perfectly maintained.

It appears this Djinn has a flair for the dramatic.

"Are we inside a pocket realm?" I asked.

"Yes," Silva said as she stepped through behind me. "And no. This is still part of Do'shan, it is just different from the rest of the city. Separate. Be careful, everyone, the rules may not be the same here."

"Rules?" Imiko asked. It was somewhat comforting that all my friends followed me into the sphere. Far less of a comfort when the doorway closed behind us. We were locked in.

"Up may still be up, but down may not be down." Tamura strode ahead and took the lead, wasting no time as he headed towards the amphitheatre. "Rules are what gives the world stability. They set expectation."

"So, the crazy old man is saying things may work differently here?" Ishtar asked.

"Maybe," Silva said. "The rules of our world cannot be broken, but it's possible that in here they can be bent."

"Will a sword still kill?" Ishtar asked.

"Probably."

"Then let us put an end to this, not-so-terrible student." Ishtar gave me a shove in the back, and it prompted me to follow Tamura. "The sooner you kill this Djinn of yours, the sooner we can make ready for the Terrelans snapping at our heels."

A nervous apprehension took hold of me as we made our way towards the amphitheatre. I couldn't help but remember my conflict with Vainfold. Mezula claimed it was a victory, a blow struck against the Djinn, yet I felt it was anything but. Even with Ssserakis aiding me, I hadn't bested Vainfold, I had barely escaped his clutches. It had

taken everything we had, all our combined power, and all
we had managed to do was distract the Djinn long enough
for Ssserakis to pull us back to my body. Retreating is rarely
winning; it is a defeat anyway you look at it.

I was stronger now, I knew things I didn't back then,
and I had the support of my friends, but part of me knew
it wouldn't be enough. The Rand and Djinn were as gods
to our world. They shaped it, shaped us. Even diminished
as they were, their power was still unimaginable. Silva
claimed I was prophesied to kill the last of the Djinn. Mezula
was betting her daughter on those odds, and even Tamura
seemed confidant. I have never believed in prophecy or
prediction. Chronomancers have tried for hundreds of
years to use their magic to see the future, and all they have
earned for their efforts is blindness to the present, their eyes
withered to dust in their skulls. The shield, Madness, is
said to show those who look upon it visions of the future,
but those visions often contradict each other as the future
is ever changing. I found it somewhat hard to believe that
thousands of years ago a Rand had seen me kill the last
of the Djinn, and somehow, despite everything that has
happened in between, that prediction was still coming to
pass.

We said little as we passed under the entrance arch
of the amphitheatre. I think we were all nervous, even
Ssserakis seemed restless. It is hard to explain the feeling
of a horror writhing about inside your soul, as though it is
a snake inside coiling and uncoiling in an attempt to find
comfort. The horror's apprehension did little to soothe my
own worries. The stone of the building did appear to be
onyx, black but not nearly as oppressive as the sphere that
surrounded us. There were streaks of white within the stone,

patterns that stretched out maddeningly and looked oddly familiar yet entirely incomprehensible.

Inside the amphitheatre, there were stands all the way around a large arena in the centre. It was, in many ways, alike to the coliseum in Polasia with a sandy dirt floor unstained by blood. Of the Djinn, there was no sign, but I wagered there was nowhere else he was likely to be.

"Spread out," Ishtar said, already moving along one of the walls. "Be ready."

The others did as ordered, gripping what weapons they had tightly and trying to keep their backs to the arena wall. I was not nearly so cautious. My weapons were inside of me, my magic, and Sourceblades, and Ssserakis. I strode towards the centre of the amphitheatre, bolstered by the fact that Silva came with me. She, too, held no weapons. She, too, carried hers inside.

"It might help to know which attunements you have?" I said as we crept forwards.

Silva drew in a deep breath and let it out as a sigh. No doubt she was considering how much she should tell me.

You cannot trust her words. Lies drip from this one's lips.

"It doesn't work like that, Eska. Aspects don't have attunements and we don't suffer from rejection. I can use whichever Source I have and can hold as many as I can comfortably swallow, for as long as I need to."

I turned an incredulous stare on Silva. "You've had that kind of power all along and you didn't tell me?"

A cold wind blew through the amphitheatre and we all knew the source. Aerolis had finally come to confront us.

CHAPTER FORTY SIX

THE WIND BLEW IN FROM ALL OVER THE amphitheatre, rushing through the arches and over stands, stirring the dirt beneath our feet and whipping coats into a flapping frenzy. It blew not in one direction, but converged on a spot in the middle of the arena, just in front of Silva and I. And as the winds rushed in, they collided, forming into a twirling vortex roughly in the shape of a terran. It was maddening to look at, distracting and impossible to focus on. Grains of sand were picked up by the blowing wind and thrown out of it constantly. Just as Jagran had taken the form of lightning, it seemed this Djinn was the wind itself.

Such a grand entrance. But for whose benefit, I wonder? This creature seeks to impress us.

"Aerolis, I presume?" I had to raise my voice to be heard over the howling of the wind.

The Djinn's head shifted. I had the distinct impression

it was looking at each of us in turn, but without a face it was impossible to discern which way it was looking. When it spoke, its voice was as the howling of the wind, only it didn't need to shout, the sound reached us all with ease. "I did not expect her to send two Aspects. Which of you is supposed to die today?"

Tamura giggled and raised his hand. "Failed Aspect. My mother was Raither."

"Ah." The Djinn looked as though it nodded. "I am sorry for your loss. Raither was ever the most reasonable of the Rand. It is a shame she thought to kill herself to stop my brother."

"Aranae needed to be stopped," Tamura said, spreading his hands.

"Yes," Aerolis agreed. "His attempt to tear open the rift and allow the creature through was misguided. We would have stopped him ourselves."

"Raither would still have died."

"True." The wind shifted and I couldn't help but feel the Djinn's attention had turned my way. "So, this is the one."

Caution, Eskara. This creature is stronger than Vainfold.

Caution has never been one of my strongest traits. I took a step forward and created a Sourceblade in my right hand, a thick bladed short sword with a serrated edge. I had no idea how to go about killing the wind, but I would tear it to pieces if I could. "I have been sent to kill you, Aerolis."

The Djinn seemed to shift a little, the wind pulsing. I squinted against the madness. "Does this form confuse you, Sourcerer? Let me help you."

The wind collapsed, as though whatever had been holding it together was released and it rushed towards the ground, blowing grains of sand to all edges of the coliseum. I tensed, crouching down into a combat ready stance with my blade held out to the side.

"Eska," Silva said, her hand landing on my shoulder. Of all of us there she was the only one standing as though completely unconcerned. When I glanced at her she shook her head. "Just wait."

Where the wind form of the Djinn had blustered earlier, the ground beneath it seemed to bubble. Dirt and sand fell away as a lumps of rock rose up from the earth and slowly stood. It was not a single rock, but more like hundreds of small stones somehow glued together to form something vaguely terran shaped, but easily twice as large as even Horralain. They grated together as the Djinn moved, sand and dirt falling from the gaps between the little rocks. Its head still had no face and so there was no way to tell which direction it was looking. This time when it spoke its voice was deep and rumbling, like a distance avalanche. If I hadn't known there to be only one Djinn left in the world, I might have suspected this one to be a different creature entirely.

"Is this better? Am I easier to look upon now?"

I was no more certain my Sourceblade could cut through rock than I was it could tear apart the wind. We had fought Vainfold with icy shadows, it seemed a natural counter to the Djinn's light and fire, perhaps there was some way to counter each element a Djinn formed itself of. Again, I felt Silva's hand squeeze my shoulder and when I glanced back, she smiled at me.

"Aerolis, the Changing," Silva said. She took a step forward so she was next to me and bowed. "My mother, Mezula, the Lasting Dawn, has sent us—"

There was a sound of rocks cracking as the Djinn laughed. "Such formality from an assassin. I know why you are here, Aspect." Again, I felt the weight of its attention shift towards me. "But I wonder if your Sourcerer does."

Horralain had continued to circle around the arena wall, inching slowly with every step. His axe was gone, shattered against the sphere, but he held a vicious curved dagger in his right hand and he certainly had the strength to put it to good use. Many people would let out a roar as they begin their fatalistic charge. It sounds like foolishness and it is, but I have seen it happen many times. Perhaps they think to scare the enemy with a bloodthirsting bellow, but in reality all they do is tip their hand. Horralain was not so foolish. The big thug launched into a sprint, pushing off against the arena wall, and closed the gap between himself and the Djinn in a frighteningly short time. It was like running into a wall at full pelt. Horralain bounced off the Djinn, his eyes going blank as his consciousness failed him, his head cracking against the stone of Aerolis' form. To Horralain's credit, the knife bit home, sinking deep and scraping stone. But what can a simple knife do against a god that chooses to wrap itself in rock? Nothing. Despite the force of the charge, Horralain and his knife came off far worse. The big Terrelan stumbled backward, swaying on his feet. I've always wondered how someone can be unconscious yet remain on their feet.

I started forwards, shrugging off Silva's hand on my shoulder and drawing on the Arcstorm inside, sending lightning jolting along my Sourceblade. The others charged as well, everyone except Silva and Imiko, who had already vanished from sight, as she liked to do. It is a true credit to my friends that they didn't hesitate. I moved in to save

Horralain. For all the bad that monster had done, he had thrown his lot in with mine and I felt a loyalty to him for that. There was no way I would let the Djinn crush the man while I stood by and watched. The others moved when I did, not for Horralain, but for me. We were all fools.

The Djinn exploded outward in a wave of force and rocks. I took a small boulder to the chest and found myself rolling in the sandy dirt, struggling to draw breath. The others didn't fare any better. All of us were down, collapsed on the ground. All of us, except Silva. The woman I loved stood still, right where she had before, a shimmering purple light in front of her. A kinetic shield formed the instant Aerolis had attacked.

Stupid, Eskara. This creature is beyond brute force.

Rocks started rolling past me, drawn from all over the arena, dragged towards the centre where they reformed into the figure of the Djinn.

"Can you help? Like you did in the crown?" I asked Ssserakis.

Not like that. This place is still your world. The rules here limit my form. I will use your shadow to shield you as best I can.

"Get up, Eska," Silva said, her voice sharper than normal, like a gong struck with force. "The rest of you should leave." Her eyes were fixed on the Djinn.

I struggled back to my feet and winced at the new hurts my body claimed. Luckily, Ssserakis' shadowy sutures held where I had no doubt normal ones would have ripped free. Only Horralain didn't stir. "Hardt, get Horralain out of the way and stay back."

"Are you sure about this, Eskara?" Ishtar winced as she stood, rolling her left arm. I thought it quite miraculous that the woman had kept hold of her sword even in the storm of rocks that had hit us all.

"You cannot help, Ishtar," Silva said. "Save your strength for the Terrelans."

I nodded my agreement and turned my attention to Hardt. "Don't get involved, no matter what."

It says a lot about the Djinn's confidence that he simply waited while my friends collected Horralain and quit the field. They climbed up into the stands. I wasn't certain they were truly safe there, but it would certainly be safer than down with Silva and I.

Tamura approached me before he joined the others, leaning in close enough so that only I could hear his words. "The true enemy is rarely those you fight, but your own ignorance." With that he giggled and skipped away like a happy child. The words meant little to me at the time, but I recognise them now as another quote from Belmoroes' Treaty of War. A wise man, was Belmoroes, at least when you stop to truly consider his teachings.

That left just Silva, myself, and of course Ssserakis to fight the Djinn. Aerolis did not appear concerned, though in truth it was difficult to tell while he waited.

"Do we have a plan?" I asked.

Silva let out a soft laugh. "I thought you were in charge. How did you beat Vainfold again?"

We didn't.

"With trickery mostly."

The Djinn, it appeared, was done waiting. "Do you know why you are here?" Its voice resonated around the arena, rumbling the earth like a quake.

"To end the War Eternal between you and the Rand," I said. The foolhardy should never speak as though they are wise.

Aerolis laughed, the amphitheatre shaking with it.
"How can a war be eternal when its only possible outcome is
the death of all those who fought in it? I doubt Mezula even
remembers why we are feuding." The Djinn's head moved
a little, the large rock that should have been its face rotating.
"Did she tell you who started the war?"

"I'll go left, you go right." Silva whispered. "We'll
have to try hitting it with different Sourcery to see what
works."

I ignored her, taking a single step forward. "You did,"
I shouted to the Djinn. "You killed one of the Rand."

"We struck first, true. But that does not mean we
started the war."

Silva stepped up beside me. "You can't trust the word
of the Djinn, Eska."

I looked at her, the woman I loved. "But I can trust the
word of the Rand?" I shook my head and raised my voice
again. "The war started because of the Other World. The
Djinn created it; the Rand filled it with life."

*Still asking others for all the answers, Eskara. You already
have everything you need.*

The Djinn rumbled for a moment. "The Rand did not
tell you this. Yes, we created Sevoari, the place you name the
Other World. Our greatest achievement, to rival the power
of whatever made us. A place where the laws are what we
choose. We built cities and mountains, oceans and deserts.
But we could not fill it with life. In our gracious generosity,
we asked the Rand to help us. We gave them access to
Sevoari, and they filled it with nightmares."

"That's what you are," I whispered to Ssserakis before
raising my voice once more. "Horrors and monsters, ghosts
and demented creatures." I actually laughed as it all finally

fit into place around me. "They filled the Other World with our nightmares. Plucked straight out of the dreams of terrans and pahht and all the other people of Ovaeris. We created the inhabitants of the Other World, the Rand just brought them to life."

"An insult to our greatest work," the Djinn rumbled, a menacing tone to the grating of rock. "The Rand mocked us. Made an abomination of what we hoped to achieve."

"What are you, Ssserakis?" I asked, turning my attention inward.

I am your fear of the dark, Eskara. The terran fear of the dark. A collective nightmare as old as your people. I am everything that you fear waits in the darkness. But I am also me. Ssserakis, one of the thirteen lords of Sevoari. I have grown far beyond my creation. The Rand and Djinn are stuck in the past, locked in the moment their war started, yet both worlds have moved on without them. They are, both of them, a dead people, irrelevant. They must remain that way.

Silva was talking, though I hadn't been listening. "... cannot trust it, Eska. The Djinn twist truth..."

"Is that what the Rand have been telling the world?" The arena rumbled with the Djinn's laughter. "It is easy to spread misinformation when you control the history books. Ask yourself this, Sourcerer. Why is the Rand so determined to see me dead, when I am locked in here? I can no more escape this sphere than Mezula can leave her palace. She has bound my city with unbreakable chains and made me a prisoner. And even that is not enough for her. Still, the Rand wants me dead."

It was a strange feeling to be in the centre of things. I felt as though the Djinn were tugging me one way, and Silva the other, both trying to bend me to their will. Both trying to convince me that theirs was the right cause. Part of the prophecy, perhaps? The Auguries may say I was to end the War Eternal, but they did not specify which side would ultimately lose the conflict.

Why should there be only be two sides? Kill both the Rand and Djinn. It would certainly put an end to the war.

"Eska," Silva gripped my hand in her own and squeezed. "We have to work together now. We can kill this thing, but only together."

"One more question, Sourcerer," the Djinn said. "Why is she here?" A single rocky arm raised and pointed towards Silva.

Silva tore her hand from mine and drew them together, forming a spear of ice between her palms. She threw it at Aerolis, and the Djinn did not move. The spear shattered against the rocks and a creeping frost swept over the Djinn. Within mere moments it was encased in ice. I had never seen Pyromancy used like that before. Silva turned to me and pulled me close. I could smell her, a combination of sweat and flowery perfume, and Silva. A scent I knew so well. A scent I remember even to this day. I stared into her eyes and saw desperation there. Even in the middle of such a conflict, all I wanted in that moment was to wrap my arms around her and let the rest of the world fade away.

"Eska, don't let it confuse you. Unless we kill it now, it will never let us leave this sphere. Not just you and me, but all of us are trapped here unless we kill it." Her voice trembled, imploring. Her face so earnest.

I shook my head, trying to free myself of Silva's intoxicating closeness. "Aerolis said it was trapped in the sphere, a construct of your mother's making."

Lies on top of lies, Eskara. You cannot trust anyone but us.

"Do you know why the Aspects were created, Sourcerer?" The Djinn's voice sounded clearly despite the prison of ice. "Would you like to tell the truth, Aspect? Or shall I?"

Silva shook her head, tears in her eyes. "Don't."

The Djinn laughed again, and the icy prison shattered, collapsing to the earth. "When the war started, we struck the first blow. Until we killed Yuestethan, the Light, we weren't even sure we could die. And as soon as her essence solidified into crystal, my brother, Purran, the Sun Honed, died also. There was no final blow struck against him, no sneak attack from hidden Rand. He simply died as Yuestethan did."

There was a look on Silva's face like grief. As though the Djinn telling its story pained her. "Please," she whispered. "Let's just end this now."

I couldn't. Not before I learned the truth. My world was built on too many lies, those told to me by Silva, by Mezula, by Ssserakis. By myself. This once, I needed to know the truth before I acted. It was important.

"We are linked by the rules of this world," Aerolis continued. "Laws that govern even us. Bound together in life and power and death. Whenever one of my brothers died, so too did one of the Rand. And whenever one of those hateful creatures perished, so too did one of my brothers. You would think it would convince us to cease our war, but it didn't. We fought even harder, even knowing that it would only speed our demise as well as their own. One thing both the Rand and we Djinn share is our stubbornness."

"That's why some of you created the pocket realms. Not to escape the war, but to escape the laws that bind you to the Rand," I said.

"You've met one of my trapped brothers?" The Djinn

asked.

"Vainfold."

"In his crown of fire, yes. How is he?"

I shrugged. "He tried to usurp my body and use it to burn Ro'shan from the sky." I have never liked being reminded of how that Djinn took control of me.

"Vainfold never could accept the futility of war." Aerolis face rock kept rotating and I wished it had some representation of eyes so I knew where the Djinn was looking. "I assume Mezula has him now?"

"Locked away."

Silva gripped my hand again. "Eska, stop. Please don't do this. Don't side with the Djinn."

I frowned, still not understanding. "I'm not siding with anyone, Silva. I just want to know the truth. The truth you've apparently been keeping from me."

"I had to," Silva was pleading now. "If you'd known, you'd never have agreed to come here."

"Yes," the Djinn's rumbling cut across us. "The pocket realms were our attempt to escape the laws that bound us together and assured our destruction by our own hands. And the Aspects were the Rand's attempt at the same. They never managed to perfect it during the war, but then I suppose Mezula has had a long time to solve the riddle."

I turned hurt eyes on Silva and she nodded. "We were created to take the place of our mothers. A shield between the Rand and the laws that bound them to the Djinn. A part of themselves, a part of the Rand to…" Silva's words failed her.

"To die in their place." I struggled to speak past a tight throat and tears. Whether they were of sadness or anger, I still can't say. "You didn't come here to fight the

Djinn with me, Silva. You came here to die."

Silva nodded, eyes down, not willing to look at me. Anger and hurt warred within and I didn't know which one to feel. I clenched my hands so tight I could feel my nails digging into my palms. Tears welled in my eyes and I let them fall rather than wipe them away.

"Why? Why would you agree to it?" I couldn't keep the hurt from pouring out.

"Because she is my mother."

"Mezula is making you do it. Forcing you." It was my turn to plead. There had to be a reason Silva was willing to throw her life away.

Silva shook her head, tears shaking free to water the ground between us. "She asked me. I do it willingly."

"Why?"

Silva looked up at me then, determination and sadness at war on her beautiful features. "Because it's my purpose. It's the entire reason I exist. By being here, I save my mother from death. I save Coby and Gol and Iron and Mercury. All my brothers and sisters who might die instead. This way, they get to live."

"But you don't." I spat the words as an accusation.

She nodded. "Some sacrifices have to be made."

"Fuck that!" I hissed. "Fuck it! Fuck your mother and fuck this Djinn! Here's another option. We leave. Now. We just walk away and let your mother and this Djinn hate each other across the world for the rest of eternity. I will not fight this thing if it means you die, Silva. I won't kill you."

She shook her head sadly. "Whether you help or not, my mother's will is set, Eska. I will fight Aerolis with or without your help. Please help my final act be one of glory. To protect those I love."

"So that's it? One way or another you die here because your mother is too much a coward to accept her own fate."

Silva nodded. Tears still rolling down her cheeks.

The arena rumbled. "Does she really have a choice? This construct is merely an aspect of Mezula. Life, but only as far as the Rand wishes it. What she believes is free will, is only an inbuilt desire to do whatever her mother wishes. Tell me, Sourcerer, what has the Rand offered you? To come here and throw your life against mine?"

"Power." The word was bitter as Spiceweed on my lips and I didn't turn from Silva as I said it.

"Sources?"

I stared at the woman I loved and she stared back. We were so close, but there was a rift growing between us. "As many as I want."

"Is it so cheap to buy your loyalty?" The stones of the Djinn groaned as it moved backwards towards the arena edge. "I offer you a different deal with better terms. A far easier price and much greater reward. Kill the Aspect, and I will give you Sources *and* teach you how to use them."

An impossible deal. An impossible choice. "I already know how to use…"

"You have no idea what a single Source is capable of, Sourcerer," the Djinn said, cutting me off. "You hold fragments of gods inside of you and think that paltry balls of fire are power? I will teach you the true potential you hold inside of you."

Take it! Learn what you can and turn it against the teacher, Eskara.

Silva shook her head. Her tears had run dry, but there was a profound sadness to her. "Please don't do this."

"Your mother has sent you here to die, Silva. Worse still, you'd die by my hands. What am I supposed to do?" How could she do this? Give me no choice but to watch her die, to be the instrument of her death. To be the weapon. I didn't want it anymore. I didn't want to be the weapon anymore. I just wanted to be Eska, and I just wanted to be with Silva.

I wiped tears from eyes. "If I help you, you die. If I don't help, you kill yourself. It doesn't have to be this way. You don't have to do this. We don't have to do this. Walk away. We'll steal the flyer and go to Polasia, never step foot here or on Ro'shan again. Let's just leave. Please."

Silva let out a ragged sigh and shook her head. "I can't. I have to do this, Eska." She took a step back and let out a steadying breath. "You're either with me, or in my way."

What else could I have said? What could I have done? Could I have convinced Silva somehow to alter her course? Should I have made a different choice? Questions that continue to haunt me to this day. An impossible choice with no right answers. With no good outcomes. I was confronted with causing the death of the woman I loved, and all I could do was either honour Silva's final request, or spite her fucking bitch of a mother who put us all in that situation. I did what I have always done. I chose the option that offered me the most power to gain.

CHAPTER FORTY SEVEN

WE LIVE IN A WORLD OF OPPOSITES WHERE one cannot be appreciated without its antithesis. You can't truly appreciate the light without experiencing darkness. Pleasure has no meaning without the existence of pain. And you cannot love something without also hating it. I loved Silva. And I hated her.

Attack!

It took only seconds to will a Sourceblade into existence in my hand. Silva was faster. I had to roll to the side as a blade of ice formed along her arm and very nearly took me in the chest. Pyromancy and an affinity to ice, the first of her Sources revealed.

With flames rippling across my Sourceblade, I charged back in as soon as I made my feet. I hoped the flames would help, perhaps crack the ice of her blade. We traded blows, and I realised for the first time that Silva must have also been trained in combat. She was not Coby, but neither was Silva weak. In fact, she proved then that she was stronger than I, beating me back with staggering blows that very nearly crushed through my defences.

I drew the Arcstorm into my left hand and thrust, even as I parried her attack with my Sourceblade. It might have worked, had the ground not shifted beneath my feet. Geomancy, the second of her Sources revealed. I found myself carried backwards on a rolling wave of dirt, and Silva did not follow. The icy blade fell away from her hand and she drew in a deep breath. And started floating. Her feet lifted off the ground and her hair and skin began to glow a dazzling, glorious silver so bright it hurt to look at. It shone through the seams of her leather jerkin and made her eyes appear aflame. She was beautiful. Photomancy, manipulating light and darkness to her will. That was when I realised Silva was taking the fight seriously. She was there to kill the Djinn, and if she had to go through me, she would. I think I had been holding back during our first exchange. A part of me wished it was all for show, or a dream. Part of me wished I wasn't involved in a fight to the death with the woman I loved. I knew that part of me was lying to myself. I knew it, and I didn't care. Silva was bringing her full power to bear. And she was an Aspect, a fragment of a god. She had a considerable amount of power to bring.

Squinting against the light, I almost didn't see the attack coming. I think, perhaps it was my power and Ssserakis' combined that dimmed the world around me, allowed me to see. An icy spear flew towards me and I swung, shattering it with my Sourceblade just in time. Frost crept along the blade and I dropped it, the kinetic energy dissipating in a rush. I wasted no time, forming a new blade and drew on my Pyromancy Source, creating a whip formed of searing flame in my left hand. Silva seemed to have an affinity for ice, but it was a side of Pyromancy I had never been comfortable with. I prefer to burn.

I cracked the whip towards Silva, ready to launch myself into a follow-up with my Sourceblade. She caught the whip in her hand and a moment later ice raced back along the flames and up my arm. I felt the chill of it, numbing my fingers and turning the skin blue. Icicles formed along the sleeve of my winter coat and the frost kept spreading. I had to light my arm on fire to ward away the ice and bring feeling back into my fingers. As I struggled to free myself from my coat, flames eagerly catching on it, I realised my mistake. I had taken my eyes off Silva.

Silva swept her arm in a broad arc and the sand of the arena reacted to her will. Jagged spikes of sand rushed up from the ground in the direction she swept, all across the arena floor. They would have skewered me if not for Ssserakis. My shadow rose up around me in an inky shield and the sand shards that hit it burst apart into harmless grains. Still I felt a sharp pain in my leg and looked down to see blood spreading out from a gash in my thigh.

This creature is trying to kill you, Eskara. Stop holding back! I couldn't. I couldn't bring my full strength to bear, no more than I could really believe she meant me harm.

My shadowy shield withdrew, and I felt sutures piercing through my skin, pulling the wound closed. Before I could form my own plan of attack, all the sandy spikes burst outward, filling the arena with floating sand. She was using Sourcery in ways I had never dreamed possible.

"Where is she?" I whispered, trying to shield my mouth and eyes with a raised arm.

I cannot see anything in this floating cloud of grit.

Something large hit the ground nearby. I heard it, felt the impact, but could not see what it was.

She cannot see in here, either.

I drew on the Arcstorm inside and let it out, bolts of lightning ripping free of my fingers and snaking their way through the cloud of sand. I had no idea what I hoped to achieve. No target for the attack, only a desire to do something. I suppose I got lucky. Silva screamed as the lightning found her and the cloud of sand dropped away in an instant, falling harmlessly to the arena floor. She was on the ground, whatever magic keeping her afloat had gone, but her skin still glowed with a radiant light. A smouldering patch of seared leather beneath her right breast told me all I needed to know.

She is injured. Finish her before she has a chance to recover.

I hesitated. How could I not? A part of me, a large part of me, still wanted to believe it was all a lie. With a new Sourceblade forming, I rushed in, still wondering if I had the courage to strike the final blow. Still hoping I could somehow incapacitate Silva instead, drag her away from the conflict between her mother and the Djinn. This wasn't her fight. It didn't have to be her fight. She didn't give me the chance. Silva reached up with a hand and clicked her fingers. I heard the noise even a dozen paces away, unnaturally loud. It echoed around the arena, growing louder and louder with each passing moment. So loud I couldn't think, couldn't stand. I stumbled to a halt and collapsed onto my knees, another Sourceblade lost as I clutched hands to my ears, trying desperately to block the noise. It was no use. Silva was using Vibromancy, amplifying a simple sound to deafening levels. The others were just as affected, my friends in the stands clutching their heads, mouths open in wordless cries of pain. Only the Djinn and Silva seemed unaffected by her magic.

Silva raised her hand to the sky, and I glanced up to see hundreds of shards of ice forming above me. There was nothing I could do. Caught in the reverberating sound trap she had created; I couldn't even move. Silva dropped her hand and the ice storm flew towards me. I had seen what such an attack could do, at the battle of Orran I had watched ice storms rip entire units of soldiers apart, regardless of armour. I was one woman wearing a leather jerkin and doubled over in pain, clutching at my ears. I was already dead.

My shadow shifted once more, black wings bursting out from my back and rising above me, shielding me from the falling shards of ice. Ssserakis growled something in my mind, but I couldn't hear anything over the sound of Silva's clicked fingers echoing around me, inside me. The noise was everywhere.

The storm of ice stopped, shards dropping around me and the black wings Ssserakis had formed shook the last of the icicles free. There were still a dozen paces between Silva and I, an uncrossable eternity with the noise between us.

Jump!

I didn't wait for an explanation. With a kinetic push I launched myself upward and my shadow wings gave a single beat, carrying me forwards at a reckless speed. I crashed into Silva bodily, sending us both rolling in the sand. My wings vanished, the shadow fading away, and I felt Ssserakis' weariness, as tangible as my own. But the attack worked. Silva's concentration was broken, and the noise died away, leaving a painful ringing in my ears, but it was nothing I couldn't handle.

We wrestled there on the ground for a moment, Silva and I. She was the stronger of us, a power that had nothing to do with muscle, but I fought with a savage, unleashed fury. I punched my lover in the face and saw her recoil, blood leaking from her nose. It was the first time I had ever seen Silva bleed and I felt my heart ache inside at the guilt of it. I wanted to end the fight right then, go to Silva, take her in my arms, and hold her until both our pain faded. I dropped my guard.

A blast of kinetic energy hit me in the chest and I rocketed backwards, crashing against the wall of the arena. Something broke inside. A rib maybe. The pain was excruciating.

Ignore it. Attack! Ssserakis was right about that, as long as I drew shallow breaths I could just about continue through the pain. I brought two Sourceblades into existence, one in each hand, fire and lightning, daggers meant for close combat. And I charged her.

Silva was still recovering and barely managed to form her blade of ice again in time. She blocked one of my knives, but the other bit home, trailing fire across her midsection. She fell back with another scream and I followed with a savage snarl. For a few moments I had her pressed, retreating with every step and struggling just to stop me from planting both daggers inside. I had no choice but to keep up the pressure. Sourcery requires concentration, and I could not let her regain that control of the fight. I knew now which Sources she carried, but the things she could do with them put my own knowledge to shame. Silva would win any battle of magic. I had to rely on my martial skill and Ssserakis' dwindling power. Even as I realised it, Silva took control once more.

A solid wall of sand rose up in front of me. I bounced off it, unable to arrest my momentum, and stumbled back. The wall burst apart and rushed towards me so fast I barely threw my arms up to shield my face. Hundreds of sand clusters and little stones pelted me, opening up new scrapes along my skin and bruising me in countless places, and when it was over, I collapsed onto a knee, gasping in pain. It hurt to breathe, hurt to move, hurt to exist. Another icy spear came my way, too fast for me to react, and Ssserakis shifted my shadow once more, a single black shard brushing the spear aside.

Silva was glowing again, a brilliant light making her skin shine, her golden hair looked like fire. "Your horror cannot keep saving you, Eska," Silva said, her voice trembling.

I'm not done yet.

I stood, my shadow shifting like black flames rising all around me. "We're not done yet." The words hissed from my mouth, a sound like Ssserakis' voice and my own merging into one. The Arcstorm raged inside, flashing behind my eyes and crackling from my fingertips. An anger I could barely control, a rage I couldn't contain. Crouching down, I took a low stand, hands held down by my side, pointed backwards, and I brought a Sourceblade larger than any I had before into existence.

Silva realised what I was doing a moment too late, I think. Her right arm was coated in ice, a flat blade extending out past her hand, but she raised her left hand and clicked her fingers once more. I struck before she could amplify the sound. The blade I held was at least a dozen paces long, thin as a reed but strong as steel and far lighter than it should have been. Even so it took all my strength and as much as Ssserakis could lend me to swing it. Silva raised her right arm in time to block the attack, but the blade bit home, shattering the ice on her arm and sending her flying. Her Vibromancy failed, the sound dying away before it could incapacitate anyone, and Silva rolled in the sand.

I dropped my huge Sourceblade and formed a new one, shorter and lighter, a much more manageable size. Silva was still struggling to her feet, golden hair glowing and skin radiant. I levelled the blade at her chest and charged. Silva threw both hands out to her sides just before I hit, and a shimmering purple shield formed around her. My Sourceblade stopped without a sound. Well, I say no sound, but I certainly hissed with the effort and pain of bouncing off another solid wall. Her shield was not something I had ever seen before. It was not like the shields I could create, solid things I could carry with me. This was a bubble of kinetic energy with Silva at the centre.

Silva looked up at me, golden hair framing her glowing face, and there were fresh tears rolling down her cheeks. This fight between us hurt her as much as it did me. There was determination there, too, a will so strong she would bear the pain of killing the woman she loved in order to fulfil her mother's wishes. I could never hope to match that sort of drive.

Silva stood, arms thrust out to the sides and the kinetic bubble moved with her. I backed up a step, frantically searching for a way around her defence. The Arcstorm still raged inside of me, lightning striking at random, and one of those little bolts passed through the shield as though it weren't there. Silva noticed it at the same time I did. I dropped my Sourceblade, useless against her bubble and summoned the Arcstorm to my hands just as Silva dropped her shield and formed a blade of ice around her right hand once more.

The black sphere surrounding us shattered.

We all paused as the world outside reasserted itself. Night rushed in to replace day and shards of black energy rained around us, disintegrating to nothing even as they fell. In the gloom of night Silva glowed even more brilliantly. Even more beautifully.

"How?" The Djinn's word rumbled around us.

I looked back to Silva just in time to see her confusion replaced by determination and I knew the source of it. The lightning had died in my hands the moment the sphere shattered, my concentration broken, but Silva still held her ice blade, extending out from her hand. She thrust it at me, and I lurched to the side, going down on one knee and feeling the ice bite across the top of my shoulder, its freezing burn tearing a scream from my lips. I thrust my hand forward, towards her. No blade, no lightning, no weapon of any kind. I couldn't do it. I couldn't. In that brief flicker of time, I realised I would rather die than kill Silva. My hand touched her chest, a flat palm resting between her breasts.

I looked at her, the woman I loved. True love the likes of which I had never felt before and knew I never would again. I smiled at her. "It's over," I said.

Ssserakis shifted my shadow, forming a blade around my hand and I watched it slide easily into Silva's chest.

CHAPTER FORTY EIGHT

LIFE IS ABOUT CONNECTIONS. THE BONDS WE make and those we break. Some friendships, even those made accidentally, can last a lifetime. A connection made on a whim can alter the rest of those lives in every conceivable way. Enemies made by a careless insult might dedicate themselves to your demise. A bond severed before its time can cause untold misery, not just to you, but to all those connected to you.

I have no doubt that without my connections I would have floundered and lost my way, even died many times over. Without Hardt's support and indomitable strength I could not have made it through the pain that my actions had caused. I would have given in to Lesray Alderson's insidious suggestion to end my own life long ago. His comfort and reassurance are what allowed me to make the decisions I have, even when doubt convinced me I must surely be wrong.

My connection to Tamura made me think. His advice and his riddles both not only influenced the decisions I have made in my life, but the way I think about those decisions. I have always been bull-headed, but Tamura's cryptic nature forced me to consider perspectives outside of my own.

In Imiko I found something I never had before. A friendship born not out of necessity, but out of pure choice. Neither of us needed the other, but we stayed together all the same. And even in those frustrating moments where her actions drove me near to madness, I found I would not have traded them, or her, for any other. My connection to Imiko made me consider what it was to choose my own path, rather than tread one already laid out for me.

With Kento, I forged a connection that led to a determination I had never felt before. Without my daughter and the love I felt for her, I would have given up and let Vainfold have my body, as well as his vengeance. Though I only knew her for a few days, my little girl gave me the will and the strength to resist. She made me strong.

My connection to Ssserakis, my bond to an ancient horror, gave me a power I had never dreamed of before. Without it, I would never have had the strength to battle a god within a world of its own making. I would never have found my way back to my body. It taught me of the price all power carries with it. Ssserakis provided me with power, but it also made me doubt my every action, fear the consequences of them and what might happen to those I loved.

Silva introduced me to love. Not the love I felt for Hardt, nor even that for Josef. Not like the lust I felt for Isen, and not like the maternal love I felt for Kento. Silva

introduced me to a passionate love born from true desire.
She opened my eyes in many ways to my own feelings. I
have never loved anyone as deeply as I loved Silva. Our
connection shifted my world, sent me hurtling through it on
a new course. Without her, I would never have met the Rand
or the Djinn. I would never have matched power and wit
with gods. Without her, I would have died.

There is one more connection that shaped that time of
my life. Prena Neralis, first blade of the Terrelan Empire. It
was her dogged pursuit of me that set us all free.

For a brief moment, I thought it a lie. My shadow a
harmless thing without true form. That was the lie, the one
I tried to convince myself of. The truth swept in without
mercy. Silva's glow faded, like a flickering candle slowly
shrinking to wisps of smoke. Blood welled up around the
edges of my shadow blade and stained her leather jerkin.
Ssserakis pulled back, the blade vanishing, and Silva fell.

I rushed forward, catching my lover in my arms
before she hit the ground. The blade had bitten deep through
her sternum, a wide wound no amount of time or Biomancy
could heal. I dragged my gaze from it and found Silva
staring at me, her eyes unusually dark. Blood leaked from
her mouth, staining her teeth and making her a ghastly sight.
Still beautiful to me. Always. She reached up and cupped my
cheek in one hand and I felt it sticky with blood.

"Don't blame… yourself." Silva's final words
designed to absolve me of my guilt. How could she do it?
How could she be thinking of helping me even as she died.
Even as I killed her.

Silva died in my arms. Her eyes went distant and her
body gave two final spasms, and she was gone. Her hand

fell away from my cheek. Gone. Dead. She took the best of me with her.

My memory of those moments is fuzzy at best, but there was a lot of blood. I knew I should have felt angry or sad, but in those few moments all I felt was numb. All I wanted to feel was numb. My mind refused to process the shouting and the clash of steel on steel. I struggled through my own mind, wading through emotions I couldn't identify, tears streaming. And then I found my anger.

The Arcstorm exploded to life around me, bolts of lightning sparking from my skin and striking the ground nearby. A new energy suffused me, chasing away the exhaustion and making the pain of my broken rib a distant thing.

"You killed her!" An accusation whispered.

I protected you, just as I said I would. Just as you asked. Lay the blame where it deserves to be, Eskara. Not on me, and not on yourself. All of this is product of a war none of us ever wanted a part in. You want a culprit, a target for your grief and pain? There is one right there.

As if following the horror's accusation, I turned my head to where the Djinn waited. Aerolis' floating rocks hadn't moved, despite the shattering of the sphere. I think, perhaps, the Djinn was trying to reason out the cause of its new freedom.

I lay Silva's corpse down as gently as I could and stood amidst a crackling storm of lightning. My eyes flashed bright, the arena clear to me even in the gloom of night, and I formed two new Sourceblades, ignoring the pain in my stomach, the first signs of Source rejection. Shadowy wings burst out of my back once more and I leapt into the sky, two beats carrying me across the distance to the Djinn.

"What are you doing, Sourcerer?" Aerolis rumbled. I didn't reply.

We attacked in a fury that was all power and no finesse. Two Sourceblades, charged with fire and lightning, clashed against the Djinn's rocky body again and again. Ssserakis helped, shadowy wings ending in icy talons striking with every swing of my blades. The Arcstorm raged around me, lightning ripping from me and searing the rocky body of a god. This was all Mezula's fault. Her will. Her plan. She had sent Silva here to die. Well I couldn't strike at Mezula, but if I could kill Aerolis, she would die also.

"I tire of this, Sourcerer."

I didn't let up. Despite the pain inside. Despite the strength fleeing me. Despite Ssserakis' exhaustion. I didn't stop.

Aerolis groaned, rocks falling away from his form and the arena shuddering around us. It was pain. I knew then, we couldn't beat a god, but we had just made it bleed. That was just about all we had left.

Rocky hands shot up and gripped hold of my Sourceblades. Ssserakis reacted with one final strike, burying both wings deep into the Djinn's body.

"Enough!" The Djinn's shout cut through my rage and brought a dizzying sobriety with it. My Sourceblades shattered in my hands, but not from my own doing. The shadowy wings crumbled away, Ssserakis retreating inside, exhausted and spent. Even the Arcstorm quieted, frenzied bolts ceasing. It still raged inside though, behind my eyes and across my skin.

New rocks rolled across the arena toward us, replacing those I had cut away from the Djinn. Aerolis stared down at me, its face rock rotating in place of its head. "Very amusing, Sourcerer. But you waste your energy on me. I made you a deal…"

"You killed her!" I hissed. Now I stopped my attack, I was finding it quite hard to stand. Every breath was agony and my limbs felt leaden. And yet there I was, throwing blame anywhere it might stick. Anywhere but myself.

"No. You killed her," the Djinn rumbled. "I will hold up my end of the deal as payment. Unless you attack me again." There was a menace to its voice that hadn't been there before. "Besides, I think you have more pressing matters."

I turned to find a battle raging inside the arena.

Everywhere I looked my friends were fighting against Terrelan soldiers. Horralain was conscious once more and held a spear in one hand and a great sword in the other. Three men wearing Terrelan uniforms were trying to flank him, but the giant already had four bodies at his feet already and was working to extend his collection. Hardt was loose, not the kind compassionate man who had been my companion for years, who had held my daughter and made faces at her. No, this was the violent storm he struggled against inside. Bones crunched and soldiers died at Hardt's gauntleted hands. Wounds didn't stop him, only spurred him on to greater violence. This was the man my friend feared of becoming. The man I had driven him to once more. To protect me. Always to protect me.

Tamura appeared unconcerned, despite the three soldiers harassing him. He flowed around strikes and disarmed his foes with twisted wrists and swept legs. Every now and then Imiko would dart in, appearing from the darkness and stabbing at a soldier with her little knife, before once again vanishing into the gloom. She was not one to stand and fight.

Ishtar and her two remaining mercenaries were perhaps the deadliest of those we had left. Ishtar herself was a blade maelstrom no one could stand against, and her mercenaries were trained and used to backing her up. Despite this, the numbers were not on our side. This became even more evident when Prena and her knights strode into the arena. Four of them wearing gleaming golden plate over red leather and black uniforms, each one carrying a weapon straight out of legend. Josef's ghost stood nearby, his hands clutched before him as he stared at me. I couldn't take the intensity of that gaze. Forced to look away by a ghost of my own making.

Prena gave some orders and her knights split up to help deal with my friends. Prena herself walked toward me, straight through the centre of the arena, heedless of the Djinn that stood behind me. Josef's ghost drifted closer, following her at a distance. Of course, my best friend only appeared to me when I was going to die.

"Can you help?" I asked Aerolis.

"Yes," the Djinn rumbled. "But I won't."

"Arsehole!" I sent a glare at the Djinn over my shoulder, but I doubt he cared. "Ssserakis?"

I have nothing left to give you, Eskara. I could feel the weariness in the horror's words. It had taxed itself to exhaustion in our assault on Aerolis. It was small, curled up around my soul, eagerly sucking at any fear it could find.

I forced a weary grin. "Just me then." I formed a Sourceblade in my hand and winced at the cramp in my stomach. I knew what that meant, I was close to rejection, but I couldn't think about it. Without my magic I had no chance against a warrior as skilled as Prena Neralis.

She wasted no time with words. They had no meaning between us. This was not an emotional fight. There was no personal reason for her relentless pursuit. Prena had been ordered to kill me by her emperor, and that was exactly what she would do, no matter how long it took, or how many lives it cost. That sort of fanatical zeal is rare. And useful.

Prena ducked into a broad upward slash that would have cut me in half. Her blade, Neverthere, glistened with that sickly yellow colour, the pattern on the blade swirling like smoke. I blocked with my Sourceblade and both swords met without a sound. There was a moment of surprise in Prena's eyes as our blades met. Neverthere passed through metal as though it wasn't even there, but my Sourceblades were something else entirely. The shock was fleeting and a moment later I was backing up step after step after step, frantically parrying and dodging just to stay alive. Perhaps Ishtar could have won that fight with skill alone, but I was not my tutor, and I knew I was outmatched.

I reached for the Arcstorm and found it raging, as always, but I struggled to draw it out. It felt, and it is strange to say it, raw. Like wounded skin tender to the touch. Yet I managed a single bolt of lightning as Prena advanced upon me. She raised an arm and her golden vambrace absorbed the lightning, the runes etched into it glowing pink for a few moments. I have always hated enchanted armour, but it is standard equipment for those who hunt Sourcerers.

The fighting was most intense towards the amphitheatre entrance where Ishtar and her mercenaries held back a much larger force. I glanced that way to see a brute of a man wearing red on black and carrying a great hammer. Prena's companion, and one who had tried to kill

me once before. I truly thought Coby had killed him back in the ruins of Picarr, but luck was not with us that day. He was horribly scarred, burned all along his left side and his chest plate was seared into his very flesh. It did not seem to bother him all that much. The monster swung his hammer at Yemin, and the mercenary's sword shattered against the blow.
A moment later Yemin himself shattered as the hammer connected. You have likely never seen a body shatter before. It is messy. And quite horrible to see. But that is the power of the hammer, Shatter. It can break anything.

"I see," Aerolis rumbled. "That's how you broke my prison."

Prena let up the pressure, as though noticing the Djinn for the first time. Her brutish companion, wielding Shatter, started forward. Aerolis raised a single rocky hand and the brute stumbled to a halt in the centre of the arena. His chest piece crumpled inward in a spray of blood and the man, so large and alive just a moment ago, dropped dead in an instant. "If anyone touches that hammer, they will die next to him," Aerolis said, his voice shaking the arena. "Continue."

Such a brutal display of power, dismissed as though it was nothing. I realised just how lucky I was to have survived my attack on Aerolis. We might have hurt the Djinn, but only by his restraint was I still alive.

Prena's attention snapped back to me and her sword came with it in a flurry that had me stumbling and wishing I had any strength left to defend myself with. On the third strike, my Sourceblade went spinning from my hand, disappearing in a rush of kinetic energy. I tried to form another, drawing on the Source inside, and my stomach cramped. The pain made me cry out, dropping me to a knee.

I felt something hot and sticky dripping down my nose and into my mouth. My hands were shaking. Rejection. At the worst possible moment. I had no time left. Either Prena killed me with her sword, or I killed myself with my magic. She didn't give me time to make the choice myself.

There is something terrifyingly efficient about a killer detached from the emotion of her actions. If Prena had hated me, she might have stopped to gloat at her victory or taunt my defeat. But she didn't. I was nothing to her but an order from her emperor. Neverthere shone in her hand, the sickly yellow of its blade a maddening pattern of smoke. And I realised I had seen this moment before. One of the many futures the shield, Madness, had showed me so many years ago. That was how I knew to look to the right just as Josef's ghost barrelled into me, knocking me aside and taking the strike meant for my heart.

CHAPTER FORTY NINE

IT TOOK A FEW MOMENTS FOR THE REALITY TO sink in. Josef was taller than I remembered him, and broader too. He was wearing a servant's uniform and his hair was longer than it had ever been, almost down to his shoulders. A scraggly beard covered his cheeks in curly brown hair, and a ragged scar stretched from one side of his neck to the other where Yorin had slit his throat. This was no ghost. It was Josef. My best friend, the other half of me, back from the dead. I glanced at the sword poking out through his chest. Only to die once more, this time saving me, rather than trying to kill me.

Prena grunted, a pained expression on her face, and then let go of the sword, clutching her hand as though it burned. Josef just stood there with the sword through his chest.

"Josef?" My first word was uninspiring, but in my

defence, I was still reeling from the shock that he was alive. And suffering from mid-stage Source rejection.

"Hello, Eska." Josef's voice was slow and croaky, as though he wasn't used to using it.

The yellow colouring on the sword was glowing, the smoky pattern swirling around Josef's blood. All ten of the weapons that fell from the moons were nothing but metal before Sources were attached to them, fused by some combination of Ingomancy and Augmancy that has long since been lost to us. The Source attached to Neverthere glowed briefly for a moment, then crumbled to rock dust.

"What's happening?" Josef croaked.

"Well this is interesting," Aerolis rumbled. The Djinn came closer.

I tried to get back to my feet and another series of cramps twisted my insides. I tasted blood and felt it dripping down from my ears. New tears felt hot and sticky as crimson leaked from my eyes. Did I say mid-stage Source rejection? It was late-stage, mere moments from death. Carrying four Sources inside my stomach, I was certain breaking down in rejection would have been cataclysmic at best. With a trembling hand I reached into my snuff pouch, grabbed a handful of Spiceweed and shoved it into my mouth, sucking for a few seconds and then spending a while retching into the sand. Bringing up four Sources at once is agonising. If Prena wanted to take the chance to kill me, there was no longer anything I could do about it. But I think she was just as confused as to why Josef wasn't dead.

When I looked up again, Josef was wincing in pain and rigid as a pole. The patterning on the sword and the glow looked as though they were being drawn inside of him. I struggled to my feet and staggered a few steps, leaving my

Sources behind. "Breathe," I said uselessly. I grabbed Josef's bearded chin in my hands and forced his eyes to meet mine. "Breathe." He did, though shallowly. And finally, the last of the patterning faded from the sword. It was dead metal once more, though still lodged in my friend's chest.

"Amazing," Aerolis rumbled. "What are you, little terran? I think you just absorbed my brother's corpse."

"He did." I recognised the voice. It was far away, reaching us by the magic of Vibromancy and it undoubtedly belonged to Loran Orran. I glanced up to see a robed figure standing atop the amphitheatre, watching the battle as it took place below him. A moment later a portal opened close by and the Iron Legion stepped through, his eyes fixed on Josef with a fanatic intensity. "I always thought it would be the Necromancer rather than the Biomancer."

Kill him. Ssserakis voice lacked the savage energy it had last time we had seen the Iron Legion. I think the horror knew all too well we were both far beyond the fight. The simple act of standing was taking every bit of will power I had left.

"You can stand down now, First Blade Neralis," the Iron Legion said as he approached. "There's no need to fight any more." He sucked in a deep breath and when he spoke again it boomed around the arena. "Everyone stand down. The fighting is over. I assure you the emperor will be very pleased."

Intense fighting never stops immediately and at least a couple of soldiers died even after the Iron Legion's appearance, but his orders held. Even the surviving Knights of Ten backed away from the fight. I glanced around the arena and found all my friends still standing, though it was taking both Horralain and Tamura to hold Hardt back from continuing the fight. He would calm eventually, and I would be there for him when he did, preferably with a bottle of something strong to drown both our sorrows.

Prena stepped in front of the Iron Legion, her hand on a knife hanging from her belt. "I do not recognise your authority. I am here on the orders of Emperor Aras Terrelan to kill the last Orran Sourcerer."

The Iron Legion laughed at that. "I'm sorry, that's quite funny. There are at least three Orran Sourcerers still living, and they are right here in this amphitheatre. Regardless, your orders were to pursue and kill Eskara Helsene, no matter the cost or where she might run to. And they were issued by me, not your emperor. He was just kind enough to relay them. Anyway, there's no longer any need." He then put on a very regal voice. "You have served your purpose well, First Blade. Your emperor will be proud. And there will be a medal or something. Now take your troops and retreat."

Prena didn't move. Even without her sword she looked the very definition of dangerous, tall and strong and steel willed. "I do not recognise your authority. My orders are to kill the last Orran Sourcerer, no matter how many of you there are."

The Iron Legion sighed at that. "You know the interesting thing about enchanted armour? It's surprisingly easy for the Sourcerer who created it, to break it." He flicked a hand towards her and Prena's golden breastplate glowed for a moment, the runes flaring pink and then going black. Another flick and Prena Neralis rocketed sideways, struck by some unseen force, and crashed against the wall of the amphitheatre hard enough to shatter bone. She did not rise.

"I gave you orders to retreat," the Iron Legion said,

his voice carrying to the whole arena once more. I have always hated Vibromancy. "Your commander is most likely still alive… probably. I suggest you collect her and go before I decide to force the issue."

The Djinn's laughter rumbled the arena even as the Terrelan soldiers backed away from my friends and collected their injured before quitting the battle. "I never thought to see you again," Aerolis said.

"One moment, Aerolis." The Iron Legion stood tall and straight despite his ancient body. If anything, he looked even older than the last time I had seen him, his hair all but gone from his head and his skin wrinkled and sagging. "I have a miracle to perform."

The Iron Legion approached Josef and looked down at the sword. "This needs to be removed, young Yenhelm."

"How is he still alive?" I found my voice pitifully weak.

"His Biomancy is trying to heal the wound even with the sword still inside," said the Iron Legion.

Josef shook his head. "I don't have a Source." His voice sounded raw.

The Iron Legion laughed; a rich sound full of true mirth. I felt my spirits rise with the sound of that laugh and recognised it for what it was, Empamancy subverting my true feelings. Once I knew it, I could chase away the false emotion.

"Surely by now we both realise you're a little beyond needing a Biomancy Source, hmm? Now hold still. I'll help patch the wound as we go, but your own magic will do most of the work. You clearly have power aplenty." The Iron Legion placed one hand on Josef's back, blade between his thumb and forefinger, and gripped hold of the hilt with the other, and he began to pull the sword slowly back through Josef's chest.

My best friend screamed from the pain of it, but he remained standing and the extrication took a blessedly short period of time. When it was done, the Iron Legion held the bloodied sword and Josef patted down his chest, pulling apart his tunic to find the wound already sealing.

"Interesting metal, this," the Iron Legion said, inspecting the sword. A moment later and the blade started compacting, bending with a horrific scream of metal resisting the force acting upon it. "It bonds so well with a Source and yet resists my magic. Fascinating." After a few more moments the Iron Legion held a ball of metal in his hand just slightly larger than a grown man's fist. He quickly tucked it away into one of the folds of his robe then turned his attention back to Josef. "How are you feeling, Yenhelm?"

"Alive," Josef croaked.

"Well, yes. You would be."

Josef turned on the Iron Legion. "You did this to us. What did you do?"

The Iron Legion smiled at that. He had a grandfather's smile, kind, compassionate, and full of wisdom. "Feel free to look around, but don't go too far and don't touch the cages. I'll be with you soon enough."

"What..." Josef didn't get to finish his question.

The Iron Legion snapped open a portal behind my friend and with a flick of his fingers sent Josef tumbling through it. The portal snapped closed a moment later. It all happened so quickly. My reunion with Josef was so short lived. I didn't get to talk with him, to find out how he had survived, or how he came to be with Prena Neralis. I didn't get to tell him about Silva or my struggles. Or Kento. Josef had come back to life, and just like that he was gone again.

"Bring him back!" I would have shouted the words if I could, but all I could manage was a savage hiss.

The Iron Legion glanced at me. His grandfatherly smile was gone, replaced by a critical stare full of authority. "You look exhausted, Helsene. Sit down." The Iron Legion stamped his foot lightly and the ground rumbled beneath me. I collapsed onto a small pillar of solid rock that had not been there before. Of course, I tried to stand, but I had nothing left and there was a pressure against me, keeping me in place. I was helpless against it. The Iron Legion turned his attention to the Djinn.

"Aerolis." If the Iron Legion was intimidated at all by the Djinn, he didn't show it.

"You're looking old, Loran," Aerolis rumbled. There was familiarity there, but too much tension to be friendship. I wondered if the bards' tales were true. Had the Iron Legion matched wits with a Djinn and won? With this Djinn.

"Chronomancy does that to a terran. You have no idea how it feels to be so young in such an old body."

Aerolis laughed at that. "Young. Old. Mortal concepts. I assume you'll be dead soon?"

This time the Iron Legion laughed. "Not if I can help it."

"I told you before, Loran. Immortality is beyond your kind. You are motes on the wind. Meaningless in scope."

"We'll see." The Iron Legion glanced over his shoulder.

The Terrelan soldiers had all but gone, leaving their dead behind but taking their wounded, Prena among them. My friends watched the encounter from a distance. Hardt was on his knees, head buried in his hands, body shaking with giant sobs. Ishtar was tending to her last remaining mercenary who looked wounded. Imiko and Tamura drifted closer to us. I tried to rise once more but I had not the strength left to resist the Iron Legion's magic.

"I'm going to need the hammer back eventually," the Iron Legion said, waving a hand to where Shatter had fallen. No one had gone anywhere near it since the Djinn had crushed the wielder's chest.

The arena rumbled. "I make the same promise to you as to the others. I will kill anyone who touches that thing."

It must have power if the Djinn fears it so. Take it. Use it. Ssserakis sounded quiet and distant.

The Iron Legion turned back to Aerolis. "Do you think you could? I've grown stronger, Aerolis, and you seem diminished." Silence held for a few moments between the two. "Besides, you'll give it to me willingly soon enough."

"Don't count on it, terran."

The Iron Legion laughed and turned his attention away from Aerolis and back to me. A second rocky pedestal rose up in front of me and the Iron Legion lowered himself onto it with a groan. With the man so close, I could feel Ssserakis' rage, but the horror did not have the strength left to fight.

"I owe you answers, Helsene. For all I've put you through."

"Where is Josef?" I strained against the magic holding me in place to no avail.

"Safe. Safer than you. He's very important, and together we're going to right the wrongs of the world." The Iron Legion glanced back toward Aerolis. "We're going to right your wrongs, Djinn."

Aerolis moved closer, looming over us both. "What

are you planning, Loran?"

The Iron Legion smiled, a dangerous grin. "I'm done with you for now, Djinn. I'm answering her questions."

"You dare…"

"I do," the Iron Legion said quietly, not even standing to meet Aerolis. I think it said a lot that the Djinn backed down first.

"What did you do to us?" I asked. Josef had said something earlier, about the Iron Legion having done something to us and now I thought about it, there were memories locked away behind a door I couldn't open. Light spilled out around the edges of the door and I could hear creatures inside, rattling cages.

The Iron Legion let out a sigh and nodded. "I changed you. Part of my research, an experiment that has finally come to fruition in young Yenhelm. Exciting times. I forced you both to absorb a Source. With Yenhelm it was Biomancy, and with you it was Necromancy. I truly thought you would ultimately be the one I was looking for, Helsene."

Isen floated nearby, his ghostly form pale and insignificant. Gen was there too, and the hunters from the Forest of Ten. When I looked up, I saw more of my ghosts, as though they had all turned up to finally discover why they existed. How they existed. Silva was not among them. She once told me that when she died, everything she was would return to her mother. I think that is why I have never seen her ghost. And yet, I would give the world just to see her face once more.

"Why?" I asked.

The Iron Legion shrugged. "Has Tamura told you about the Auguries?"

I glanced over to find the crazy old Aspect waving.

He let out a giggle. "The truth is never where you leave it. Has a habit of wandering off."

"Fusion of life and death. Renewal of body. Unity of purpose," I said quickly. "Signs to find the one prophesied to end the War Eternal."

The Iron Legion laughed then. "No. No. No. Raither was as crazy as Tamura. Her prophecy was a riddle."

"So, what are they?"

The Iron Legion smiled at me and leaned closer. "The Auguries are not signs that the chosen one has come. They're instructions on how to create one."

Books by Rob J. Hayes

The War Eternal
Along the Razor's Edge
The Lessons Never Learned
From Cold Ashes Risen
Sins of the Mother
Death's Beating Heart

The Mortal Techniques novels
Never Die
Pawn's Gambit
Spirits of Vengeance

The First Earth Saga
The Heresy Within (The Ties that Bind #1)
The Colour of Vengeance (The Ties that Bind #2)
The Price of Faith (The Ties that Bind #3)
Where Loyalties Lie (Best Laid Plans #1)
The Fifth Empire of Man (Best Laid Plans #2)
City of Kings

It Takes a Thief...
It Takes a Thief to Catch a Sunrise
It Takes a Thief to Start a Fire

Science Fiction
Drones

Lightning Source UK Ltd.
Milton Keynes UK
UKHW040656260622
404878UK00005BA/101/J